PART OF HER LIFE

Anne buried her face in her hands. "I'm sorry I got you messed up in this," she said. "All you wanted to do this month was fish and think."

"I'm not sorry," David said.

He crossed the room quietly until he stood behind her. He lifted his hands to her shoulders and with deft, sure strength began kneading her knotted muscles.

She moaned a little and surrendered herself to his touch. No, she wasn't sorry, either. Not really. She didn't know if she would have had to face the problems in her upstairs room if he hadn't been there. She suspected she wouldn't. But he *was* here, and she *did* have the problems, and she didn't know how she could face them without his help.

And she didn't know how he had so quickly become a part of her life, or why his touch was so impossibly familiar. So blessedly welcome.

Too welcome.

Books by Modean Moon

The Covenant
A Little Peace and Quiet

Published by HarperPaperbacks

A LITTLE
PEACE AND
QUIET

Modean Moon

HarperPaperbacks
A Division of HarperCollinsPublishers

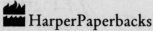 HarperPaperbacks
A Division of HarperCollins*Publishers*
10 East 53rd Street, New York, N.Y. 10022-5299

This is a work of fiction. The characters, incidents, and
dialogues are products of the author's imagination and are not to
be construed as real. Any resemblance to actual events or
persons, living or dead, is entirely coincidental.

ISBN 0-06-108315-1

Cover design by Jon Paul

First printing: September 1996

Printed in the United States of America

Visit HarperPaperbacks on the World Wide Web at
http://www.harpercollins.com/paperbacks

❖ 10 9 8 7 6 5 4 3 2 1

A LITTLE PEACE
AND QUIET

Prologue

The wind forced its way in from the north, drinking up moisture as it crossed the Great River and sounding its way through the leaves remaining on the trees. It hesitated at the ring of low-built earthen mounds, and the torches there flared as the wind shared its breath with its brother, fire, gently so as not to extinguish him or enrage him, then hurtled its way across the plaza.

Woman-From-The-West paused as she felt its chill embrace of her face and her bare legs. Her life would change this night. The two warriors who had been sent with her to bear the Warrior's burial gift to the Priest paused when she did, waiting silently.

Woman-From-The-West turned slowly, heavy with child. From where she stood, between the house of the Priest and the raised earthen platform of the temple, she could not see the mortuary on the burial mound, readied and waiting for the bones of the honored dead, but far to the east, across the smaller river which flowed from the south, from a raised earthen work much the same as the one on which the temple stood, a signal fire glowed.

She continued in her slow circling. To the south she saw the lights from the fires of those who had come bringing their dead; to the west and to the north, the fires of the villages, swollen now with still more arrivals.

So many had come. And from so far. But the Warrior had said, "It is time," and the word had gone out. Had he known the Priest would die? Or had it been only that the mortuary house was full? Woman-From-The-West could not know, and the Warrior would not say. Had he known that he, too, would die?

Woman-From-The-West felt the chill that was not caused by the wind. It prickled her arms, raised the fine hairs on her neck, and misted her eyes. She had not known these people two winters past, but now two lives connected her with them: the one that grew within her, and the one that ebbed from the man in the house where she had lived since the time of the green corn.

She heard a low growl, different from but carried by the wind, and with a pain she could never share, she knew what that meant. The Guardians were restless. The Warrior's time grew short. Drawing about her her soft cloak of colored fiber woven from the sturdy cane that grew near the Great River and from the hair of the rabbit, she turned to the two warriors who waited. They, too, had heard the growl. They, too, knew what it signified. They, unlike some others, had remained loyal to the man who lay dying.

Quickly, accompanied by them, protected by them and by the spirits of the Guardians, Woman-From-The-West returned to the man who had taken her from the caravan of slaves being shipped to the great water of the south and had chosen her to be his mate. For him, to accompany him, she would gladly give her life, but that was not to be allowed, even though at this moment the wives of the Priest readied themselves to join their mate in burial. For the Warrior, another service was required.

The smell of death was strong in the house. None of her healing arts had been able even to slow its relentless approach. The Warrior lay near the fire, his great length stretched out on a litter she had ordered brought close to the warmth. Although he did not raise his head, she knew he watched her. "You heard them?"

"I heard them," she said.

"Then it is to be tonight. You will prepare me?"

She heard no fear and no sorrow in his voice and vowed that he would hear none in hers. "I will prepare you."

She knelt beside him, testing the water that waited near the fire, and drew away the furs that covered him. He was silent as she touched the damp cloth to his chest, as though knowing she mourned his wasted strength. Silent. Leaving her in silence to bathe him as she had bathed him before, as once, he had bathed her. She had fought the women he sent to her that first day, her greater size and strength and fear easily overcoming their efforts to prepare her for this giant who had claimed her for his own. He had laughed and dismissed the women. "What a mate you will make for me," he said. "You will never cringe from me. You will bear me many fine sons. And you will stand by my side through this life and the hereafter."

She had never cringed from him; from that moment she realized there was no reason. She carried his child, the only child she would ever bear. And because of that child, she was preparing him to go into the hereafter without her.

He caught her hand in his. "I will miss you."

She looked up, seeing the pain that glazed his eyes. "And I will miss you."

"I must wear the armor," he told her. "There are those who would try to claim the position of Warrior. For their sakes, as well as the sake of our people, I cannot allow them to do so. And you —" He groped beneath the edge of the litter and brought forth a copper breastplate with his likeness engraved upon it. "You must wear this. No one will harm you while you do. The Guardians will see to that. As they will see that I am not disturbed. I cannot command them to leave me until a new Warrior arises. I have copied the designs. You will find them on a scroll hidden beneath our bedrobes. When our son is ready to assume his place as the Warrior, you will have new armor made for him. Then they will come to him. You will do this."

"I will do this," she promised. "And then *I* will come to you."

He dropped his hand on the rise of her belly where their child lay protected. "Woman-From-The-West," he said softly, and she knew he was remembering. It was he who had named her. With a gentle sigh, he left her.

1

1985

Anne had returned to *Allegro* to heal, and
sometimes she almost felt that she had. Her body had,
of course. Even before she closed up her apartment and
practice and ran from Chicago, she knew there would
be no problem with that. It was the other, the emotional
and mental wounds, that seemed in no hurry to close or
scar over. But on that crisp, clear Saturday morning in
late November, with the forest and the hills of south-
eastern Oklahoma spread out around her, surrounding
her, enclosing her, protecting her, she felt almost whole
again.

It was strange, but lying there in that hospital bed in
Chicago, something within her had said, *It's time to go
home,* and she had known she had to return to Allegro,
even though she had never truly considered this tired
little town as home, even though she had not been here
but a few times in her life, and those with her mother as
a child or as a very young adult, before medical school.

The people of Allegro had needed a doctor for too
long not to accept her back into the fold, even if she

wasn't sure just how long she could stay in medicine. Besides, Great Uncle Ralph had once owned more than half the town, and she still had family, numerous though not close, living here. But she wasn't really welcomed back like the prodigal son, although some seemed to think she was a "prodigal." And, to quote Bobby Preston, an eight year old with a penchant for broken arms, split lips, and black eyes, she "talked funny."

She wasn't thinking of any of those things, though, when David Huerra came, literally, crashing into her life. She was sitting in Agnes, her brown Ford pickup, at the end of the lane leaving Johnson's sawmill, thinking about the vagaries of one-by-sixes, how all lumber is not created equal, or even the same size, and about the ongoing objections Willie Johnson kept voicing about her renovations to the house that had been a landmark in Allegro since before statehood.

She was mildly miffed that she had to have the trim lumber for her hundred-year-old house specially sawed because modern techniques had reduced what she'd always thought to be the actual measure. A one-by-six ought to be an inch wide, not three-quarters, not five-eighths. And she was more than mildly pleased that Willie Johnson was willing and able to custom-saw the lumber she needed even though he never failed to lecture her.

"Ah, Anne, my girl, you should have let your cousin Joe take the house," he'd said today, as he had already said a dozen times since she bought the house from Aunt Ellie and Uncle Ralph's estate. "He would have done good. He would have torn it down and built those apartment houses like he's been wanting to for years."

So that was what he had wanted with it, she thought, as a troubling puzzle piece tumbled into place.

"You wouldn't have been bothered with it," Willie said, drawing her attention back to him and the present.

"You wouldn't have been worried about hurting your fine hands."

Willie worried about her hands. Not because she needed them in the practice of medicine, but because he was one of the few people who had actually looked at the jewelry she used to make before she became consumed with medicine and success, had in fact bought a piece of it from her when she was just a fumbling adolescent who thought she knew where her life was going.

"Why'd you want to go and buy a big old place like that, anyway?" he'd asked her.

She'd had to laugh, and she'd had to be honest; that was the only thing you could be with Willie Johnson. Although she didn't tell him that buying the house hadn't truly been her decision. At least not at first.

"I don't know," she told him. "I just felt it was something I had to do."

"Well, you ought to hire somebody to do that work for you," he said, not willing to back off completely from his subject. "Just move out, turn it over to a contractor, and don't go back till the work is finished. You got better things to do than worry about power tools and hammers and lugging this lumber up and down the stairs."

She'd laughed again, thanked Willie for the week's worth of materials he'd loaded into Agnes, and left. In retrospect, though, she sometimes wondered if he had been right. Not about letting Joe have the house—that would only have made things worse—but about hiring someone. If she had been able to, and if after doing so she had been able to keep any of those she had hired working long enough to finish the job, if she hadn't personally been so involved in cutting and trimming and measuring, would she have noticed the discrepancies?

And there she was, sitting at the end of the lane, waiting for a log truck to turn into the narrow road from the highway when her life changed once again. She had fought back an irrational moment of urban impatience at the truck for taking so long to turn, and at herself for being too timid to turn onto the road when she'd probably had the chance, accepting that she wasn't in so much of a hurry that a few more minutes of her time were really going to be of any earth-shattering importance.

She had taken those moments to look again over the magnificent view spread out in front of her and was letting the beauty of that view calm her, as it always did when she surrendered to it. Fall had come late to this isolated area. There hadn't yet been a killing frost or even a harsh wind or heavy rain to complete the job of denuding the trees. Yellows, pale greens, oranges, and shades of red marched up the mountains before her in step with the dark greens of pine and cedar, crowned in the distance by a veil of rising fog from the meandering river.

Granted, surrendering to the calming influence of nature was a little difficult, because the log truck was groaning and creaking under its load of pines loudly enough, almost, to drown out the sound of its straining, belching diesel engine, and definitely loudly enough to disrupt her amateur attempts at meditation, but she was working on it.

That's when she saw the approaching car and abandoned all attempts at meditation. And that's when the driver of that car saw that the log truck was all but stopped in the middle of its turn in the road in front of him. He hit his brakes. There wasn't anything for him to do but try to stop; a hundred-foot sheer drop marked the other side of the road, and although Anne shoved Agnes in reverse gear and was frantically trying to back out of his one alternate path, there was no way she could do so fast enough to help him. He stopped, with a controlled skid and a more responsive car than she had seen in a long time, just inches from the back of the protruding logs. She saw him slump over the steering wheel in relief. And then she saw Hank Foresman's souped-up red one-ton truck come around the curve so fast he hadn't a prayer of stopping in time, even if his brakes had been in order. And the driver of the car saw him, too.

How long had the lights behind those mud-encrusted reflectors been glowing? David Huerra swore swiftly and violently when he realized that the heavily laden log truck on the grade below him was stopping and beginning a tortured left turn. He hit the brakes while scanning for an escape route. Not to the right; that meant at least a hundred-foot drop off the side of the mountain to the first rock outcropping, with nothing to break the fall but a few scrubby pines and winter-dead oak trees. And not to the left; the truck was already into its turn. Even if he could beat it to the side road he couldn't squeeze between it and the brown pickup truck waiting to turn onto the highway.

He heard the borrowed fishing tackle and gear he had stacked so carefully on the backseat crash to the floor as the car shuddered to a stop barely a foot from the end of the logs protruding from the back of the truck. He let out a long breath and slumped against the seat.

Swearing, he thought as he felt the effects of adrenaline racing through his system and remembered the oath that had spewed so naturally from him. He swallowed once and began taking deep, even breaths. That was something else he could work on this month. Swearing was becoming a matter of routine, a thought-less response to almost any situation. Like this one, he told himself, seeing the slight tremor in his hand when he released his death grip on the steering wheel. If he were going to swear over this, he ought to be swearing at himself for not paying more attention to the unfamiliar road, not at the truck driver for making a left turn.

Swearing. Yes, he definitely would work on that. Clean up his language while he cleaned up his life.

He glanced again at the drop to his right, then into the rearview mirror. His jaw clenched when he saw the oncoming truck, a bright red one, nose down as it approached, coming around the curve too fast to be able to stop in time.

All thoughts of cleaning up his language fled, chased out of his mind by a swift, certain knowledge: *that idiot is going to kill me!*

And then, as had happened to him too many times for comfort, as if he were considering it from the safety of his office or his living room or in some secluded spot well away from all danger, everything slowed down. Slow motion with occasional stop-action. With him completely unable to act in any way to prevent what was happening. The truck still came toward him, the knowledge of his impending death still danced around the edges of his consciousness. He felt a moment of sadness for his brother, for his niece, for those whose lives had touched his, for the words he had often spoken heedlessly, for the words he had left unsaid in spite of all his good intentions.

There was no time for fear. That had come earlier, when there had been a prayer of his saving himself. Now there was nothing to do but accept the inevitable. But his hands still gripped the wheel, twisting it in an effort to turn away from the protruding logs, his feet slammed onto the brake pedal, shoving down, without his knowledge but with all of his strength, in an effort to stop the unstoppable, and his body twisted sideways in an effort to avoid the unavoidable.

"Son of a bitch," David whispered in what only he would recognize as a convoluted prayer before the windshield shattered, his head slammed forward, then back, and the slow-motion action stopped. Silenced. Darkened.

The sickening sounds of metal on metal and green-pine log on metal and glass released Anne from the paralysis that had held her immobile through the slow-motion video. The driver of the log truck had stopped in the middle of the road. He slammed out of the cab of his truck, and she, even knowing what she must find, jumped from hers.

Hank Foresman wasn't hurt; he had the advantage of the weight of his truck and the slack-muscled responses of the slightly drunk. The driver of the brown Chevy was a different story. One of the protruding logs had gone through his windshield, missing his head by no more than a thickness of skin; he had a nasty knot already rising on his forehead; and he was out cold.

She slapped Hank's hands away as he tried to release the man's seat belt. "Get my bag out of my truck," she told him, knowing she'd have to distract him or he'd yank the man out of his car without respect for any possible injuries.

"What can I do, Doc?" the driver of the log truck asked from behind her. Anne hadn't recognized him, but she breathed a sigh of relief that he wasn't one of those locals who felt the need to take charge.

"Give me a minute," she told him.

Her examination was perfunctory at best but, given the decided smell of gasoline, as adequate as she could make it. Only when she had finished did she realize that her recently too-familiar sense of panic hadn't overwhelmed her. But then, there hadn't been any blood. Thank God.

"Help me get him out of here and across the road."

They stretched him out on the grassy slope beside her truck. Hank shoved her bag at her, and she quickly checked for vital signs. When assured that the man wasn't in imminent danger of dying on her, she began checking for other injuries. He was a slender man, a little under six feet tall, with muscle tone that spoke of a strength not evident from his size. His features were slightly Hispanic, his eyes a dark brown, she discovered, and showing no signs of a serious head injury. Altogether, he wasn't bad looking. And he was definitely a stranger to the area, with a smashed car and a whale of a headache coming on.

"Damn!" he muttered, thick tongued and groggy but quite succinctly. He raised a hand to his head and opened his eyes. Giving up the effort to focus, he closed one eye and peered at her with the other. Apparently deciding she was no threat to him, he relaxed again. "I'm going to quit swearing," he said experimentally, as though not sure his voice would work. "That's what I promised myself just before that— *Son of a bitch!*"

His open eye widened; his other popped open.

"Move away from him, Doc."

She twisted around at the menace in Hank's voice and came eyeball to gaping black barrel with the rifle he held one-handed and trained on her semiconscious patient.

"What?" she choked out as involuntary fear sank its claws into her. Yep. *There* was the panic. But she didn't have time for it now.

"Put the gun down, Hank," she ordered quietly.

"No, ma'am," he said. "You move away from him."

"Put the damned gun down, Hank, before you get into more trouble than you're already in."

"It's not me that's in trouble," Hank said. "And it's not my gun you ought to be worried about. It's his." He held up his left hand, brandishing a deadly looking blue revolver.

"Found it in the front floorboard of his car. No telling what all's in those bags in the back."

"Fishing tackle," she heard from behind her.

Hank snorted. "With Texas tags on your car? Likely story," he said, ignoring the fact that the entire area around Allegro and the man-made lake with which it shared its name derived most of its meager income from catering to fishermen.

"No." He took a shaky step closer. "With the way you look, you shouldn't have any trouble coming back and forth across from Mexico. I think maybe you're one of them drug runners. Or maybe one of them folks that brings in illegal aliens. I think old Hank's just caught him a wanted criminal."

Most of the people Anne dealt with were decent, hard working, and too concerned with their own survival to worry too much about who or what other people were. But occasionally prejudice reared its head. She didn't like it here any better than she had in Chicago. Less, because it seemed so out of character with the history of this area and the natural beauty that ought to have seeped into the pores of every living being.

"Hank Foresman," she said as indignation overcame the residue of her fear. He wasn't a threat to her, only to her patient, and perhaps, to himself. She could stop him. Yes. She could do this. "If you don't put that gun down, I'm going to stick you with a megadose of tranquilizers that will have you singing lullabies for three days."

"I can explain," her patient said, reaching for his pocket.

"Don't move."

The man sighed and looked over her shoulder. "You look sane," he said to the truck driver beside her. "Will you see if you can find a blue windbreaker in the back-seat of my car? My wallet is in the pocket."

They waited, with only the sounds of Hank's heavy breathing and distant fumbling noises from the car until the driver returned. "You caught yourself a bad one all right, Hank," he said, and she saw that he was trying not to laugh. "David Huerra, Dallas P.D. Detective."

"Oh, shit," Hank said, lowering the rifle just before his knees gave out and he sank into a loose-jointed pile on the road. The truck driver walked over and relieved him of both the rifle and the revolver.

She heard the squeal of brakes, followed by Willie Johnson's shout. "Sheriff's on his way. I've got him on the CB. Do we need an ambulance?"

"Yes," she shouted back, only to be overruled.

"No," David Huerra said quietly.

Anne could have insisted. Maybe she should have. Instead, she heard herself saying, "Tell him we'll let him know."

By that time quite a crowd had gathered. With Hank collapsed at her feet, her conscience prickled until she gave him a cursory examination to make sure that nothing other than alcohol contributed to his blackout. As she finished, she heard the scream of the sheriff's siren approaching.

The tableau in the highway made what happened obvious, and any answers that might be needed seemed to her to be supplied by Hank snoring, blissfully ignorant of the stories that were passing through the growing crowd of spectators from those who had witnessed his big arrest.

David Huerra, the Dallas cop, was trying to get to his

feet when she put a hand on his shoulder and pushed him back toward the ground. "Unless you want to pass out like your buddy Hank, maybe you'd better sit still for a minute or two," she told him quietly. He grimaced but apparently decided she might know what she was talking about, because he didn't struggle against her restraining hand.

Sheriff Blake Foresman pushed his way through the crowd toward them, and knelt beside his brother Hank, looking up at her with concern written in every weathered line of his face. When Hank snored and belched in his sleep, Blake backed away from him. "Oh, hell," he muttered and turned to survey the wreckage on the road. "I don't suppose that brown Chevy ran into the truck and then backed into my brother," he asked wryly.

The driver of the log truck chuckled. "Don't think so, Sheriff."

Blake looked at him, trying to place him. "Sam Wilson?"

"Yep," the driver said.

"You saw what happened?"

"Yep," the driver—Sam—said again. "Me and the doc, and of course Detective Huerra, here."

"Oh, hell," Blake said again, raking his hand across his forehead. He looked at her with weary resignation. "You want to draw me a blood sample?"

"I'm sorry, Blake," she told him, meaning she was sorry for him and for Hank's wife Ida. "He's really done it this time."

"I'm sorry, too," he said, looking at her patient. "Are you going to be okay?"

Huerra nodded, then winced. "It could have been worse. It could have been a car full of kids he ran into."

Anne cringed at still another unwanted reminder of something she had managed to put out of her mind for almost half a day.

Blake sighed. "I know. He promised he was dry. I told him I'd lock him up if I caught him driving drunk. I guess he didn't believe me. Detective?" he asked. "What jurisdiction?" And Anne knew she heard in his voice his almost futile hope that Sam had been wrong.

"Dallas P.D."

"Great. Just great," Blake muttered. "Thank God I just got reelected. The county paper's going to have a field day with this. Are you sure you're okay?"

"No, he isn't sure, Blake," Anne said, needing this diversion from the ugly track her thoughts had taken. Once again, she put her hand on his shoulder to push Huerra back down into a semblance of sitting. "And neither am I. A log came within less than an inch of taking his head off." She saw Huerra wince when she said that, and once again he stopped struggling to rise. "He's got a whale of a headache, assorted cuts and bruises, maybe a cracked rib or two, and possibly a concussion, not to mention a wiped-out car and a ruined fishing trip."

"Oh, hell," Blake said still again, dragging the word hell into more syllables than she had ever thought possible.

She softened toward him. Blake was a good man. And it was only moderately his fault that Hank was still driving around the country. "Get the consent form," she said gently. "Shake Hank awake enough to sign it, and I'll draw the blood sample for the blood alcohol analysis."

"Right," he said, but his heart wasn't in it. He looked toward the road, where a deputy was taking pictures and measurements of the accident. "I'll need a statement from you, Huerra."

David Huerra managed a wry grin of his own. "I don't think I'm going very far in the near future, and it looks like you've got plenty on your plate right now. Why don't I come by your office in the next day or so?"

Blake nodded. "Yeah. Sam? It looks like you can move that log truck now." He looked toward her. "Do you need an ambulance?"

Anne glanced at Huerra and shook her head. "No. But I'm going to take him into the clinic for a checkup. Would you ask someone to unload his luggage from the car and put it in the back of my truck?"

"That isn't necessary," Huerra said.

She shook her head. "It's either that or a thirty-mile code-three ride to the county hospital in Fairview with an ambulance driver who thinks he's training for the Indy 500."

He raised an eyebrow as though questioning her truthfulness.

"Trust me," she said, then smiled at him. "Do you have reservations for someplace around here?"

"Yeah. The Tompkins fish camp."

Anne nodded. She knew where the Tompkins place was. "That's not too far from town," she told him. "I'll take you there after I get a good look at your skull and ribs."

She took hold of his arm to help him rise, but he glared at her as though she had just insulted his manhood instead of merely offering the help she would have given anyone.

"I'm all right," he said. "My head's hard."

Somehow that didn't surprise her. But she didn't say anything. She just gestured toward her truck and forced herself not to offend his pride by insisting on helping him as he struggled to his feet.

The last of the crowd remained until after the wreckers carried off the car and the pickup truck, the sheriff's car left with Hank once again snoring, and David Huerra reluctantly allowed Sam Wilson to help him into Agnes's cab after he discovered he wasn't quite as steady on his feet as he'd thought he would be.

A couple of the hardier gawkers began following Anne's truck toward town, but she knew how to handle that. She slowed Agnes down to about three miles an hour and after less than a mile the two voyeurs pulled out and passed them.

"You handled that well," Huerra said in the tight voice that told more about his pain than he would want her to know.

She grinned at him, using that excuse to take a quick look at his face. He was pale, but not more so than he had been.

"I meant it," he said, apparently recognizing her surreptitious examination for what it was. "My head is hard. I've had worse bumps in the past. I'm fine. All I need is a shower and a change of clothes to get rid of all of this glass grit, a meal, and a bed. I don't want, I don't need, and I won't sit still for any x-rays."

While she pondered her response to that, he used the closeness of the truck cab for an examination of his own—a long, detailed examination of her face, her hands, and the rest of her five feet four inches visible in jeans, sneakers, and the heavy fisherman's knit sweater and knit cap she wore. Without speaking, he reached over and tugged the cap from her head. Most of the hairpins had either already slithered out of their moorings or were caught in the cap, and her hair tumbled in a willy-nilly disarray of unruly auburn curls over her shoulders.

His lips quirked in a grin. "Doc?" he asked. "Do you have another name?"

She snatched the cap from him but realized there was no way she could stuff the mass of hair back into it without pulling off the road. She dropped the cap onto the seat. "Anne. Anne Locke."

His lips twitched again. "Annie?"

"Not if you want to live to catch another fish," she said tightly.

"Annie," he said, smirking only a little. "I bet you keep that hair of yours whipped into submission and pinned to within an inch of its life when there's any chance anyone's going to see it." Apparently he just couldn't let it rest. "Doesn't anybody call you Annie?"

She acknowledged defeat. She really didn't mind. Her need for maintaining a perfect image had been blasted out of her life along with her need for success at any cost. "Only one person," she said, "but he's only ten years old and lives half a world away."

He leaned back against the seat, mouth drawn tight against pain for a moment, then took a deep breath and let it out slowly.

"I mean it," he said again. "All I need is a shower, a meal, and a bed."

"Yeah, right," she said. "But if you've had your hard head thumped before, you know there's no way I'm going to let you go to sleep until I'm sure you haven't cracked or scrambled something up there." However, his insistence that he needed food was a good sign. "Tell you what," she said, making a quick decision. "I'll feed you and lend you my shower. And if you're still doing okay after a couple of hours, I'll take you to Tompkins and let you out of the x-rays."

"Ah," he said. "A sensible woman."

And that was the last he said until they reached her house.

He opened his eyes as she pulled into the driveway and downshifted for the climb. She glanced at him for his reaction and wasn't disappointed. Few could fail to react to the Victorian monstrosity perched near the top of the hill overlooking the town of Allegro.

He swallowed once and then looked at her as if to see

if she had grown some additional appendage or sprouted some outward sign of instability. "Did I say sensible?" he asked. "My God woman, that house is purple."

She fought to keep from laughing. Purple was too kind a word for the colors her aunt had painted the house after Uncle Ralph's death. All shades of purple. As many shades of purple as there were in the hedge of crape myrtle, rose of Sharon, and weigela Great Aunt Ellie had planted along the back property line and which now tangled together in drooping, inseparable branches, effectively fencing her yard from the forest behind her.

"Yes," she said. "It is. At least in those places it still has paint."

"But it has running water," she reminded him. "And the kitchen is functional."

"Sorry," he muttered. "I have better manners than that. Maybe I did get thumped a little harder than I thought."

She let her laugh escape then.

"You're obviously working on it," he said. "That's why you've got a truck full of lumber, isn't it?"

She pulled to a stop in the back yard and turned to face him. "Your brain seems to be functioning again," she said. "We may not have to amputate after all. Sit still," she told him as he reached for the door handle. "I'll let you out."

"I can manage," he muttered.

"Right." she hopped out of the truck and walked around to the passenger side.

He hadn't managed—at least not to get the door open—as she had known he wouldn't.

"Agnes has character," she told him as she opened the door. "That means not all of her parts work, including the inside door handle on this side." She winked at him. "It comes in handy sometimes. Like today. Now, put your arm over my shoulder and lean on me until we get you into the house."

He hesitated, as she knew he would, and then leaned on her as he got out of the truck. She sensed his hesitation and looked up to see him studying the house.

She followed his glance, seeing it with the first shock as he must be—the turrets, the gingerbread, the outlandish clashing shades of purple in the walls, trim, and sash—and then with the familiarity she had grown into.

Her attention snagged then lingered at the second floor rear bedroom, at the solid wall of faded purple, a solid wall when all other walls were studded with windows—rectangular, square, round, arched, or diamond-shaped windows. This weekend, she had promised herself.

This weekend she was going to explore the reasons for that wall, the reasons why it, of all the walls, was not riddled with windows, when it was so perfectly positioned to overlook what must once have been a superb herb and perennial garden.

This weekend, she promised herself again, just as she felt David Huerra slump against her. "What's this," she asked. "Weakness, Detective? Do we need to go to the clinic after all?"

He grinned back. "Why, Annie, that was my best wounded warrior ploy. I'm disappointed in you for not succumbing."

"Fat chance," she told him, managing a lightness at odds with the dark emotions his innocent words triggered. "Warriors . . . Warriors aren't my style at all. Now come on." At last she felt herself back on steady ground and able to maintain an—almost—easy banter. "Let's get you into the house. I swear I've just about worn myself out lugging you all over the country."

He stiffened and started to withdraw his arm.

"I'm teasing," she said hurriedly. "My goodness, you are touchy, aren't you?"

"Not . . . usually," he answered tightly, and she didn't believe him for a minute. But after a quick, almost panicked look at the house, he relaxed his arm over her shoulder, and she took the first step up to the porch. A chill, as unexpected as it was unexplainable, shuddered through her, and she stopped there on the first step, for the moment unable to go any farther. He glanced at her with a wary question in his eyes.

"Uh—" she cleared her throat. What on earth was happening?

This was her house, for goodness sake. True, she'd heard the rumors that it was haunted, but only after she'd found herself committed to purchase it, and she suspected those rumors had been started by Joe to keep the place vacant, and to keep anyone other than him from even thinking about bidding on it. Hadn't she walked into it in the dark on countless occasions and not bothered to turn on a light? Hadn't she'd slept in it every night for almost six months and never even heard a board squeak after she got to sleep?

"You too, huh?" David asked.

"I don't know what you're talking about," she told him. Admittedly her words lacked conviction, but she tried.

"Sure," he said. "But if you don't know what I'm talking about, then why do you look as if someone just walked over your grave?"

2

1926

The man stood hesitantly beside the back of the farm truck. Dust covered him and the truck, and dried mud coated his boots and the legs of his overalls.

Ralph Hansom kept well back from the mud and the dust and the man, as if by doing so he could hold himself aloof from the poverty that had spawned his visitor. "What did you bring, Jackson? I've got better things to do than stand out here all morning playing guessing games."

Tom Jackson gestured toward the tarpaulin-covered bundle in the back of the truck, almost invisible among the spare tire and boxes of broken tools and debris.

"Haul it out. You know I have to examine it. Too many of you people have tried to pawn off bogus trash on me."

Grimacing, Jackson climbed into the back of the truck and wrestled two baskets from beneath the tarp and to the rear of the truck bed. Only then did Hansom step forward. The first, a peck basket, obviously the one Jackson thought the prize, was over half full of objects Hansom had long ago identified as fresh-water pearls. He plunged his hand into the basket, confirming that pearls actually filled it, and not a hidden layer of dirt or gravel or bone. Then he turned his attention to the other, larger, bushel basket.

A pile of thin leaves of copper, engraved but green and fused together, lay wedged near the top. He glanced at the copper but moved it out of his way. A half-dozen conch shells were next. And then—Hansom told himself to breathe, to betray no emotion—as one by one he lifted six engraved shell gorgets from the basket, finding only one of them chipped, and then pushed aside four bones, leg probably—why the hell did these people think he was interested in bones?

Something lay on its side in the bottom of the basket. Tentatively, not letting himself hope, he touched it, then lifted out a stone statuette almost a foot tall and in the shape of one of the recurring heathen images he had seen engraved on the shells.

A pipe. Without the stem, of course; the stem had probably long ago rotted away. But a pipe? *God!* He fought not to suck in his breath. He had heard of these pipes, but this was the first he'd seen.

"Well," Jackson asked. "It's good, isn't it?"

The little girl had come from behind the house, unnoticed. Barefooted and almost as dusty as Jackson, she stopped by the rear of the truck and reached for the pile of copper. "Pretty," she said, touching it reverently.

Ralph Hansom looked at his four-year-old daughter. The child's Choctaw blood showed in her dark hair, her bronze-gold coloring, in the fineness of her hands. Ralph's stomach revolted when he thought of this child springing from his loins. She had no class, and as she had just demonstrated by reaching for the junk copper, no taste and no knowledge. Just like her mother.

Her mother, however, had had the advantage of money and land.

"Ellie!" Ralph yelled. "Come and get your brat out of my way!"

A woman appeared on the long back porch. "Lucy," she called softly. "Come in the house. You know better than to bother your father."

Bitch, Ralph thought. She'd said that deliberately, goading him in front of this piece of white trash. But maybe he could make it work to his advantage.

Lucy clutched the copper. "Pretty," she said again. Ralph disengaged her fingers from her treasure. "*Pretty!*" she screamed.

"*Ellie!*"

Soundlessly the woman left the porch and walked to the truck. She reached down and gathered the child in her arms, crooning softly to her in her own language as she carried her to the house. For once Ralph bit back his habitual order for her to speak English. Jackson had seen and heard enough.

"How much?" Jackson asked.

Ralph sifted a few of the pearls through his fingers and waved dismissively toward the rest. "Ten dollars."

Jackson paled beneath the dust. "Ten dollars? God, man. I've snuck in there every night for two weeks, digging all night and hiding the hole the next day, lied to my brother-in-law to get this truck, drove down here—more'n a hundred miles before I get back home. I got a family to feed."

"Sorry," Ralph told him. "But this stuff is broken and rusted. I won't be able to get much more than ten for it myself. So if you know someone else who'll buy it, take it to them."

"Wait!" Jackson called out as Ralph turned to leave. "Twenty. And I'll get you more. Not broken. It's there, Hansom. And I know where it is."

Ralph looked at him. Slowly and carefully he reached

over and picked up the copper. "My kid liked this," he said. "I'll give you twelve fifty. You bring me more, not broken, and we'll work out a deal."

3

The porch door opened into Anne's kitchen, cavernous beneath the skeletal framework for a dropped ceiling. She pulled one of the mismatched oak chairs out from the round table, and with only a sharp glance at her, as though he wanted to argue the necessity for sitting but knew he'd lose, David Huerra sank onto it. She left him there while she went back out to the truck to retrieve her bag and his, but when she returned, he'd recovered enough to go exploring.

Just off the kitchen, also at the rear of the house, was a room that might have once been a sleeping porch or possibly a housekeeper's quarters. The double glass-paned doors argued for a more formal use, but the location denied it. She thought it would probably be perfect for her jewelry workshop if she ever got the courage to do what she already suspected was inevitable, but for now that same location made it just as perfect for her renovation tools and clutter.

She found him in that room, studying what had to be the oldest table saw in existence. He traced his hand along the homemade rip-fence and looked up, grinning. "This is vintage. It came with the house, I presume?"

She chuckled. "It's not quite that old. And it came with two cases of chicken pox and a broken ankle."

"And a pint of blackberry jelly?"

"I wish."

He reached for his bag, but she stepped back, holding it away from him and studying him. Thank God for safety glass. Without it, he'd have been a maze of cuts and slashes, but even safety glass had its limits when bashed by pine logs. "Come on. I'll show you to the downstairs bathroom and let you wash away some of that glass grit."

He nodded and followed her back into the kitchen and out the door she'd had knocked through the wall into the front hallway. The bathroom under the stairs would eventually be little more than a powder room, but because she was more or less confined to the ground floor until she did major work upstairs, she had finished this one with new fixtures and a small, tiled shower enclosure.

"Nice," he said, when she opened the door to the tiny room.

Yes, it was, Anne admitted to herself as she saw it for the first time through a stranger's eyes. "Thanks." She stepped back to let him enter and handed him his bag as she pointed out the obvious: fresh towels and washcloths on the wicker shelf, a basket holding soaps and even a package of disposable razors, the hair dryer in its tole-painted rack. "Call out if you need anything," she told him. "I'll be in the kitchen. Oh—and don't even think about putting those clothes in your bag. I'll run them through the washer and dryer with a load of my work clothes."

"Have you ever been told you're pushy, Doc?" Huerra asked her. But there wasn't any heat in his words. There wasn't much energy either, and she could tell he was far from the "all right" he had insisted he was.

"Yeah," she said. "Probably about as often as you've been told you're stubborn, Detective."

He absorbed that, gave her a weary smile, and closed the door against her.

She listened outside the door for a moment until she was sure he wasn't going to collapse on the floor and then went back into the kitchen.

And realized what she was doing.

She gripped the edge of the poor, beat-up old kitchen sink. She'd brought a complete stranger home with her, bossed and bullied him into stripping off and bathing in her private space, and was now preparing to cook for him and do his laundry?

Maybe the house was haunted, after all. *Something* had her acting like *she* was the one who had gotten thumped on the head.

Nonsense, she told herself. She was a doctor, for God's sake. She had chosen and had been trained to nurture her patients.

But she had also been trained not to take unnecessary risks with her safety, and that lesson was one she'd sworn she'd never again forget.

He was a cop, she reminded herself, not an ax murderer or a drug dealer, not a danger to her. Well, at least not to her physical safety. The last thing she needed in the wreck her life had become was a cop. She'd had enough of cops—and all the pain that they drew like magnets—to last her the rest of several lifetimes.

But he was injured. She reminded herself of that, too. "He's your patient," she whispered to herself. "Remember that."

And she did, at least until he walked into the kitchen several minutes later, all scrubbed from his shower and dressed in jeans and a shirt so fresh from the laundry that the creases fairly crackled. He held a small stack of his clothes carefully away from his body.

"I don't think you want to wash these with anything

of yours," he said. "If you'll give me a bag of some sort, I'll let a commercial machine take the risk." He grimaced. "Or maybe I'll just throw them away."

He didn't look like a cop, and except for an unnatural pallor, a few nicks now visible on his jaw and throat, and the burgeoning bruise near his left temple, he didn't look like a patient.

"Nonsense." She reached for the clothes, but he held them away from her. "Okay." She smiled and pointed to the washer and dryer across the room.

Huerra nodded. In only moments he had competently loaded his things into the washer, added soap, and started the cycle. Well, well, she thought. Maybe his clothes were commercially starched and pressed because he liked them that way, and not because he didn't know how to take care of them himself.

Which was none of her business. None at all.

"Any dizziness?" she asked, as he closed the lid and turned to study the wreck of the kitchen. "Blurred vision? Blood where it shouldn't be?"

He grinned and shook his head, then winced and leaned back against the washing machine. "You've got a he—heck of a bedside manner. Anybody ever tell you that?"

"Yeah." She pulled out a chair and pointed at him, then at it. "Sit."

"I'm only letting you get away with that because I see a coffeepot on the counter and I haven't had my quota of caffeine this morning," he told her as he eased himself onto the chair.

"And you're not getting any from me, either, until I'm sure it won't do you more harm."

"Come look in my eyes, Doc, and feel my pulse. No concussion. And, to answer your last, oblique question, no signs of internal bleeding. No lumps or bulges," he volunteered, "that don't appear superficial, manageable, or normal. Nothing requiring stitches, intensive care, or even taping up. So, please, Annie," he said, giving her what she suspected was his best good-little-boy grin—a grin that had probably gotten him just about anything he'd ever asked for. "Please, please, please can I have some coffee?"

She gave him a laugh as seemingly easy, and as false, as his grin and reached for the second of two canisters. He didn't have to know it was decaf. "Is that how you solve your cases?" she asked, determined to continue their light, meaningless patter. "Beg until the perpetrator confesses?"

His grin faded, and although he made a quick attempt at recovery, it wasn't quite successful. Ah hah, she thought. Secrets. And definitely a man who wasn't as superficial as he'd tried to make her think. Well, she understood secrets, and the necessity for keeping them private, quiet, and contained. "I suppose the next thing you're going to ask for is cholesterol. And carbohydrates."

"And calories?" The little boy was back, more naturally now, with just a touch of flirt. Not so much that she couldn't handle it. Not so much that for a little while she couldn't enjoy it.

"I've heard nasty rumors that those things are bad for you," she told him as she filled the coffeepot and turned it on.

"Yeah. Me too. Problem is, those same rumors would have you believing everything's bad for you. You do have sausage, don't you?" he asked, looking at her in feigned horror. "You do have . . . eggs?"

"Of course I have sausage and eggs."

He put his hand over his heart and grinned again, but as she turned her attention to the refrigerator she glanced at him and realized that he was fading fast. If she was going to feed him, it would have to be soon, or he'd be sleeping at her table. And feed him she would. He was displaying no signs of concussion or internal injury. Of course, if he lost his breakfast, she'd have to do some fast rethinking.

And it would be all right for him to sleep. She was confident of that now. In fact, it would be better for him if he did. The human body had miraculous powers of recovery, as long as it was given time and, in some cases, permission to recover.

In deference to his failing energy and her less than wonderful kitchen skills, she opted for toast instead of biscuits, but she did dig out a jar of blackberry jelly—purchased, not homemade—and for once everything else she cooked turned out better than just edible . . . pretty good, in fact. It was amazing what six months without a McDonald's had done for her kitchen chemistry.

Huerra was exhausted but trying to hide it when he finished off the last slice of toast. "That was great, Doc. Now if I could just trouble you for a ride out to the Tompkins place—"

She shook her head. "I said a couple of hours, and I meant a couple of hours." She picked up their plates and carried them to the sink. "If your breakfast doesn't come up—" He raised a hand as if to assure her. She ignored it. "—and if you don't start seeing four of me, I'll deliver you out there before noon."

He winced again, and turned in his chair in a surreptitious effort to get comfortable. Before he realized what she was doing, she returned to the table and captured his face in her hands, looking into his eyes.

"Are they crossed?" he asked.

She released him. "No. And they're not dilated, either." She nodded toward the front of the house. "Come with me. Your body's got to be screaming for some rest."

He rebelled at the bedroom door, looking in at her unashamedly romantic comforter and curtains. "That's your bed."

She nodded and pretended to write on a chart. "Very good. Abstract thinking and cognitive skills appear unimpaired."

"Come on, Annie," he said, "I can't take your bed."

He'd dropped all pretense of humor; so did she. "You can barely stand up," she told him. "You need to rest. Your choices are exactly two: my bed or a sofa with about as much support as a marshmallow."

"Or my own rented bed at a fishing camp just outside of town. I can rest there."

"Maybe," she admitted. "Probably. But I wouldn't feel good about abandoning you there, and since I can't leave until my weekend carpenters show up, the question is not debatable. Another hour," she said, relenting when she saw how uncomfortable her skewed impersonation of Marcus Welby must be making this big-city cop. "Humor me for an hour longer."

She gestured toward the bed. "There's a phone. Make any calls you think necessary, and then lie down before you fall down."

He looked at her, still dubious, she knew, but nodded. "An hour." he said, as though confirming a contract. When she nodded, too, it was as though all the argument went out of him. "All right," he told her, "I'll rest. But I won't sleep."

He slept for three hours.

She checked on him frequently, but after the first time she unplugged her bedside telephone so he wouldn't accidentally be awakened and fought her own battle with her conscience about awakening him deliberately to check on him. He'd shown no signs of concussion, and he slept the sleep of the exhausted, not the injured.

She amended that thought as she stood in the doorway and watched him sprawled in sleep across her bed. The exhausted *and* the injured. Because the collision he'd been through today would take its toll on his body—in bruises and sore muscles he didn't yet suspect. But something else, something more, had already taken a toll, as evidenced by the dark shadows under his eyes, of the way, in sleep and without his deliberate attempt to hide it with smiles and animation, his face seemed drawn and lined beyond his years.

Secrets.

She had enough of her own.

She didn't need his, too.

She shook her head. Food, a shower, and a couple of hours observation. That was all she had promised him. That was all she—owed him. And she did owe David Huerra in some strange, off-kilter way. If she hadn't been stopped at the end of the lane, he might have had an escape route.

After he woke up, after she delivered him out to Gene and Gretta Tompkins's place, she would have lived up to her obligations. He could have his fishing trip and then take his secrets and his big-city problems back where they belonged, to the city, and leave her in the peaceful small-town solitude she had sought out and was so carefully wrapping around herself.

Solitude or not, Anne was pretty close to cursing small-town living hours later when Huerra carefully walked his bruised and battered body back into her kitchen.

"You let me sleep longer than an hour."

He headed immediately for the coffeepot—now filled with the fresh, real coffee she'd decided she needed instead of decaf—helped himself to a cup as though he had every right in the world to do so, and leaned back against the counter frowning at the lumber she'd carried in from Agnes's bed and stashed mostly in the room with the power tools, with only a little over-flowing into the already cluttered kitchen.

He pointed to his left temple, to the bruise that promised to spread colorfully over most of that side of his face. "Did you see this?" She nodded, but he didn't seem to want an answer. "If your good buddy Hank could see me now, he'd really think I was one of the bad guys. How the hell did I get bruised on that side of my head?"

"And other places?" she asked.

"Yes," he admitted. "Oh, hell, yes." He glared at her. "You knew, didn't you?"

She suspected that if he had been shot, if he had been seriously injured, he would have borne it with stoic acceptance, but he hadn't been, and he didn't. "Didn't you ever work traffic detail?" she asked.

He slumped against the counter. After a moment, while they both considered the unexpected trauma even the mildest wreck could inflict on a person, he took a drink from his cup and looked across to where she sat with her feet propped up on a nearby chair. "Too long," he said. "Sorry."

"Apology accepted." She dropped her feet from the chair and gestured toward it with her coffee cup. "Maybe you'd like to sit for a while?"

He nodded. "Do you think I could have a couple of aspirin now?"

"On the counter beside the sink." She'd put them there earlier, knowing he was probably going to need them. She watched while he swallowed three with his coffee and then came over and eased himself onto the chair.

"So what's got you down in the dumps, Doc? And where's your help?"

"It's the same question," she said, saluting him with her cup. "And the same answer."

"Are they coming later?"

Her glower at her now empty coffee cup had to have answered him.

"Well," he said, "the economy here can't be so good that there's not a half-dozen other people waiting in line for a job."

She transferred her glower to him, knowing he didn't deserve it but needing to vent her frustration in some way. "That was my fourth crew. This one didn't even bother to tell me they weren't coming. When I called the lumberyard here in town to find out what the holdup was, the clerk there told me they hadn't even been in to pick up the drywall and other standard supplies I need. And that they'd started a different job."

"And left you with a half-finished kitchen ceiling, at least one unfinished doorway, and—and what else?"

She felt a grin trying to break through. She didn't have to waste her energy getting indignant. David Huerra, the big-city cop, was doing it for her. "An upstairs that is practically uninhabitable."

"And a fading purple paint job."

Inside the house she could and often did forget how bad it looked from the outside. Apparently Huerra's first impression was still too new for him to forget. "That, too," she told him. "But an outside paint job is way down on my list of must dos. First I'd like to make sure I'm warm and dry for the winter."

"You could import a crew or two and have this done in no time," he said.

Antsy, frustrated, and needing the release of movement, she got up from the chair and paced to the coffeepot. She filled her cup and carried the pot back to the table. "In case you haven't noticed, I practice family medicine in a small town, not a specialty in some affluent suburb. I'm not exactly rolling in money."

For the first time she saw a touch of cynicism in David Huerra's eyes, but it was gone almost before she saw it, replaced by—what? chagrin? "So what do you do now?" he asked.

Good question. What did she do? She poured him some coffee and sat back down. "I guess I do the things I can do around here, put out the word at the lumberyard and at Willie Johnson's sawmill and among my patients, and hope to find a couple more out-of-work carpenters."

He lifted his cup and tried to hide his body's reaction to his sore muscles. "Four crews?" he asked. "In how long?"

"Not quite six months." But for the first time since he'd entered the kitchen, she didn't want to talk about carpenters and repairs. She suddenly remembered what discomfort he had to be in.

"Isn't that stretching bad luck a little far, even in a place as small as Allegro?"

That echoed her own earlier thoughts too closely for comfort. "Or good luck," she told him. "Since it seems that everyone I manage to find winds up with a job that's both bigger and better than the one I offered."

The cynicism she now saw open and unmasked in David Huerra's expression was not new to her. It was one of the reasons she had fled Chicago. It was something she sometimes still saw in her own bathroom mirror. But she had never expected to face it across the oak table in her disaster area of a kitchen.

"Are you hungry?" she asked him.

He let her change the subject. "No."

But he was still tired, still sore, and still needing rest. "I called Gretta Tompkins while you were asleep. Gene is out on the lake with some fishermen, but she promised to hold your cabin and have it ready for you when we get there."

Why was she dismissing him? Maybe it was because he was far from recovered from the accident. But maybe, and the thought nagged at her like a toothache, maybe it was because for the first time in months she didn't want to cut herself off from anyone and everyone who knew what life away from Allegro was like. And maybe, just maybe, it was because she sensed more of a tie between the two of them than just that knowledge.

Gretta Tompkins had done more than keep the cabin for him. She had stocked the pantry and the small refrigerator, and turned up the heat and turned back the covers on the only moderately lumpy bed. Obviously she'd heard about the accident. Of course, David thought, remembering. Anne had probably told her when she telephoned earlier.

And Pete—her son and his captain—had undoubtedly called and warned her about the short fuse David had been traveling on for so long, maybe even told her he'd ordered David to vacation and all but ordered he do it with them.

"Well—" Anne turned in a circle, surveying the room, taking note of the roaring panel-ray heater and the empty spot on the nightstand where no telephone sat. "You'll be all right?" she asked, sounding anything but convinced that he would be. "It's pretty basic out here. You might need a telephone."

"I'll be all right," he said. He was no more convinced than she was at the moment, but he hoped his voice didn't give his doubts away. Damn. All he wanted right now was to crawl into that bed and sink into oblivion while his body healed. He must really have taken a battering if he could stand in a rented room with a woman who looked as tempting as Anne Locke and desire only—well, almost only—rest.

Anne smiled at him. Taking a package from a pocket

in the light windbreaker she wore, she placed it on the nightstand. "It isn't much," she said hesitantly. "Just something a little stronger than aspirin in case you need it. You'll call me if you have any problems?"

"Yeah." He nodded, too fast, and his head began pounding again. "But I won't have any problems."

"Right." Her face lit with a crooked grin before she gestured toward the minuscule kitchen. "You probably won't, but you should avoid caffeine for a while. And definitely no alcohol for a couple of days. Rest. Yes. That's—"

"Doc." And damned if she wasn't. A doctor that was. He was having trouble remembering that. "I told you. I've been thumped before. I know the drill."

"Right," she said again. "Then I'll— I'll see you if you— I'd like to check you over—I mean . . ."

He almost laughed. He would have if he hadn't known how much it would hurt. Slowly, he walked to the door, holding it half open while she backed out, embarrassed and tongue-tied. "Thanks for everything," he said.

"Go home, Annie," he told her when she continued to stand on the small porch, obviously reluctant to leave him in the primitive cabin. Finally though, she gave an abrupt nod, spun on her heel, and marched away toward her parked truck.

David watched until she climbed into the truck and drove away. Agnes. The woman had actually given her truck a name. He wondered for a moment if she'd named that purple monstrosity of a house.

Cautiously, he worked his arms out of the windbreaker and dropped it over the back of a chair. The aspirin he'd taken earlier hadn't begun to cut the bone-deep aches that had started sometime during his unexpected nap. He picked up the bag she'd left, took out one of the sample packages it contained, read the label, and shook out two of the capsules.

The water from the kitchen tap was icy cold and free of any chemical taste. He downed the capsules with a generous swallow, then finished the remainder of the glass. A well, he thought. Deep and clear and clean. It had been a long time, years, since he'd tasted water so pure.

Maybe that was something else he had to think about this month.

As if there wasn't enough already.

He managed to get his boots off and stretched out on the bed, fully clothed, giving in to the groan because there was no longer any reason to hide it.

A doctor for God's sake. He'd been rescued by a doctor.

He glanced at the wooden planks of the ceiling, and beyond. He'd been a scrawny little kid in west Texas, growing up poor and Hispanic and Catholic. He'd been a scrawny, scrappy adolescent, still poor, still Hispanic, still Catholic, when he fell in love with Marla Hamilton, the rich, Anglo Protestant daughter of the county's only private-practice doctor.

He hadn't been good enough for her. That was the lesson he'd learned the summer of his seventeenth year. That was the lesson her daddy had made sure he and all his family learned.

Lying through his teeth but smiling all the while, Dr. Hamilton had fired David's mother from her job as his housekeeper and accused his brother Patrick of stealing his medical bag. Of course, Dr. Hamilton's word had been taken over David's, his mother's, and his brother's. In that county, at that time, doctors were ranked right up there with God. His payment for dropping the false charges was David's leaving the county, leaving the doctor's precious daughter. David had left to save his brother from prison, but Marla hadn't been willing to leave her father, his money, or his prestige.

Yes, that had been a hard lesson, one David barely

survived and one he had stubbornly, angrily rejected. But he'd absorbed another one, not even realizing he had, until his prejudice against all doctors had come crashing into his professional life. He'd been a good cop. At least he thought he had been. Impartial, objective, even dispassionate in a job that exposed him to all human passions and emotions. Until he'd been blindsided by a hatred as irrational and as deeply ingrained in himself as the one that had spawned his own.

And apparently his childhood Catholicism was as deeply ingrained. "I don't need more lessons," he said to a spot somewhere beyond the ceiling. "I've already had those. Remember? We did that last month. What I'm here to do is—"

Is what?

Decide whether or not he had more blind spots ready to jump out in ambush.

Decide whether he had what it took to be a cop. No. To be a good cop. A decent cop.

And after fifteen years of living with the dark side of humanity, to learn whether he still had—if he'd ever had—the ability to be a decent human being.

And for that, he didn't need another lesson. He didn't need another doctor in his life, no matter how . . . human she seemed. No matter how appealing he found her. How attractive.

No matter how much he felt as though the God of his Catholic childhood had put her in his path.

No. What he needed was solitude, peace, and quiet for at least long enough to examine what was in his own heart and psyche, and then, if he still thought it necessary, the strength to say good-bye to a job he loved but was no longer competent to perform.

4

Sometime around midnight the Saturday before Thanksgiving, winter found Allegro, Oklahoma. Grateful for even the increasing cold that dragged her from the dreams that continued to haunt her, Anne still had to force herself out from under the electric blanket. She knew that some folks swore electric blankets were as bad for a person as sausage and eggs, but she happened to think terminal frostbite was worse.

She also knew that she couldn't just crawl back under that blanket and ignore the drop in temperature. Shivering in the chilled room, she struggled into fuzzy slippers and a cotton terry-cloth robe. Then, still shivering, she worked through the house lighting small gas heaters.

The idea of central heating was appealing more and more as she made her way through the drafty hallways and back to the warmth of her bed. Flick a thermostat before retiring and never have to get up to protect plumbing or plants? Heaven, maybe, but she still hadn't made up her mind about the economy or practicality of one huge gas burner in a house this size.

Surprisingly though, it wasn't thoughts of giant gas bills or miles of snake-like ductwork that kept her awake after she settled back into the cocoon of her bed and upped the thermostat on the blanket. Nor was it the all too frequent fear of falling back into her troubled dreams. It was that out-of-the way bedroom upstairs. The one with the lavatory. And the off-center light fixture. And the blank wall that should have been filled with windows looking out over the garden.

And a cop. A cop who had come crashing into her life and was spawning thoughts, emotions, and memories she couldn't afford, didn't want, and wouldn't tolerate.

By noon it appeared that winter had come for more than a brief visit. The bright, crisp blue sky of Saturday had settled into something between pewter and wet fireplace ash in color, and periodically spat little needles of cold rain against the equally cold expanses of windows in the kitchen.

Anne had begged and bartered for a delivery from the lumberyard yesterday, and now rolls of pink insulation and four-by-eight sheets of drywall spilled out from the overflowing tool room, but she hadn't been able to beg or barter anyone to install it, or even to help her do so.

She'd lit all the burners on the charming but antiquated gas range, and cranked the new, highly touted gas heater up to full roar, so the old kitchen wasn't too bad, except when the wind rattled the windows. Then she shivered and cursed the naïveté that had lulled her into thinking she was going to be forever warm in the winter just because she had moved back to the south. While she shivered, she huddled over a cup of coffee and continued toting up the cost of something that should have been so simple: making this monster of a house into a home.

Maybe Willie Johnson was right, she thought in disgust. Maybe she ought to have let Joe have the house. That would be one more way of simplifying her life. Maybe she ought to call him now and see if he was still interested. But she knew she wouldn't. This grand old relic deserved a better fate than demolition to make room for a pile of lookalike boxes like the ones Joe Hansom owned on the other side of town.

Between bouts of feeling sorry for herself, she spent a few minutes in silent sympathy for her unwilling houseguest of the day before. She had signed on for the long haul in this part of the country; he had come looking for rest and recreation. What a vacation he was having.

What the hell was he doing?

David shook his head, letting his attention wander from the rain-slick road and the lumbering shock-sprung Blazer he was driving long enough for the rattling relic to try to take a dive off the twisting road. Hell and damnation. He needed another wreck even less than he needed what he was inviting by what he intended to do.

He'd convinced himself last night that he could spend the next month in Allegro without seeing Anne Locke.

Yeah.

But that had been in a fit of self-righteous self-examination.

And before Blake Foresman had come by for him this morning and driven him to the Sheriff's Department to take his statement about the collision, before Blake, a basically decent man, had helped find him transportation, and before he'd just happened to mention Dr. Locke.

"She's a fine woman," Foresman had said. "And from all accounts a fine doctor. She doesn't need the grief that cousin of hers is trying to give her. Hell, everybody knew he thought that place would be his. It's not her fault that his grandmother didn't inherit it. Or that he didn't have enough sense to suspect someone besides himself might want it."

David didn't need this. He had enough on his plate as it was. He wouldn't get involved. Nope. Not him. Under orders from his captain, this was vacation time. This was reflection time. This was her problem.

"What kind of grief?" he heard himself ask.

"Oh, hell," Foresman said. He rubbed his hand across the back of his neck and shrugged. "It's gossip. Just gossip. I shouldn't have said anything. They'll work it out."

"What kind of grief?" David repeated, looking steadily into Foresman's eyes until the sheriff shifted, turned, sighed. "It's ancient history," he said finally. "Katherine—that's Anne's mama—moved away from here years ago, as soon as *her* mama died. To get away from family. To get away from gossip. Unfortunately, some folks have long memories. They remember the mistake Katherine made as a girl, never mind how much she turned her life around and raised that little girl into a fine woman. Never mind that Joe's side of the family never gave her a lick of help."

Foresman met his steady questioning inspection. What he hadn't said was where Anne's father had been during all this time. But then he didn't need to, did he? So old family gossip was again circulating. And Anne had lost four work crews in six months. Nice cousin. Welcome home, Annie.

She deserved better.

It wasn't any of his business, he'd told himself when he'd headed the Blazer out of Fairview. He didn't need to go riding to the rescue like some damned cowboy. It wasn't any of his business, he'd told himself when he reached the turnoff to the Tompkins place, and passed it. It wasn't any of his business, he told himself again, when he reached the bottom of Anne Locke's driveway and turned in, when he stopped beside that fading purple wall and felt the back of his neck prickle, when he crossed the yard and stepped up onto the back porch and felt a chill that had no relationship to any cold-weather chill he'd ever felt before shudder down his spine.

He didn't owe her anything. Except maybe payment for a medical bill and a genuine word of thanks.

None of his business.

Right.

He raised his fist and knocked at the door.

Anne almost kicked over the chair she had her feet propped on when she heard the knock on the kitchen door. On Sunday? In this weather?

She carried the cup of coffee to the door with her and cautiously moved the curtain to one side to peer out at the shadowed porch. David Huerra stood there, bare-headed, hunched into his blue windbreaker.

She fumbled the deadbolts open with one hand and stepped back in a wordless invitation which he didn't hesitate to accept. He entered, stamping his feet and blowing on his hands. She didn't bother to ask, she just parked her cup on the table, went to the counter, and poured him a cup of coffee. When she turned around, he'd already gravitated to the open heater and stood backed up to it. She handed him the cup, and he took it in both hands.

"Thanks."

She cocked her head, looking up at him but resisting her initial impulse to order him into a chair and begin an examination. Instead she went to the basket of folded, clean laundry beside the dryer and returned to his side with a towel.

"You look—"

"Like your buddy Hank's worst nightmare?" he finished for her. He smiled, but smiling did little to dispel the image of desperado his assorted bruises and cuts had hung on his already dark looks.

"I was going to say cold," she told him. She held the towel out for him. "And wet."

He traded her his cup for the towel and wiped still glistening drops of rain from his hair, then followed her to the table where she set his cup and retrieved her own. He grinned at the arrangement of chairs, probably realizing she'd had her feet propped up again, and looked around the room as he sat down. His grin faded when he saw the stacks of new supplies.

"What brings you to town?" she asked. "Figuratively and literally?"

He laughed softly. "Sheriff Foresman came to the cabin this morning. It seems he didn't want to wait to see how much trouble his brother was in, or if he could somehow mitigate it. He took me into his office in Fairview to make my statement, then tracked down Hank's insurance agent and the owner of the Chevy dealership." He shook his head. "I'd forgotten how different small towns could be."

She chuckled. She'd had that same slightly dazed feeling herself for the first several weeks, before she'd remembered there was a flip side to the good things a small town offered—such as long memories and a surprising lack of choices in the matter of craftsmen and carpenters. "So when is Blake coming back for you?" she asked. A sudden thought sobered her. "Are you in pain? Discomfort? Did I miss something—"

He waved his coffee cup in dismissal of her fears. "I

feel like hell," he admitted, "and I probably will for a few days, but no, you didn't miss anything. And Foresman's not coming back, because he didn't bring me here. Thanks to his influence with the Chevy dealer, I have the use of what is probably the oldest Chevy Blazer still on the road until my car is either repaired or replaced."

"Then what—"

"Annie, Annie," he said on a long sigh. "I came to say thanks and to take you out for Sunday dinner to repay you for yesterday's meal, provided of course you don't mind being seen with someone who looks as bad as I do right now."

Oh.

Oh, my.

Decision time.

She grinned at him. "I suppose if I refuse, you'll blame it on your appearance."

He grinned back. "Anything that works, Doc."

Allegro offered only two places to eat the midday meal on Sunday: a really good restaurant in the downtown business district that catered to the after-church crowd, and a rustic looking but also excellent restaurant at the lake where casual clothes were the norm, not the exception. They opted for the lake.

The hostess was not a patient of Anne's, although Anne did recognize her. She glanced from Anne to David, cocked her head, and pursed her lips, but she didn't say anything until she had seated them beside a wall of windows overlooking the wooded hillside and a cove of the lake below. They were well away from, but not out of sight of, the table where Anne's cousin Joe sat with a group of men, engaged in an avid discussion.

She'd heard rumors that Joe was going after a state

senate seat in the next election, his reason having more to do with proposed oil and gas legislation that threatened his mineral holdings than with a need to serve. It looked as though the rumors might be right. The group with him consisted of the powers that be, the movers and shakers of the south end of Pitchlyn County.

Joe broke off his part of the conversation long enough to shoot Anne a long, unwelcoming stare not seen, she hoped, by anyone but her. Then the hostess called out to a passing waitress, "Hey, Susie. Come take care of Doc Anne and the Dallas cop. And be nice," she added as she plopped their menus down on the table. "We want him to have a better impression of us than the one Hank must have left him with."

Anne saw David's lips twitch, but he controlled them and gave the hostess no more than a polite smile before he hid his face behind the menu.

"I didn't think Allegro had a Sunday paper," he said.

That was just what she needed to take her mind away from why Joe Hansom couldn't even pretend to be friendly. "It doesn't," she told him, feeling a smile of her own threatening to get out of control. "It doesn't need one."

She glanced at her menu. "The catfish is always good," she said. "It's local, and fresh. So is the prime rib. Good, that is. Although I'm pretty sure it has seen the inside of at least one freezer." She read further, sharing her knowledge of the offerings because she knew how wary one could get of strange restaurants. "The German fries are to die for, and—oh, great. They do have it today. Sometimes they don't—save room for the deep-dish apple pie. They serve it heated with a scoop of double-rich French vanilla ice cream."

She heard what could have been a cough, could have been the sound of someone choking, and looked up to see David Huerra watching her cautiously. "Doc?" he said when he saw he had her attention. He raked an appraising glance down all of her he could see, from forehead to tabletop, then back up to her face, and she felt the warmth of a flush threatening her embarrassingly fair complexion and the freckles that no makeup, even if she had been wearing any, could hide.

His appraisal wasn't blatant, but neither was it dismissive. And it didn't offend her. Well, well. Imagine that. Maybe she was coming back to life after all.

"I thought anybody coming out of med school these days had to swear allegiance to the carrot stick and celery brigade. Did you miss a few nutrition classes? Or maybe learn something that the American Medical Association isn't letting the rest of us in on?"

She grinned at him. She'd heard that question before. "Or maybe the rest of us just haven't listened to?" she asked him. "Such as 'moderation'?"

He raised an eyebrow, silently requesting her to explain.

She moved her hand in a sweeping gesture to catalogue her less-than-imposing features. "I weigh a hundred and ten pounds. I don't have an exercise regime, but I park at the back of the lot when I do go to a mall, rarely take an elevator when the stairs are accessible, and walk to work five days a week. Those same five days I eat baked, broiled, or low fat. On the weekends I usually wear myself out toting, sawing, and hammering in my house, so if I want to treat myself, I don't think I'm hurting my chances for a long and healthy life.

"Besides," she added, "I was just telling you what's good on the menu. *I'm* having the baked chicken."

He gave her a rueful grin and a two-finger salute, and she realized that once again, with little or no provocation, she'd climbed on a soapbox. She dropped the menu onto the table. "Sorry," she told him, giving him a rueful grin of her own. "If you push the right button, I can argue the flip side of that, but probably not with as much fervor."

They were laughing when Susie came to take their order. They both had the baked chicken. And the German fries. And the deep-dish apple pie. They talked with an ease and companionship that Anne had found with very few people. It was almost as though they had known each other forever instead of barely twenty-four hours, yet with an underlying awareness of each other as strangers: distant, somewhat mysterious, possibly dangerous to each other's peace of mind. That awareness was visible, in an occasional sharp glance, a marginally nervous handling of the flatware or dishes, a shifting in the mismatched but comfortable chairs. But it was unspoken, as were other things.

She learned that David Huerra, surprise of surprises, had actually seen Placido Domingo in *La Traviata*, that he frequented museums in Dallas and elsewhere, that he had seen the Tutankhamen exhibit, had been to Teotihuacán, and had even been dragged to the Thorne room display in Chicago by a niece who had then demanded that her father, his brother Patrick, build her dollhouse furniture that looked like the museum-quality miniatures she had seen on display. He glossed over his childhood, but he said enough for her to understand what he wasn't saying: for a man who had been raised on what he called a west Texas dirt farm, he and some members of his family had ranged far and wide from their beginnings.

She didn't learn why he had chosen to take a vacation in November, nor did she learn why his expression became withdrawn, almost painfully so, when he mentioned his job. That was all right. She really didn't want to learn too much about the pressures of the Dallas P.D., any more than she wanted to reflect on why she had really left the clinic in Chicago. She did share the story of how she had come to own a sprawling purple monstrosity on a hillside in downtown Allegro.

"My mother put the bid in for me," she said.

"She what?"

Anne nodded. "I didn't even know about the family's lawsuit to partition the property, only that I wanted to come home. At least for a while. I had no idea that I would enjoy renovating an old house. I did ask Mom why, if she thought the house was such a great buy, she didn't buy it herself. She just said that she knew herself as well as she knew me; she'd found her haven and now it was my turn." Anne smiled with the memory of her mother's impassioned speech. "She said that even though Allegro hadn't been particularly good for her, it was probably just what I needed. At least for now."

"So you bought it?"

"Once I saw it, I knew she was right. Purple paint and all." Anne laughed in self-conscious acknowledgment of Joe and all the unpleasantness. "But along with it, I have acquired what appears to be a family feud. It seems they were a package deal, and if my mother knew about it, she kept that knowledge to herself."

"Is this a long-standing feud?"

"I don't know. No one seems willing to admit it exists, much less talk about it."

For a moment she glimpsed the cop in him. "Is it a dangerous one?"

Loud laughter erupted from across the room. In one of those odd coincidences no one would believe, the laughter came from the men with Joe, the main perpetrator of the very feud they were discussing. Their party was breaking up, and Joe, after ignoring her, this time for more than a month, stood up, snagged his leather jacket from the back of his chair, and walked to where she sat.

He stood there with his jacket caught by one finger over his shoulder, pearl snaps gleaming on his white-on-white western shirt, knife-edge creases accenting black denim jeans, tooled leather and triple-stitching marking his boots as custom-made.

"Anne," he said, with all the warmth of an IRS auditor.

"Joe," she answered, marginally warmer.

"I hear you've had more trouble up at the house."

Now where would he have heard a thing like that?

"No," she said. "Not that I know of."

"You haven't lost another crew?"

As if he didn't know. He probably had a pipeline to the lumberyard, if not to the carpenters themselves. "Why, Joe, I'm getting so used to that, I don't consider it trouble any more, just a fact of life. Let me guess—you're starting a new project, and my two carpenters were the very ones you needed for a special phase of that job."

"Winter's coming, Anne," he said, ignoring her gibe. "I worry about you up there all alone. That house has to be almost uninhabitable. When are you going to give up in this effort to inconvenience me?"

"Joe, Joe," she chided. "If you hadn't been so sure of yourself that you only bid ten cents on the dollar, you'd own the house now."

His smile slipped slightly. "Yeah, but that was all it was worth, sitting there going to ruin. I bid fair market value for the land. I suppose you're going to want a profit on what you've done—"

When she shook her head, he grimaced. "You won't last the winter," he said. "You might as well get someplace comfortable before it gets really cold."

David picked up his coffee cup and set it back in the saucer, a nonthreatening action that somehow managed to convey all sorts of unspoken menace. Joe wasn't unaware of him; he'd just been ignoring him. Now he glanced down, taking in David's desperado appearance in one sweeping, disdainful glimpse. He had to know who David was—everyone in the restaurant did—but he chose to pretend that he didn't. That didn't surprise her; his words did.

"You're starting a little early, aren't you? Even for someone with your track record."

No. Winter wasn't coming early; it was already here. Anne felt the chill clear through her bones. What had she ever done to Joe Hansom that would cause him to make such a malicious, mean-spirited attack? Other than buying a house that was up for grabs anyway? Nothing. At least nothing that she was aware of.

She saw David lean forward in his chair and wondered if they were going to have a major scene in the Lake Café. No. She wouldn't give Joe that satisfaction. She smiled at him. "I got a letter from my mother last week. From Australia? You do remember that's where she lives now, don't you, Joe? She asked me to give her regards to your grandmother. Since you won't tell me where she is, please pass the message on to her for me, will you? Or maybe I should just ask around until I find her."

Joe's smug grin became a little strained. He nodded abruptly and left without saying another word.

David Huerra studied her silently for a moment. He glanced in the direction of the door to make sure Joe had left, then rose and held his hand out for her. "I think it's time for us to leave, too."

Yes, it was.

The rain had eased, but the wind was just as cold as they drove back toward town.

"I take it that was an example of the feud," David said.

She nodded. "It's a lovely family, isn't it?"

"Obviously you were adopted."

"Thanks." She sank back against the cracked seat and looked out the window, silent for perhaps another mile, debating with herself, knowing she had to tell him. "Joe has a vicious mouth."

"You don't owe me any explanation," he said, and she knew by the way he said it he'd thought Joe had been making some sort of sexual innuendo. And maybe he'd already heard the stories circulating about her birth. About her mother. "By this time tomorrow everyone else in Pitchlyn County is going to know what he said and what he was talking about. I'd rather at least one person heard it from me," she said, hoping she didn't sound as weary of Joe's unending rumors and innuendos as she felt.

They were still a couple of miles outside of town. Huerra found a wide shoulder and pulled off the road, set the emergency brake and flashers, and turned in the seat to face her. "Okay," he said. "Shock my socks off me."

"I wish." Was there any good way to say this? Damn Joe anyway. She sucked in a deep breath. "He was making allusions to your visible injuries, not to the fact that we were sharing a meal. It seems I— Well, the men in my life . . . They die."

She'd shocked him all right. Maybe he still had on his socks, but for several seconds it seemed he'd lost his voice. "Oh, hell, Annie. Damn that son of a bitch!"

She tried to rake her hand through her hair, got it caught in the pins and gave up. "The first one was in high school. We'd gone steady for three years, two eggheads who didn't fit in with anyone else. Someone decided it would be fun to spike his drink to see how a nerd acted drunk. Then they put him in his car and let him go off alone. He drove off the side of a mountain."

"Annie—"

"It's all right," she said. "I can tell you. Maybe I need to tell you. The other one was a man I had been engaged to. We'd decided we didn't really have what it took to make a marriage work, but Anthony and I did have a fine friendship and a good working relationship. He was murdered—killed in a clinic robbery."

"Hell."

"Yeah."

She thought for a minute that David was going to reach for her. She thought for a minute she needed him to do just that. She hadn't talked about Anthony in months—not to anyone—and just mentioning him brought back too-vivid memories that had stubbornly refused to fade. Instead, David turned in the seat and started the Blazer back toward Allegro with what she suspected to be an uncharacteristic clashing of gears.

David stayed silent—so did she—until they were back in her kitchen. There, he looked at the supplies spilling from the tool room. "Joe is responsible for your crews being hired away from you, isn't he?"

"No one will admit it, but, yes, I think he is. Men who haven't worked for weeks, some of them for months, are suddenly offered long-term projects just as I get them lined up out here."

"What does he want with this place?"

"I think he really does just want the land. Willie Johnson at the sawmill told me Joe wanted to put up another set of apartments like the ones south of town."

"You mean the ones that look like prefab mini-storage buildings?"

She caught her hand to her mouth as an unexpected laugh broke from her. "Yes," she said. "That's exactly what they look like."

He pulled off his windbreaker and draped it over a kitchen chair. "Why don't you show me what needs to be done?"

"Why—"

"I don't like your cousin Joe," he said. "Your cousin Joe is not a nice man, and he's had everything his way for much too long."

"But you're on vacation."

"Yeah," he said, and grinned. It was not a nice grin, not at all like the easy, companionable ones he had shared with her and that had coaxed return smiles from her. No. This one gave her a glimpse of a side of David Huerra she wasn't sure she was ready to know. "Against my will and for a month. And it just so happens that this west Texas farmboy worked his way through night school on a construction crew."

"You're injured. And you came here to fish."

"Wrong," he said. "I came here to think, and I can do that just as well helping you as I can killing bait. Besides, you were the one who told me my brain was still working. Do you remember what the weather is like outside? With the windchill it's about ten degrees, and that's on dry land. God only knows what it is out on the lake in a boat. Come on, Annie, isn't there some part of you, buried way down deep, that wants to rub good old Joe's face in it? Let's do it, Annie. Let's fix up this house. And let's see who offers me what to leave you stranded."

He was offering her retribution for all the slights and slurs Joe had been responsible for giving her since she'd inadvertently thwarted his latest plans. Already he knew her well enough to know what her answer had to be.

Knew it before she did.

And he was right.

In spite of his stated intent, David Huerra didn't start work on Anne's house that Sunday. After a tour and a discussion of what had been done and what remained to be done, after a slice of Sara Lee pound cake topped with the last of her precious stash of Häagen-Dazs, after a yawn and a stretch and a groan she knew he didn't intend for her to hear, he left, banished by her to his rented cabin on the lake for much needed rest.

What she wanted but wasn't able to do that afternoon was to finish lowering the kitchen ceiling so that she'd have one room where the heat didn't hover twelve feet above the floor. What she was able but didn't want to do that afternoon was some minor finish work in the butler's pantry, which, until she'd knocked the doorway through to the hall, had been the only access to the kitchen from the rest of the house.

What she did was something she hadn't done in years. Her things were packed away in a jumble of unlabeled boxes in an abandoned parlor off the living room, and it took some time to locate them, and then to drag the kitchen table closer to the gas heater, and to find a floor lamp to use until her magnifier surfaced.

Her tools and supplies were in three modified tackle boxes. She scooted her pile of invoices and bills to one side and arranged all three cases on the kitchen table within easy reach.

Anne opened the first tackle box and glanced at the battered and well-used metal snips, shears, and soldering irons. She hadn't been able to spend a lot of money on her hobby, and for the last few years she hadn't even been able to spend a lot of time on it. For Anne's high school graduation, her mother had presented her with an unorthodox gift. Anne lifted the fitted case from the bottom of the tackle box's deep tray and opened it, too, tracing her fingers over the matching precision scaled awls and punches and rasps, the calipers and pliers and hand drill with its assorted bits.

Her mother *did* know her well. Any doubts Anne might have harbored about that disappeared when she touched the set of tools that she had coveted for years but had never mentioned to her mother, had no idea her mother knew anything about, until she had opened her gift expecting to see something imminently practical for college and found these.

Somewhere Anne had a padded work surface, but she hadn't uncovered that or her anvil or grinder in her search through the packing crates. She took a folded jeweler's cloth from the second of the boxes, spread it on the table in front of her and began opening the trays and drawers of this case. She'd never used many stones in her work, preferring the beauty of the metal she'd worked with, but she did have a small hoard of them. She lifted them to the cloth, along with the few finished pieces she hadn't yet given away, a couple of partially completed pins, and a scattering of loose findings.

Then she opened the third box.

And knew what had compelled her to drag out these icons of her youth.

But not why.

Not yet why.

She felt a strange tightness in her throat and chest— apprehension or anticipation?—and a betraying tremor in her hands as she lifted the carefully wrapped bundle from the third box and placed it on the cloth in front of her. She'd foregone lunches and movies in high school, and later even necessities, to keep herself supplied with what she'd long ago determined was as essential to her well-being as the air she breathed.

And she hadn't even looked at it in years.

Did she want to now?

This wasn't the material she had cut so that she could shape the smaller pieces. This was intact, although some of it—very little—was worked. She remembered that, too well, and how she had agonized over the designs and the execution. But the other was clean, pristine, just waiting for—for what? For a skill greater than hers had been or probably ever would be, she suspected.

Another gust of rain battered the windows, and in it she heard what she very much feared was ice. What little daylight there had been was fading fast, and the kitchen was illuminated now only by the circle of light from the floor lamp and from the open gas flames of the heater and range. She shivered, cold again, even in her heavy sweater. The chill extended to her fingers. She flexed them once, twice, before reaching again for the bundle and folding back the cloth.

The metal should have been cold. Everything she knew or had been taught told her that. Each exquisite and finely prepared leaf should have absorbed the chill from the unheated room where it had been stored, from the draft now scooting across the kitchen, from the years of having been abandoned to the darkness. But it wasn't. She dropped her hands to the top sheet, unmindful for the moment of fingerprints and damaging oils, and felt the warmth and the soft, beckoning glow of the copper fill her with the same inexplicable longing it always had.

5

1935

     Son of a bitch, but it was cold. Ralph Hansom leaned against the truck and shrugged deeper into the long wool coat he'd bought on one of his trips back east. The hicks in Allegro had laughed at him the first time he'd worn it on the streets there. No one would ever need a coat like that this far south, they'd told him. Well, he was the one laughing now. Maybe they hadn't had so much as a killing frost until a week ago, but those bastards digging and crawling through the tunnels not a quarter of a mile away were freezing their asses off now.

    He stamped his feet, feeling the crunch of frozen grass beneath them. There was one blessing to the cold. With all the rain they'd had, even the abandoned roadbed where they'd parked wouldn't have been protection enough, but maybe Jackson wouldn't get mired down trying to get out of here after all.

    Not that he was worried about Tom Jackson. He'd paid the man enough over the years for him to take the risk. And if Jackson hadn't figured out he was risking more than losing his new truck in the river bottoms if it mired down, if the men who owned the leases for digging found out what he was doing—and had been doing since long before they had taken steps to legitimize their own plundering—then who was he to tell him?

Should he be here? He hadn't bothered to return since his first visit two years ago, when dealers had been invited but were treated like beggars for the grave goods being brought out. He'd long before learned the general location of where Jackson was obtaining the objects he'd been bringing him for almost a decade, just not exactly where and how, something he'd rather not be too familiar with. Rather than submit himself to the haggling, the bickering, the total lack of respect he'd found on that one trip, he'd decided to continue his more than lucrative association with the one-time dirt farmer. And Jackson hadn't been averse to doing so. Granted, it was a little more risky for him than it had once been, but the artifacts more than made up for the increased sums the man demanded.

Ralph could see the flare of bonfires from the site, smell—what? cedar?—burning, and hear the noises from the digging, oaths and groans and shouts all carried on the wind from the northwest that hurried across the river but seemed to gather strength when it reached the grove where Hansom and the truck waited.

Oaths and groans and shouts and—and what? For a moment Hansom thought he heard footsteps in the frost-bitten underbrush beneath the trees surrounding him. The footsteps of something large and restless. Pacing. Pacing. Back and forth. Back and forth. For a moment he thought he saw a glow— Someone coming with a torch? But that was gone. And then it wasn't his eyes that were alerted to strange goings-on but his ears. A growl?

The wind.

Moaning through the dead leaves still clinging to otherwise bare branches.

Moaning around the hills to the west that had been built by a race far removed from the one that now scrabbled to find the treasures hidden there.

Moaning in the dips and hollows of the river-bottom lands and erosion creeks.

Still—

A branch snapped beneath something heavy, and Ralph Hansom swung around with an oath of his own.

Another branch broke in the underbrush. Hansom twisted in that direction, reaching for the Colt revolver in his overcoat's deep pocket. This time he was sure he heard a growl. Mountain lion? It was possible farther south, but here, along the river? Whatever it was, it was big. Damned big.

He heard the wind moan again, recognizing it this time for what it was, and told himself to relax. He was getting too old for skulking in the bushes. If tonight hadn't been the last chance, if Jackson hadn't sworn it would be worth his while, if he hadn't had a buyer with more money than China had people, he wouldn't be here now. If he hadn't been here before, if he hadn't known what was causing those sporadic leaps of flames, his imagination might not be playing these tricks on him.

He understood the diggers burning the cedar poles and beams they brought out of the mound. Unless they were written on or painted or carved, they had no value except as firewood, and God knew the diggers needed something to burn for heat.

But the bones?

He didn't want them; no buyer he knew of wanted them. What the hell did he expect the diggers to do with them? Take them back into the mound after they'd made sure they contained nothing of value? Call a preacher out here to say prayers over the heathens? They didn't have time for that. Ralph knew it, even understood it. Midnight, which was coming soon, marked the end of the lease and the end of the only job the few, trusted hired workmen had been able to find in months. Marked the end of the time the state of Oklahoma had insisted the leaseholders had before they had to stop, forever, the private excavations regardless of what kind of a deal they could work out with the landowners. Marked the end of the time that Hansom, with Tom Jackson's help, would be able to provide his carefully cultivated group of collectors with the items they had grown to covet.

Well, hell, whoever the bones had belonged to was dead. Long dead. Each and every one of them. Think of this as a delayed cremation. Some ancient civilizations had cremated their dead, hadn't they? He wasn't too sure of that. He could recite the going price for an Egyptian scarab or a Mayan celt or a Spiro gorget dead drunk or in his sleep; his knowledge didn't extend to the people who had made these things. Hadn't had to. Wouldn't need to.

It was just a bone pile, he told himself. Just a damned bone pile. Every rancher he knew had one. A place in a ravine or gully or grove of trees, where he dragged the carcasses of his disease- or predator-killed livestock and left them there to rot or be scavenged, until the ravine or gully or copse was full of bleached white skulls and bones.

It meant nothing there; it meant nothing here.

What did mean something here was that one strange, carved pipe and the wealth of arrowheads and pots and engraved shells that Jackson had been bringing him for almost a decade.

What meant something here was the comfortable lifestyle he had made for himself placing those arrowheads and shells and heathen treasures with so-called connoisseurs of history. Connoisseurs, hell. They were greedy bastards, every one of them. But they had served him well. Ellie's family didn't dare look down on him now, didn't dare say that he wouldn't have a home or two dimes to rub together if it hadn't been for her land and money.

Some said the people who had built these mounds were the ancestors of Ellie's people, not that anybody knew for sure, but wouldn't that be justice of the nicest kind—that in the long run the very people who had proved so tight-fisted with the money from their land and coal and gas roy-alties had provided him with the means to tell them all to go to hell, that he didn't need them anymore? Not them. Not Ellie. Not the brat she had presented him with.

He heard a shout from the direction of the mounds and a strange silence before voices broke out in a con-fusing babble of sound, and then a crashing through the underbrush as of something heavy running. He felt a bead of sweat pop out on his upper lip and chill in the night air. He yanked the Colt out of his pocket even as he opened the truck door, preparing to leap into the cab.

Jackson. Ralph sagged against the truck door. Only Jackson. Running. For his life? And then Ralph noticed what he should have seen at once. Jackson was empty-handed.

"Get in the truck," Jackson called out in an urgent hiss. "Now!"

Other sounds intruded over the calls from the exca-vation, and three men broke from the woods carrying a strange, long litter of some sort, canvas covered, sagging between the poles and with at least three baskets jum-bled on top. Ralph hesitated at the truck door while Jackson lowered the tailgate and directed the dumping of whatever the men carried into the bed of the truck. One man crawled in with the litter, but when the other two tried, Jackson waved them back. "On the running boards," he told them. "And for God's sake, be quiet."

Ralph slipped into the cab of the truck and eased his door shut. Jackson leapt into the driver's side, glanced at Hansom and jerked Ralph's hat down to cover his eyes just as one of the men jumped up onto the running board beside Jackson, the other beside Hansom and looked into the cab. "Who's this?"

"Never mind, Billy Ray. You don't want him to know who you are, either."

The man called Billy Ray grunted an acknowledgment. "You got that right. Let's get the hell out of here."

"Not yet," Jackson said grimly.

Jackson sat in tense silence behind the wheel, not reaching for the starter, obviously waiting. But for what, Ralph wondered.

When the explosion rocked the ground even as far away as they were parked, he had his answer. And the leaseholders had their revenge. Jackson fired the engine and spun them out of their hiding place, slewing chert and shale and frozen mud behind them as the two on the running boards swore and grabbed for purchase. Jackson didn't stop or slow down until they reached the old Fort Coffee cemetery, where he wheeled in and skidded to a stop.

Jackson left the engine running while he got out of the truck and joined the three men at the back. Ralph stepped out in time to see Jackson lift a basket from the back and hand it to the one he'd called Billy Ray.

"There's enough here to keep the two of you well for a long time," Jackson said. "Just don't be in too big a hurry to let anyone know you've got it. And if you're thinking about coming back on me for more, I can see that the other men who paid your wages tonight find out that you were working for more than one. You got that clear in your minds?"

Ralph caught only a glimpse of the contents of the basket. Beads, pearls, a few broken shells. For a moment he considered arguing Jackson's method of payment, but he recognized the wisdom of it. What the men were taking wasn't that valuable in the overall scheme of things, depending on what was in the other baskets and under the canvas, and giving it to them made them more active participants than just hired hands. Well, well, maybe the dirt farmer had learned a few of the finer points of stealth and deception while he was grubbing around in the back of a man-made hill. Of course, knowing that made Hansom realize just how much he'd have to keep his eye on Jackson.

Two of the men left. When Jackson turned to get in the truck, he waved the third man from the back with a gesture that said plainly he was to ride up front. "My son," Jackson told him.

"Am I going to get a chance to look at what you've got before we get out of here?"

Jackson laughed. "What difference does it make now? We've got it, and if that blast was half as successful as I think it was, we're not going to have a chance to get more. Let's head to your place before someone from the site stumbles on us and decides they want to have a look at our cargo, too. I don't think either one of us would like what would happen if we're caught."

Ten miles outside of Allegro, on a muddy and pot-holed mountain switchback with no way to go but down, Jackson again stopped the truck and turned in the seat to look at Hansom.

"I've been thinking," Jackson said, "that I've learned a little about the stuff I've been hauling down to you over the years. I've been thinking that I've learned a little about the other folks that deal in this kind of stuff."

Ralph tensed. Maybe he'd been too trusting for too long. Maybe he should have started watching out for Jackson a lot sooner than this abandoned road in the predawn hours. Cautiously he felt for the Colt in his pocket. How big a shakedown was coming? Casually, almost without effort, a hand came from behind him and clamped his in place before it ever reached his pocket. Jackson's son. Shit.

"What else have you been thinking, Tom?"

Jackson smiled at him, his teeth white in the darkness of the cab. "I've been thinking that all in all, except for the first few loads when you cheated my socks off me, you've been fair. Fair enough so that I'd hate to have to break in that fellow down in El Dorado, or one of those men from Missouri. But those first few loads do stick in my craw, Hansom. You know, like something you just have to drag out and chew on every once in a while? It leaves a bad taste, a sour stomach, and sometimes even a hangover. I sure don't want to have to add to that mess of stuff I'm already chewing on. Sure would appreciate it if I could get rid of some of the old stuff, too. So I figured I'd talk to you, maybe come to a real clear understanding about what this night is going to mean to me, especially now that I won't be able to get anything else."

Hansom drew in a shallow breath, trying not to suck in air, trying to ignore the hand clamped on his. "I thought we'd come to an agreement about what the different things were worth. Are you suggesting that we change that agreement now?"

Jackson shook his head. "No. I've been talking, casual like and real careful. I figure you were paying me right for them. It's just that I ain't never brought you anything quite like I've brought you tonight, and I think we ought to have an understanding before we get to your place."

"Or?"

"Or I let you out here, you walk home, and me and my boy drive to Missouri."

Hansom relaxed marginally. As a shakedown, it wasn't too bad, nothing, maybe, that he couldn't talk his way out of. "Just what in the hell do you have back there?"

As he appeared to relax, so did Jackson. He leaned back against the door. "There's been an archaeologist fellow there, wringing his hands and watching us dig. He even went in once, but when he found out we weren't shoring up the tunnels, he backed right out and went to moaning and groaning about the way we were treating stuff, first of all by even daring to touch it, and then in the way we handled it when it came out. You'd have thought we were in his grandmother's casket the way he carried on.

"Well, what I learned from him was that these things have more value if they're treated a certain way. Like records kept of where they were found. Like some things being kept together. He kept talking about 'intact burials' and 'integrity of the find,' or dictionary words something like that. So when we found what we found, I knew what I had to do. I'd have liked to get that other one. Whooee, that cloak was something else, all feathers and beads woven in with only God knows what. Must have been seven, eight feet long, but somebody else grabbed that right off the skeleton, and I knew I couldn't take the chance of trying to get it back.

"So me and the boys, we threw a little dirt over this one then hauled it out in wheelbarrows until I could get the tarps laced onto the poles—we got all of them, too, that archaeologist would be right proud of the way we made sure of that—and hauled it out. It's all there—or most of it. We dropped some, and then we had to give that little stuff to the crew—"

Hansom leaned forward. Jackson's enthusiasm was catching. "What are you saying? Just what did you bring out?"

Jackson grinned. "Hey, partner," he said, and Hansom didn't bother to correct him, "I think we got ourselves one of their gods."

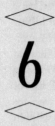

6

Anne didn't expect David Huerra to arrive the next morning. That's what she told herself as she leaned against the sink while she ate her English muffin, surveying the wreck of her kitchen and listening to the rain as it battered the windows.

She hadn't expected him, but when she heard the knock on the back door, she wasn't surprised.

He wore a disreputable pair of jeans and his boots—not the cowboy kind she was used to seeing around Allegro, but a pair that made her wonder if he'd ever done motorcycle patrol—his blue windbreaker, a gimme cap from Tompkins fish camp, and of course his spectacular bruise that tied his bad-guy-run-amok costume all together.

"Don't even think about walking to work today," David said as he took off his cap and hit it against his thigh, sending raindrops and ice pellets scattering on the porch.

She stepped back to let him enter the kitchen then hurriedly closed the door behind him.

He stopped just inside, sniffed deeply, and smiled at her. "Good. Real coffee. I knew you couldn't be the early-morning-instant type."

Anne nodded toward the counter, feeling a reluctant smile of her own. What was there about this man that gave him the ability to creep behind her armor? What was there about him that she found so appealing? Especially since she suspected that with any encouragement he could be totally overbearing. "Help yourself," she told him. "And by the way, good morning to you, too."

She heard a mumble from him that could have been a belated greeting. So David wasn't a morning person? That did surprise her. She studied him a little more carefully as he reached into the cabinet for a cup and poured himself some coffee, noticing then the care with which he moved. Men! Why on earth did they have to be so—so damned macho? And why on earth did David Huerra think he had to hide his physical discomfort from her? After all, she'd been there when the accident happened. She'd cared for him then and since, and she'd continue to—

Whoa!

She'd continue to *what*? The eerie feeling of déjà vu, of having cared for this man before, hovered around her. For a moment she fought it but when that did no good, she searched frantically for a logical reason for the feeling. When she found it, she couldn't stop the relieved laugh that broke from her. Saturday. Of course. When she had found herself completely and uncharacteristically tending to more than his health needs.

He turned and peered at her over the rim of his cup. "Are you okay?"

Maybe she wasn't, because it seemed so natural for her to go to the fridge, take out another muffin, split it, and drop it into the toaster. For him.

"Sure. What brings you out this early? What brings you out in this weather at all?"

"Cabin fever," he said. "And the fact that your place is warmer than mine."

She raised an eyebrow at that and glanced pointedly at all four of the burners on her kitchen range, which were turned up to maximum, one of them with an upended clay flowerpot on top to act as an improvised radiant.

"And to take you to work," he added.

She'd started to tell him she hadn't planned on walking that morning, that she'd already decided to drive Agnes. His next words stopped her.

"It looks as if that four-wheel drive Blazer is going to come in handy after all."

"The roads are icy?"

He nodded. "The highway and downtown streets are bad enough, but that ski slope you call a driveway is nearly impassable."

"In November?" she asked, incredulous. "I thought this was the South."

The muffin popped up from the toaster. He looked at her questioningly. "For you," she said. "I've already eaten."

He slathered butter on it from the open container and munched reflectively. "Texas is south, Doc," he told her finally. "I'm not sure what this place is anymore." So saying, he carried both muffin halves and his coffee across the room and backed up to the gas heater. "So what time do you have to be at the clinic?"

"Soon," she said, and glanced at her watch. "Oh lord, yes. Real soon." If the streets were as bad as David said, most of her morning appointments would probably cancel, but that time was sure to be filled with work-ins of people who didn't have enough sense to stay in off the ice. "Let me get my snow boots," she told him, glad that she hadn't gotten rid of them when she made the move from Chicago.

When she returned to the kitchen, wrapped and bundled like she'd thought she'd never have to be again and carrying her bag, she found David standing at the table, gently tracing his finger along the narrow sheet of copper with the design she had worked on until well past midnight. She'd mentioned to him Sunday that she'd once worked at jewelry-making, but she had been deliberately vague about the depth of her interest; it wasn't something she had shared with many people. At least not since starting med school.

Now she wondered why.

Slowly, almost reluctantly, he turned his attention from the sheet of copper to her. "You're good, Doc. Real good."

His words warmed her more than her down-filled coat and fleece-lined boots. "Thanks."

"It reminds me of—" He hesitated. "I'm not sure just what it reminds me of. It's vaguely meso-American, but not really Aztec. Not really Mayan. Not really anything I've seen before."

She knew what he meant, because when she had first begun the series of designs, of which this was but one of many, she'd wondered if she was being derivative, and if so, of what.

"Maybe it's just 'Anne Locke,'" she said.

He touched the design once again: a salute? a farewell? "Maybe it is at that." He pulled the folded cap from his jacket pocket and settled it on his head, but waited while she put her supplies back into the tackle boxes and closed them. "So what would you like me to work on first, boss? I'm not sure I'm up to putting in the ceiling without a helper, but I'm game for just about anything else."

Anne might as well have stayed at home. She ran the clinic with the help of Margaret Samuels, an extremely efficient registered nurse who had been out of the workforce for almost a decade, but had kept her license and her training up to date and announced she was ready to return to work when Anne arrived in Allegro looking for an office assistant. Margaret had the doors unlocked, the heater turned up, and the coffee made by the time David Huerra delivered Anne to the front steps and into the building before leaving.

Margaret had also noted the cancellations who had already called, and had begun a list of those she was willing to wager a week's worth of coffee-making just wouldn't show up.

One of those who didn't show up, but who did eventually telephone—just before Anne called Blake Foresman's office to get someone to search for her—was Nellie Flynn, part-time office help, inexperienced, never before employed, who had turned out to be as dependable as the chimes in the Methodist Church in Fairview and, after an almost nonexistent training period, as competent at her job as Margaret and Anne were at theirs. Nellie had slid her car into a ditch halfway down the mountain between her house and the highway and had walked back home before she'd been able to call. After Nellie assured Anne that she wasn't hurt, and that she had a neighbor who could retrieve her car for her, Anne made her promise to stay home until the roads thawed, which Margaret assured her would be soon.

Not soon enough, Anne thought with grim resignation as the day dragged on and she realized that she might have been overly optimistic about how well the people of Allegro had welcomed her. In a day when only three patients showed up, she had to admit that her practice wasn't exactly growing by leaps and bounds. While she undoubtedly got to treat most of the kids for colds and sprains and childhood diseases, and even their mothers for viruses or confirming pregnancy, she seldom saw anything serious walk through her clinic doors. If it was serious, if there was even the slightest suspicion that it might be, the patient bypassed her, usually bypassed the facilities in Fairview, too, and went directly to Fort Smith or to Texarkana.

But that was what Anne had wanted, wasn't it? She'd certainly told herself it was when she'd turned down a position on staff at an Indianapolis hospital and another with an aggressive and growing clinic in Lincoln—both among the places she'd applied while her life was in the process of going to hell but before it actually got all the way down there.

At three o'clock the snow started. All day the rain had been mixed with freezing rain and sleet. It gave way entirely to big white flakes that quickly built up on fences, tree branches, and windowsills. Margaret and Anne shared a long, discouraging minute in front of the rapidly fogging doors.

"Well, hell," Margaret said, sighing. "Three days before Thanksgiving. Who'd have thought it?" She grinned. "I sure hope the deer hunters are having a good time."

Knowing the hunters she'd met in Allegro, who seemed to live for deer season, or turkey season, or some even for no season, Anne suspected a little friendly malice in Margaret's words. "You'd better get home while you still can," she told her nurse. "I can take care of things here for the rest of the day."

Margaret laughed in that earthy, abrupt way Anne had first resented because she didn't understand and now had come to appreciate. "Honey, the roaches from that closed-down tavern out on Highway 59 can take care of all the business that's going to come through this door today. Grab your coat while I turn on the answering machine and tell the county to call you just in case there is an emergency, and then I'll give you a lift home.

Unless you want to call tall, dark, and dangerous to come after you."

Anne shot her a glance, but Margaret was all innocence as she turned on the answering machine, made her telephone call to the sheriff's dispatcher, and began turning off lights. Tall, dark, and dangerous, huh? Anne wondered what David Huerra would think of that description.

Margaret drove an oversized truck as down to earth and as efficient as she was. But she didn't immediately point it toward her house. When Anne turned to her to question her, Margaret shrugged. "Bet you don't have your holiday groceries bought yet, do you?"

Holiday groceries? For whom? And while Anne couldn't quite imagine turkey for one, she resisted the impulse to feel sorry for herself. Her mother, her stepfather, and her two half-brothers were on the other side of the world, the cousins her age had all moved away to find work, and Joe's part of the family hadn't seen fit to do any inviting.

"You've got that right," Anne said. "As a matter of fact, I don't even have my weekly groceries bought yet."

"Busy weekend?" Margaret asked, doing her best to leer suggestively.

Anne spluttered out a laugh. "Don't tell me the stories made it all the way up your hill. And you didn't say a word all day?"

"I was waiting for you to," she said. "Especially after I saw how you got to work."

"But—"

"Easy, Doc," she said. "Everybody in town may know he drove you to work today, but they also know he spent the night in Gretta Tompkins's Number 4 cabin. Alone.

"They also know your latest crew quit on you. And that Joe stopped to say sweet, loving words to you at the Lake Café yesterday."

Anne shook her head. "Is anything ever kept secret around here?"

"Nope," Margaret told her. "Not unless you work at it real hard." She frowned. "Some do." After another moment she added, "Joe usually does."

The truck skidded a bit as Margaret turned into a half-empty parking lot. She tapped the brakes lightly and brought her truck to a stop four spaces from the front door of the grocery store. "We're either real lucky or real late," she said. "Whichever, we need to stock up while there are still groceries of any sort available."

"Stock up? You sound like we're in for a blizzard," Anne protested. "Isn't this supposed to go away in a matter of hours?"

"It isn't supposed to happen at all," Margaret admitted. "Not this early. But since it has, you've got to realize that nobody knows how to drive on ice down here so you might as well be prepared. Then if the temperature goes up to seventy tomorrow, the worst that can happen is you'll have a full pantry, but if it stays cold or gets worse, you're ready for it." She grinned. "Especially if you just happen to get iced in with someone who can't get back out to a certain uninsulated cabin on a very bad road."

The house smelled like fresh paint and turpentine and simmering, spicy chicken when Margaret and Anne made the slippery run from the truck into the kitchen. Best of all, it felt blessedly warm after the buffeting they had taken from the wind in just the short distance from the truck to the porch.

And when Anne saw David Huerra standing at the kitchen sink, it felt like home.

She didn't have time to explore that, though. David whirled around from the sink when they came bursting through the door, but when he saw her he leaned back against the counter, drying his hands. "You're home early."

"Yes," Margaret said, giving him a blatant once-over. "That's because we wanted to get home. Hello." She bumped the two grocery bags she carried up onto the counter beside the ones Anne had just placed there and thrust out her hand. "I'm Margaret Samuels, Doc Anne's nurse. You left the clinic before I got to meet you this morning."

David returned her admiring smile, but Anne saw an easy humor in his eyes, not seduction. "My loss," he said, taking Margaret's hand. "I'm David Huerra—"

"The Dallas cop," Margaret finished for him. She gave a deep sigh and patted his hand. "Why couldn't it have been me out at Willie Johnson's sawmill Saturday?" She glanced at the paintbrushes that lay on the counter beside the sink, and the open toolbox that sat beside them. "I'll bet Joe's wishing pretty much the same thing."

David chuckled before he turned serious. "How bad are the roads?"

"Strictly four-wheel drive," Margaret told him. "But the snow's actually helping by covering up some of the ice. Or at least it will until it freezes over, too." She shrugged and drew her hand from his. "And I'd better get back out on them if I'm to have any hope of getting up my hill tonight."

"You could stay," Anne offered, remembering how cautiously Margaret had had to drive to get the short distance from the clinic and up her potholed driveway and dreading the thought of the miles the woman still had to travel. "I have plenty of room."

Had Anne surprised her nurse? Was her offer of hospitality so out of line? Maybe. Margaret seemed startled for a moment, but shook her head. "Thanks, anyway. But I have—responsibilities. Livestock, you know. Chickens."

Margaret left in a flurry of admonitions and cautions and promises to be careful. When Anne turned from the door and at last began unbundling from scarf and gloves and coat, she realized how much Margaret's presence had filled the room and how inexplicably awkward she felt being alone with David Huerra as the snow swirled outside and early darkness threatened.

Awkward. How strange. Especially after that one burst of . . . of belonging she had felt only minutes before.

"I'd better change clothes," she said, clutching her coat to her chest.

David looked at her, cocked his head to one side and tugged at his earlobe, but all he said was, "Watch out for the wet paint."

Awkward. Since she had met him she had felt many things, but always she'd had this underlying sense of having known this man forever, and well. What had changed? What could have changed in the few hours since he had left her at the clinic door? Nothing, she told herself. Not a thing. She dredged up a smile for him and left the room.

He'd told her to watch out for wet paint. She just hadn't realized how much of it there was. He'd finished framing and hanging the new kitchen/hallway door and replacing the trim along the hallway wainscoting and bathroom door. All of it gleamed with new gloss enamel. But that wasn't what drew her attention.

Anne stopped at the bottom of the stairwell, her attention drawn upward. For a moment she stood there with her hand on the old age-blackened varnish of the railing and her foot on the bottom step, listening—longing. Had she heard something? Or had she only wanted to hear something?

And then she realized how bizarre the last few minutes would seem to anyone else—as bizarre as David Huerra's first reaction to her house?—and gave a self-conscious chuckle as she forced herself to turn away from the stairs and go on into the bedroom to change into jeans and a sweatshirt so that she could rejoin David in the warmth of the kitchen and get on with the nev-erending project of making this old house into a home.

If anyone had asked her the previous Saturday morning before she went to Willie Johnson's sawmill, Anne would have said she didn't want a man in her life. She didn't need a man in her life. She didn't need anyone in her life until she figured out what *she* was doing in her life.

After having had seven roommates while in med school, and never a moment to herself afterward because of the pressures of her practice and her clinic work, and the sheer number of other people who lived in the building where she had finally leased a tiny one-bedroom apartment that was all her own, after she'd seen how crowding too many persons in too small a space with no hope for more destroyed the humanity in those crowded, Anne had hoped she would be for-ever happy, or at least content, to rattle around in her small town and her big old house without having to worry about offending, bothering, or annoying anyone else. Or being offended, bothered, or annoyed by someone.

David Huerra didn't offend or annoy her. Bother her, yes. But that was something she was trying very hard not to think about.

There was something pleasant about coming home

from work and finding him there, something familiar about working together and sharing with him the meal that he had begun but that together they finished preparing; something almost . . . almost intimate about how easily they settled into each other's lives while the evening settled around them. At least that was how it seemed until he pushed back from the table after their meal and walked over to the pile of drywall and rolled insulation.

"You had company today, Doc."

"Here? At the house? Everybody knows I'm at the clinic on Mondays."

He nodded. "That's what I thought. But I couldn't be sure whether his surprise was at seeing me here, or at seeing anybody at all when the house was supposed to be empty. He covered it real well, though."

"He?" Anne had lived in the city too long. Her paranoia was working overtime. "I don't suppose it was my loving cousin Joe with an invitation to Thanksgiving dinner?"

David quirked a grin at her. "What? You'd accept and waste that runt bird I saw you stash in the freezer?"

She shook her head. There'd be no invitation to join that part of the family. She'd known that since the day she won the bid on the house. "Don't malign that bird," she said. "If you're really good, I might decide it's big enough to share with you."

His grin softened. "Thanks, Doc. And if *you're* really good, I might share my Aunt Elena's cranberry relish recipe with you. But no, it wasn't your loving cousin Joe. At least not in person."

It looked as though she wasn't the only one suffering from a little paranoia. "Then who? The weather today certainly wasn't conducive to casual, drop-in visitation."

He nodded. "Our buddy Hank."

"Hank Foresman?" That made absolutely no sense.

"He's never so much as spoken to me if he had to cross the street to do it. What on earth did he want?"

"Work."

"Work? Here? Why?"

David snagged a card of paint samples and brought it to the table. "He said—" He set the card on the table and himself in his chair. "He said he was in Alcoholics Anonymous. You may not know, but one of the twelve steps to sobriety is to make amends for any harm you've caused."

Anne nodded. She was familiar with a number of twelve-step programs. "But he hasn't—"

"He said he'd fallen off the wagon and that his wife—Ida?"

She nodded again. Ida Foresman was as straitlaced and honest as any woman her patriarchal God ever created.

"Ida," David continued. "Anyway, apparently Ida tore a strip off him once Blake brought him home Saturday. Said he could either get back in the program or find a new home. And since I was up here helping you, he'd be able to make some amends to me by helping me out."

"Right," Anne muttered into her coffee cup. "Did you believe him?"

"For about thirty seconds. Until I saw how he looked when I explained how I could use him to help hang the new ceiling in here. And until I realized he was a lot more interested in what you were doing upstairs than in what I was so obviously doing down here.

"What are you doing upstairs, Doc?"

"You didn't take him up there?"

"I took him down in the cellar, which needs a new door, out to that old garage or barn on the back property line, which needs a new roof, even to the well house, which only needs a good shoveling out, but we just never got around to going upstairs before I told him

I'd have to check with you about giving him a definite answer. But I was tempted. Real tempted. If for no other reason than to see what he thought was of so much interest up there. What do you think it could be?"

"Nothing." But Anne shivered as she remembered the feeling that had gripped her as she stood with her foot poised on the first stair, that sense of being both drawn and repelled by something unnamed and unnamable. "Absolutely nothing. There's only more old house and . . ."

"And? Come on Annie."

She grimaced. Why was she stretching for an explanation when she probably didn't even need one? "And one strange room that makes no sense."

"Strange? In what way?"

"Just—" How did she explain it? "Didn't you go upstairs at all?"

He shook his head, but not before she noticed an uneasiness in him, too. At least she thought she did.

"Then let's go upstairs and I'll show you. I need to check on a stove anyway."

Yep. There was an uneasiness all right. He stood, but not quickly, and he walked to the front of the house with her, but not with any enthusiasm, and when they got to the base of the stairs, he rested his hand on the newel post but kept both feet firmly planted on the old pine floor.

And she knew why. In no way did she want to walk up those stairs in the dark of the night. Something was up there. Something that was going to change her life. And if David felt it, did that mean his life would be changed, too?

She forced a laugh and turned toward him. "It's all your fault," she said. "If it hadn't been for your comment about someone walking over my grave, my imagination wouldn't have gone wild."

But it hadn't. She'd gone up those stairs last night without so much as a quiver and lighted the stove. Only tonight, with him in the house, had she felt any uneasiness.

"My fault, is it?" he said as he reached for her hand. "I'm not the one who bought a haunted house."

His hand enveloped hers, holding it, wrapping it in familiarity and—and safety. "Haunted house?" she managed to splutter. "Where did you get an idea like that?"

He tugged on her hand, pulling her closer, and they started up the steps together. "From your buddy Hank. He kept making all sorts of allusions to mysteries and danger and an Indian curse."

"And he was sober?"

David chuckled. "If your cousin Joe was trying to scare me away, it didn't work, Doc."

Amazing. Anne felt her own answering laughter. Why had she feared going upstairs with this man?

"It didn't work with me either," she told him. "Especially since I think it was all an invention of Joe's to keep anyone from wanting this wonderful old house."

There were five bedrooms upstairs, two bathrooms, a sleeping porch, attic stairway, a couple of rooms not large enough for anything but storage, and the room where Anne had left the stove burning the night before. They poked their heads into each room, turning on lights where there were working bulbs, rattling dresser drawers, cabinet doors, and windows, and opening the rare closet door, and finally she led him to the one room in question.

An ornate art deco light fixture hung from the ceiling, about three-quarters of the way across the room. The art deco vanity backed up to the wall that adjoined the bathroom in that end of the hall and had probably been installed about the same time as the light fixture. Instead of having, at the most, an old wardrobe or a corner that had been framed in for a closet, the entire back wall of the room had been converted into a closet. The decorative little stove that at one time must have seemed the height of sophistication glowed merrily. Instead of the floral paper she had found in every other room, this one held the remnants of a boldly striped paper with a swag border, except in one corner where it was shredded as though someone, at some time, had made a valiant, if heedless, attempt, at stripping it from the wall.

The furniture remained. All art deco. A long couch that had once probably matched a stripe in the wallpaper, although both were now badly faded. A couple of chairs. An octagonal table with a stained-glass lamp and huge ashtray. A mirrored dressing table with its matching bench. All of it lay covered with a grime that not even the years of neglect the rest of the house had suffered could explain.

David looked around the room with what Anne recognized as his cop's eyes. "I don't suppose there's a lock on the outside of that door."

"No." She could answer that. "At least, not one that can't be opened from the inside with a key. But there is a slide bolt on the inside."

"And the closets? Was anything left in them?"

"No."

Still holding David's hand, she led him to the nearest door and opened it. Light from the room went only partially into the closet, but it was enough to see that it was one deep closet extending the width of the room, empty of anything except a single, long rod and a few bare wire hangers below a narrow shelf.

"This is the back of the house, isn't it?" he asked. "The outside wall with no windows?"

"Yes." She'd known he'd realize where they were, even though they'd gone almost in a circle upstairs.

He stepped back and appraised the overhead light,

then looked back into the closet. "If the closet was added later, that might explain why the light's not centered."

He'd noticed that, too.

"But not why they took out windows for this closet when there's a perfectly good inside wall," he said. He stepped into the closet and then back out, pacing the distance between the closet's back wall and the overhead fixture, then the distance from the fixture to the opposite wall. "It's short a few feet."

"I know."

"I thought you would. Any ideas?"

"No." The room wasn't cold, but Anne was. She tugged on David's hand but found him almost as reluctant to leave as he had been to climb the stairs. Eventually, though, he did follow.

"That was what I was going to do this past weekend," she told him. "Explore the possibilities."

Once again in the kitchen, both of them backed up to the stove, fighting a chill.

"How?" David asked. "How were you going to explore the possibilities?"

Anne should have known he wouldn't drop the subject. Why should he, when it was still so very much on her mind?

"I thought I'd go up into the attic," she told him. "Maybe measure the distance from the ceiling fixture wiring to the outside wall of the house."

"And if there's a discrepancy? What then?"

She shrugged, as though it really wasn't too important. But it was. She knew it, and apparently so did David Huerra. "And then, maybe knock a hole in a closet wall and see why."

"When?"

Restrained impatience. How interesting. And how

very much like her own feeling. "Wednesday," she said. "I close the clinic at noon. There'll still be daylight. And maybe it will be warmer." Then, knowing on some level that she was probably doing the worst thing possible, that she hadn't felt any of these strange reactions until David Huerra came to this house, she looked up at him and said it anyway. "Want to help?"

"Yeah." He turned slightly, looking down at her upturned face. "Yeah, I do." Then as casually as if he'd been doing it all his life, he gave her a quick but thorough kiss. A kiss that went from casual to heated in the space of a heartbeat. A kiss that lasted no more than half a minute but seemed to have gone on for centuries.

"Damn," he swore softly as he clamped his hands on her arms and pulled away from her. "I don't . . . "

Then, before she found her voice or any words to use with it, he grabbed up his jacket and let himself out. Anne watched as he skidded across the backyard, buckled himself into the world's oldest Blazer, and slid his way down her hill.

And that's when her questions, and doubts and—yes—longings really began.

Longings that weren't based on the physical.

Yeah, right.

David Huerra was a literate, sensitive, attractive man. And in the six months she'd been in Allegro she hadn't even been out for a drink with a man. Let alone a literate, sensitive, attractive one. Now she'd had him in her house from daylight until long after dark, and to herself for most of the evening hours.

And what had they done? They'd talked, yes. They'd laughed. Yes, that, too. And they'd worked on woodwork and insulation and drywall and old wiring.

All of that she could have taken in stride. All of that she could have accepted as nothing—well, not too much, anyway—out of the ordinary. But then he'd kissed her, and she realized that she'd been lying to herself since the moment she helped pull him from his mangled car.

Oh, God, she didn't want to feel this. She didn't want to feel anything. Not yet. Maybe not ever. And not for someone who regularly and consistently put himself in danger.

But when he was with her, she didn't slink back into any of those pseudo-healthy techniques she'd developed to keep from thinking about what had really brought her back to Allegro. She didn't have to. When David was with her, she didn't think about screaming children or fear or even about Anthony, her fiancé for all of six days, and how he had died.

So maybe it was a decent trade-off. A little feeling—surely she could restrain herself to that—in exchange for a little, maybe a lot of, peace.

7

1935

Lucy loved the garage—at least the loft of it, all quiet and dimly lighted and private. There wasn't any place private in the house anymore, not even her hidey hole in the attic, since Aunt Marian and the baby had come to live with them.

Lucy tried to like the baby, she really did. It would have been easy to love the little boy, if Aunt Marian had just let her hold him once in a while, if she had just let her play with him, if she wasn't always telling her to be quiet or still so she wouldn't bother him.

If Papa hadn't liked the baby better than he liked her, and Aunt Marian better than he liked Mama.

Lucy felt guilty for thinking that, just like she felt guilty for not really liking her little cousin. It wasn't *his* fault. But was it hers? Had she done something that made her papa not love her?

It was all right, she told herself. She had Mama to love her, and Mama was better than Papa and Aunt Marian and Cousin Joseph all put together.

And now she had Walter, too.

Walter sat in the desk beside her at school. He was new this year. He didn't have a papa to buy him new clothes or shoes and sometimes he looked like he was hungry, but he didn't make fun of her when she couldn't spell the words or make the reading behave and he wouldn't let the others make fun of her either.

She didn't think he was going to have a Thanksgiving dinner, and she knew Papa wouldn't let her invite him and his mother to theirs, but Mama had made an extra pie for her to give to them. Just as soon as he got here. Just as soon as she showed him the secret she had hidden in the loft over the garage.

Papa kept the garage locked, even when his big, new car wasn't in there, but he didn't know about the two boards at the back, under the window, he didn't know that she came in here whenever Aunt Marian got just too bossy to stand, and he didn't know about the mama cat and the kitten upstairs in the loft.

Papa was gone now. Lucy didn't think he'd come home all night. Maybe he wouldn't come home. Would Mama make Aunt Marian leave if he didn't? She'd heard her grandpa talking once—more than once—telling Mama it was her house, that she didn't have to be a servant to any white man. Mama had always hushed him when she saw Lucy, so Lucy wasn't too sure what Grandpa meant—not about the white part, but about the servant. Wasn't Mama just doing what mamas did?

Lucy hopped up and down, stomping her feet. Her coat was warm, and the garage walls kept out most of the wind, but Mama wouldn't let her wear overalls except when she visited Grandma and Grandpa, and her legs were cold. And if Walter didn't get here soon, everybody else would be here and she wouldn't be able to show him the mama cat and kitten.

She heard a two-note whistle outside and looked out

the window. Yes. There was Walter coming through their secret place in the hedge. Lucy inched the first board to one side and answered his whistle, and in a moment Walter squeezed through into the garage.

"Wow," he said. "This is big. Almost as big as a barn."

"It used to be a barn—well, a stable, anyway," she told him as she led him to the ladder in the corner and up to the darkened loft that created a ceiling over half of the building. She couldn't really remember when, that was when she was a real little girl, but Mama had told her it was, and that was why there was still some hay up in the loft. "I wish it still was. I'd sure like to have a horse."

"In town?" Walter asked. "Could you do that now?"

Lucy nodded. "Out here. If my papa would let me. Grandpa told me."

Walter scuffed his already worn shoe in the dry, loose hay scattered across the floor. "Bet you'd have a whole lot of friends if you had a horse."

Lucy might not be real smart, she'd heard Papa tell Mama she wasn't, but she knew why Walter hung his head and kind of shriveled away from her. "They wouldn't be real friends," she told him. "Not like you. And you'd always be my best friend."

He didn't look real convinced. "Promise?"

Lucy nodded.

"Blood brothers?"

"Ah, Walter, we don't do things like that." At least she didn't think they did. None of her cousins from her mama's family ever told her if they did. Hunting for words that were for now as slow in coming as they always were when trying to read, she pushed aside a stack of old feed sacks. The mama cat looked up and gave a welcoming twitch of her tail but didn't try to raise up on the injured leg Lucy had cleaned and bandaged. She was yellow and scrawny, not at all like

Mama's fat tabby. Quickly Lucy checked the dishes of food and water, then petted the cat. The kitten was getting braver every day. It crept toward her. Lucy curled her fingers gently around the wiggling, mewling little ball of yellow fluff and pulled it out of the shadows. "And besides," she said, offering her treasure to Walter, "I'm showing you my best secret even without that."

"I don't care," he told her, obstinately stubborn as she had learned he could be. He gave the mama cat a comforting pat before he tickled the tiny little kitten on the belly and under the chin, and she saw his smile dart out of hiding for only a moment. He shrugged and pulled out a scratched up pocketknife. "I been thinking about it, and I want us to make an oath that we're always going to be best friends. And I figure the best way to do that is share blood. That way when Harvey Skinner tells me I don't have any right to butt in when he's giving you a hard time, I will, too, have."

Lucy looked at the knife and shivered. It wouldn't do to let anyone, even Walter, know she was afraid. But she was. Oh, yes, she was. "You mean cut each other? Like in the movies?" She dragged her head slowly from one side to the other and held the kitten closer. "I don't think so. Mama would be real mad if I got blood on my clean dress."

"Come on, Lucy." He opened the knife and held the blade against his finger. "It would only be a little bitty cut, it's not like we're going to cut open our arms or anything—"

"Hush!" Lucy twisted away from him and the sight of the knife. Something scarier than that was getting ready to happen. "Someone's coming."

"We've got to get out of here."

Lucy heard the scrape of the padlock. "It's too late,"

she said, dropping to her knees in the hay and scooting back from the edge. "Quick. Get back here, out of sight."

It wasn't her papa's car. Instead of the big black Buick, a new but unbelievably muddy pickup truck that she recognized as belonging to Tom Jackson backed into the garage. Three men, her papa, Mr. Jackson, and someone she didn't know, got out of the truck and pulled the garage doors shut, sliding a board through the braces to keep them shut, and walked to the back of the truck.

Quickly Papa pulled the baskets off whatever was wrapped up in a big piece of canvas and tugged the canvas away.

Silence. Utter silence.

And they were too far back from the edge to see what kept her papa and Mr. Jackson and that other man so quiet. She and Walter shared a questioning look. She put the kitten to one side and quietly, stealthily she and her best friend slithered to the edge of the loft to look down.

Oohh.

Lucy pressed her lips together and prayed she hadn't let that moan escape.

A man lay in the back of the truck, all crumpled, surrounded by what looked like a whole lot of Papa's treasures, and covered in that metal that Papa always threw away when Mr. Jackson brought some to him. But this was different. It wasn't all green and mangled and stuck together. It glowed, and there were designs on it, strange drawings of the big birds she had seen in some of the shells Papa sometimes had out on his desk, and cats, big cats like she had never seen before. And it covered him from the top of his head right down to his feet.

Then Papa reached into the truck and picked up something and moved something else, and she saw that the man wasn't a man—well, wasn't still—

She felt that funny sound trying to get out of her

again when she saw that beneath the copper he was just bones. White bones. Bones that seemed to her to gleam with as much life as the copper. But not to her papa she guessed, because he tossed what looked like an arm bone to one side while he looked at the metal and then snatched up a—a what?—a statue and turned it from side to side.

"Didn't I tell you I did good?" Mr. Jackson asked. He reached into the back of the truck, too, and raked up a double handful of those round shell things Papa got so much money for when he sold them, put them down and lifted up two big shells—really big shells—that looked like dippers or gourds or pots, and turned them over and spilled out the beads Papa called pearls.

Papa put the statue down. He was trying to look like he wasn't impressed, but Lucy knew better. She'd seen him look like that sometimes when Grandpa would be talking about how much coal they were taking out of the mines on the land he had bought next to his allotment.

"It will take some time to move all this," he said. "If I even can. I know where it came from, but some folks might question it, except for the regular stuff, since I doubt anybody's seen anything quite like—

"What about the other one? The one you couldn't get. Did he have these copper plates all over him, too?"

"Nah," Mr. Jackson told him. "Just that big feather cape I told you about. And piles of stuff like these beads and shells and pipes. But it was broken. All broken. I ain't never seen so much unbroken stuff at one time before."

"Neither has anybody else," Papa told him.

"And they just let you walk out of there with it?" Now her Papa had his disgusted tone of voice, the one he used when he told her how bad her teacher said her

reading was. That one. Had Mr. Jackson done something wrong, too? Was that why Papa was trying to
make him feel bad?

"Hell, no, they didn't just let me walk out of there. I
told you how we got it. And you were there, so don't think
you're going to be able to weasel out of being part of it. If
someone else just happens to figure out what I've done, I
figure they'll be able to figure out who I did it with."

"I'm not trying to weasel out, Jackson. I'm just trying
to be fair about what it's worth, and I'm afraid we won't
know that until I manage to move it."

"Until you— Oh, no," Mr. Jackson said. "I'm not
leaving this with you, so you can just forget all about trying that. You take it, all of it, now, and pay me for it like
we talked about."

"It's Thanksgiving Day. The banks are closed. Where
do you expect me to get any kind of serious money?"

Mr. Jackson smiled, but it was not a smile Lucy
would like to see aimed at her. "I expect you to get it
from that safe in your office. The place where you keep
the money you don't want the taxman or your wife to
know about. And I think I'll just go along with you to
make sure you don't try to send anybody around to pay
a surprise visit on me or my boy."

Papa had a safe in his office? With money in it? Was
that where it all was? She'd heard her Grandpa ask her
mother once what happened to all of Papa's money so
that he never had any extra to spend on his family.
Nobody knew. But Mr. Jackson did. How?

Unless it was just a guess, and a wrong one at that.

She hoped her papa would tell him he didn't have a
safe and that he wasn't going to buy the dead man in the
truck. She hoped her papa hadn't already done something real wrong, like helping to steal the dead man in
the first place.

Her papa stood up real tall. He looked at Mr. Jackson first and then at the dead man in the truck for a long time. Finally he nodded his head, just once. "Come on then," he said.

The third man, the one Mr. Jackson had called his boy, stayed in the garage with the truck, keeping her and Walter trapped in the loft. Walter looked at her while the man locked the doors back, and she could see the worry and questions in his face.

She shook her head, wanting to tell him not to worry, that they'd get out just as soon as Papa finished his business. She wanted to tell him to be quiet because she knew her papa would be real mad if he caught them watching what he was doing today. It was wrong. Real wrong. And nothing anybody could say to her would convince her it wasn't. But it was a big secret that she knew they all had to keep or something real bad would happen to all of them.

She felt the soft brush of fur against her cheek and reached out to catch the kitten before it fell off the edge of the loft. A little hay slithered down, dropping into the back of the truck. Mr. Jackson's son didn't see it though. He was staring at the door. Until he turned and went back to the side of the truck and looked in at the dead man.

He had his papa's nasty smile. Lucy saw that as he stuck his hand into the pile of treasures and pulled out a small carved piece and stuck it in his jacket pocket.

The growl seemed to come from everywhere.

She felt Walter jerk to attention at her side and clutch her hand. But he didn't say anything. Maybe he couldn't. She sure didn't think she could.

What was it? And where was it?

Mr. Jackson's son looked around, nervous like, then shrugged and, trying to act like he wasn't as scared as she was by the sound that shouldn't have been there, reached back into the truck for another piece and stuck it in his pocket, too. Maybe he wasn't. Maybe he didn't hear it. Maybe he just felt them watching him as he stole that stuff from the dead man.

It was inside the garage. Downstairs, under the part the loft covered. And it was not mad, not yet, but getting there. The kitten Lucy clutched in her hand heard it, too, and its little ears flattened back and the fur rose up on its neck. Walter's hand tightened on hers.

Mr. Jackson's son grabbed a third piece of the treasure and eased his way to the doors, looking around a little, even up toward the loft before he scooted outside and slammed the doors shut behind him. Lucy heard the bar go across outside just as the cat—it had to be a cat, a big cat, maybe more than one—downstairs growled again. Over the pounding of her heart, and Walter's because she could hear that too, she heard the sound of restless pacing and then—silence.

The kitten relaxed in her grasp and began purring. Walter released her hand, slowly, and pulled himself closer to the edge so he could hang his head over and look back into the part of the garage beneath them.

He jerked back with a a nervous laugh and scrambled to his knees. "There's nothing down there."

"What do you mean there's nothing down there?" Lucy put the kitten down, crawled forward, and peered over the edge and into the corners. "I heard it. You heard it. Even the kitten heard it."

But there was nothing there. Only a pile of tires and tools in the corner and a bunch of old harness and tack hanging on the wall. And the man, the dead man, gleaming and glowing with the warmth of copper, jumbled and hurting and all alone in the truck.

"We've got to get out of here," Walter whispered. "While we can."

She didn't seem to be able to move.

"Come on, Lucy!" He tugged at the collar of her coat, pulling her back from the edge. "They'll be back after a while, and maybe that thing will be, too."

He pulled her to her feet and half pushed, half carried her to the ladder. "Hurry!"

"Wait!" No matter how much she wanted to run, she paused long enough to put the kitten back, safe with its mama.

She scrambled down the ladder, not believing until she looked around that the cat or whatever it had been was really gone. Walter scrambled after her and took her arm, tugging her toward the window and the loose boards at the back of the garage. But she couldn't go. Not yet. Digging her feet into the dirt of the floor, she stopped. Walter turned to see why.

She couldn't leave him. Not that way. There wasn't much she could do about him being all jumbled up like that, but she climbed up on the sideboard and reached in and put his arm back with the rest of him, only shivering a little when she touched the bare bone. When Walter saw what she was doing, he took a deep breath but climbed up to help her.

She had to touch the metal. Just like she'd had to touch it all those other times when Mr. Jackson brought some. This was different from all those other times. This was warm. Even though it couldn't be. Even though everything else in the garage was cold. Slowly she traced her fingers over one design—a cat, pacing, mouth open in an eternal growl.

She heard voices outside the door, and Walter tugged on her arm. She nodded. But before she left, she took the edge of the canvas and tossed it over the dead man.

It only partly covered him, but when she reached for the other end of it, to toss it, too, Walter already had the corner in his hand. He looked at her, not smiling, then climbed into the back of the truck and finished the job of covering the corpse.

Maybe she would trade some blood with him, after all, Lucy thought. Anyone who knew her as well as he did, who knew without her saying anything that she couldn't go off and leave the dead man like so much trash, had to be worth a little pain, a little blood. But she had a feeling that what she and Walter had shared this day in the garage was worth a lot more than any oath would have been before—

Before what, she didn't get a chance to explore. The voices outside the garage were getting closer. Walter jumped from the back of the truck and held his hand out to her. She smiled, quick like, because there wasn't time for much else, and jumped down, too. Then they slipped out beneath the loose boards, hearing what Lucy thought sounded like the low warning growl of the kitten's mama, only bigger, coming once more from inside the garage. Because they couldn't leave the boards dangling open to tattle on their having been there, they slid them into position and ran together for their secret place in the hedge, just as the garage doors banged open.

Lucy whirled around. "Papa," she whispered. "Will it hurt Papa?"

Walter dragged her down into the undergrowth beneath the hedge. "Sshh. Listen."

But there was nothing to hear. Nothing but the muted sound of voices within the garage. Then she saw Mr. Jackson's son walk to the shed beside the henhouse and come back dragging two big barrels, returning again to the shed for packing crates.

"What are they doing?" Walter asked.

Lucy shook her head. Were they putting him in a barrel? Was that what—

Her papa came out of the garage and marched up to the back porch. "Ellie!" he called out. "Ellie, get out here now!"

Mama came out onto the porch, wearing her apron.

"I want you to go the post office," Papa told her. "And then I want you to run over to McPherson's and pick up that book I lent him last week."

"Now? We have company coming in less than an hour. I have dinner on the stove."

"Marian will watch it," Papa said. "Take her Ford and go. And take Lucy with you."

Mama didn't like it when Papa talked to her like that. Now she stood up straight. "Lucy isn't here right now. And Marian can run your errands."

"Marian can't leave the baby. Just go. For once don't give me grief in front of my associates. Just go and get the mail and get the book so I can lend it to Jackson here."

She might not like it when he ordered her, but she always did what he said. Frowning, she took off her apron and stepped back into the kitchen, saying something, probably to Aunt Marian, before she went and got into Aunt Marian's spotless new Ford and left.

Aunt Marian came out of the house and said something to Papa that Lucy couldn't hear. Papa hugged her and whispered something to her. Aunt Marian laughed, and then Mr. Jackson and his son drove away in their dirty, empty truck, and Papa and Aunt Marian began hauling barrels and crates into the house.

"What do you suppose he told her?" Walter asked in a whisper.

"I don't know," Lucy said. "She never laughs. Never.

Walter? Did they put him in those barrels? Did they break him up even more and stuff him in those boxes?"

"I don't know. Wait here while I go see."

"No—"

But it was too late to warn him to be careful. Walter crouched and ran for the back of the garage and pushed aside one of the boards to peek inside. He was there for a long time, quiet, and Lucy saw him kind of slump there until he turned and then not even trying to hide came back to the hedge and sat down heavily beside her.

"Well," she asked when he just sat there saying nothing.

"Yep. That's what they did all right," he said, and his voice sounded strange. "Every bit of him and all the stuff that was with him is—is gone, out of sight, probably in the crates. Except for those long poles that were in the truck. Those are stacked up against the wall."

"But he's too big to fit in just one of them, unless . . . unless . . . "

"Yeah," Walter said. "I know."

"It's not right," she whispered. "It's not right to do that to someone!"

"Lucy, he's dead. He's been dead a long time."

"I don't care. Papa's wrong. Mr. Jackson's wrong. We've got to do something."

"We're just kids," Walter said. "Your papa isn't going to give him back just because we say to, and even if he would, who would he give him back to? So what are we going to do about it?" Walter asked. "What can we do? What will whatever it was that made that noise let us do?"

"I don't know." For the moment, Lucy admitted defeat. For a moment she believed all the things her teacher and her papa said about her being dumb or stupid. But she wasn't. She just couldn't read too good. Lots of folks couldn't read. That didn't mean she couldn't think. "I don't know," she repeated. "But there's got to be something."

8

Wednesday finally arrived—cold, but not as cold as Monday. And clear, with enough sunshine to filter through the ancient windows and vents of the attic. A perfect day for prowling.

In the day and a half since that brief and unexpectedly devastating kiss, David had managed to act as though it had never happened. Because his actions echoed her own admittedly conflicting desires, she had done the same. At least she hoped she had. She wasn't looking forward to an entire afternoon of guarding her words and emotions, but she also wasn't looking forward to an afternoon of searching out a mystery without David's steady presence beside her.

The attic stairs took them up into the northeast corner of the house, completely opposite to the area they needed. She had been up there, once before, right after she took possession of the house, but the profusion of actual walls, as well as those created by the studs of the walls below rising to the roof trusses, had confused her then, and it confused her now.

"My God," David said when she led him through a cut in what had to be the original wooden-shingled roof into the main part of the attic. "You have enough floor space for most small city halls. How many rooms are there up here?"

"I don't know. Not as many as it looks right now. If I remember correctly, the area we want is in the original part of the house, and it's basically open."

"Let's hope so," he said, testing the flooring beneath him with a cautious foot before he trusted it with his weight.

The attic wasn't completely floored, and in those parts where it wasn't they stepped over the roll insulation someone had installed long enough ago for the pink to be distinctly gray, making their way carefully along planks laid across thick, sturdy cross members.

Considering the condition of the rest of the house, the attic was surprisingly free of clutter. But then, except for furniture and some household goods, Anne had found nothing resembling Great Aunt Ellie's personal property, and she wondered, not for the first time, who had come for it and when. Since her bid had been for the house and furnishings only, she supposed she didn't really care who had divided up the essence of Ellie Hansom that probably had remained in the house after her death.

There were no halls, but brick chimneys, sloping ceilings, and, of course, the rising studs helped guide her, until they reached the south side of the house. A change in the roof line placed what windows there were in the end wall at the front of the house, and only a slatted vent lighted the rear. Cautiously, carefully, Anne made her way to the chimney flue for the small parlor stove below, and directed the beam of her flashlight along wires she found snaking their way across studs and insulation toward the wiring box for what she suspected must be the art deco light fixture.

They'd brought a metal tape measure with them, but they didn't really need it. The box lay off-center of what was clearly a rectangular area approximating that of the room below. And what she had thought to be a framed-in closet wall rose as a stud wall through the ceiling of the floor below, as did the walls of all the other rooms of the second floor.

"Another room?" she asked David, who had made his way to the other side of the stud wall.

"Yeah." He knelt down and began pulling at the insulation until he uncovered some ancient electrical wiring and followed it to a lighting box. "And it looks as though it's been wired."

She walked to the stud wall and looked toward the back of the house. There was enough space for a good-sized bedroom behind that wall, not just a three-foot-deep closet. "Why?"

David pulled back the insulation. There, as in the rest of the house, the ceilings were solidly framed and covered with thick boards. He knocked on it, and she almost expected an echo, but all they heard in the silence was the sound of their breath.

"Want to go find out?" he asked.

Anne shook her head, a reflex action, surely, because at that moment she didn't want to find out. She wanted to leave the mystery of that back wall in limbo as it had to have been for fifty years or so. But she couldn't. And David couldn't either.

The room was as eerie as it had been Monday night. She glanced at David and found him studying her. He felt it. Oh, yes, he felt it too, but neither of them said anything.

Taking a deep breath for the courage she suddenly needed, she opened the closet door and stepped in. The back wall inside the closet had been papered-over drywall. David knocked around on it looking for studs, tapping on it and the front wall, listening for differences. Even she could hear them.

She hefted the hammer. "Anywhere?" she asked.

"Looks like it."

She found a spot out of sight of the open door and waited for David to come to her side. Now that the moment had come, she didn't want to do this—but she knew she had to.

She raised the hammer, gripping it, and swung it. The ease with which it penetrated the wall stunned her. For some reason she had almost been expecting a vault or a fortress. She stepped back, and David bent to step closer beneath the rod and looked into the gaping hole before he moved aside for her. Nothing but darkness greeted her. Darkness, a chill, and that same attracting, repelling force that had gripped her Monday night at the foot of the stairs.

She handed the hammer to David. He nodded, and began knocking hunks out of the drywall, while she switched on a flashlight.

This time, the hole was large enough for both of them to look through it at the same time. The circle of light from the flashlight played across windows, still in place but covered on the outside by the wooden ship-lap exterior siding, across a small floral paper, across a bare bulb hanging from a broken fixture in the ceiling, across years of dust on the bare pine floor, across something that gleamed faintly from that floor in the far corner of the room.

Anne dropped the flashlight.

"Was that—"

"I don't know," she said quickly. "I don't know."

Both of them stood silently for a moment, then, without speaking, they began tearing chunks of drywall away. Why, she didn't know. She wanted to run away, to leave the room as they had found it, to forget all about windows and measurements and secrets. God, yes, secrets. And she suspected David did, too. Instead, they worked silently but almost frantically at enlarging the opening while the beam of the flashlight reflected off whatever it was that lay in the corner.

Once they'd torn away enough drywall to make an opening large enough to squeeze through, David laid a restraining hand on her shoulder. Foolish man. Did he think she was going to argue with him about who went through first? She didn't want to go through that opening at all. But she did, easing her way in behind him as he stooped and retrieved the flashlight. Instead of doing the obvious, going immediately to the corner, he shined the light on the bare bulb and broken fixture above them. A long cord dangled from it. Miraculously, when David pulled on the cord, the bulb lighted, casting its forty-watt glare into all corners of the small room.

Illuminating what lay there on the floor.

"Oh, my God." Anne caught her hand to her mouth, tasting the chalk of drywall as she fought to hold in a moan.

Four wooden poles outlined a large rectangle covered with beads, pottery, shells, weapons—axes, celts, maces, and assorted blades and points—and what appeared to be small statues. Two others served as bracing. And in the center, covered with glowing, engraved copper plates—

"It's a body," she whispered.

"No." David spoke softly. He walked to the edge of the first pole and knelt down, reaching out but not touching the abundance of artifacts that surrounded what her eyes told her was definitely a skeleton. A human skeleton.

"It's a burial," he said, his voice hushed. "My God, it's a—it can't be—complete archaeological burial. But who? What? He must be—what do you think, Anne? Six feet seven? Eight?"

He. Yes, this—had been—a man. A tall man by anyone's standards. The copper that covered him had to be a form of armor. Thin, engraved with warlike hawks and snarling, prowling cats, it was impractical for any protection so it had to be ceremonial. It had to be . . .

And then she recognized the copper feathers that sprang from his mask, the human representations with their distinctively outlined eye that adorned a breastplate, the almost abstract snakes, the swirling repeated designs, and most of all, the cats. It couldn't be. But it was.

"My designs."

Slowly she sank to her knees at the foot of this impossible find. She too stretched out her hands, drawn to the man but like David, unable to bring herself to touch him.

"Who—" She lost her voice entirely for a moment and only managed to recover a small part of it. "Who is he?" Did she know? *Should* she know? Somehow she thought she must. But *how?*

"A monarch of some sort. Obviously a powerful warrior, because of his armor and the number of weapons." David shook his head, still speaking in hushed tones. "But how did he get here? Into a closed-off room in Allegro, Oklahoma. How did he get into your house, Annie? And why is he still here and not in some museum?"

A small box rested near the warrior's left foot, from which the covering had long ago disintegrated, leaving the bones visible and strangely vulnerable. Cautiously Anne reached for the box, almost expecting a crack of thunder or an ominous voice demanding that she stop.

The box appeared to be—cedar? It was hard to tell. It had a fitted, almost transparent top, with a design etched in it. She held it for David's inspection. He touched it as cautiously as she had lifted it.

"The top is mica, I think," he said.

She nodded, swallowed, and began carefully working the top from the box. The inside of the box was lined with copper and contained only two items. Small shell cameos lay among the remains of some woven fabric. They were perhaps two inches in diameter, each bearing the representation of a person: a man and a woman. The man pictured was this one. She knew it. She felt it in every chilled inch of her being. She looked at the items surrounding him. Possessions. Awesome in their diversity and antiquity, but only possessions. "But where is she?" Anne asked.

She sensed David's eyes on her and looked up to see him watching her warily. She tried to smile. When that didn't work, she handed him the box containing the two cameos. "The woman whose likeness accompanied him," she explained.

David took the box from her and lifted one of the cameos, turning it in the light of the bare bulb. Carefully he replaced it and the mica lid and settled it back in its original place.

"Come on, Annie," he said, rising to his feet and putting his hand on her arm. "Let's get out of here for a minute."

"No, I—"

"Come on, Annie," he said more forcefully. "We need to get out of here."

He sounded so convinced she hadn't the heart to argue with him, until he reached to turn off the overhead light.

"No—"

He shook his head, but he pulled the cord, plunging the room into darkness except for the small beam of light that seeped through the opening they had made. Then, holding her arm firmly—for her support or his?—he walked her to the opening and all but pushed her through it.

They didn't make it to the warmth and familiarity of the kitchen. At the base of the stairs, Anne stumbled. David stopped and turned to look at her. He muttered an oath and threw his arm around her, almost dragging her to the front of the house, to the safety and sanity of her bedroom. There, he pushed her down on the side of the bed and shoved her head down between her knees.

Anne sucked in a deep breath and tried to raise her head. His hand on the back of it wouldn't let her. "I'm not going to faint," she protested.

"Could have fooled me. Breathe. Slowly."

As she struggled for air, she dimly realized that his words were as ragged as hers. "I've seen worse," she choked out.

"Yeah. Me, too."

She felt the pressure on the back of her head ease and the mattress dip slightly as he sat beside her, heard him working as hard at controlling his breathing as she was, and knew as she fought her reaction that it was all out of proportion to what had gone before. And that David Huerra, the big-city cop who had to have seen more carnage and mayhem than even she, had reacted just as strongly.

Eventually his hand slid from the back of her head to the nape of her neck, and his touch gentled. Eventually her breathing settled into a rhythm that would supply her body with the oxygen it needed. Eventually she heard him draw a deep breath.

She looked over at him to find him pale beneath his bruises. Paler even than when she had pulled him from his car. He looked back at her. Both of them had questions; neither of them had answers.

And at almost the same time, both of them realized that David's hand had begun tracing a pattern on her neck that was more sensuous than protective.

Anne tensed. He withdrew his hand. And she once again felt the chill of the house. But at last she was able to begin to identify the emotion that had gripped her so strongly when she looked at what remained of that bare, vulnerable foot. Not horror. Or perhaps, not entirely horror, because that was mixed in with it. But grief. A grief so intense, so all-encompassing, that it threatened to paralyze her.

Fighting it, she reached for the bedside telephone.

"What are you doing?"

"I'm calling the sheriff," she said. For the moment that seemed the only thing to do. "We've got to report this."

"Annie, however he got there, he's been there for a long time. A few more minutes won't make any difference. Let's think about this. Blake Foresman is a good man, but I'm not sure his department is what we need right now. I'm not sure he's up to handling what—whatever it is that we just exhumed."

He was right, of course. Anne knew that. A few more minutes wouldn't make any difference. Whoever was up there had been there for—what?—fifty years or so, and, if she allowed herself to think clearly about him, had probably been dead for a lot longer than that.

He was definitely not anything Blake Foresman would want to be responsible for.

She sighed and slumped back onto the bed, releasing the telephone, and nodded. They did need to think about this. About who and what and when. And about why it had affected both of them the way it had. David squeezed her hand and released it with a sigh of his own.

"Good girl."

Anne glared at him. "Don't be patronizing, David Huerra. I'm not the only person in this room who just fell apart."

He managed a grin, a lopsided one that didn't quite disguise the fact that he was still as deeply affected by their find as she was. "Damn," he said. "I was hoping you hadn't noticed."

Her laugh surprised her. And as weak as it was, as reluctant as it was, it was enough to bring them both out of the morass of emotions and into a semblance of normality.

Anne had no alcohol in the house. David brewed coffee so strong she choked on the first swallow. But that jolt of caffeine was what she needed. That, and his touch, which she no longer had. Even though he sat beside her at the round kitchen table with its familiar nonmealtime clutter of phone books and construction invoices and a pile of opened but unsorted mail, he kept his hands securely wrapped around his mug of coffee. As she did.

She was weakening though. She could tell that at any moment she would give way and act on her uncharacteristic need to be connected to someone, anyone.

David stood and paced the length of the room before returning to the table. "You worked the emergency room during your internship, didn't you?" he asked.

"Yes."

"And I've been in homicide for five years." He sat down. "So why did we react the way we did?"

She looked up to find him fighting to find answers that just weren't there. To hell with it, she thought. She needed human touch regardless of how proud or stubborn he thought he had to be. She reached for his hand. Without looking, he grasped hers, and slowly, gradually, she felt the tension begin to leave her, begin to leave him.

Remembering his words the first time he saw her house, she attempted a lightness she didn't feel. "Maybe someone walked over our graves?"

He smiled, or grimaced. It was difficult to tell which. "Maybe," he said. "But it felt more as if *we* were the ones doing the walking."

Yes. Now that he mentioned it. Yes it had. And the graves had been their own.

"I don't suppose this uncle of yours was a grave-robber?" he asked tentatively.

She shook her head. "I don't know much about him. Only that for a while he was, or at least was thought to be, extremely wealthy. He owned half the town. And then he lost his money, had to sell off his holdings."

"But not this place?"

"No, and I think everyone wondered why. But we found out, just months ago in fact, that this was always Aunt Ellie's place, part of her allotment from the Choctaw Nation, and he never owned any part of it."

David glanced around the kitchen, and she knew he was seeing the size and scope of the house of which this room was just a part. "Somebody had some money."

Yes, someone did. "He did, early on. And of course her family had coal and gas and lots of timberland."

"When?" David asked.

He hadn't released his grip on her hand, but he turned over an envelope from her untidy pile of mail and began, idly, she thought at first, drawing a design on the stark white with a fine-line black pen.

"When what?" she asked as she watched a design

emerge. A design she had just seen upstairs on a round piece of shell.

"When did he lose his money? The depression? That far back?"

"I don't know. Is it important?"

"I don't know. I don't know what is and what isn't anymore. Damn!"

"David?" What was happening here was serious enough, but she sensed his frustration came from more than just—just?—this afternoon's bizarre happenings.

Again he smiled. Or grimaced. "I told you I came to Lake Allegro to think, didn't I?"

She nodded.

"But not what I had to think about."

He knew he hadn't. That was one of those secrets she had sensed in him.

"I blew a case, really blew it, because I had closed myself off in my preconceived notions."

She didn't see the relevance, not really, and he must have sensed that she didn't.

"I almost cost a couple of nice people their lives, maybe did cost one woman hers, because I insisted on seeing something the way *I* knew it had to be. And then I learned that I didn't know it all after all."

"So you came here to—?"

This time it was definitely a grimace. "To learn whether or not I could ever be a cop again. To learn whether or not there was enough left in me after fifteen years on the force to rejoin the human race.

"I didn't want to," he continued slowly, "but I was ordered to come here or someplace like this. I thought I'd spend my thirty days staring at strange walls and feeling my brain turn to mush. I had no idea that I would have to face something that had no apparent logical explanation."

She had to set aside what he said about self-discovery, for the moment, to address the second part of his statement. "There's a logical explanation," she insisted. "Just because we don't know what it is—"

"I'm not talking about just what we found upstairs, Annie. Or maybe I am. Maybe it's all tied together."

And of course, she had no answer for that.

David squeezed her hand. "Okay," he said. "For now, let's not dwell on our reaction to what we found in that room. If we do that, maybe we *can* find something logical in why there's a copper-armored skeleton with most, if not all, of his grave goods surrounding him in a carefully constructed secret room in your house."

"Uncle Ralph was a grave-robber?" she offered tentatively.

"Maybe."

"David, I was not serious."

He flashed a wry grin at her. "There are different kinds of grave-robbers," he told her. "Some of them operate within the law. Maybe your uncle was a collector. The question is, which particular set of graves did our friend upstairs come from?"

"No. The question is, why is he still here? I may not be knowledgeable about archaeology and artifacts, but it seems to me that there's a fortune hidden here. Supposedly, Uncle Ralph sold everything of value he owned, so why didn't he sell what . . . what we found upstairs? Unless there's something really bizarre going on and the skeleton isn't as old as we think it is."

"Good point, Annie. Let's find out."

"Right. And just how are we going to do that?"

He scooted the drawing toward her. "I know a collector. I wouldn't call him a friend, but he's reputable, probably even honest. Let's ask him—discreetly—

about some of these designs. They seem familiar, but I can't place them. Maybe he can."

She thought about that for a moment. *Discreetly* was the operative word here. Since he'd stopped her from calling Blake, she'd realized she didn't want cops, or now collectors or reporters, crawling all over her house. Finally she nodded. "And I have a friend who just finished a residency in pathology. I can ask her to assure us we're not dealing with a reportable corpse."

"Is there any way you can get more information about your uncle?"

"Maybe. Probably not from anyone around here," she admitted. "But maybe my mother knows something."

"Okay." He chuffed out a breath. "If we hurry we can get this started before the holiday officially begins so that maybe by Monday we might know something."

She glanced at her watch, knowing it was far too late to accomplish anything before Monday, only to find that barely an hour had passed since they had started their search. "You first," she said.

David brought the phone to the table and dialed information in Dallas, asking for the number of the collector he knew, while she dug through her junk drawer for her address book containing Karen Ready's new, unlisted Chicago phone number. David had his number before she found hers and had dialed by the time she returned to the table. While the telephone rang at the other end of the line, he continued drawing on the sketch he had started.

"Jack?" he said. "David Huerra." He laughed. "Yes, it has been a long time. How was your trip to Peru? Oh, really. I'm sorry to hear that. Maybe next year."

He waited, listening for a moment. "Well, yes, there is something you can do. I'm hoping you can identify an artifact for me.

"No, not official business. As a matter of fact, I'm on

vacation. It's something that's— Well, hell, Jack. It's personal."

David laughed again, but the pen in his hand pressed down on the envelope. "How about me sending you a drawing—okay, a tracing of a shell gorget?"

He frowned slightly. "Oh, yeah, it's engraved all right. . . . A couple of heavily dressed figures with speech symbols. They're holding some sort of vessel with a cat-headed snake, the world or four winds symbol and a couple of other things I don't remember seeing before.

"Yes. Oh, yes, there's enough to identify. It's intact. No, it hasn't been killed. I don't know. Let me check."

He held his hand over the mouthpiece and frowned at her. "He's excited, but trying to hide it. He says he needs to see the real thing."

"Should we send it to him? Can he be trusted?"

"Probably," David said. "And it's either send him a piece or invite him here if we want any kind of positive I.D."

"Not here." That much she was sure of.

David nodded. "FedEx? UPS? Do we have time to make their pickup schedule?"

"No, not this late. We'd have to drive to Fort Smith. How about overnight mail? It takes two days to get most places from here, but that would put it there Friday."

"You're sure?"

She wasn't, but they had to do something. This at least was a start. "Yes."

He lifted his hand to her cheek and held it there for a second. Encouragement? Who knew why at that time? She didn't; David probably didn't either. But that small gentle contact was needed, oh, so needed.

Slowly he withdrew his hand and lifted the receiver. "Okay," he said to the man on the line. "We'll get this out to you tonight. Where do you want it sent?" He scrawled the address on the envelope beneath his sketch. "Right. No, I don't know whether the owner will want to sell or not. I'll ask, and I'll certainly recommend you. Yeah, thanks. Right. I'll call you what—Sunday morning? Will that give you enough time? Okay. Thanks again, Jack. I really appreciate this."

Reflective, David replaced the receiver and scooted the telephone toward her. "Your turn."

She reached Karen at the apartment she still shared with two of their original roommates, although that would change soon. Anne knew Karen had been chasing a slot at a university med center somewhere in the west—Wyoming, Montana, Utah, Colorado. Anywhere closer to the mountains she loved and away from the man she didn't.

"It's about time you contacted somebody, Locke," Karen told her with a laugh. "We were all beginning to think you'd either fallen in that lake down there, or taken root and started to sprout. How the hell are you? And what's it like not to have to chase yourself around the clock?"

"Excuse me," Anne said. "I thought I'd reached the mature and eminently respected Dr. K. Ready. I must have misdialed."

"So, kiddo." Karen dropped her voice half an octave and affected a mixed-eastern European accent. "You call, you joke, you must vant somet'ing. Tell Dr. Ready how she may help. But remember—none of my patients survive."

Karen had been the one who held the roommates together back in those early crowded years. When tempers, already short because of stress and long hours, threatened to get out of control over whose turn it was for the shower or who should have carried out the trash, she was always there with a joke when needed, a soft word, or even an occasional dressing-down.

Anne and Karen had gone through a residency in internal medicine together, but Karen had learned early on she couldn't stand losing a patient. She was the only person Anne knew who'd gone into pathology because she was too softhearted to watch the living die. In pathology, Karen swore, she'd have a chance at finding out how to fight disease and trauma without risking her heart. Knowing Karen, Anne thought she probably would.

"I've missed you," Anne told her friend.

"Yeah." Karen lost the accent. "Me, too. Damn." Anne heard a strange muffled noise and then a sniff. "Did you just call so we could have a good cry together, or was there a more important—excuse me—*another* reason for you spending long distance dollars I know that practice down there doesn't provide?"

That comment was part of one of Karen's ongoing gibes, made without malice, and Anne let it slide. Besides, Karen's opinion of her practice wasn't so very far off the mark. "Yeah," Anne said. Now that the moment had come, she almost relished her reaction. It was all too seldom that she got the best of Karen Ready. "I want you to look at a bone and tell me if I have to call the cops."

Absolute silence filled the line. Finally, Karen whispered softly, "You're serious?"

"Yeah."

"But you're qualified. Surely you can tell if it's—"

"I can tell that it's human, and that it's dead. Long-time dead. But I need your expertise to tell me how long, and whether I need to call a homicide division or a museum."

Anne looked at David to see him frowning and shaking his head as though to tell her to be careful about how much she said. But this was Karen, someone she'd trust with her life. Still, when he leaned closer she held the receiver so he could hear both parts of their conversation.

"Oh. Oh, well, sure I can do that. I do that a lot. But generally it's the cops who bring me the bone. Are you sure you don't want to go the regular route—of course, you're sure. I'm sorry Anne. You have a reason for not contacting the cops, right? Something to do with that godawful old house you bought and that mean-spirited cousin of yours?"

David glanced at Anne and grinned, and his eyes taunted her with his knowledge that no matter how circumspect she had tried to be with him about her family, she had not suffered in complete silence.

"I can send you a right femur," Anne said.

Again silence filled the line. "You have more than the one bone, don't you?" Karen asked. "You have the whole damned thing. What did you do, literally find the skeleton in the closet?"

David's frown grew fierce. And not without cause. He didn't have any kind of shared history with Karen on which to base trust. And for now, maybe the less Karen knew, the better—for her own sake, if they were wrong about the age of the man upstairs.

"I have a right femur," Anne repeated. "Will you look at it for me?"

"Oh, hell yes, you know I will," Karen said with only mild exasperation blunting her words. "I suppose you want it yesterday, and in complete confidence, too?"

"Got it in one," Anne told her and laughed softly, knowing Karen's eyes were dancing and her mouth was drawn in a mock pout. "With overnight mail to your door, it should get there Friday morning, and I'll call you Sunday morning for an unofficial report. Okay?"

"You're damned right it will be unofficial. Do you have any idea—"

"Lots and lots of ideas, Karen. You know that. It's the reason you put up with me all these years. When you couldn't get into enough trouble on your own, I was always able to help you out. And I'll owe you for this. Big time."

"Big time and big explanation," Karen added. "Anne . . ." Her voice was hesitant. Anne knew why, of course. Karen couldn't fail to ask, yet she didn't want to bring up harsh memories. "Are you all right? Really all right? We worried about you so much when you left. You know, you had some pretty serious injuries, lady. Physical and, well, and otherwise."

Anne didn't miss David's sharp glance. Only inches away from her, his already dark eyes took on an even darker glitter. She wanted to take the telephone receiver and pull away from him, but the damage had already been done.

"I'm fine, Karen," she told her. "Really. The practice is every bit as slow as we thought it would be, and so is the town. I've had lots of time to rest. And to heal."

"And to find skeletons in the closet," Karen added dryly. "Yeah, it sounds as though you've found a perfect place to recuperate."

"Better dead skeletons in the closet, than live, persistent secret admirers. Have you found out who he is, yet?"

"Pu-leeze, Anne. Jeeze. You could have gone all day without mentioning that."

Anne chuckled. Karen still sounded more provoked than frightened by this unknown suitor. "More flowers?"

"Twice a week," Karen told her. Maybe provoked wasn't a strong enough word, because Anne definitely heard more in her friend's voice than that. She also heard hesitation, as though Karen were holding something back.

"And what else?"

"Nothing," Karen said. "Nothing except my paranoia. You know I never could keep track of my things. And with Rae and Molly in the apartment, it's no wonder that I occasionally lose something."

Anne felt David tense beside her. She shook her head as she saw him reaching for the receiver. "Well, if it's clothes, check Molly's closet," she told Karen. "And if it's more serious than that, maybe you'd better reconsider talking to the police."

"Yeah. I can just see the headlines on something like that: 'Bone doctor blows whistle; flowers mask scent of formaldehyde.'"

"Karen—"

"It's okay," she said. "I promise. Now send me your femur and start practicing for the time when you're going to give me this wonderful explanation. Is it too much to hope there's a living man mixed up in it somewhere?"

"Dream on. I'll talk to you Sunday, but let's keep in touch, okay? I worry about you. And thanks."

Anne sank back in her chair after she hung up, as drained as if she had just taken a major test. Concerned, David asked, "Are you up to calling your mom now?"

"Doesn't matter whether I am or not," she told him after a glance at her watch. "I never can remember whether it's a seven-and-a-half or an eight-and-a-half hour time difference. They get up early, but if I call them now, Mom's fully capable of putting a contract out on my life."

He had to have heard the affection in her voice in spite of her words. "You love her, don't you?"

"Yeah," she told him. "A lot. And I miss her. A lot. But I'm so damned glad she's happy at last."

David dropped his hand to her shoulder, and it was like his touch to her cheek had been earlier. Necessary. Too much. Not enough.

"Okay," he said, squeezing her shoulder gently before

releasing it and standing. "Let's go get the stuff to send."

Anne didn't want to. God knew she never wanted to go back into that room. But she knew they had to. "Right," she said. "Just let me find some boxes first."

The two items they were mailing were fragile and would need a lot of protection. She grabbed two boxes left over from her move and scooped up a double handful of polystyrene peanuts and a couple of lengths of bubblewrap.

David stopped her as she was reaching for tape and scissors. Stilling what even she recognized as nervous procrastination, he put everything but the boxes on the table. Those he took from her. "This is all we need for now," he said. "We'll bring them down here to pack."

She stood looking at him in silence, every fiber of her being rejecting her conscious decision to go back upstairs. *We'll bring them down here to pack.* David had said that, linking himself with her even though she knew he didn't want to return to that travesty of a grave either. She swallowed once, still silent, wishing he didn't have his hands full with the boxes so that he could at least touch her, and then realized that she could reach out. She could offer the touch that maybe he needed, too. She rested her hand on his arm. He glanced at it then back at her eyes. "Okay," she said abruptly, sounding much braver than she felt. "Let's get this over with."

9

What waited in the secret room was as overwhelming as it had been earlier. For both of them. Anne felt David standing close behind her at the foot of the array heaped up around the copper-covered skeleton within the confines outlined by the cedar poles.

But maybe it was getting easier to view this scene, or maybe her eyes were just becoming more accustomed to the forty-watt lightbulb.

The area defined by the cedar poles was perhaps six feet by eight feet. The body—she couldn't think of it in any less personal terms—lay in the center of that area on the remains of what appeared to be some kind of mat, although it was difficult to see for the profusion of items piled upon it.

She saw two wooden barrels and several boxes in the corner of the room. She made her way over to them and found them empty except for a small amount of dirt in the bottom of each of them. The same dirt, probably, that she felt sliding beneath the soles of her shoes. The same dirt that she saw in small piles among the artifacts and which lightly dusted everything within the boundaries of the cedar poles.

"Did you find anything?" David asked from the other side of the burial.

"No. Just dirt. And maybe the way he was brought up here."

"Then let's get on with it."

The harsh, bleak sound of his voice echoed her own emotions too closely for her to begin to examine. Deciding it fell in that area of things they wouldn't dwell on, she nodded, carefully walked around the perimeter of the burial and knelt beside David.

Almost reverently, he touched a round, engraved object four inches or so in diameter that rested on top of a pile of other engraved shells. Anne recognized the design on it as he lifted it and held it so the uneven light could illuminate it. "This is a gorget," he told her, again turning the item in the light so that she could see. "It's engraved on a circle of conch shell and made to be worn as a neckpiece. These two small holes here?" He pointed at a place near the top of the disk. "These were drilled so that a thong could be inserted." For a moment she thought he was going to place it back with the others. "I hate to separate this," he said.

"I know."

"I'll want to make a tracing of this before we send it away."

"Is it very valuable?" she asked.

"Yeah. Oh, yeah. If it's authentic, and I don't think there's any doubt of that, it won't really matter where it originally came from. It— Yeah. It's valuable."

"Something your friend Jack might decide actually belonged to him?"

He was silent for a moment. "I don't think so, Annie, but greed's a strange thing. It can make thieves of people you'd swear on your life were honest. So just to make sure Jack stays honest, we'll do the tracing, or photocopy it if we can find a copier, and— I don't know. Can you register overnight mail?"

"I don't know. I've never tried. Doesn't it have to be signed for anyway?"

He didn't answer, but he put the disk in the small box she had selected for it and then moved the larger box closer to her. "Do you want me to get it?" he asked.

He didn't have to say what "it" was. The unspoken words hung between them, all out of proportion, as everything had been since they'd pounded their way into this room. Leg. Thigh. *Femur.* She snatched onto that clean, impersonal word, hoping it would bring reality into their own private twilight zone. It didn't.

Did she want David to get it? Did she want David to be the one who desecrated an already desecrated grave? Anne didn't want either one of them to, but that was irrelevant now. She shook her head, trying to erase images of the skeleton before them as he once must have been—living, vital, dynamic—and leaned forward.

The copper plate covering the warrior's right thigh was in two pieces. It had been hinged. The remains of what appeared to have been leather thongs were still clearly visible. It also mirrored the copper plate on his left thigh. Two cats looked out from the armor, upright on their haunches. Their bodies twisted to one side for protection, but they were writhing, snarling, ready for battle. And she didn't want to touch either of them, but she knew she must. As reverently as David had lifted the gorget, she lifted the copper plate and lay it beside the thigh.

As much as she could see of the femur was intact. Part of it was still hidden by the copper plates that had covered the man's abdomen and groin. All connecting muscle, all flesh, had been gone for years, for centuries, but without the harsh intrusion of weather, the bone had taken on a soft, white patina, curiously unmarred by the green tinge ancient copper should have given it. Hesitantly, she reached for it.

A low growl seemed to come from all around them. Anne jerked her hands away and her head up, to meet David's frantic search of the room.

"What was that?" she whispered.

But then the wind rose outside and she recognized the scrape of that branch from the pecan tree that periodically threatened the roof as it raked against the side of the house. And sighed. "Wind," she said. "Just wind."

But still, she didn't want to go on. "Do we have to do this?" she asked David. "Can't we just sheetrock and paper over the closet wall and pretend we never found him?"

"And leave him here for your cousin Joe or someone else out for the quick buck to find?" David asked. "How long do you think it would take him and your buddy Hank Foresman to pick through and scatter this collection?"

Not long, Anne knew, and not with any respect. She reached again for the femur and couldn't help apologizing. "I'm sorry. I wouldn't do this if it wasn't absolutely necessary, and I promise to put it back just as soon as I can."

Walking over a grave? Yeah. They were doing that. Big time. And it didn't help that she felt an undue bond with the long-dead man whose grave they were desecrating. It didn't help that she sensed that David felt that bond, too.

David's hand covered hers as she placed the femur in the box. His sigh echoed hers as they released the partially calcified bone. They remained kneeling there for a moment, then stood, not speaking. David was the one who reached over and replaced the copper armor to cover the length of missing bone. He picked up the boxes and stood, but waited until Anne had passed through the opening into the closet before he turned out the light and followed her.

Downstairs, the kitchen seemed abnormally normal. Anne left the room long enough to locate a package of white tissue paper in her gift-wrapping supplies. She gave it to David and he carried it to the round oak table where he made a tracing of the gorget. Together they located a box more suitable for the femur and carefully wrapped the bone and the gorget. They packed with the hope the fragile items would reach their destinations without damage and that the recipients would treat them with equal respect.

"I have labels and postage at the clinic," she told him when the items were wrapped and securely taped into their boxes.

"Good. It will mean Jack knows about you, but it might be better if it looks like these are really going out from the clinic. That way, no one around here will be curious about what we're sending overnight delivery on a holiday weekend."

"Do you really think anyone would even notice?"

"Annie, Annie," David said, with a grim sort of humor. "This is your small town. You know someone would. And if Cousin Joe is already suspicious about what you're doing in the house, you know it would be only a matter of hours before he or one of his friends began to wonder what you'd shipped off, and why."

David was right, of course. Joe might not know about their friend upstairs, but since he'd so obviously sent Hank around to snoop he probably suspected something. And wasn't that a nice little piece of a puzzle she hadn't even been aware of until David Huerra came crashing into her life?

Anne looked at the long, squat box with the femur in it. Strangely, handling it, being responsible for it, caused her more concern than any thought of the small artifact David had said was so valuable. "You'll go with me?" she asked, but it wasn't really a question. She couldn't visualize carrying those two boxes through town without him by her side. She couldn't visualize him letting her do so.

"I don't think that's such a good idea. Not with that hole in the wall upstairs and with at least one person real curious about what's up there."

"Oh." He was right again, damn it.

David carried the packages for her, out to where she had parked Agnes, near the old barn. He opened the driver's side door, slid both boxes over the center hump until they rested on the floor on the other side, and turned to her. "Be careful."

For a moment as she looked up at him, she considered pleading with him to reconsider, to go with her. Pleading. Her. She had begged exactly once in her life. It had done no good. She couldn't suppress the shudder that ran through her.

"Annie?"

She shook her head. She couldn't bring herself to tell him that nothing was wrong, because she wasn't sure that everything wasn't wrong. But there wasn't anything either one of them could do about it right now except exactly what they were doing. "I'll be all right," she said as she climbed into the truck. "You be careful, too."

David watched until Anne had backed her truck to the wide, sparsely graveled area nearer the house, turned, and disappeared down the driveway.

Be careful.

His warning? Or hers? His concern? Or hers?

Did it matter?

Was it necessary?

He felt an all-too-familiar prickling along the back of his neck. Carefully, but with all appearances of casualness, he turned. Nothing. Nothing but the old barn, weathered, decrepit, all but falling down. Unless there was something or someone inside. He'd walked out here with Hank Foresman Monday, but they'd done little more than crack open one of the hinge-sprung doors.

Cautiously he began walking, pacing off his steps to the north wall and then to the rear of the barn.

Nothing. Nothing except a hastily made but ancient repair to the board and batten siding beneath the grime-blackened window on the rear wall: four one-by-fours laid unevenly across the siding and hammered in place with oversized nails. Nothing in the now bare, skeletal branches of the overgrown hedge.

He continued on around the barn until he once again stood in front of the doors.

Inside then?

Because the sensation of being watched was as real as when he first felt it. Because he had been through this too many times to disregard whatever warning system sparked this feeling.

Inside then.

He faced the doors. His service revolver lay safely stashed beneath the seat in the Blazer, half the oversized yard away. The locked Blazer. And the keys were on Anne's kitchen table. Whoever or whatever could be long gone by the time he retrieved them and his revolver.

He could risk a quick look. Joe was a bully but not necessarily dangerous. Hank was a blowhard and so out of shape David could outmaneuver him easily. The odds of him being physically harmed were minuscule so long as he wasn't taken by surprise, and there was little chance of that now that his early warning system had kicked in.

He stopped for a second with his hand on the ancient

door. What an interesting qualifier his thoughts had just produced. Physically harmed. He shook off that thought and lifted the crossbar. He pulled one of the double doors open, keeping it between himself and the dark interior of the building. Then, moving quickly, he stepped to the other side and pulled that door open, too.

A hole in the roof helped light the back of the barn, although an old loft kept the north side in shadows. He stepped to one side to look into the dim interior to make sure that no one waited in ambush there, and saw only the rusted remains of an abandoned car, wheels and rotted tires sunk into half-composted leaves. It was an old Ford—fifty years or so old—with its windows rolled tightly up and covered with decades of grime. No one had touched those doors in years, just as no one had cleaned those windows, but to be on the safe side, he yanked down on the door handle, finding it every bit as filthy as it had looked. Finding it locked. He eased around the car. The other door was locked too, but the vent window on the passenger side cocked out at a slight angle. He found it stuck, but not locked, pushed it open and bent to look inside.

The car was empty, a rusting, mostly rotted hulk. He reached inside and jerked up on the door handle to free the lock. Damn. It didn't budge. He wiped at the lower corner of the window, smearing the dirt. The lock button sat squat and fat and still down, and what appeared to be an acre away from the vent window opening. He grimaced, but there was no other way. Leaning sideways against the filthy car, he stretched his arm inside along the base of the window until he felt his fingers touch the flattened top of the lock button. Thank God it was still there. He caught it, scissors fashion, between two fingers. Now, if he could just—yes! He felt a stubborn tension on it, but it did ease up. He sagged against the car for a moment, and then withdrew his arm and opened the door.

What had he expected to find? He and Anne had used their quota of surprises in an upstairs bedroom. Or had they? A miasma of despair pervaded the interior, from the oversized dashboard with a key protruding from the ignition next to the starter button, to the small rear bench seat with its rusted springs clearly visible. Years of despair. A lifetime of despair.

Swearing, David slammed the car door, holding it shut with splayed hands as he leaned against it.

And then he realized what he had seen but not noticed before. Rust. In the humidity of this town, of this entire area, anything not zealously protected would rust and corrode in record time. Why hadn't the copper corroded? Other than the light sprinkling of dirt, barely more than dust, the entire hidden trove in that upstairs room had remained remarkably clean. Pristine. New.

Even the conch shell core pendants had still carried the opalescent glow of new shell.

Why? How?

Not now! he told himself as he felt the despair from the car leaching its way out into his hands, up his arms. He jerked away and turned to continue his study of the barn. Four rotting tires without wheels rested against the wall along with what appeared to have once been harness and tack that had fallen from hooks on those walls.

Behind him, ladder-type stairs led to the loft.

And the back of his neck still warned him of something . . . Something.

He tested the flattened rungs of the ladder and found them surprisingly secure, and when he gripped them and released them, his hands came away covered with still more previously undisturbed dirt.

He looked at his hands, at the ladder, and up toward

the loft. Nothing was up there. Nothing could be up there unless it had wings. But still he climbed up and cautiously peered over the ledge into the loft. It was empty, entirely visible except for one corner which housed a pile of wooden boxes. David eased himself onto the flooring. Testing it, he found it sturdy. Sturdy enough, he thought, for a quick but careful examination of those boxes.

If the boxes contained anything, examination would have to wait, he decided when he reached the corner and discovered their primary purpose. Stacked as they were, they created an alcove, hidden from view, just large enough for—*for what?*

A gust of wind whistled through the barn, bringing in a chill and a scattering of dead leaves, and sounding at one moment suspiciously like the furtive laughter of young children, at the next like the sigh of a lover. David turned rapidly and felt the floor, not so sturdy after all, shake beneath his feet.

"There's nothing here." He spoke aloud, and the sound of his voice startled him almost as much as the wind had. But there *was* nothing there. If ever there had been, it was gone. Long gone.

He eased his way back to the ladder and down to the ground. Little remained in the rest of the barn. A pile of rotted lumber, a stack of discarded, beyond saving, furniture, the frame of what looked like an old hospital bed, an ancient trunk, empty, with the lock missing and the lid hanging crazily from one hinge. Nothing to explain the warning he'd been given.

Nothing.

Nothing except the car. The rusting, dead car. And the depression it had invoked in him.

Enough!

David whirled and marched out of the barn. He and

Anne had enough to worry about without adding an abandoned car to the list.

Unless the car was part of the mystery.

He stopped. They had no way of ever learning if it was. Did they?

More carefully than he had opened them, mindful now of their age and disrepair, David closed the double doors and dropped the wooden brace into position, sealing whatever was in there, if anything was in there, securely inside.

Where the hell was Annie?

It was getting dark. Not really late, but dark. Too dark to be working in an unlighted closet, and David didn't want to open the frayed draperies in the upstairs sitting room or turn on any lights to advertise to anyone who watched that he was in that room.

And hell, yes, it was late. Too much time had passed since Anne left with the packages. She could have driven them to Fort Smith in the hours she'd been gone. She'd had more than enough time to fill in a couple of labels and waltz those two boxes over to the post office.

Unless something had happened to her.

"Damn!" The staple gun twisted in his hand, slamming his thumb between its handle and the edge of the panel he was constructing. He shook his hand, muttering at the minor pain. Carelessness. Stupidity on his part. He should have gone with her, would have gone with her if it hadn't been for that hole in the wall.

Well, that was just about fixed.

He had prenailed the remaining piece of trim. Now he aligned it along the edge of the paper-covered drywall and tapped it into place. He carried the drywall into the closet and fitted it over the opening that he had enlarged until it stretched between the two-foot centered studs, from the base nailed to the floor to the brace he had nailed between the existing studs just below the closet shelf. The paper matched, compliments of a cheesecloth backed strip he'd cut from the inside closet front wall above one of the doors. And the trim matched those pieces he had nailed in place over each of the studs, making the stained vertical strips appear to be part of the original finish of the closet rather than an afterthought.

It would do, he thought, as the makeshift door eased snugly into place and blended into the surrounding wall.

Like it had never been disturbed.

He'd done most of the cutting and trimming downstairs, so with a minimum of pickup, this room would look like it had never been disturbed, either.

And then, by God, if she wasn't back, he was going after Annie.

He was returning the last of his tools to the converted sleeping porch adjacent to the kitchen when he heard the kitchen door open.

"David?"

"Where the hell have you been?" His growl burst from him before he'd even thought the words, surprising him as much as it must have surprised Anne. He dropped the armload of tools and drywall leavings and trim and whirled to face her.

And saw the blood.

"Annie?" His voice came out soft and shocked.

"Annie," he said again, louder but still not much more than a whisper as he moved into the kitchen, as he crossed to where she stood, as he gripped her shoulders. "What happened?"

"What?"

She followed the direction of his eyes, to the blood splattered on her shirt, clearly visible between the edges of her open jacket. "Oh, damn. That."

"Hell, yes, that," he said, drawing her toward the table. "Sit. Are you all right? What happened?"

With his hands still clutching her shoulders, he used his foot to nudge a chair out from the table and pushed her onto it. God, she was small. Why hadn't he ever noticed before just how small? Just how fragile? He felt the bones of her shoulders, of her arms, beneath his hands, but he couldn't ease his hold on her, not even to pull her jacket away and search for her injury. He shouldn't have let her go on alone . . . go *out* alone. She wasn't prepared for the dangers. "Who did this?"

"David." Anne looked up at him with confusion at first darkening her eyes, then concern, before she smiled gently. "Bobby Preston. It's his blood, not mine. He was playing Superman and tried to fly off his parents' garage. He landed in his mother's rosebushes. He's the reason I'm so late. Now. Are *you* all right?"

Was he? Or had he gone completely over the edge? He didn't like not being in control, and he hadn't been. Not once today. Not since finding the body. Not in the barn. Not even now when any fool could look past the blood splattered on Anne Locke's shirt and see that she was not bleeding from any wound but that she was pale and drawn and that probably the last thing she needed was some madman interrogating her and shaking her hard enough to dislodge the pins in her hair.

And any fool could also see she was trying desperately to distract him from the subject of his interrogation.

He dropped his hands from her shoulders and spun around. "Yeah. Oh, hell yeah. I'm just dandy."

"Then why—" Her voice cracked, hoarsened. "Then why are you carrying your revolver?"

Damn! He felt for the small of his back, where he had tucked the revolver into his jeans.

"What happened while I was gone?"

He looked at her and tried for a grin—anything—to erase her worried frown. "Would you believe nothing? At least, nothing with a rational explanation."

She shook her head, and her chin came up a notch. "Everything has a rational explanation. Sometimes we just have to look harder for it than at others."

"Like our friend upstairs?"

He saw the change that clouded her face, saw the shudder she couldn't quite suppress. *Low blow, Huerra,* he thought. *What are you going to do next? Find a puppy to kick?*

"Yes," she said firmly. "Exactly like our friend upstairs. Now, please tell me what else has happened."

He sighed, dragged out a chair and sank onto it. "Nothing, Annie. Absolutely nothing. I guess I just let my paranoia get out of control."

"How?"

Let it go, he wanted to tell her. But he sensed she wouldn't. And maybe she ought to know how far out of control he had let his imagination get.

"I— When you left today, I had a bad feeling about your garage."

"Bad enough so that you armed yourself to investigate?"

"Bad enough that I would have, if my weapon hadn't been so far away and if I hadn't been so sure the intruder would escape if I took the time to go get it."

"And did he?"

"Hell, Annie, there wasn't anyone there. Just a falling down barn, a rusted-out, locked hulk of a car, and a pile of clutter."

"Then what was the problem?"

"The problem was—" He reached across the table for the envelope with the drawing he had sketched only hours earlier, but he couldn't hide behind studying it.

Not now. "The problem was, it felt as though there was someone there. There was no reason for the emotions I felt as I broke into that car."

"Like upstairs."

He heard no question in her soft voice, only a resigned statement of fact. For a while, he'd wondered if maybe he'd imagined the intensity of feelings—his and hers—in that upstairs room. Now he knew he hadn't.

"Yeah," he said. "Like upstairs."

"God." Anne folded her hands in her lap and sat up very straight. "Do I have to go out there, too?"

"No. Not now. Maybe not ever. But haven't you been in there? Haven't you—"

"I've been in there," she said. "Six months ago. I wondered about hauling off the old car. I considered trying some kind of renovation on the trunk but decided it was too far gone. And I climbed far enough up the ladder to see that the loft probably wasn't secure enough for exploring, and that except for those boxes in the back, it was empty."

"And felt nothing?"

She shook her head. "But then—and you're not going to like this—I never felt anything strange in this house or around it, until last Saturday morning."

She was right; he didn't like it. Whatever was here had been here a lot longer than a few days. It had been firmly in place before he felt the first chill shudder over him as he stepped down from Anne's truck. Unless— Unless Anne wasn't being as forthright as he had thought. Unless Anne had an agenda of her own that he knew nothing about. And now he needed to change the subject.

"With all the excitement at the clinic, were you able to get to the post office?"

She grimaced. "Not exactly. But I did get them mailed," she said quickly. "Margaret—you remember my nurse?—saw the crowd at the clinic and stopped to help. I had the packages ready to go when Bobby's family brought him in. I'll admit, I worried about it, but it was either that or run the risk of letting them sit until Friday, so I asked Margaret to carry them to the post office for me."

"And she did? You're sure?"

"Yeah, you're right," Annie said. "Your paranoia is working overtime. You met Margaret. What's not to trust? Besides," Anne fumbled in the pocket of her jacket and dropped a square of folded paper onto the pile of invoices, "she brought me the receipts."

He tried for a grin. Maybe he made it. "Once upon a time," he told her, "I was a reasonable, sensible person."

"You're sure about that?" She delivered the words deadpan, but he saw a glimmer of humor in her eyes.

"Come on," he said. "I'll show you what I've done while you've been off hobnobbing with the small and famous. And run something past you that I think will provide some additional protection as well as a reason for you to be up in the sitting room at odd hours."

"Do you really think someone is keeping tabs?"

"Do you want to accept at face value that Cousin Joe really doesn't suspect anything about our friend, and that Hank Foresman is just trying to make amends?"

She didn't answer, but she didn't have to use words to tell him that she trusted Joe and Hank no more than he did.

10

Woman-From-The-West *lay* on the robes near the fire. That she lay in the same place where the Warrior had died brought her scant comfort. Soon she would die. As he had. As their child within her had.

And their separation would be for nothing. *Nothing*.

Would she be allowed to join him in the hereafter if she had not kept her promise to him? Or would she be forever separated from the man who had grown to mean more to her than her own soul?

His burial chamber was covered now but no one had yet smoothed the top of the sacred mound. No one had yet begun to build another mortuary house.

Just as no one had burned this house and all its contents after his death.

As no one had killed the grave goods that accompanied him on his journey.

As no one had been allowed to disturb him once his armor-clad body had been placed in the chamber with the ceremonially robed body of the Priest.

The Guardians would not allow it.

They had allowed no one to approach him, to harm

him, to touch him in any way, since she had knelt by his side and returned to him the small cedar box he had given her containing their images on shell.

And they had allowed no one to approach her, to harm her, to touch her in any way she did not wish while she wore the medallion, while she carried his child. But even they were not powerful enough to force someone to give her aid.

The pain came in unrelenting waves now as her body tried futilely to expel the body of their child. He was dead; he must be. Too many hours had passed since he began his journey into this world.

Too many hours had passed since she'd sent her sweet child of a maid to find help for her. Too many hours had passed since the one still living member of the Warrior's guard had come to her side bringing his own mate, telling her the maid would not be allowed to return. Too many hours had passed since she'd heard the last of their moans and cries as they had died, poisoned before they even came to her, she was sure—not by the black drink of honorable death but with something sly and secret—to prevent them from offering her even succor in her last moments.

And for what?

More power for one person?

Three had ruled when she came to these people. The Chieftain, the Priest, and her mate, the Warrior. They had ruled well; their people had prospered.

Now, only one ruled. And greed ruled that one.

No Priest had been allowed to rise up.

If the Warrior had lived, he could have confronted the despot the Chieftain had become, could perhaps have prevented it happening.

But he had not lived. And his successor had not been allowed to be born.

What would happen to his people now?

When the greed of one destroyed the hope of many, would they all just cease to be? Would they fade from the earth as though they had never been?

What would happen to her?

Would she float in limbo, forever alone?

The Warrior was safe. She held onto that thought as the last light in the house faded. He was beyond the touch of the Chieftain, in the hereafter. And his body was safe from depredation and degradation. The Guardians would see to that. Yes. She raised her hand to the likeness of the Warrior she wore on her breast. As was hers. *He* had seen to that in his last moment. And his likeness was all of this earth she needed to accompany her.

Even in limbo. Even alone.

11

Anne had spent too many years getting up before dawn for something as sane as a holiday to keep her lazing in bed. She didn't like it, but she was up and dressed in jeans and a sweatshirt, leaning against the kitchen sink, not quite awake enough yet to tackle any work on the house, and waiting for the coffee to finish dripping into the pot long before eight o'clock Thanksgiving morning.

David hadn't returned to his cabin until after midnight the night before. Even then, he hadn't been happy about leaving her alone in the house with the warrior and at the whim of whoever might decide to come looking for him. Which was pretty silly, Anne thought in the dim, cool light of early morning as she rubbed her neck and stretched and tried to wake up.

She'd been alone in the house with the body upstairs for the past six months. And vulnerable to whoever decided to come looking for him. She shuddered at that sudden thought. Maybe David hadn't been quite as arbitrary as she had believed last night.

She wondered where David was. She wondered why, for probably the ninetieth time, she hadn't told him she didn't give a hang what small-town gossips said and asked that he stay with her last night. She wondered why—and how—he had so quickly become a part of her life.

She heard the groan of an engine and pushed aside the faded kitchen curtain to look out the window over the sink, just as the gray-green Blazer David drove topped the hill of her driveway.

She dragged open the back door just as he stepped onto the porch. "Morning."

"Good morning to you, too," he said as he thrust a brown paper bag at her.

She took the bag and stepped back in mock alarm. "My God, you're actually awake. What happened?" She opened the bag enough to glance inside. "And doughnuts? Where on earth did you find someplace open this morning?"

He headed directly to the coffeepot, eased the carafe from under the stream of dripping coffee and one of the waiting cups into its place. While the cup slowly filled, he stood facing the window, not looking at her. "Are you in a better mood this morning, Doc?"

Uh oh. *Doc* not *Annie.* And she heard no teasing in his voice, only a weariness that might be explained by lack of sleep last night. He had thought she'd been incredibly stupid in refusing his protection last night.

But he had brought a peace offering.

"Yes," she said quietly, "I am." She extended the bag toward him. "And thank you for breakfast."

He did a quick juggling act with the two cups and the coffeepot and turned, handing her a filled cup. "Come on," he said. "There's something we both need to see."

Maybe if he'd pulled her along behind him, she'd have protested. He didn't; he simply led the way out of the kitchen and down the long, wide hall.

What did they need to see? To visit the room upstairs again? Nope. David passed the stairwell. And before she could become even remotely suspicious, he passed the door to her bedroom, too.

The door to the front porch was a massive, carved relic from an older age, complete with an etched glass window showing a woman in a rose garden. Anne had fallen in love with the window the first time she saw it but in the go-for-nothing pace her life had once again assumed—couldn't seem to get away from—she seldom really saw the door any more, simply passed it on her way from one job in the house to another.

And if she seldom paused long enough to admire the door she loved, she certainly hadn't taken the time to open it and step out onto the long covered porch. Now David did, and led her outside into the brisk November morning.

A grouping of nondescript chairs and a settee made of what appeared to be small branches had been left on the porch. Anne noticed that a tarp had been thrown over the settee. David gestured toward it and with more than one unspoken question, Anne sat.

So did David. Close enough to her on the small settee that only inches separated them.

"I'll take one of those doughnuts now," he said, leaning against the tarp-covered back of the settee and drawing in a deep breath.

Anne handed him the bag. "So what is it we need to see?"

David stopped with his hand half in the bag and looked at her incredulously. "Annie. Oh, Annie. You can't still be that asleep." He lifted his hand and pointed toward her front yard and beyond. "Open your eyes."

Maybe she was asleep. Maybe she had been asleep most of her life. She had marveled over the view once, twice, maybe even three times when she first moved into the house, had promised herself that she would never grow used to it, and then, like the door, it had become a mere prop in the background of busy work. She gave David an apologetic smile and leaned back against the tarp, looking out into the distance.

The town of Allegro, with its ancient brick buildings and tree-lined residential area, sat on the edge of a hillside, the hillside her house topped. The lake was farther to the south, in the valley, fed by a northern flowing river that, once freed by the dam, continued its meander north, marked in the distance by a tree line not visible at this early hour because of the fog rising from the water. Mountains rose on the south and the east, surrounding them like friendly, aged sentinels. The sun had already risen far enough to have lost the miraculous glowing colors she had once—but only once—seen from this porch, but its early morning slant lighted and highlighted the various shades of green and tan of forest and cleared field on the closest mountains.

Now Anne, too, took a deep, cleansing breath. "Thank you."

She heard the rustle of the paper bag, then felt it as David nudged it back toward her hand. "My pleasure," he told her.

Not willing to look away from the peace of the view, Anne groped in the bag and retrieved a doughnut. The two of them sat there in companionable silence, until Anne shivered, and David shifted his weight beside her.

"Cold?" he asked."

"A little."

"Here." She felt his arm settle around her shoulder and draw her against his side. She tensed slightly, until she realized he offered nothing but warmth, then relaxed against him, loathe to give up the peace they had found on the porch. Not yet. And at the same time realizing David was merely continuing—on a different level—the campaign she had recognized and rebelled against last night: protecting her.

Well, this protection she could take.

"So what do we do now?"

His words were an intrusion and a reminder that she didn't want. Once again she tensed. This time, she moved away from him. And he let her go.

She sighed, stood, and gave one last, reluctant glance at the valley before turning toward the door. "Now, I start cooking. And getting the house as ready as I can for Thanksgiving dinner."

The fool woman had invited people for dinner. And not just dinner—televised football and parades and all the attendant folderol of a holiday feast.

David lugged the last packing crate from the downstairs sitting room into place in the upstairs sitting room.

People who would want to see what she had done with the house.

People who would be marching through room after room, opening closet doors, and giving in to natural curiosity. Or maybe not so natural.

He straightened and stretched and looked around the now carefully cluttered room.

Well, this would help. Moving Anne's unpacked goods up here had freed a reasonably sized room downstairs for her television and had given her a reason for the lights in this room to be on at night. And the things he had stacked in the closet helped hide the back wall from any but the most determined of searchers.

Maybe it wasn't such a bad idea after all, he thought. Maybe a little enthusiastic gossip about how normal everything up here looked was just what the doctor needed.

He heard footsteps behind him and turned as Anne entered the room. She paused at the doorway and looked around, at the boxes so neatly stacked, at the portable sewing machine he had found and opened and set on a small side table he'd brought in from another upstairs room, at the small stove he'd lighted to heat the room and the bar of soap and clean towel he'd placed on the vanity. At what had become a cozy and efficient work room, a place to sort through boxes and yet keep the clutter from the rest of the house. A place to be comfortable and warm while doing so. A place to clean up afterward.

"Oh," she said. "Oh my. You have been busy."

Almost as though against her will, she crossed the room and opened the closet door. The boxes he'd stacked there were not heavy, could easily be moved, even by her, but seemed to fill most of the closet. She stepped inside, silent, looking at the boxes, then placed her hands on the small portion of the back wall not covered by crates and stood there for a moment, head bowed, quiet.

"He's—all right?"

David knew the emotion that fueled her question; he'd felt it, too, as he'd begun the job of further hiding the warrior. He knew it, but didn't like at all the fact that Annie felt it.

"Annie. He's dead."

She whirled to face him. "I know that!"

But did she? he wondered. Did *he*? Because even he had to admit what they were doing seemed much more personal than hiding an already hidden treasure.

The kitchen was redolent with the aromas of Anne's childhood and as sparkling clean as two people could make it. The supplies had all been either stashed in the room off the kitchen or hidden away elsewhere. The small sitting room had been dusted and swept and the dining room truly cleaned for the first time since she'd moved into the house. And her plain white china looked almost festive on her grandmother's Battenburg lace tablecloth.

She didn't know why David had fallen so willingly into helping her prepare for this meal, but she knew she couldn't have done it without him. She doubted that she *would* have done it without him, but knowing he would be alone for Thanksgiving unless she invited him to dine with her, knowing that *she* would be alone, had started her thinking about others who might be alone. Nellie, her receptionist, and her small daughter, and Margaret, her nurse.

But it seemed Margaret wouldn't have been alone. Not according her response to Anne's invitation. She wanted to come, but she wasn't sure about other plans—and if she did come, could she bring someone.

Anne heard the first car groan up the drive just as she and David stashed the last tool and closed the double doors to the supply room. Anne wiped her hands on the dishtowel she had tied around her waist, then, after looking around distractedly, dropped the towel into the hamper by the washing machine.

"Nervous, Annie?" David asked. "Don't tell me you've never entertained."

Anne shook her head. "Not for a major holiday. Not anyone other than roommates or close family."

He dropped his hand onto her shoulder and gave her a gentle push toward the door. "You'll do fine."

She shot him a disbelieving look. "And what if I burn

the pie, or the turkey's dry? What if I absolutely ruin this meal?"

"Then we'll eat cornbread dressing and Aunt Elena's cranberry relish and start practicing the stories we'll tell for the rest of our lives about your first Thanksgiving feast." He grinned at her. "Provided, of course, you ever open the door and let your guests in."

Nellie Flynn stood on the porch with her hand resting protectively on a four-year-old, scrubbed clean, wide-eyed, miniature version of herself.

The little girl smiled shyly and held out the pie carrier she held. "Mama said be real careful, 'cause this is special for Doc Anne. Are you Doc Anne?"

Anne knelt and took the carrier from the little girl. "Yes, I am. And who are you?"

"I'm Lilly, silly." The girl giggled. "I made a poem."

"Oh, my word." Nellie shook her head and sighed. "It's Lilly that's being silly. You know better than that, cupcake. Apologize to Dr. Locke."

"Grownups aren't silly?"

Anne chuckled. "Sometimes grownups are very silly. Just like we are right now for standing out here in the cold." She stood, lifting the carrier, and stepped to one side. "Why don't we go on in so I can see what's in here that smells so good. You know you didn't have to bring anything, Nellie, but I think I'm going to be real glad you did."

When Nellie didn't move except for her hand tightening on her daughter's shoulder, Anne looked up to see her staring into the house. At David. In all his bruised and battered glory.

She had no idea what caused Nellie's tension, but worked quickly to defuse it. "Nellie Flynn, meet David Huerra." She smiled at David and handed him the pie carrier. He lifted an eyebrow but dropped right into the

domestic role she had just assigned him as though he suspected Nellie might not set foot in the house if he didn't.

"Nellie's my receptionist," she told him. She turned
her smile on Lilly and took her hand. "David is the
Dallas police officer who was hurt in the wreck with
Hank Foresman. He's been helping me with the house.
My goodness, you're a big girl, Lilly. Your mother tells
me you're four?"

"Yes." Nellie held up four fingers. "This many. Are
we going to have turkey and gravy?"

"You bet," Anne told her, at last ushering the small
party into her kitchen.

"I like the leg."

Anne laughed and bent to help the little girl with her
jacket. David set the pie carrier on the table. She
noticed that although he stood close, he made no effort
to help Nellie with her jacket until she had freed herself
from it and was looking for a place to put it down.

"Why don't I hang those up?" he asked, holding out
his hand but not aggressively reaching for them.

Nellie kept the large bag she had carried and slung it
once again over her shoulder as she handed him her
coat. She then turned quickly to her daughter, fumbled
in the bag and brought out an obviously well-loved rag
doll.

He'd just hung the two coats over pegs in the battered coat rack on the wall next to the back door when
the sound of another engine, this one considerably
more powerful than Nellie's Escort, announced the
arrival of her other guests.

"It must be Margaret," Anne told him. "She was able
to come after all."

Not only had Margaret managed to come for dinner,
she had brought the "someone" she'd mentioned.
When Anne opened the back door, she found her nurse

and a tall, lanky man with hard, suspicious eyes standing on her back porch. And in a replay of the earlier arrival, he, too, was staring over her shoulder. At David.

Margaret thrust a covered casserole dish at Anne. "Thanks for inviting us," she said. "Anne Locke, this is my husband, Wayne Samuels."

Anne didn't let her eyes widen, but she knew her shock must be evident. Husband? Margaret?

Instead, she took the dish and smiled at the man. "I'm happy you could come today, Wayne." Then, because he was still staring past her, she half turned. "Have you met David Huerra yet?" she asked, knowing that he probably hadn't. "David's—" For some reason she didn't examine, she didn't want to tell this man that David was a police officer. "David's a friend of mine who's been helping me with renovating the house."

"Huerra." The man's voice was abrupt, almost curt, and rusty as though little used.

"Samuels."

Anne looked from one to the other of them. Honestly! she thought. Men! They were facing each other, measuring each other, like a couple of territorial dogs. She stepped between them and considered handing David the casserole the way she had the pie carrier, but decided she probably wouldn't get away with it this time.

"Come on in," she said. "We finally got the television tuned in, and it's almost time for the parade. I know Lilly is really looking forward to seeing it."

With relief she saw Margaret's lip lift in a shadow of a smile, acknowledging Anne's diversion. "Lilly isn't the only one," she said as she entered the kitchen and held the door open, encouraging the man she called husband to follow her. "I love the Thanksgiving parade, too, but there's no way on earth we can tune it in at our place enough to tell even one band from another."

Anne set the casserole on the table and watched as the man entered cautiously. With great care and gentleness for such a dark, rough-looking man, he helped Margaret remove her coat and hung it on the rack before removing his own.

David closed the kitchen door but stood braced in front of it, Margaret spoke quietly but with what could almost have been forced cheer about how much better the kitchen looked than it had only days before, and Nellie looked as though she wanted to run away.

"Doc Anne? Doc Anne?"

Anne felt a tug on her skirt and looked down to find Lilly pulling on it.

"Are we going to watch the parade, Doc Anne? Really?"

Thank heavens for babies and their sublime self-absorption. "You bet, cupcake," she told Lilly. She glanced up at her assorted guests. Had this been such a good idea? She wasn't sure now, but she was in for the duration. Unless Nellie bolted or—good grief, who was Margaret to call David *tall, dark, and dangerous* when she had her own edition of that hidden away on her mountaintop?

"How about something to drink?" she asked. "I have coffee, hot cider, and tea. David, would you mind showing everyone the way to the small parlor while I fix a tray?"

"Let me help," Margaret said.

Anne looked toward Nellie and doubted that she would walk through a strange house with two strange men. "No," she said. "Thanks, Nellie will help me. But why don't you make sure that Lilly doesn't miss anything?"

Nellie shot her a look of pure gratitude and turned toward the cabinets as the others left the kitchen. Anne considered asking her why she was so uneasy. Was it because of David, or this house, or even something that had happened before she arrived, but decided that Nellie would only speak when she felt safe in doing so.

The little downstairs sitting room was really quite pleasant, Anne admitted later as she and Nellie carried the trays containing beverages and snacks into the room. At the end of the living room, it had double windows that faced the long front porch, French doors that faced the covered porch that wrapped around from the dining room, and a wall of fireplace and book shelves.

Unfortunately, until she had a chance to check out the chimney, the room had no heat. David had solved that by somehow coercing Gretta Tompkins into letting him borrow a kerosene heater, which he had set in front of the open fireplace.

A heater which he and Wayne Samuels were standing by, discussing, just before coming to words about when Anne entered the room.

"Let me ask her."

And before she had time to more than set the tray on a small table, David grasped her arm and led her from the room.

"That's quite a crowd you called together today, Annie," he said when they reached the front hall, well away from any chance of being overheard.

"Ask me what?" she said, deciding that might be a safer topic than her guest list.

"You know he's done time, don't you? Hard time, and I suspect not too long ago."

"No. I— He's— Well hell, David." Sometimes there was nothing to do but swear. "I thought Margaret was a widow. I didn't even know he existed until ten minutes ago."

David looked at her in silence for a moment before he chuckled and pulled her head against his shoulder.

"Well hell, Annie," he said, mimicking the exasperation in her voice. "A woman who can keep a secret better than I can, a hard-time con, a woman who's either been raped or seriously assaulted, and a four year old. Nobody's ever going to accuse you of a dull mix at your parties."

"Nellie—"

"Sshh. I shouldn't have said that."

"But—"

"Annie, if she wants you to know, she'll tell you."

"But—" How on earth had she worked with the woman and not picked up on anything even hinting at that kind of past until today?

"We have something more immediate to discuss," he told her. "Samuels doesn't like kerosene heaters. Says he doesn't think they're safe. He's volunteered to help me check out the chimneys."

His shoulder was nice. Too nice. And she shouldn't be leaning on it. Even if he had tucked her head against him, he obviously had meant nothing by it. Anne pulled away.

"You don't have to if you don't want to."

David shook his head. "That's not the point."

Confused, she looked at him. "What is?"

"We'll have to go on the roof," David told her. "And in the attic."

"Oh." Now she understood his reluctance.

"And he volunteered."

"Oh, dear. Do you think— No. Not if he's with Margaret. She— If she doesn't hate Joe, she at least considers him a lower life form than algae."

"I don't know what I think, Annie. I do know there's nothing in the attic for him to see. Maybe he needs to know that, too. And maybe I need to check him out some. Working together, I could do that."

"Is he— Do you think he's dangerous?"

"Who the hell knows, Annie? But the next time my captain tells me to go off and rest for a month, I'm going to introduce him to you and tell him about this trip."

Samuels knew what he was doing. That didn't surprise David. A man as hardened as Wayne Samuels wouldn't suggest doing something he wasn't competent to do. Not even as an excuse to snoop where ordinarily he wouldn't be able to.

He didn't appear to be snooping. That didn't surprise David either. Any man as hardened as Samuels would know how to hide his interest.

It seemed that his only interest in the dim light of the attic was the construction of the old house. He played his flashlight beam across the unplaned lumber of a massive roof truss and a smile as unexpected as a bolt of lightning cracked his hard face.

"They knew how to build," he said, then fell silent and stonefaced again as he went unerringly to the chimney for the downstairs sitting room.

David was respectably familiar with modern chimney construction, but he stood back and watched as Samuels inspected the bricks for discoloration and the mortar for failure. "This one looks okay, at least under the roof. You want to check out the other ones while we're up here?"

There were three other chimneys for wood or coal fireplaces, and two chimney flues for stoves, including the one for the small upstairs sitting room. David shrugged. He knew how to hide his interest, too. "Might as well."

So they did, finding all the brick unstained, all the mortar intact, and David learned absolutely nothing about Wayne Samuels other than that he knew chimneys, he worked with an intensity that blocked out everything else, and he showed no interest in Annie's attic other than an appreciation for the craftsmanship that had gone into building it.

Well, hell.

Well double hell, he thought when they walked out to Samuels's truck and he saw, stashed neatly under the low camper shell, all the equipment necessary for cleaning the chimneys, and most of the supplies for any repair they might have decided was necessary.

Maybe he had lost more than just his edge.

"You always come to dinner ready to clean and repoint chimneys?"

Samuels had draped a coil of rope over his shoulder and had begun pulling an extension ladder from the back of the truck. He stopped and leaned against the tailgate. "Maggie said the doc was cold." Whatever accent the man had had once had long since vanished into his rusty voice. "You got a problem with neighborly help for your lady? Or is this just your cop working its way out?"

His lady. The town gossips had been working overtime if they'd already paired the two of them, in spite of all his precautions about going back to that permanently air-conditioned cabin each night. But the gossips weren't the issue here. And neither was his relationship, or lack of one, with Anne. Or his right to question any guest of hers. Damn. He had no *right* to do what he was doing, but it sure seemed as if he did.

"Maybe both," he told Samuels, in a voice as uninflected as the other man's had been. "Where'd you do your time?"

For the first time he saw life in Samuels's eyes. A glimmer of what vaguely resembled humor lighted them for a moment before fading back into their flat darkness.

"Not did I do time? Or why did I do time? But where?"

It had seemed a logical question to David. He knew it had happened, and he wasn't interested in any explanation of mix-up or setup. A nice clean *where* would give him all the information he needed for finding out the rest. "Yeah."

Samuels bent back to the truck and hauled out a stack of plastic sheeting, a long-bristled chimney brush, and a burlap-covered weight on another length of rope. He hefted the burlap and pushed the sheeting at David. "Take this to Maggie. She knows how to set it so we won't have rooms full of carbon and soot and bird skeletons to clean up. Then come back for this stuff. I'll meet you on the roof."

Neatly done. David watched Samuels slowly but deliberately walk away. He hadn't argued or denied David's assumption; he'd just acknowledged and then ignored it. But the day wasn't over yet.

Margaret—there was no way he could think of that stately woman as Maggie—met him on the back porch and took the pile of plastic from him. He knew she'd watched his brief exchange with her husband; the tension in her eyes, her hands, and the set of her jaw all told him she had. She glanced once toward the side of the house where Samuels had passed on his way to the front chimney. "He's a good man, David Huerra. Don't ever doubt that. Not for a minute."

Maybe he was a good man, but maybe Margaret only thought he was. And what the hell difference did it make to him anyway? If the man wasn't interested in the secret in the closet, he could keep all of the secrets he wanted to. After today he'd be gone and Annie—and *he* would never see Samuels again. Right? Right.

Then what the hell did he care if the man had a rap sheet three miles long?

Because he was married to Annie's nurse. Because he would be in Annie's life long after David had gone back to Dallas. Because—

"Ready down here." Margaret's voice floated up the chimney only seconds after David had climbed to where Samuels waited.

Samuels stood staring at the overgrown, wooded area beyond the back hedge. With visible reluctance he turned his attention from the hillside to the chimney. "All right," he called down the open flue. "We can handle it from here, but it will be a minute."

A minute? Why the wait, David wondered as he hefted the long-handled brush up onto the roof and glanced pointedly at the weight and rope. It looked to him as if their party was all ready and waiting.

But maybe not for chimney cleaning. At least not yet.

Samuels stared once again at the hillside. This time, David followed his example, seeing nothing but wild land. "Is there a problem?"

"Maybe," Samuels said. "Maybe not." He stooped, picked up the brush, and looked at it as though wondering how it came to be there, how he came to hold it. "But I reckon you've got a right to know. I'd want to know if my lady was at risk.

"I wasn't going to come today. I don't get out much, don't mix with folks too well, didn't figure I needed the hassle of you asking me all sorts of questions I don't plan to answer. But Maggie likes the doc. Maggie wanted to come. So I drove up last night just to look around, check out the place.

"It was late. Your Blazer was gone, and the house was dark except for a light from a downstairs room about there." He pointed to the opposite side of the house, in the general direction of Anne's bedroom. "And one from an upstairs room at the back. I thought at first that one was from a television but the color was wrong, more amber than blue. Outside it was dark. Real dark. So I could be mistaken about what I saw."

David's warning signals kicked in with a vengeance as the back of his neck started its too-familiar prickle. "You saw someone?"

"Nope." Samuels put down the brush and picked up the weighted bag, resting it on the chimney ledge. "Something. Two actually. Might have been mountain lions. Big ones. But I don't recall ever hearing about them coming this close to town before. At least, not in any way I believed. Just thought you ought to know," he said, tightening his hold on the rope and lowering the bag into the chimney. "Maggie'd be real upset if something happened to Doc Anne."

David turned once more to look at the hillside, remembering the sound he'd thought he'd heard the day before but had dismissed as only a trick of the wind. "Maybe we ought to look for tracks," he suggested.

"Already did." Samuels said.

"And?"

Samuels turned to look at him. "There weren't any."

12

The night wrapped itself around the old house. Anne leaned back, making herself as comfortable as possible on the sprung and lumpy Chippendale-style sofa that Ellie Hansom's estate had left in the downstairs sitting room.

The glow from the remains of a fire in her newly cleaned fireplace mingled with the soft, rose-colored circles of light from two fringed and beaded floor lamps, and a Chopin étude whispered from her portable tape player set up on the library table across the room.

The day had been almost perfect, in spite of its rocky beginnings, but now all her guests were gone, Margaret and her desperado who had been so remarkably gentle, Nellie and her delightful daughter, Lilly, who had begged hugs and good-bye sugars from everyone, including an astonished Wayne Samuels. Only David remained—and the man in the closet—to keep her company in the echoing, suddenly lonely rooms.

She knew she ought to be helping David as he made his rounds checking to see that all the doors and windows were locked and secure, but for the moment contentment held her quiet and still. This was why she had returned to Allegro. This sense of belonging. This sense of family that might be only an illusion but seemed so real. This sense of safety, in spite of Joe's continuing feud, that told her that only David's cop persona saw any real need for his double-checking the locks. Here there were no muggers lurking on every corner, no drug dealers invading the school or clinic, no danger waiting to jump out in ambush.

She heard footsteps on the hardwood floor and slanted her head to look at David as he entered the room. He stopped by the French doors leading out to the rear porch and tried the handle, then glanced warily at the old draperies that obviously were meant to frame but never to cover the doors.

The remains of the last log in the fireplace dissolved in a sparkle of glowing embers, sending a few errant flames dancing across the grate before they faded away. David secured the screen in front of the firebox and leaned back, resting his arm on the oak mantel. "I believe your first dinner party was a success, Dr. Locke."

Anne grinned lazily. "Yeah. Which of us did it surprise more? You? Or me?"

He returned her grin before turning serious. "Are you up to trying again to reach your mom?"

A little of her contentment faded, and she sighed, knowing that when she left this room, when she returned to the brightly lighted kitchen and the questions that still had to be answered, the rest of it would, too. She patted the couch beside her. "Sit with me just a while longer?"

David nodded, acknowledging her need to remain cocooned in the peace of this room for at least a few more minutes. He sat on the other end of the sofa, extended his long legs toward the fireplace, and stretched his arm along the back of the sofa, toward her.

"What a mixed bag of people we were to have come together so well," she said softly, remembering how they had at first faced each other warily and then had reached some sort of uncertain truce as the afternoon wore on.

"Not so strange," he said on a sigh and a stretch. "Considering we all had something in common."

She turned her head to look at him and found that he had shifted closer to her. "What?"

His hand dropped to her neck and began kneading muscles she hadn't known were so tight. She closed her eyes and surrendered to the massage, vaguely wondering why the touch of a man she had not known a week ago felt so natural, so familiar, so right.

"What?" Both his voice and his touch remained gentle, but she heard an underlying tension in his words. "Surely you noticed, Annie, that with the exception of Lilly, everyone at your table today was hiding from something."

How had he known?

She gave him the smile that had fooled everyone but Karen and her mother. "Surely not everyone," she said.

He wasn't fooled; she could see that in the speculation in his eyes. "Oh, yes," he said. "Everyone."

And then she realized that not only had he included her in that statement, he had included himself.

"And what are you hiding from, David Huerra?"

"I suspect from the same thing you are, Anne Locke."

No. He couldn't be. He couldn't have the memories she had. Or could he? His hand had stilled on her neck. She leaned against it, needing, wanting his support but not able to take more than this. "Maybe—" she said, groping for a way to deny his words. "Maybe we're not hiding from something so much as we're looking for something."

"Maybe," he said, giving her that much as he moved

and at the same time pulled her toward him until she found herself held tight against his side with his arm around her. "That's better," he said.

Better? For whom? And in what way? Because the comfort she had felt only moments ago had fled. Now her awareness of him was much more primal, much more demanding, and even though she might have told herself she could handle a flirtation with this man, right now she wasn't so sure.

"David," she said, putting her hand against his chest to push away but finding and being trapped by the beat of his heart beneath her palm. "This isn't a good— This isn't wise."

"Don't you think I know that, Annie?"

When he'd kissed her before, she'd been too surprised to savor the touch of his lips and the hard strength of his body. She'd had no warning, no time to anticipate. Now she did. He tightened his arm around her shoulder and lifted his other hand to her cheek, holding her still as he looked down at her in the dim light, searching her eyes for answers, for permission. The music swirled through the room, accenting the moment. "Nothing about this is wise," he said. "We'd both be making a mistake, a big mistake, to get involved with each other. It can't go anywhere, Annie. You know that. In less than a month, I'll leave; you'll stay."

She wanted to deny his words, but she couldn't. She would stay. Allegro was her haven, her safe place. And no matter what demons had brought David here, he would leave. He would have to leave.

"I know," she said.

"Damn, Annie, you're supposed to tell me not to do this."

"I can't."

The music ended, leaving the room in silence as

David stared down at her, as she felt his heart racing beneath her palm.

"Stop me, Annie," he said, bending toward her. "Before we both get hurt."

A sound as sharp as a shot cracked through the hushed room. David jerked away from her and twisted in a warrior's stance, searching the room as he thrust her behind him, protected between his body and the sofa.

For a moment, even Anne didn't recognize the sound. For a moment the adrenaline pumping through her had nothing to do with pheromones and hormones and attraction and fledgling affection and everything to do with fear and blood and the sound of screaming that never seemed to stop. For a moment she was trapped in the nightmare that had brought her back to Allegro and would never let her leave.

For a moment. Then sanity returned and she recognized the sound as the faulty shut-off mechanism on her ancient tape player. "Oh, God," she moaned, sagging back against the sofa. "It's nothing," she told him, gesturing toward the tape player. "It's—nothing."

The tension drained from David as rapidly as it had from her. He glared at the tape player. But he stood, the moment lost, the mood broken, and after a moment he held his hand to her. "Let's go make that call," he said.

She nodded. What else could she do? She couldn't very well drag him back down on the sofa with her; that wouldn't be smart. That wouldn't be wise. That could very possibly be emotional suicide. But she didn't take his hand. Instead, she offered him a tentative smile, one acknowledging her own withdrawal from him, and managed to get herself to her feet.

"Wait," David said as she left the room. When she looked at him questioningly, he again checked the lock on the French doors, went to each of the lamps and turned them off, and as they left the room, he closed and tested the door behind them. "Is there a key for this door?" he asked.

She raised an eyebrow. "There's a whole box of keys in a kitchen drawer," she told him. "Is there a reason to search for one?"

He shrugged, grimaced, and finally gave her a wry smile. "A cop's paranoia?" he offered.

She didn't return the smile. He might be joking about a cop's paranoia, but his request and his words had activated her own, and she didn't like it one bit. Not here in her house. Damn it, until he'd come along she'd seldom worried about keys for the outside doors, let alone for interior ones.

"Good enough for me," she told him. "But I'll let you go through the box."

He dropped his hand onto her once again tense shoulders. "Annie, I'm sorry. There's probably no reason in the world to lock that door."

"But you'd feel better if I did?"

He nodded.

"Are you going to tell me why? Who do you think might try to come through it?"

"Not who," he said. "What. Samuels saw what he thinks were a couple of mountain lions near here last night. All the glass in that room would make easy access. I'd just feel better if you had some solid wood between you and it."

Mountain lions? This close to town? Surely not. And yet— And yet she remembered the sound, so like a growl, that she had heard when they were in the secret room, the sound she had hastily, gratefully attributed to the wind, and shuddered. "Well, hell, David." Once again she threw the words she had heard him mutter under his breath as he worked in the house back at him and laughed weakly. "What else is going to happen? What else can happen?"

He pulled her to him, and she went easily into his arms. Yes, the sensation fluttered through her again— *Natural. Familiar. Right.*

He hugged her quickly, tightly, and released her. "We're going to call your mom for some answers about your uncle," he told her. "Then I'm going to check the locks on all the doors and windows one more time, I'm going to look around outside just to make sure nothing and no one is or has been lurking around out there, and then I'm going back to my cold, drafty cabin, while you get some much needed rest. Okay?"

It wasn't, but she supposed it was what had to be done. "Okay," she said.

"Anne?"

Her mother's voice carried clearly over the long distance lines, and in its soft drawl Anne heard all the sounds of home, though now tinged with the flavor of *down under*. "Honey, what's wrong? Are you— Oh, gosh, it's Thanksgiving Day in the States, isn't it. I'm so sorry. We're in such a rush getting ready to go to the ranch—I mean station—I forgot. Are you all right? Did you have a good day? Did any of the family come through with an invitation for you?"

"I love you, too, mother," Anne said when her mother paused for breath. "And, yes, I'm all right, and no, no one came through with an invitation, so I invited friends to the house and had dinner here."

"You did? In that wonderful old dining room? I just knew that would be a great house for entertaining. I always wondered why Aunt Ellie didn't do more of it. Of course, Marian was a pretty heavy burden on her time, and she was just about as grim as they come, but anybody who would paint a house purple had to have a sense of humor, even if it was dry—"

"Mom?" Anne hated to break in on her mother's enthusiasm—for too many years Katherine Locke had had no time or energy for enthusiasm, only for the fight she waged daily to raise her daughter alone and in a home that Anne would never have reason to be ashamed of. But she wasn't single mother Katherine Locke any longer; she was Katherine Hudson. And she no longer balanced precariously on the edge of poverty. Tom Hudson had seen to that. Sometimes Anne resented Tom for taking her mother so far away, for making the long visits they had once shared impossible, but when she heard the life in Katherine's voice, she knew that the missed visits were small enough payment for the happiness her mother so richly deserved and had at long last found.

"Yes, dear?"

Anne glanced at David, who had pulled his chair close to hers at the kitchen table, and tilted the receiver slightly, wordlessly inviting him to listen in on the conversation. "What do you know about Uncle Ralph?"

"Oh." A faint crackling sound filled the silence. "Is it important?" Her mother laughed abruptly. "Of course it is, or you wouldn't have called. What's happened, Anne? My God, I didn't get you in any trouble, did I? I really thought Allegro would be a safe place for you to recover. Is it Joe? He always was a mean little brat, but I thought surely by now he would have grown out of it."

"No. I'm not in any trouble. At least none that I can't handle, I think. And it's not Joe, not really, although he still is a mean little brat. But there's— We— I need to know what— I need to know everything you know about Uncle Ralph. Do you . . . Do you remember him?

"No. He died when I was still real small. We? Who is *we*, Anne?"

Anne sighed. She loved her mother; she really did. But sometimes she wanted to shake her. Fortunately Katherine was well out of her reach. She looked at David and saw him fighting both a smile and a serious case of frustration.

"Mom, please. Uncle Ralph? What did he do for a living? How did he lose his money? And when?"

"And this is really important to you?"

"Yes."

Anne heard the clink of ice in a glass thousands of miles away while her mother took a sip of her inevitable strong southern sweet tea. "Marian would be the one to talk to about what happened to Ralph's money," Katherine said slowly. "Of course, she's always been crazier than a bessie bug. At least since her accident. And depending on her mood, she might blame it either on the curse or the cats—"

"*Mom!*"

"But according to the letter I got from Harriet—you know, my cousin who lives in Kansas City—Joe's had her in a nursing home in—where? Jeez—Texarkana, I think, since Christmas. But he may have moved her again. He does that, you know."

"No," Anne said. "I'm afraid I don't know very much about his side of the family."

"Well, honey, they're not family. Not really. Well, maybe . . . "

"Thank God for small favors," David whispered. "But ask her what she meant—"

Anne shook her head and cupped her hand over the telephone speaker but removed it when he gave her a quick, reassuring smile.

"I need answers, Mom, please. And if you don't have facts, would you please let me have the gossip?"

Katherine laughed. "What on earth have you gotten yourself into now?"

"A purple house, remember? You put the bid in for me."

"Yes. I did. Are you sorry?"

"Only when Joe hires another work crew away from me."

"He's done that? Why?"

"He wants the house, Mom. Or the land. I'm not sure which."

"Damn. So did his grandmother. But she wasn't entitled to it, either."

"Because even though she was Ralph's sister, the house belonged to Ellie?"

"Yes. At least that was what the grownups said when there were any outsiders around. But there were a lot of us kids around—at least for a while, before everyone started moving away to find work—and we heard things. So bear in mind that what I can tell you is filtered through a child's perception of cryptic conversations. Except for the things Marian actually said. And God knows how that's been filtered."

Anne could only shake her head. Maybe this meant her mother accepted that she had finally grown up. Amazing. David's hand clamped on hers where she held the receiver and his other caught her chin, stilling her.

"I never knew exactly what he did for a living. Not much at the last, I remember hearing that."

"Did he go broke in the Crash?"

"Oh, no, honey. He came through that like a champ. And he made money hand over fist all during the depression. I remember hearing that said, time after time, and not with any admiration. It seems he had cash—lots of cash that no one really knew where it came from—so he was able to buy up forfeited tax lands and even some delinquent mortgages before the government put the brakes on foreclosures."

"Then what happened?"

"Marian said it was a curse."

"Yeah, right."

"No, just listen, my young skeptic. Ralph dealt in antiquities. Of course, no one I overheard called them that back then. They simply referred to his 'treasures.' But he apparently had quite a little network of sources and markets for archaeological items. Probably a black market network, but a lucrative one just the same. Until he got greedy.

"The story is that he was involved in those excavations at Spiro, on the sly of course, and that he bought a load of contraband that wiped out all his resources and then couldn't get rid of it."

David's hand once again tightened on hers, and he leaned closer. Anne felt her throat go dry. "Why?"

"Why did he buy it? Or why couldn't he get rid of it? Or does it matter? He bought it because he thought he could make a dollar. And if he couldn't get rid of it, it was probably because somebody finally pulled one on him and unloaded a bunch of fakes. Fitting justice, I'd say."

"Spiro?" Anne asked. "As in LeFlore County, just north of here?"

"Yes. There was a big discovery made there in the thirties. Didn't you study that in— Oh. We were in Tennessee by the time you got to state history in school. Anyway, I think he just got caught in a scam and never got over the blow to his ego or his pocketbook. Marian insisted that he had infuriated some ancient god.

"In fact, she insisted that same god, in the guise of giant yellow cats that just happened to be roaming around the upstairs hallway, killed two of his suppliers as well as causing the fall that broke her back."

Anne heard the humor in Katherine's voice. She knew

there was not a malicious bone in her mother's body, not even after the hellacious time she'd gone through as a young woman surrounded by these people she now discussed. She glanced at David. He wasn't smiling.

"Cats?" *Samuels saw what he thinks were a couple of mountain lions near here last night.* Coincidence, surely. She felt her hand slide on the receiver.

"Yeah." Katherine's voice lost its laughter. "Cats. Forgive me, darlin'. I'm sorry Marian broke her back. I'm sorry Ralph died, but Ralph treated Aunt Ellie like dirt. And after he died, Marian kept it up, propped up in that room upstairs, expecting Ellie to wait on her hand and foot—which Ellie did—expecting her to care for her young son—which Ellie did until she just couldn't handle it anymore and sent him to stay with a cousin—refusing even to sell the car that Ralph had bought her, not his wife, to help with the expenses of her care. These things I do know.

"And I know that when Ralph died Marian tried real hard to take Ellie's home away from her, but never produced so much as a birth or baptism or confirmation certificate to prove she was really his sister, and that Joseph, her son, as nice a kid as I could hope to meet when I was growing up, looked a hell of a lot like that framed picture of Ralph that used to dominate the mantel in your living room. I am so damn glad that we're on Ellie's side of the family." Katherine paused to draw in a deep breath and remained silent a moment. "And I am off my soapbox as of now. I'm sorry, Anne. I thought I was over all the hard feelings. I guess I'm not."

From laughter to bleak despair in the space of a heartbeat. So her mother's memories were as sneaky about ambush as Anne's were. "No, Mom. I'm sorry. I shouldn't have dragged you into the past."

"And why not, darlin'? Every family has a skeleton or two in the closet."

Anne turned to David. This was her *mother* for God's sake. If she couldn't trust her, who could she trust? Slowly, almost reluctantly, he nodded his head.

"That's just it, Mom," Anne said. She took a deep breath. "This family— We— It wasn't actually in the closet; it was behind a false wall in an upstairs sitting room."

She heard an abrupt clank—her mom's glass hitting the ceramic tile of her kitchen counter—and a sharp, indrawn breath. "Lucy?" Katherine whispered. "Did you find Lucy? She didn't run away with that Briggs boy? Oh, God, no one really believed she'd go off and leave her mother, even if Marian was doing her best to make her life holy hell, but there wasn't any other answer . . . Have the police identified her? Oh, God. Oh, God. In the house all this time?"

"Mom? Mom, back up a minute. Who is Lucy?"

"Lucy Hansom. Ellie and Ralph's daughter. You found a skeleton? A human skeleton? In Marian's room?"

"No!" Anne shouted the word to break through her mother's frantic questions. "Well, yes. But not— Mom, what we found was probably the contraband you said Ralph got stung with. Not a—not a woman, not anyone we have to call the police about. At least I don't think so. I've asked Karen to give me her opinion so we can be sure. And asked a collector in Dallas for an opinion on one of the items with it. But other than that, I'd just as soon no one else knew about it. At least not yet."

"Oh." Again, only a faint crackle filled the silence for one second, two, three. "Oh. It was true then? He did get stuck with what he thought was treasure? Someone did pull a fast one on Ralph Hansom?"

Again Anne looked at David. He shrugged.

"I don't know, Mom," she said. "I don't know. It sure

looks real to me, but I won't know until some time next week." And then, to keep any more of her mother's questions unspoken, Anne asked one of her own. "That was Marian's room? The art deco one?"

Katherine laughed softly. "Ellie didn't change it? Good. It has to be pretty worn by now, but when I was growing up, I used to peek in the door when Ellie had Marian out for her bath or for some other reason, and I thought that must be the most sophisticated room ever designed.

"You're all right with this, Anne?" she asked abruptly. "Finding it wasn't too much for you so soon after . . . "

"I'm fine, Mom. How are the boys?"

Again Katherine laughed. "They are holy terrors. Tom has them out now for some last minute 'manly' shopping before we take off. They'll be sorry they missed your call."

"I'm sorry, too. How long will you be gone?"

"About a month. You do have the emergency numbers in case you need to contact us?"

"Yes. Yes, I do. But don't worry. Everything here will be fine."

"I just hate it that you're all alone there with this mystery to solve."

"Face it, Mom." Now Anne laughed. "You're just sorry you aren't in the middle of it with me."

"Maybe," Katherine admitted.

"And besides," again Anne looked toward David. Hesitating only slightly, he nodded. "I'm not alone."

"Ah hah! The *we* that kept slipping out when you were talking to me? Who? 'Fess up, Anne."

God! She felt about ten years old. And David's grin didn't make things one bit better. She felt her face turning red and every one of her freckles glowing. "He's a Dallas police officer on vacation, and he's helping me with the house."

"Good. You tell him hello for me. And you tell him to take good care of my little girl."

He'd moved away slightly, she hoped to give her privacy for the rest of her conversation, but she was pretty sure he'd heard that last bit, anyway. She glared at him, even as she softened her words to say good-bye to her mother.

"What else can happen?"

At David's question, she looked up from her studied inspection of the telephone after she had replaced the receiver.

"I believe you asked me that just a few minutes ago," he said.

Sighing, she leaned her elbows on the table and rested her chin on her hands.

"Anne?"

She couldn't answer his question; she couldn't answer her own. And she couldn't sit there pretending that those questions weren't racing through her. She jerked to her feet and paced to the kitchen sink where she gripped the edge and stared out the window. David must have turned off the porch light while making his rounds, because blackness pressed in, capturing the lighted kitchen like a mirror, throwing her image back at her. Throwing the image of David standing behind her back at her.

He dropped his hands to her shoulders, then traced them along her arms, before enfolding her.

"I don't need this," she told him. But she wasn't sure whether she was talking about the complications her mom had just brought up, or the complications that her reaction to his embrace could cause. "I came back because I wanted a slow, uncomplicated life. Not a mystery, not a . . ."

"Not an involvement?" he asked.

She stared at his image in the window and found him

just as intently watching hers. "Not an involvement," she admitted as she released her grip on the sink and raised her hands to capture his arms as they held her.

He didn't comment, not on her words, not that she held him locked in the embrace he had initiated, not that she had leaned back against him, absorbing his warmth. He didn't comment about her crazy aunt, her greedy uncle, her missing cousin, incest, or adultery. He just held her as the two of them stared at their reflections against the midnight black backdrop of the kitchen window. He just held her, until she felt the comfort he offered her turning to something warmer, something more intense. Until she felt the changes in his body signaling that he, too, had taken a step beyond comfort.

No, she definitely didn't need this, she thought, even as she canted her head to one side, exposing her neck as David lowered his head toward her. She felt his breath on her cheek, on her throat, as his arms tightened around her. "David . . ." she murmured in protest.

"I know," he told her. "I know, Annie. I don't want this either. Help me out, here, lady. Tell me to get lost. Tell me that all you want from me is someone to hang drywall. Tell me . . ."

If only she could. Slowly she turned in his arms.

"Tell me why you're running," he persisted on a groan of need. "Tell me what brought you back to Allegro."

And that was all it took. She still stood within his embrace. And she still needed his warmth. But now it was to protect her from the chill that shuddered through her.

"Annie?"

"What makes you think anything happened?"

"Maybe because your best friend and your mother have both been concerned about your recovery? Maybe because when I asked, you tensed up like a rubber band about to snap? Maybe because I sometimes see the weight of the world in your expression? What happened, Annie? Is it so bad that sharing won't make it easier?"

Nothing would ever make it easier. But maybe it was time to share. "I got shot," she said.

She felt his arms tighten around her, felt the protest he wouldn't let himself utter.

"I was lucky," she told him in a soft monotone. "I only lost my spleen. Anthony—the man I had been engaged to—two mothers and four children at the clinic, and eventually two cops, and one of the six young men who were convinced we had to have drugs at the free clinic we staffed twice a week, died."

She heard him moan—for her—and let herself accept that small comfort.

"Sounds to me like you lost a hell of a lot more than your spleen," he said, restraining her when she would have pulled away.

Yes, she had. But those closest to her had not seemed to give more than lip service to the fact that much more than the physical trauma needed healing. How had David? And just how perceptive was he? "Such as?"

"Such as your innocence, a dear friend. Your career, maybe, and the lifestyle you had chosen and cultivated. Those are part of the losses. I imagine you also picked up a trailerload of guilt, too, didn't you? Because you'd worked hard to convince people to take advantage of your clinic?"

He was too damned perceptive. Anne tilted her head back so that she could look into his eyes. They were clouded with pain—for her. And she didn't have to admit anything, because she saw in them his knowledge of just how much of that guilt she carried.

"Yeah."

"So you came home, to lick your wounds, to recover, to assuage your guilt by providing medical care where it hadn't been available before, maybe even to recapture your courage, and ran straight into Cousin Joe and a half-century-old mystery?"

She couldn't have put it more succinctly; she *wouldn't* have, because she couldn't have been that honest with herself. But she could admit the truth when it was slammed down in front of her. She nodded once, a mere jerk of her head.

"And a man who is no more sure of his future than you are."

When she looked up, the pain she saw in his eyes was now his own.

"No, you definitely do not need this, Annie," he said, using his hands on her arms to hold her still while he stepped away from her. "Unfortunately, I don't know how to back up and take the mystery away. And I don't know how to change Joe's attitude. But I can keep from adding myself to the load of stuff piling up on you."

She wanted to argue with him—God it was lonely without his arms around her—but she knew he was right. And she also knew that he didn't need any more of her problems than he had already shouldered; he had his own to work through. That was why *he* was in Allegro.

"I want you to lock the door when I leave. And stay inside. I don't know how much stock to put in Samuels's story about the mountain lions, but it's just too much of a coincidence that your crazy aunt claims they crippled her.

"Tomorrow we'll talk about what your mother said. And we'll try to figure out the what and why of the man upstairs. You'll be all right until then, won't you, Annie?"

Of course she would be. She was strong. Didn't he realize that? Otherwise she would have already broken.

Otherwise she would have given in to the demand she felt rising within her to beg him to stay.

"Of course," she said, and even managed to dredge up a small smile. "And you be careful."

He caught her face in his hands and looked steadily into her eyes. Was he convinced? She wasn't sure. But eventually he nodded and released her.

"I'll be back first thing in the morning," he told her.

Anne watched from the locked screen until the Blazer's taillights disappeared down the drive, then closed and locked the back door and leaned against it.

She hadn't wanted him to leave. But until she was sure why she wanted him to stay—for protection, for comfort in the lonely hours of the night, for physical gratification, or for some reason that was all of those, and more—she couldn't ask him to stay. Wouldn't ask him to stay.

Slowly she crossed the kitchen, turned out the light, and started toward her room. She was at the top of the stairs before she realized it, and then, drawn, she found herself in the upstairs sitting room, opening the closet, stepping into it. She caught the edge of the strip that bordered the drywall insert. Boxes blocked the way. Boxes that she could easily have moved but which provided enough deterrent to bring her to a halt.

She pressed her hands flat and leaned her head against the wall. Why was she doing this? She didn't want to look on what lay beyond this fragile barrier. She never again wanted to see what lay on the cedar litter.

But it seemed that she couldn't raise her head, or move her hands, or leave the chill darkness of the closet. Not yet. But maybe soon . . . soon, she could leave him alone in the dark.

13

1935

The scream echoed through the house, waking
Lucy from a troubled sleep and bringing her upright in
her bed. It sounded again, this time accompanied by
baby Joseph's angry demand for food, or for changing—
sometimes they sounded the same—or maybe just for
comfort because he had to be frightened; his mama was
the one who was screaming. Unless, oh please no, there
was something wrong with him.

Lucy swung her legs over the edge of the bed and
tugged her long flannel nightgown down to cover them.
She shivered in the chill early morning air and made
herself hesitate long enough to find her house slippers
before she ran toward the screams.

Aunt Marian's room was on the other side of the
house, halfway to the back, at the end of the first hall.
Papa got there before Lucy did, and neither he nor Aunt
Marian saw her when she skidded to a halt in the doorway between Aunt Marian's sitting room and bedroom.

The light on the table beside the bed was on, and Lucy
saw Joseph in his crib, screaming and waving his little

arms and legs. Aunt Marian was all but collapsed against Papa, crying and every once in a while pointing, but not toward Joseph—toward the other side of the room.

The barrels and crates they had brought in earlier were there, in the corner, only now they were tumbled and open, and between them, in the shadows on the floor—

Lucy sucked in a big breath. There he was. All spread out like he had been in the truck, only better, neater, taking up much more space, with the poles around him making a kind of frame for him, and with all his treasures heaped around him.

Mama came into the room behind her and stopped in the doorway with her hands on Lucy's shoulders. Then Papa noticed the two of them standing there. "Go back downstairs, Ellie," he said, moving a little to stand between Mama and the man on the floor. "Everything's all right up here. Marian just had a scare."

Didn't Mama see it? Maybe not. She just nodded toward the crib and frowned. "Take care of your baby, Marian."

"Go," Papa said again. "And take Lucy with you."

Of course Mama left, using her strong hands on Lucy's shoulders to propel her along with her. She always did what Papa told her to do. But at the top of the stairs, she stopped and looked at Lucy. "Will you go back to sleep if I send you to your room?"

Lucy nodded.

"I mean it, child. I know you've got more curiosity than any ten other girls, but you don't need to be sticking your nose in where you might get it cut off."

Lucy looked up at her mama. She wanted to ask her about the man on the floor, but maybe she hadn't seen him. Maybe Lucy hadn't *really* seen him, not like she'd thought she did. She wanted to ask her what she could poke around in that would get her in trouble, but she knew better than to do that. So she nodded again. Her mama hugged her. Her mama gave the best hugs in the whole world, Lucy knew that for a fact, and this morning she smelled real good, like she'd already been in the kitchen, like cinnamon and apples and nutmeg. "Go back to bed, child."

Lucy didn't say she would; she couldn't say she wouldn't. Instead she smiled and headed down the hall toward her bedroom while Mama went back downstairs. Then Lucy turned around and went back toward Aunt Marian's room.

Joseph was quiet at last. And she didn't hear Marian crying anymore as she slipped into the sitting room and tiptoed across it to the bedroom door. Papa and Aunt Marian were just standing there, staring at the man on the floor, and Papa was not happy.

"What do you mean, you don't know how it happened? You expect me to believe someone came into your room and spread this out and neither you or that screaming kid heard anything?"

"Well, that's exactly what happened, Ralph Hansom. And don't you dare yell at me. I didn't want that dirty old mess in my bedroom anyway—"

"The hell you didn't! You couldn't stand the thought of something worth that much money being out of your control for even a day."

"My control— I'll have you know—"

"And how do I know you didn't do this?" He waved his hand toward the man on the floor. "Why in God's name you'd scream about it, though—"

"Me! You think I had anything to do with—with rearranging that corpse. Oh, wait. Is it all there?"

"How the hell should I know? We didn't inventory, remember? You were in too much of a hurry to get it all stashed before Ellie's family showed up. I doubt anyone knows just what's supposed to be there, even Jackson."

"Jackson." Aunt Marian sounded like Grandpa some-times did when he said Papa's name. "I wouldn't put it past that piece of white trash to have come looking for a little more of the take."

"Oh, Ralph, do you think it could have been Jackson, that he came in while we were all asleep. My God, he could have killed all of us in our beds."

Now why would Mr. Jackson do a thing like that, Lucy wondered. But she didn't have time to wonder long. Papa turned toward the door and started march-ing her way.

"I don't know," he said, coming into the sitting room just as Lucy ducked behind the wardrobe. "But I'm damned sure going to find out." He turned and looked at Marian, who was standing, just standing there, staring down at the man on the floor with the strangest, saddest look in her eyes. "Come on," Papa told her. "I'm not leaving you here. Not now anyway. For all I know, you've been prowling through the lot of it half the night. But don't forget, Marian, that no matter what you found or find there, it's not worth a dime to you until *I* find a buyer."

Lucy stayed hidden behind the wardrobe until they'd left the room, until she heard their voices floating up the stairs, still arguing. Still mad. Then she crept out of hiding. She knew where they'd be going. Papa's study. And she knew she couldn't get close enough downstairs to hear what they were saying, and she also knew she had to hear what they were saying.

But first, she had to look once more at the strange, wonderful man on the floor. The copper covering him glowed softly in the dim light. He looked almost peaceful lying there. Slowly, careful not to disturb Joseph, who was now happily sucking at a bottle, Lucy made her way to the foot of the wooden pallet. Papa might not know what had been with the man, but Lucy counted one more basket than she had seen in the truck, and on the very edge of the pallet, half on, half off the cedar rail, sat a carved statue. Just a little one. One that looked just like— Lucy reached out to touch it but couldn't seem to make her fingers work. She shook her head. It looked just like one of the pieces that Mr. Jackson's boy had taken when he didn't think anyone was watching. But it couldn't be.

A small box rested near the man's foot. Lucy knelt and this time had no trouble picking it up. It had a delicate, engraved top, which she touched with gentle fingers then slid open. Inside, in a nest of shattered fabric, lay two small medallions. Lucy turned the box toward the light enough to see that each carried an engraved likeness, one of a man, the other of a woman. And they made her hurt to look at them. Hurt almost to tears, and she didn't know why. She sucked her lower lip between her teeth as she knelt on the wooden floor and rocked back and forth, seeking—comfort?—seeking something she couldn't understand, until Joseph gurgled and tossed his bottle to the floor. Quickly Lucy replaced the box and rose to her feet. Just as quickly, she found Joseph's bottle for him and silenced him as he opened his mouth to wail a protest at being left alone.

Papa's study was at the north end of the house. The room directly above it was a guest room, almost never used even though it had one of the few closets in the house. This one was in the sloping space beneath the attic stairs, and one end wall was made by the brick chimney of Papa's fireplace. She'd found a loose board there ages ago, and while she knew she couldn't see anything—she'd given up even trying to do that—she didn't know if she could hear anything. She'd never tried while Papa was in his room.

Now she thought it was worth the risk of being caught.

She lifted the board and bent down until she had her ear to the opening. She heard Papa cranking the telephone. He didn't like telephones, said he thought the nosy old operators listened to every word, so he had to think this was important.

"Yes, Gladys," he said. Mrs. Porter was the operator. "Get me Tom Jackson at Atwood. I know what time it is. Just ring the number will you? Yes, Gladys, I know it's long distance. My God, woman, I don't care if the Atwood operator is asleep. Wake her up."

Then Papa was quiet for a moment. Aunt Marian said something, but Lucy couldn't understand her words, just her tone, and she was still mad.

"Mrs. Jackson?" She heard her papa's voice distinctly. "I'm sorry to bother you at this— What? No. No, this is Ralph Hansom. I need to talk to Tom. What? I'm sorry. I can't hear you over the static." There was silence, and Lucy strained to hear, to make sure she wasn't missing anything. "I see," her papa said at last, and this time he didn't use his 'important man' voice. "I see. Yes. I'll call back later. No. No, it was no trouble. You— You take care now."

"Well, what did she say?" Aunt Marian all but shouted.

"Tom isn't there."

"So he was here!"

"I don't think so. There was a crash. The brakes on that new truck of his failed, up in that straight, flat farmland, and the car hit the one tree within three hundred yards. Jackson's son was driving. He was alone when it happened, and they only found him an hour or so ago. Jackson's still talking with the sheriff and the undertaker."

14

David awoke long before dawn Friday morning, compliments of the wind-up alarm clock that seemed to be standard issue for the cabins at Tompkins Fish Camp and the nagging feeling that he shouldn't leave Anne alone too long to deal with all the problems her home had brought her.

He turned up the panel heater in what he suspected was a wasted effort to take the chill off the room, and lit the burner under the old blue coffeepot and its two-day-old brew, knowing that if he hurried he could be in and out of the shower before the thing boiled over. Icy cold well water lost most of its appeal when it came straight from the showerhead, but this morning, he needed the extra kick it would give him to get started.

He glanced out the tiny window in the bathroom. Yep, those idiots in the next cabin were already up, probably chomping at the bit to get back out on the lake. He guessed it took all kinds, but why Pete Tompkins had ever thought, and he'd ever agreed that he might be the kind who'd actually enjoy sacrificing helpless bait from a boat in a subfreezing windchill, he'd never know.

He emerged from the shower in time to lift the pot off the burner as it started spewing over and poured himself a cupful of reheated sludge. He needed that extra kick this morning, too.

Gretta Tompkins was just stepping out of her cabin when he drove past. She smiled and waved. His captain's mother was a nice woman, someone who had no bones to pick, no ax to grind, no ox to gore. Just a genuinely good person.

Nice. Not earthshaking. But nice.

Something he hadn't realized he'd needed in his life. Something he hadn't realized had been gone until now.

He'd found the convenience store on Monday, halfway around the lake on the way into town. Straight out of his concept of a step into the past, it offered bare wood floors, a pot-bellied stove, decent coffee, fresh doughnuts, and usually two or three fishermen and local residents gathered around the stove or the live-bait boxes, swapping stories before they started their day. To his surprise, within less than a week, he had become an accepted part of that early morning crowd. He didn't kid himself that anyone was going to spill any deep secrets around him, but the camaraderie was a welcome change, a reminder of early days on the force before even the small talk between officers got dragged down into the cesspool their investigations invariably led to.

That too was nice. Not earthshaking. But nice.

Something else he hadn't realized he'd needed, hadn't realized he'd missed, until he felt the warmth and welcome wrapping itself around him.

Only one car sat outside the store when he arrived. A

sheriff's patrol car. David approached warily, but the car was parked, not slewed in, and the lights and radio were dark and silent.

He eased in the front door. Blake Foresman looked up from his propped-back chair beside the stove and lifted his foam coffee cup in welcome.

"Henry's out in the storage shed," the sheriff said. "It's strictly self-service till he gets back."

David felt the tension release him. He hadn't meant to stick around this morning, only grab a cup of coffee to go, but maybe he ought to take advantage of this chance meeting. He nodded and headed toward the coffee counter.

"You're out early," Foresman said when David settled into the chair next to him.

"So are you. Or is it late?"

Foresman grunted, which David interpreted as meaning late. "I'm two men short," he said on a yawn, "and I like to give the men with families as many holidays as possible."

David's respect for this man had been slowly growing since the day of the accident. Now it took a giant leap. He nodded his understanding and appreciation of Foresman's work assignment and took a cautious sip from his cup. The brew was as hot as asphalt in August and as strong as it could be and still be liquid, but it was fresh. "You make the coffee?" he asked the sheriff.

Foresman grinned at him. "I figured I'd need all the help I could get to make it the rest of the shift and thirty miles home. Too strong for you?"

David returned the grin and they sat there in companionable silence for a few minutes before David broached the first subject. "These woods around here are pretty wild. Ever have any trouble with predators?"

"Every now and then a bear gets curious and we have

to call the wildlife people in to chase him back to his part of the woods."

"How about cats?"

"A bobcat or two has been reported, usually by a tourist who's had too much to drink and can't tell the difference between a wild animal and something like Gretta Tompkins's twenty-pound yellow tabby."

David thought of his neighbors in the next cabin. Yeah. They'd be likely to do something like that. But he was concerned with something much larger than Gretta's house cat. "How about mountain lions?"

Foresman peered at him, not alarmed, but alert. "They're not unheard of around here, just rare enough to make a sighting real newsworthy. Why? You hearing strange noises around your cabin?"

David shook his head. "Wayne Samuels said he thought he spotted a couple on the hill behind Dr. Locke's house."

"Well," the sheriff said. "Well, now. Samuels, huh? Heard he was up at the doc's for dinner yesterday. He ought to know. Well, hell. That's all I need—a couple of wild animals practically in town."

Was there anything this sheriff—anybody in the whole county for that matter—didn't hear within a day? Somehow David doubted that there was. But Blake Foresman didn't ask about Samuels, and he didn't issue any warnings about him either. That silence almost as good as told him he could trust his instincts and trust the man. But almost wasn't good enough if Annie's safety was at risk.

"Anne thought Margaret was a widow."

"So did Margaret."

David waited, silent, and after a moment Foresman shrugged. "I stood beside her six years ago while she buried what was left of a body the army told her was his.

I stood beside her last winter when we dug that body up and gave it back to the army after Wayne showed up on her doorstep one morning more dead than alive."

Damn! Samuels had done hard time all right. He'd done time in hell. "MIA?"

"Nope." Foresman let the legs of his chair drop to the floor. He stood and stretched. "Not even official prisoner of war. He came home, you see. But his brother didn't. His best friend didn't. After a couple of years, he joined up with a bunch to go back in and look for some of those who hadn't made it out. He doesn't have much to do with folks. Won't talk about what happened in those years he was gone. But he'd die for a friend."

Yeah, David thought, he would. He already had.

Which left the next topic. Anne hadn't picked up on it. Or if she had, she hadn't said anything. But Katherine's questions had triggered questions in David. Questions that couldn't be ignored. "What do you know about Lucy Hansom and somebody named Briggs?"

"Lucy?"

"Yeah. She'd have been Anne's great uncle Ralph's daughter."

"Would have been?"

"Or is. Seems she took missing a number of years ago. There might have been a search. Might not have been."

"You've got a need to know?"

David grimaced. "Maybe."

Foresman looked at him. "You got any idea when?"

"Nope."

"I grew up in this county. I've been back for fifteen years. In office for nine. And I don't remember anything about her. I don't suppose you could ask Joe?" When David just looked at him, Blake shrugged. "No. I suppose not." He sighed and crushed his empty cup.

"Give me a couple of days. I've got a room on the third floor of the courthouse bulging with old records. I'll take a look."

"Thanks."

"What the hell are you two doing up at that house, anyway?"

"Just making it livable, Sheriff," David told him while his thoughts jumped from the man in the closet, to Katherine's assumption that they had found Lucy's body, to the eerie and oppressive feeling in the old barn, to the absolutely impractical attraction growing between him and Anne, to the big hole that faced him whenever he thought about his future. "Just making it livable."

David brought doughnuts that morning, and just like the previous morning walked her out onto her front porch and sat with her for a dose of early morning air with their caffeine. But this morning he sat far enough away that they didn't touch. And this morning, although he teased her, even laughed with her as they discussed the day before and their plans for the morning, he looked as though he needed the calming effects of the view of the valley and mountains beyond. He didn't seem agitated so much as troubled, drawn in on himself as though caught in thoughts he didn't much like but couldn't avoid. Like she too often was.

"Want to talk about it?" she asked finally. She wouldn't. But maybe he would. Maybe he needed to.

"About what?"

"About whatever's bothering you this morning?"

"Nope." He stood and tossed the dregs of his coffee into the overgrown flowerbeds fronting the porch. "What I want to do is take a look around the outside of

the house to satisfy my paranoia and then finish that
kitchen ceiling."

The telephone rang as the lights of Allegro were beginning to dot the darkening landscape below the house.
The clutter of their day's work still lingered in swept-up
piles, and the remains of their leftover turkey dinner
still occupied the table. Anne gazed with satisfaction at
her new ceiling, and David, who had finally managed to
forget to worry about what he was going to do with the
rest of his life, gazed at her and wondered how she had
managed to draw him out of his dark mood.

The phone rang a second time, a sharp summons full
of its own importance, refusing to be ignored. Anne
stiffened, her smile faded, and the animation drained
from her face, but she made no move to answer the
phone, made no move to quiet the intrusion.

"Are you expecting a call?" he asked.

She shook her head.

"Do you suppose it's an emergency?"

"God, I hope not," she whispered.

He stood when she didn't, walked to the counter,
picked up the telephone, and brought it back to the
table as it rang still another time. He set it beside her.
"Is something wrong, Annie?"

"No. Of course not."

*Then why don't you want to answer the telephone?
What the hell's going on here, anyway?* "You want me
to answer that?"

She looked like she wanted him to. Hell, she looked as
though she wanted him to tell whoever was on the other
end of that line she wasn't there, couldn't be reached,
couldn't help if she were. But of course she didn't tell
him that—not his Annie.

His Annie? But before he could do more than question that thought, she gave him the cheeky grin he had seen many times and which he only now began to suspect she used when she was hiding something from someone, maybe even herself, and reached for the telephone. "What?" she asked. "And finish ruining your reputation? I don't think so."

She snatched up the receiver before the ring could shriek again. "Hello?"

She frowned slightly as she listened, but her tension seemed to ease some. She held the receiver toward him. "Too late," she said. "You're already ruined. It's for you."

Now David frowned. Who knew he was here? He coughed out a laugh. Only about half the county. But he spoke cautiously. "Huerra."

"Huerra, how in the hell did you manage to wind up in the middle of one my investigations when you're supposed to be in a boat in the middle of Lake Allegro drowning worms?"

"Captain?" *Pete Tompkins?* Calling him here? Why? "What investigation?"

He heard Pete sigh. "I was going to call, hat in hand, and ask you to break your vacation long enough to introduce yourself to the local sheriff and then ask a couple of questions there in Allegro. But when I call, my mother tells me you are with the person I need you to question, and before I can dial again, the lab turns up your name written on a notepad we've taken in evidence. So maybe I'll just ask you. What did you have going with Jack Townley?"

"Oh—" He caught himself before the obscenity erupted from his mouth. Dragging the cord up and over Anne, he sat heavily in his chair and glanced around the room that only moments before had seemed so peaceful. "What happened?"

"God knows," Tompkins told him. "At least I hope he does, because sure as hell no one else does. The housekeeper said he was looking for a package in the mail, which came about ten this morning. He took it into his study and later made a series of phone calls. Just after noon, she heard him scream, found the door locked and called 911, but was so frightened she ran outside and was halfway down the block when the first officers arrived."

"Townley is dead?" Of course he was. Pete Tompkins worked homicide. Not burglary. Not robbery.

"Oh, yes. Oh, hell yes."

Dead. And not neatly. Not with that tone in the captain's voice. "How?"

"At first glance it looks like some sort of animal attack, but the windows were closed—not locked, but closed—and I don't think any animal is going to stop to shut a window, so I'm afraid we've got some sort of Freddy Krueger copycat loose in the city."

He felt Anne's eyes on him and glanced up. She couldn't possibly have heard Pete's words, but the color had blanched from her face. "Do you have a motive?"

"His safe was open, so robbery, maybe. That's what I wanted you to find out. The package was from a Dr. A. Locke. From what my mother said, I take it that was Dr. A. Locke who answered the telephone."

"Yeah."

"And you've been there with her all day?"

"Yeah."

"Any idea what was in the package?"

"Yeah."

"Jesus, Huerra, are you going to tell me what it was or are you going to make me drag it out of you one word at a time?"

David shook his head, but the action didn't clear

away the fog of questions he felt building. "It was a shell artifact," he said. "Engraved. About four inches in diameter. Is it missing?"

He heard the shuffle of papers. "I don't see anything like that on this list, or in the pictures. Is it valuable?"

"It could be. That's what we wanted Jack to tell us." He glanced at Anne again, but he knew what had to be done, even without her consent. "We took a tracing. I'll see that you get a copy. I don't suppose you found any notes?"

"Only the sheet of paper with your name on it, a list of telephone numbers we're in the process of checking, and one other word that looks like spiral, spires, spirit, with a question mark?"

"Spiro," David said on a slow exhalation.

"What does that mean?"

"Not what," David explained. "Where. It's the provenance. We just found out last night that Dr. Locke's great uncle was an antiquities dealer who had some dealings with the excavations at Spiro in the thirties. But keep that as quiet as you can. If your perp would kill for one shell, he might decide to come see if she has more."

"And does she?"

Anne had sunk back in her chair, her face chalk white, her eyes closed as slowly she dragged her head from side to side, denying—denying what?

"I guarantee you," he said, making a quick decision that might well damn him, "that shell was one of a kind."

"Let's hope so," Pete said. "Let's hope so."

Carefully David placed the receiver in the cradle and leaned back in his chair.

"Your friend is dead," Anne said, at last opening her eyes, revealing an anguish all out of proportion with learning of the death of a stranger.

He nodded.

"And someone stole the gorget?"

Again he nodded.

"Who?" she asked. "Who knew?"

"Good question, Doc," he said. The words and the cynicism just slipped out, and once released, hung in the air between them. "Who did know?"

She recoiled from the unspoken accusation he had been unable to check.

"Ah, hell, Annie," he said. "I didn't mean that the way it sounded."

"Didn't you?" she asked softly. "On some level don't you wonder who I told about the packages? Did I open them up and show Margaret? Did I boast about the treasure we'd found? Did I make sure Joe found out so I could gloat about it?"

He couldn't answer her, because he did wonder. All of the above. And he didn't want to doubt her, but for the moment, yes, he did.

She pushed back from the table and stood. She walked to the back door and tested the lock and then crossed the room.

"Where are you going?" Stupid question, Huerra, he told himself. He knew where she was going. But instead of the acerbic reply he expected from her in light of what he'd just said, she simply shook her head. "Someone has to check on him."

Well, hell. She was right, of course. But hearing her refer to that pile of bones and grave goods as *him*, as she always did, he realized, sent a chill down his back remarkably like the one he had felt the first time he saw her house.

He stood, scraping his chair back. "Wait a minute. You don't need to go up there by yourself."

She paused but didn't turn and didn't speak when he

caught up with her in the hallway. "Did you hear anything last night?" he asked.

She shook her head.

"See anything? Did anything unusual happen after I left?"

"No," she said.

And that was all that either of them said until they reached the closet. David stepped in first and looked around, and all his alarms went off. "Someone's been in here. Those boxes have been moved."

She followed him into the closet, knelt to examine the boxes he indicated and sighed. "I was in here, David."

"You—"

"Just hush," she said. "I started to check on him last night after you left. I came this far and then realized I didn't want to go in there with him. Not alone."

It was her house. It was her closet. It was her damned treasure. And if she wanted to check on it every fifteen minutes, it was her damned right to do so. So why did he have to work so hard to remember that? Why was he glad that she hadn't gone in without him? And why was he so reluctant now to go in, either with her or alone?

He turned away from the questions and mild rebuke he saw in her eyes, pushed the boxes away, and lifted the panel from the opening.

The light from the sitting room didn't penetrate the bends and curves of the passageway enough to do more than cast the glow of the opening across the dark room. David stepped through and more by memory than by sight located the pull cord for the ceiling fixture. He yanked on it, and the glare of the bare bulb flooded the room.

The warrior lay on his litter, surrounded by his grave goods. His copper armor gleamed softly, giving the appearance of a statue, or perhaps a sleeping man, until the stark whiteness of the bones visible beneath the armor, beneath the profusion of shells and pipes and pearls and pots destroyed that image. He appeared unchanged, undisturbed since he had been placed there, only God knew how many years before, except for the slight depression where Anne had removed the right femur—and except for one shell gorget that lay alone in a space on the cedar pole near where David had knelt two days before. He'd been careful then not to disturb anything more than absolutely necessary; he'd been careful to replace everything he'd removed. He'd left nothing on the pole or outside the confines of the litter.

David glanced at Anne. *Her house*, he reminded himself again. *Her closet. Her treasure.* Her lie? There was no reason she shouldn't have come in here if she wanted. There was also no reason she shouldn't have admitted a closer examination of what could make her an extremely wealthy woman. But she obviously thought there was. And there was no reason for him to feel as though she had betrayed him in some way much more elemental than simply hiding an innocent curiosity from him. But he did.

He bent to examine the gorget.

"No way," he whispered, kneeling, taking the gorget in his hand. Feeling again the slash of betrayal.

"What is it?" she asked from the foot of the litter. "We didn't leave anything there, did we?"

So innocent. David's fingers closed around the gorget. He forced himself to release them, to remember his strength and the fragility of the ornament. But it was there—damn! For a moment he had almost allowed himself to hope there were two identical gorgets. But there wouldn't be, not both bearing the small, peculiar nick he had noticed Wednesday.

"David?" she said again in the soft voice she always used in this room. "What's wrong?"

"What's wrong," he said, exerting the same tenuous control over his voice as he did the hand that gripped the gorget, "is that this is the shell we picked out to send to Jack Townley."

"No," she said. She knelt beside him and reached for the shell. He continued to hold it, but turned it so the light reflected from its engraved surface.

"Oh." The word came out on a soft hiss of breath and Anne sank onto her heels. She looked up at David, her eyes wide and questioning. Either she was truly surprised or they still taught advanced acting in med school. "We— How? When?" She shook her head again. "No. It can't be."

He pushed to his feet and looked down at her. He heard the chill in his voice, but there wasn't a whole hell of a lot he could do about that. Too often in interrogations he'd been forced into the role of "bad cop" because at some point it became impossible for him to disguise his disgust at the ease with which the slime he was interrogating slipped into the role of innocent victim, when the true victim was on a slab in the morgue. Lying did that to him, too. Especially unnecessary lying from someone he'd begun to believe he could trust.

"We have the tracings," he said. "Let's go take a look."

Anne was as silent returning downstairs as she had been coming up them. This time, David made no effort to break that silence.

She'd carefully folded the tissue paper and placed it out of sight—she'd said because of the visitors to the house—in what had to be the safest, or the place the least likely to raise questions about why she had a series of pre-Columbian tracings—with her copper, where she already had a tackle box full of similar designs.

Thursday morning he'd watched, smiling, while she'd stashed the tackle box in a stack of boxes and cartons in the room adjoining the kitchen. "Poe," she'd said grinning. "Wasn't he the one who said the best place to hide something was in plain view?"

Now he watched as she prowled through the stack of boxes looking for the right tackle box, and smiling was the last thing he felt like doing. Damn! Was it too much to ask that finally in his long, lonely, miserable life he could have someone he could trust?

Whoa! Where had that come from?

David walked to the table and reached for the chair he had abandoned only minutes before, but he didn't sit; he gripped the back of it, one-handed. Unlike the gorget, which he still held cautiously in his right hand, the chair wouldn't break. Maybe. He had someone to trust, he told himself as he felt the bite of wood against his palm and fingers. His brother. And his brother's family. And in the past he'd had the support and, yes, love, of his overworked parents. And, damn it, he wasn't that old; his life hadn't been that long. And if he'd been alone, it had been by choice. His choice. So why was he standing here moaning because Anne Locke had so obviously and needlessly lied to him?

Because he wanted Annie. He wanted to trust her. He wanted to love her. He wanted her in his life now, this weekend, the rest of the month he was to spend here, the rest of his life.

"Son of a bitch."

When the hell had that happened?

Anne swiveled around from where she was digging through boxes. "What?"

David shook his head. Then he sat. And pushed the plates and platters and bowls containing the remains of their dinner toward the other side of the table. And set the gorget on the table in front of him, next to the telephone that they had left there when they went upstairs. And forced himself to think about lies and betrayal. "Have you found them yet?"

"Yes."

He heard the less than gentle click as Anne closed a metal box, the soft fumbling sounds as she rose from her crouch on the floor, and then her steps. She stopped beside him. "Here they are," she said.

Any hope that he might be mistaken died when he placed the gorget on the tissue next to his initialed tracing, but still he turned it over and compared the reverse, and set it on the tracing to compare the nick.

"It's the same, isn't it?" she asked. "But how? How can that be?"

"What happened, Doc?" he asked without turning to look at her where she stood near his shoulder, giving every appearance of being as engrossed in the comparison as he. "Didn't you trust me enough to let this out of your control long enough to have it identified?"

"*What?*"

He trailed his fingers along the edge of the gorget when what he wanted to do was swivel in his chair, grab Annie by the shoulders and shake her until she admitted her deception, until she—until she what? Until she wrapped her arms around him and begged his forgiveness? It wasn't going to happen. Not in this lifetime. But if it did—just for the sake of speculation—what would he do?

He buried his face in his hands, raked at his eyes and his forehead, at the alien thoughts that had crept from some unknown well in his psyche. Pete was right. He had lost it. He sighed and then he did look at her.

"Except that sometime in the last two days it has been cleaned, this gorget is identical to the one we brought down Wednesday and packaged to send to Jack Townley. I can only think of two ways it could be here. Either sometime between noon and now someone sneaked into a house where we were both working, found the entry to the closet room, and returned an artifact worth thousands of dollars, and just as quietly left without either of us hearing a thing. Or . . . "

Her expression had gone all tight and closed, and her eyes, usually alive with humor, if not laughter, had narrowed and darkened. "Or what?" she asked.

"Or it never went to Texas."

She shook her head. "Of course it went. We wrapped it together. You carried it out to the car for me. I took it to town."

"That's right. You took it to town." And Bobby Preston had chosen that day to try to fly. David snatched that memory and held onto it. God. Maybe she hadn't lied. "And Margaret mailed it for you. What did she mail, Annie?"

She shook her head. "No. No, I'm not going to do this. Margaret is my friend."

"A friend who was in the house yesterday."

"And your friend, David? I'm sorry he's dead. Oh, God, I'm sorry he's dead. But did he get an empty box in the mail and not say anything? And how did he know to write the word Spiro by your name? No. There's another answer somewhere."

"Where?"

She reached across him and picked up the tracing, leaving the gorget on the table. "Upstairs."

He picked up the gorget to follow, but she stopped him with a sharp look at his hand. "Leave it," she said. "That way we won't have any doubt when we find another, or several others, that look just like it."

He'd turned off the light in the room when they'd

brought the gorget downstairs, but neither of them had stopped, or even thought, to close the panel. Now he stepped through it and began reaching for the light cord. The sound was softer than a whisper, barely audible over the sound of Anne's steps as she followed him into the room, of the combined sounds of their breathing as she, too, heard whatever it was. Anne lifted her hand to his arm, touching him for the first time since the telephone call that had started this search, and together they listened. A padding, back and forth, of something soft-footed but heavy, across the room, between the burial and the closet wall. And then a soft, guttural utterance—not spoken word but conveying some unknown message. Annie's fingers gripped his arm with an almost painful tightness at the faint but unmistakable sound of bones and copper and shells settling into place.

David thrust her behind him and yanked on the light cord.

The room was empty. No one and nothing greeted his quick visual inspection of the confined area. Nothing but the blank windows, intact over their backing of unfinished siding; the wallpaper, dingy in the shadows but still covering the walls in an unbroken pink floral pattern, except for the exposed studs and back side of the sheetrock of the unfinished closet wall; the ceiling, with nothing visible there but the bare lightbulb suspended from a tarnished metal plate and decades worth of cobwebs. No one but the warrior on his cedar litter, still in place, still surrounded by his earthly treasures. David spun around, searching behind him, but he knew there was only one way out of the room, the way that he and Annie had blocked.

Once again, Annie clutched his arm. He pulled her to his side and held her there. He didn't have to ask if she'd heard the noises. Her always fair complexion had gone even paler, as pale as when he had been talking with Pete about the murder, and her eyes, which minutes ago had seemed dark and lifeless, now held expression, but he wasn't sure that terror was an improvement. She drew in a deep breath, then another, as though by regulating her breathing, she could regulate her heartbeat, now racing in cadence with his. Not a bad idea, he thought, and tried it himself. It worked, finally, marginally.

When she began unwrapping her arms from around him and pulling away, he realized she had been holding him as tightly as he had held her. He didn't want to break that bond. There was safety there, and comfort, and, strangely, a belonging. Eventually, the feeling of belonging was what forced him to release her. How could he feel that for someone who only minutes before he had thoroughly and completely distrusted? How could he distrust someone who made him feel so—so at home, so welcome? So wanted?

"Annie?"

She jerked the rest of the way out of his arms and stood rubbing her hands over her forearms. "I'm all right," she said tightly. But she wasn't. Any fool could see that she had gone all brittle and fragile. "I'm all right," she repeated as she thrust her chin up a notch.

"That's good," he said, giving her this lie. "I'm sure as hell glad one of us is."

She looked wildly about the room before glancing down at the warrior and taking a half step toward him. She stood there in silence for a moment, and David wondered what thoughts raced through her as she fought the tears that glistened in her expressive eyes. He took a step toward her and the sound on the old pine floor echoed through the room. Anne twisted around to look at him, stopping him even as he recognized his need to touch her. "I'm all right," she said, turning back to the burial and dropping to her knees beside it and raking through the shells. *"I am."*

"What are you doing?"

"I'm doing what we came up here to do. I'm looking for some more of those damned gorgets that look like the one we—*I*—sent to Texas. The one that got somebody killed."

"Annie, don't."

She turned at his softly spoken words and looked up at him. Her face twisted but the tears didn't escape. "I have to," she said, sinking back on her heels. "Don't you see. I have to."

"You sent it," he told her. "I believe you." And he did. At last. Too late? "It's all right. I believe you." He made another wary search of the room. Nothing. But damn it, something had been here. "Let's get out of here now. Let's go downstairs and talk about what just happened."

"No. Nothing happened. The wind blew or the house settled or we had an earthquake—"

"Annie." He dropped his hands onto her shoulders and tightened them until Anne sagged back against him. "Whatever it was, it has an explanation. Let's shut this room up and go—somewhere, anywhere, out of here—and try to figure it out."

Numbly, she nodded. He bent to help her to her feet. That was a switch. Since the day they'd met, she'd been the strong one, probably still was if he were completely truthful, because those sounds had affected him at a bone-deep level that went way beyond fear. But for now, it felt good to be doing *for* her, even if it were no more than getting her out of this room. What didn't feel good at all was knowing that anything could drain the enthusiasm from this vibrant woman the way whatever had made those sounds had. The way his suspicions had.

He felt her shudder and begin to rise, but she hesitated and looked once more toward the burial. She sucked in a shallow breath, shook her head, and reached toward the copper plates that had covered the skeleton's right thigh.

The armor that only minutes before had lain in a slight depression where the bone had once been. The armor that now lay level with that of the other leg.

The armor that once again covered a gleaming white bone.

David tightened his hands on Anne's shoulders, instinctively drawing her back from the body.

"This was here earlier, wasn't it?" she asked in a small voice. "Tell me it was. Tell me no one could have come into the house in the last few minutes and replaced it. Tell me!"

"It wasn't here, Annie." God, all the strength of his voice was gone, too. "I remember noticing the way the copper was displaced because it wasn't here."

"This isn't happening."

He knelt beside her and cautiously lifted the edge of the upper copper plate covering the femur. "This bone has been cleaned. Not much. Maybe just dusted. Like the gorget."

"It's Joe," she said. "Somehow. Some way. He's wired the house. He intercepted the shipments. But why? Damn it! Why?"

"Annie."

She jerked beneath his hands.

"No one has been in the house with us today. We can search, we *will* search, but there weren't any wires in the attic yesterday."

"Then what— How— It can't . . . "

He lifted her to her feet and turned her away from the body, toward him. She didn't help, but she didn't resist, either. "I don't know," he told her. "But I sure as hell want to find out. You were right, you know. Jack Townley didn't make those notes and those phone calls because he got an empty box from us."

She lifted her face to his as the memory of what had happened to Jack Townley, of what had brought them to the room, slammed into her. She lifted her hand to her mouth and swayed. "Karen," she whispered. "Oh, my God. Karen."

15

Downstairs, Anne fumbled through the kitchen drawer for her address book. *There's no reason to worry,* she kept telling herself, but her hands shook so badly she could barely turn the pages, barely see the number. David lifted the book from her and carried it to the table. There, he kicked out a chair for her and began dialing.

Anne couldn't sit. Did he think she could sit until she talked to her friend?

There's no reason to worry.

Why didn't Karen answer? There. Thank God. Someone picked up the receiver. *Her answering machine?*

Anne held the receiver with both hands. She didn't realize she was rocking back and forth until David scooted the chair behind her knees and pushed her onto it.

The message was blessedly brief. Anne waited for the beep and spoke as quietly, as calmly as she could, but she heard and hated the tremor in her voice.

Karen's voice interrupted Anne's garbled message. "Anne?" she asked with a shaky laugh.

"Karen? You're all right?"

"Yeah. You've heard already? My word, bad news

does travel fast. I thought you were so far in the boonies I'd have a chance to . . ." Karen's voice faded. "Sorry. It wasn't me. I don't know when they will release the name to the news media, but it was a lab assistant. Not me. And they haven't found the animal yet. If it was . . . an animal. But, hey. Thanks for calling. I'm still a little shaken. He had— He had some of my things—my driver's license—in his lab coat. The cops talked to me—it seemed like for hours. They didn't want to believe I didn't know him. Anne, he's probably the one who's been calling and, yes, stealing my things from the lab and from here, and I didn't even know him."

Karen's voice broke on a sob. Anne shivered. Cold, she was so cold and it had nothing to do with winter or high ceilings. She looked up at David, then gestured toward the telephone. He pulled a chair close and dropped his arm over her shoulder. She nodded, thanking him for the warmth and the comfort and tilted the telephone receiver so that he could listen in.

"Tell me what happened," she said softly.

"I wish I knew," Karen told her. "I wish to God I knew. Or maybe I don't. I saw him. I'm a pathologist. I work in a morgue. And I have never seen anything like that in my life."

"Karen."

"Yeah. Right. I— I don't know how to tell you this. But your bone's gone. I guess I'm glad for more than one reason that you called. I didn't know how you'd feel about my telling the police. I haven't yet. I didn't know it was gone until after they had released me to go home. I don't know if it's relevant. I don't know if he took it, or where it is. I can't give you any kind of report, except that, yes, it is old. More museum age than homicide, but I'd just gotten to the lab, just opened the package, when we had this damned impromptu staff meeting. And that went on and on and would probably still be going on if we hadn't heard the screams from the stairwell. Anyway, when I finally got back to my office, the box was in the cabinet where I'd put it, and all the packaging, but the bone was gone. I'm sorry, Anne—"

She saw David's eyes close, saw his lips thin, saw a nerve twitch in his jaw.

"Don't worry about it," Anne said. *No, Karen,* she thought, *you won't have to. There are two people right here who will do all the worrying for you.* She glanced at David. He nodded. "Do what you think best about the bone," she said. "It's no— It's no big secret. My uncle was an antiquities dealer. I was pretty sure it was something he had brought in, back in the thirties, but I wanted to be certain. You've confirmed that. Just— Are Rae and Mollie there? Or are they gone for the holidays?"

She heard what sounded like a sniff. "They're both due back any time now."

"You're sure? You don't need to be alone right now."

"I know," Karen told her. "My first reaction was to come home and hide, but I have a neighbor here with me now. I'm okay. Or I will be. I just don't know why this has upset me so much. After all, in my line of work—"

She heard the murmur of a man's voice in the background. Good. Karen might think she ought to be indestructible, but no one as softhearted as she was could face violent death on a personal level and not be affected. Anne knew from firsthand experience. "Hush," she told her friend. "See if your neighbor can find you some brandy. And for God's sake, call me if you need me. Heaven knows you were certainly there for me."

David replaced the receiver, but he left his arm over her

shoulder, and the two of them sat in stunned silence until Anne whimpered, "I almost killed her. I almost killed her. If he hadn't stolen the femur, Karen would be dead, too. Why? Why, David?" But, of course, he had no answer.

The sky outside had gone completely dark, dotted in the distance by the lights of Allegro that only a short time before had seemed so pleasant. The table remained cluttered with the remains of their dinner. The ceiling gleamed under its coat of paint. All the things that such a short time ago had brought her so much pleasure now seemed to mock her. What in God's name was happening?

And almost simultaneously the two of them noticed what was missing from the clutter on the table. David picked up the address book and moved it. He removed his arm from around her so that he could scoot bowls and plates to one side, but the gorget wasn't there. He rested his elbows on the table and buried his face in his hands. "I don't want to go back upstairs. I don't want to know if it's returned."

Feeling as though she were moving on automatic, the way she had too often in med school, Anne got up and checked the back door. It was still locked. She leaned against it. "We have to go," she said. "We left the panel open. We left the light on."

Upstairs, the copper plate had resettled over the warrior's right femur, and on the edge of one cedar pole, half on, half off, lay a four inch diameter shell gorget, marked with one unique nick, and easily identifiable as the one in the tracings.

They found no wires. No microphones. No hidden speakers. No electronic intrusion of any kind. With the aid of electric lighting where it was available, supplemented by two powerful flashlights, David and Anne searched the room where the grave goods lay, the closet, the adjoining sitting room with its chimney flue and plumbing run, the room in the north wing of the house, which must at least partially abut the hidden chamber, even the attic. They found dust. Lots of dust. And cobwebs. And, except in the attic where David and Wayne Samuels had worked the day before, no sign that anyone other than he and Anne had been anywhere near the walls, ceilings, and floors. Certainly no sign of any large animal.

And no one but the blind fool he had been only hours before could possibly believe that Anne Locke had any knowledge of what was happening, or how.

"There has to be an explanation," Anne said when they had completed their search and returned to the hidden room. "A logical, reasonable explanation."

Yes, there had to be. But God alone knew what it was. Anne stood at the foot of the litter, looking down at the warrior as though he could tell her what that answer was, and she hadn't yet noticed what David, standing just behind her, had seen the moment they reentered the room. The gorget no longer lay on the cedar pole.

They had left their flashlights in the sitting room, but David didn't need extra light to find the gorget. He knew where it would be—and it was—on the very top of a pile of beads and engraved shells near the skeleton's copper-covered right shoulder, if not exactly where he had first found it, then so close his eye couldn't tell the difference.

David lifted his hands to Anne's shoulders and pulled her against him. "Look," he said, nodding over her shoulder toward the floor.

She sucked in her breath when she, too, saw that the

shell had been moved. For a moment, she shrank against him. Then she straightened. "An explanation," she repeated. "All we have to do is find it."

Downstairs, David took a flashlight, his service revolver, and himself outside to search the perimeter of the house. Anne tried to go with him, but he stopped that foolishness by the simple expedient of glaring at her and pulling the door closed behind him. He found nothing. Of course, he found nothing. Life couldn't be that simple.

Anne spun around in alarm from where she stood at the kitchen sink when he opened the back door to return to the house.

"Nothing," he said. "I found nothing."

She didn't nod, smile, or ask any questions. "I'm putting the food away," she said, wrapping and scraping and reorganizing the remains of the holiday feast with quick, jerky motions. "What we really need on top of everything else is a case of ptomaine or salmonella."

David propped the flashlight on the table, tucked the revolver into the belt at his back, and began stacking and scraping their used dishes.

"You don't have to—"

"Yes, Annie," he said, silencing her protest and carrying the stack of dishes to the shallow sink. "I do."

They worked in silence. There were too many questions and too few answers for any conversation.

They had just finished drying the last dish when Anne heard the unmistakable sound of an engine coming up her steep driveway.

David's head jerked up and he cocked his head. Listening. "Someone's coming," he told her.

"Great," she said, sagging back against the counter. "That's just great."

"You don't get many drop-in visitors."

Anne choked out a laugh. "You noticed?"

Only emergencies. That thought sobered her. *Not now*, she thought. *Please God, not now. I don't think I can handle anything more tonight.*

Instead of coming on to the back of the house, the car stopped at the front, engine idling, where an over-grown and seldom used walk led to the front door. In the six months she had lived in the house, only three people had come to the front door: a salesman, and a pair of Mormon missionaries.

David walked to the back door and flipped on the light that illuminated the back porch and makeshift parking area, opening the door as he did so. After a moment, she heard the car resume its journey, then stop, then a door slam. She stepped to the back door beside David.

Blake Foresman. The sheriff. Oh, God, it was an emergency. Without knowing how they had gotten there, she found her hands clutching David's arm.

David glanced back at her. She couldn't call the expression on his face a frown, it was much too solemn for that, much too ingrained. But it softened slightly as he looked at her. He lifted his hand. For a moment she thought he might touch her cheek; with a shock she realized she was standing close enough to him for him to do so. Instead, though, after a lingering inspection of her face, he dropped his hand to hers in a light caress before he unlatched the screen and pushed it open.

"Blake," he said easily. "What brings you up here? Is there a problem?"

Blake wasn't in uniform. Anne grabbed that piece of information. He wore dark slacks, boots, a leather jacket, and a western hat, but he wasn't in uniform. "I don't know," he said as he stepped up onto the porch and removed his hat. "Evening, Doc." That formality concluded, he returned his attention to David. "I was across town when I glanced this way. Thought I saw a light bobbing and swaying around outside up here. After what you told me this morning, I thought I'd better check it out. You folks have any trouble?"

What had David told him? Anne found she still held David's arm. She released her grasp on him. David glanced over his shoulder, giving her a look she knew he meant to be reassuring, that he meant to tell her he hadn't betrayed any of her secrets. And she believed him. Just like that. She dredged up a smile and stepped back slightly so that he could, too.

"Come in, Blake," she said. "I was just getting ready to heat up some apple pie."

"Well, now," he said easily, smiling but wary as he entered the house. "Does that mean yes, you did have some trouble, or no, you didn't?"

David latched the screen behind the sheriff and closed the back door. "I was outside with the flashlight earlier."

"You hear something? Find anything?"

David shook his head. "Maybe to the first, no to the second." He turned toward Anne. "Do you need some help?"

"No," she told him as she reached for the coffeepot. "This will only take a minute. Why don't the two of you sit down?"

But they didn't sit, neither one of them, until she had filled and plugged in the coffeepot and started toward the refrigerator for the pie.

"Doc? Why don't you sit for a minute, too. There's something I've got to ask you."

She'd suspected Blake was a more than competent lawman; she'd heard it said and seen his quiet, calm professionalism herself too many times to doubt her instincts. But until now he had never turned his professional demeanor toward her. "What is it?" she asked.

He pulled a chair out from the table and stood behind it, waiting. With a shrug, she sat. Only then did he pull out a chair for himself on the opposite side of the table. "Huerra?"

David glanced at him but reached for the chair beside Anne.

"Is your search outside the reason you're armed?" Blake asked.

David sighed and shook his head. "Damn," he said as he felt for the pistol at his back. "Let me just put this away."

Blake grinned. "Good idea."

David stashed the pistol in a drawer and took the seat beside Anne.

"So," Blake asked. "What did you hear?"

"I don't know for sure what it was," David told him. "Or even where it was. Whatever it was, it was big."

Which was certainly true. As far as it went. Anne shuddered at the memory of those footfalls. At the memory of Karen's description of the lab assistant.

Blake nodded. "And no prints outside?"

"None that I could find."

"We might ought to get Samuels up here to look tomorrow. He's a pretty good tracker."

"He didn't find anything last time," David said.

Blake studied him steadily across the width of the table. "Just the same," he said finally. "I want him to look.

"Now, Doc," he said, smiling grimly, "I've got to ask you about a bone."

So Karen had told. Well, there really wasn't anything else she could have done.

"The Chicago P.D. called me a little while ago. They'd run your name through their computer but they wanted to know what I knew about you since you'd moved back here, and what I knew about a bone you'd sent to one of the Cook County medical examiners, a bone that disappeared today in connection with a particularly nasty homicide."

"A right femur," Anne told him.

"Yes. According to what Dr. Ready told them, an old femur. A very old one. I was just wondering, Doc, where you got it, and why you didn't run it through my office."

Those were good questions. Questions she wasn't sure how to answer. There wasn't any way she wanted to take him upstairs and show him where she'd found the femur. And where it was now. And yet, he wasn't going to leave without an acceptable answer.

"I found it upstairs," she said, deciding to stay as close to the truth as she could. "In a closet. I don't know if you knew that Uncle Ralph was an antiquities dealer, that he was involved with buying and selling artifacts and, according to what my mom told me, involved somehow in the early excavations at Spiro. I was pretty sure the bone was old enough to be an archaeological find, something left over from his days in the business, so I didn't want to bother your office with it. But believe me, if Karen had told me any different, I would have called you in a heartbeat."

"Any idea why somebody would want to steal it?"

"It was just a bone, Blake," David said. "A centuries-old bone from a very tall, very dead man. It had no monetary value. But from what Dr. Ready said Wednesday and again tonight when we talked with her, things belonging to her have been taking missing for a while. It's possible that whoever is responsible for taking those items also took the femur."

That too was true. As far as it went.

"Yeah. That's kind of what me and the Chicago detective came up with, but I had to check it out. Have you two been here all day?"

David nodded. "Yes."

"Can anybody confirm that for you?"

Alibis? Surely Blake wasn't asking them for alibis. Surely no one would think they had anything to do with a murder in Chicago. *Unless they searched and found that damned bone.*

David smiled grimly. "I saw you a little before seven this morning. Pete Tompkins called me here about six this evening." He glanced up at the ceiling. The new ceiling. "You can ask Samuels what shape this room was in when he and his wife left here last night."

"Pete got in touch with you then?" Blake asked.

"You knew?"

Blake nodded. "I was having dinner with Gene and Gretta when he called. I don't suppose you want to tell me what that was all about?"

Anne couldn't help it. She stretched out her hand toward David. He took it and wrapped it in his. "A homicide," he said. "But then I suspect you already knew that."

"Yeah," Blake said. "I know Pete. I like Pete. And when he called tonight, I talked to Pete. Doc, you want to tell me what was in the box you sent to Townley?"

"I sent it, Blake," David said. "Anne just used her supplies to mail it. You see, the bone wasn't alone. There was an engraved shell artifact with it. I sent it to Townley to see if it might shed a little more light on when and where the bone came from."

"Any idea why somebody might want to steal it?"

"Yeah," David said. "If my suspicions are right, several thousand dollars, give or take a few thousand more."

Blake gave a low whistle. "Yep. That's motive enough for murder, all right." He glanced toward the counter. "I think I'll take a cup of that coffee after all, Doc."

Anne brought cups and the coffeepot to the table. Even though she suspected Blake's request was a delaying tactic rather than a desire for coffee, she poured and smiled and resumed her seat and gave him the time he seemed to want. Gave herself some time.

"Let's see if I've got this in order. Wednesday night, Samuels sees what he thinks are mountain lions prowling around this hillside. Would I be wrong in thinking you shipped those packages out Wednesday?"

"Wednesday afternoon," David told him.

Foresman nodded. Anne suspected he'd already known that. "And Friday, noon or so, after one of your packages arrives, a man is killed in his locked house in Dallas by some sort of wild animal, and a couple of hours after that, after another of your packages arrives in the M.E.'s office in Chicago, another man is killed in a county building secure stairwell by some sort of wild animal. And tonight, you're out searching the yard because you hear something that just might be another wild animal. I leave anything out?"

Anne closed her eyes. "No."

"Did *you* leave anything out?"

Just any mention of a fortune in grave goods, Anne thought. Just any mention of an armor-clad skeleton. Just any mention that the two items sent had returned to that skeleton. "Such as?"

Foresman leaned forward. "What I'm asking, Doc, is, did you send anything else out in Wednesday's mail? Am I going to get a call from some other jurisdiction wanting to know who you are, wanting to know what was in the package, telling me of still another murder?"

"No." David answered for her. "We sent only the two items."

"Things like this don't happen in my county," Blake said. "I don't like this. I don't like it at all."

Neither do I! Anne wanted to cry. *I came back here to be safe. I came back here to—* To hide. Oh, God, yes she had, even if she had never fully admitted it until now.

"I don't like it either, Blake," she heard David say. "That's why I'm staying here tonight."

"Good." Foresman stood, picked up his hat, and looked down at Anne. "Good. You keep her safe."

"I will." Now David stood. As he walked with the sheriff toward the door, Anne knew she should, too, but as she started to rise, David looked back at her. "Keep your seat, Annie."

She heard them. Just because they stood outside on the porch, did David think she wouldn't?

"I'll be on duty at eleven," Blake said. "I'll try to stay here in the south end of the county. If you need me, holler."

"I will," David told him. "And thanks."

"The two homicides have to be connected. I know that; you know that. Any idea who might be behind them?"

David gave a short laugh. "If you'd asked me right after Pete called, I probably would have come up with all sorts of theories, and even a couple of suspects. But the lab tech doesn't fit with any of them."

"Yeah."

Their footsteps sounded as they moved across the porch, but their words still carried into the house.

"It really isn't your problem, Blake. Both murders were outside your jurisdiction."

"Yeah, right. But it sure feels like my problem. So I

guess I'll keep an eye on this place as much as I can, maybe find out where Joe Hansom was today. And I'll stop by Wayne Samuels's place tonight before it gets too late and tell him you'd like to see him up here tomorrow morning."

David stayed on the porch until Blake turned his car around and drove down the hill. Then he closed and locked the door and leaned against it. "We're going to have to tell him, you know."

"Tell him *what*, David? What in God's name can we tell him?"

"If I knew that, Annie, I would have done it already."

Anne buried her face in her hands. "I'm sorry I got you messed up in this. All you wanted to do this month was fish and think."

"I'm not."

He crossed the room quietly until he stood behind her. He lifted his hands to her shoulders and with deft, sure strength began kneading her knotted muscles, easing the tension that had gripped her since Pete Tompkins's telephone call.

She moaned a little and surrendered herself to his touch. No, she wasn't sorry, either. Not really. She didn't know if she would have had to face the problems in her upstairs room if he hadn't been here. On one level, she almost suspected she wouldn't. But he was here, and she did have the problems, and she didn't know how she could face them without his help.

And she didn't know how he had so quickly become a part of her life, or why his touch was so impossibly familiar. So blessedly welcome.

Too welcome.

David was a cop. A big-city cop. And after his vacation was over, he'd go back to being a cop. In a world

she could never return to, a world where violence and
death were commonplace, where children were victims
and attackers, where life was no longer valued, where
blood and screams—

She pulled away from his touch. "You don't have to
stay with me tonight."

He sighed but dropped his hands. "Sure I do. I just
can't decide whether I need to stay downstairs, to protect you from anything breaking into the house, or
upstairs, to protect you from anything breaking out."

"I'll be all right alone. I've lived here for months
without anything happening."

"Got a road map?"

"David, I'm serious."

"So am I, Annie. I'm staying. Now, do you have a
road map?"

"Why?"

He grinned, his little-boy-gone-bad grin, and she
knew he wouldn't answer. At least not completely.
"Because I thought that after Wayne gets here tomorrow, we might take a little day trip. Say, up to Spiro?
Check things out. And then, depending on what we
learn, we might try to find your crazy aunt."

David didn't sleep. Since Annie's bed apparently wasn't
an option, he'd chosen the downstairs sitting room to
camp out in. It was a little far from Annie's room, but
with its uncovered French doors and double windows it
was the most logical room to watch from. But damn it
was cold. He didn't want to risk the exposure the light
from a fire would bring to the room, so he wrapped
himself in a blanket and lay back against the arm of the
lumpy old sofa.

Anne Locke. What the hell was there about the

woman that made him feel as though she had been a part of his life forever? And was she completely immune to him? Occasionally he suspected she wasn't, like tonight when she moaned as he had worked the tension from her neck. Tonight, when she had pulled away from him as though he were the animal that had killed those people.

But she hadn't objected when he had taken over as host tonight, as though he had every right to: inviting Blake in, walking him out, answering the questions he had directed at Annie.

Well, what the hell was he supposed to have done? Let her go out on the porch alone to see who was coming? Flounder around wondering how to be honest and still not tell the sheriff what he really didn't want to know?

Hell, he didn't need this. Anne Locke was a forever kind of woman. He was a washed-up cop. She had a medical practice and a hundred-year-old home and roots in a small town. He had a career down the tubes, a rented condo, and a knowledge as old as he was that he could never live in a small town. She also had a not-so-small fortune in antiquities in an upstairs closet. He had, at the most, savings to hold him for a year, a police pension that wouldn't take effect for another five years, and a limp little 401K he'd been meaning to add more to but just hadn't got around to it.

So why did he feel as though he had just found a part of his life that had been missing forever? Why did he feel as though he belonged down the hall in that impossibly romantic bedroom with that impossible woman?

He looked up at the ceiling. "More lessons?" he asked. "Do you mind cluing me in as to what course we're studying this time?"

He got no answer, but then, he seldom did.

And if he was to get answers, what he really needed to know was what force, what power, had he and Anne unlocked when they knocked the hole in that closet wall.

Were they responsible for the deaths of two people?

And were they, and possibly anyone around them, in danger?

Damn! Maybe he shouldn't drag Samuels into this mess. Wayne had already been through enough hell for a dozen lifetimes.

The sound was faint, just a whisper of noise from the direction of Anne's room. David cocked his head and listened. Yes. There it was again. He threw off the blanket and rose, easing his way to the door, into the hall, toward the stairs.

It was Annie, going quietly, stealthily upstairs.

David frowned but lowered his revolver. What the hell was she doing?

He gave her a moment before following.

She'd closed the closet door, but a strip of light found its way beneath it and into the sitting room and told him all too clearly where she was.

Damn it! Didn't she realize she could be in danger?

Still, he didn't barge into the room. He eased the closet door open and just as cautiously sidestepped boxes and the panel until he stood in the opening.

She knelt on the floor at the foot of the litter, her dark red flannel nightgown pooled around her like so much blood. In one hand she held the small cedar box, open now, with its engraved mica lid in her lap. With the other, she touched the carved shell images. Tears ran unchecked down her cheeks.

The warrior was not aware of her. He'd never again be aware of anything as he lay there in solitary splendor. But David was aware of her, so aware it hurt, as she knelt grieving for a long-dead man.

He wanted to go to her, to yank her away from him, to tell her she was his, by God—

But something wasn't right.

"Annie?" he asked softly.

She didn't answer.

"Annie?"

Carefully he knelt beside her. When he reached for the box, she resisted only slightly before letting him take it. He placed the lid back on it and put it on the litter.

"Annie," he said again.

When she still didn't speak, he lowered his hands to her shoulders and turned her toward him. "Annie," he demanded. "Answer me."

She looked up at him, her eyes unfocused, then shuddered. At that moment, and only then, did she seem aware of him. Her face clouded with pain and then softened as she leaned forward and wrapped her arms around him, holding onto him for dear life. "You're all right," she said. "It was just a dream. You're all right."

Heaven. Or it could have been. But something still wasn't right. David held her away from him and looked down at her. "Yes. I am. But are you?"

"What— David?" Now he didn't have to hold her away. Anne pulled back and looked at him, questions and fear and the residue of pain all too obvious in her expression. She glanced around, and he knew that only then did she become aware of where she was. Of who he was. "How . . . "

He rose to his feet and lifted her to hers. She swayed slightly and he put his arm around her, to steady her, to anchor her to his side. She didn't fight it. Maybe she couldn't. Hell, he knew he couldn't.

"I followed you," he told her.

"But I— I never sleepwalk."

He closed his eyes and rested his forehead against her hair. "I wish you hadn't said that, Annie. I wish to God this wasn't something else that we're going to worry and wonder about."

"What did I do?"

He lifted his fingers to her cheeks and brushed across the dampness still streaking them.

"I cried? Why?"

"I don't know." He pulled her up against him hard. Damn it, he'd tried. He'd done everything he knew to avoid the hell this was probably going to cost him, but in the last five minutes, all the rules had changed. "I don't know much of anything anymore. But one thing I do know, I'm not letting you out of my sight or away from my side until this night is over."

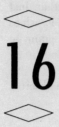

16

1940

Lucy was reading. It still wasn't easy, and it sure wasn't fun, but it was something she had to do if she was ever going to get out of school. And she had to do that. As much as she loved her mama, she had to get out of this house.

That Saturday morning in early November had started out cool and wet, but about an hour ago the clouds had finally moved on to the east and the weather had pulled one of its autumn switch acts. Now it was warmer outside than it was in the house. That's why she had the windows open in the dining room where she had her books piled around her at the end of the long dark table.

And that was probably why Papa had the doors to his study open onto the porch, just an angle away from where she sat, trying to concentrate on her homework so that she could leave when Walter came for her. Didn't they know that she could hear every word they said? Didn't they know Mama was in the house, only one more room away, in the kitchen? Didn't they care?

"It's a chance, Ralph," Aunt Marian said. Lucy had twisted around to look when she first heard their voices and knew that Marian stood in the doorway. "Maybe our last chance. My God, how can you stand being dependent on her family for every dime?"

"*Our* last chance, Marian?"

"Yes."

"And all I have to do is take the risk?"

"There is no risk. Can't you see that by now?"

"What I can see is that Jackson is dead, his son is dead. Billy Ray and that other digger are both dead. Every buyer I sent any part of it is dead— No. Adkins isn't dead. He's just a blithering idiot. And every other buyer has already heard about the damned curse on the stuff, a curse that attacks anyone who touches any part of that *marvelous* treasure of mine."

"Except us."

"What?"

"Except us. It hasn't harmed us."

"But we haven't—"

"Haven't what? We moved it into the house. I helped you pack the pieces you sold. We moved it into the attic."

"Yeah. And it moved itself right back."

"But we hadn't completely finished moving it when we stopped for the night. And that isn't the point, anyway. It's been almost five years. Don't you think if it was going to harm us, it would have done so by now?"

"Is that why you won't sleep in your bedroom any more, why you wanted it out of there, why you've locked the door on it and everything else you couldn't move into your sitting room?"

"Where I sleep isn't the issue either, Ralph. Or maybe it is."

"What do you mean by that?"

"Nothing. Just that I'm tired of living in poverty. I'm tired of being a hanger-on to a group of people I wouldn't acknowledge on the street and having those same people look down on me. You promised me more when I came here. You owe me more."

Lucy heard Papa's desk drawer slam. She closed her eyes, wishing she could close out what she was hearing, but she couldn't, because then she heard his voice, louder, as though he had moved to stand beside Aunt Marian. "And all I have to do is what, Marian?"

"I think you must take it. That seems to be the clue. We can touch it, probably because we have all of it; others can't. So all you have to do is take enough of that—treasure—to Henrik Johnson to convince him we have the real thing, to convince him he needs to buy it—all of it—and then it will be his problem and we can get out of here."

"Lucy."

Her mama's soft voice. Oh, no. She hadn't heard, had she?

Lucy opened her eyes. Walter and her mama stood at the door to the pantry. Mama beckoned to her with that same sad look on her face she had seen too many times. Lucy gratefully left her books and the sounds of her papa and Aunt Marian plotting to get rid of that poor, dead man upstairs, plotting to get rid of her mama and her. Plotting. Always plotting.

Walter was quiet when they went back into the kitchen, but he had a hard time hiding what he felt, and he was so mad now his freckles were standing out like paint against his ruddy complexion, and his blue eyes fairly sparked fire.

Mama had draped her apron over the edge of the sink. Now she folded it and placed it in the basket she kept in the kitchen for laundry. "I believe I will visit my father this afternoon," she said in her soft, slightly accented voice. "I will ask him to return me to this house at nine this evening. That would be a good time for you to return also, Lucy."

Lucy felt her mouth hanging open. She'd had to beg her mama for permission to go to the matinee at the picture show with Walter this afternoon, and now mama was telling her to stay out until bedtime? Walter tugged on her arm until she got her feet to moving, then opened the door for her and stood there, waiting for her to grab her jacket from its peg near the door and go on outside.

"Yes, ma'am, we'll be back by then," he promised, in a hurry, so that her mama wouldn't have time to tell them she'd changed her mind. But on the porch he stopped, and turned, and looked back into the kitchen, and Lucy looked, too. Her mama was just standing there in the middle of the kitchen, looking lost.

"You take care now, Mrs. Hansom," Walter said. And then, being Walter and, Lucy suspected, unable to just go off and leave someone hurting the way her mama must be, he took a step into the house. "Should we stay here with you until your father comes for you? Can we do anything for you?"

Her mama looked at him, still sad, still quiet. "No, son," she said. "Yes. Yes, there is. You take good care of my little girl for me."

"Yes, ma'am," he said solemnly. "I will do that."

And then her mama smiled. "I know that, Walter Briggs. I've known that for a long, long time."

They walked down the driveway. Even though she wanted to, even though she needed the physical connection with Walter, Lucy wasn't quite brave enough to reach for his hand. Not where Papa might look out the window and see them. Not when he might yell at her and make her come back to the house. Not when he might tell Walter to go away and never come back.

At the street, Walter turned to the left, out of sight of the house, and stopped at a dusty green truck. "Do you really want to go see that big monkey?"

Lucy dredged up a smile. All anyone had been talking about at school for the last week was that the movie *King Kong* was finally coming to the Criterion in Allegro, Oklahoma.

"A monster movie might be the only thing that could make me laugh today," she told him, "but I'm not sure Harvey Skinner would appreciate my laughing just when he's all set to protect Mary Sue Johnson from whatever might lunge off that screen after her."

Walter chuckled, and it sounded only a little forced. "I know what you mean. This will probably be the only time in his life Harvey can look like a hero without really risking anything. So," he said, patting the front fender of the truck, "would you mind going for a drive with me?"

"A drive?" Lucy looked at the truck. "You mean it? In this? Whose is it? Oh, Walter, you didn't buy a truck?"

"Not too likely," he said. "It's Abe McPherson's. I'm doing some work for him, helping him build a barn. He asked me if I'd pick up a load of posts at the sawmill and deliver them out there. I should have gone before I picked you up. I would have, if I hadn't hoped I could talk your mama into letting you go with me. We can still be back in time to go to the movie if you really want to."

Young Mr. Johnson helped Walter at the mill. He was called young Mr. Johnson because he was a Junior and it got real confusing when everyone out there was yelling for "Will." And he was young, only a few years older than

Walter, but old enough to be courting Miss Edmonds, the new high school teacher who had come to Allegro last year. He was a nice man, but then Lucy had known that forever, because she had cousins who lived on the next road over and she had visited in the Johnson house almost as much as she had visited in her cousins' houses.

But he was also a busy man that Saturday, and Lucy couldn't help but be glad, because that meant he didn't have a lot of time to tease her and Walter and ask how things were at home.

And Walter was busy. Thinking about something real hard. Something that he didn't even try to share until he had offloaded the last post, not letting her help even the least bit. She didn't mind, not really. She knew he'd get around to sharing whatever was bothering him with her soon. He always had. Just as she had always shared with him.

And besides, the homesite where Abe McPherson was building was beautiful, peaceful, sunshiny warm but alive with leaf color, set as it was on the top of a ridge, with mountains above and below and all around.

"Lucy," Walter said, finishing his job and dusting his hands on his trousers. "I've been thinking."

She couldn't help smiling. That was exactly the tone of voice he had used when he'd announced they ought to be blood brothers, exactly the tone he used for any important pronouncement he made.

"I could tell that, Walter," she said lightly.

He frowned at her, deep in concentration. "I figure you and I ought to go ahead and get married now."

Lucy leaned back against the tailgate. *Married now?* Whatever happened to *Lucy, will you marry me?* Had she missed something? Of course she would. Marry him, that was. She'd known that since the day she'd shown him the kitten in the loft and he'd gone back into the barn to see what Papa and Aunt Marian had done with the dead man. But he hadn't asked. He hadn't ever asked.

"Now?" she squeaked.

He nodded, sure of her. Sure of himself. "I love you. You love me. And I have to get you out of that house. I— I can get enough work to take care of us."

"And what about your schooling?"

"I— I'll get by. Lots of folks don't finish school."

"And the army?"

"I'll— I can still go, later.

"And your plans to learn a trade?"

"I'm a carpenter, Lucy. I've worked as one for years."

"And you're a darned good one, Walter, but every man in this county who can hold a hammer calls himself a carpenter. That doesn't leave a whole lot of work, even for someone as good as you."

"You love me," he said.

Yes. She did. "Only this morning, I was thinking how much I want to get out of that house. But not if it means giving up your future. And not if it means going off and leaving my mama alone there."

"Maybe if you left, she could, too," Walter said.

Mama? Leave her papa? Lucy shook her head. That would never happen. And if it did? "And all of us could just go off and leave him alone with Papa and Aunt Marian, with them selling off pieces of him and getting even more people killed?"

"Damn it, Lucy, they're going to sell him anyway, and we still can't do one damned thing about it. But I can get you out of there. Hell, I can even get your mama out of there. If I tell her how much you want to go."

She couldn't let him do that. Not for his sake. Not for the sake of the dead man in Marian's bedroom. Not for her mama's sake and not for her mama's pride. Lucy

lifted her fingers to his mouth to silence him. He shook
with frustration and that other, darker emotion that had
come barging into their times together only after they
had explored their friendship as children, that other,
darker emotion that sang and sizzled through her blood,
too, when they had their too-few precious moments
alone.

He clasped her about the waist and lifted her to sit on
the tailgate of the pickup, then stepped close, holding
her tight. "Say yes, Lucy."

She shook her head. "Not to this, Walter. Not until
we're out of school, that's only months. Not until after
you've enlisted, and been accepted, and done your
training."

"And if we go to war like it looks like we might have
to?"

"Then I'll marry you before you leave. I promise you
that."

"Say yes, Lucy," he said again, his voice harsh in the
way it sometimes was when he felt things too strongly,
when he wanted her too much.

"No," she said. "Not till later."

"Say yes, Lucy," he said, his voice hot against her
throat.

She felt tears welling in her eyes. She knew he didn't
think he'd be sacrificing anything by marrying her now,
but she knew he would. And she knew she could never
let him make that sacrifice.

"Only to loving you," she told him. "You know I do.
You know I will."

"Say yes, Lucy," he groaned.

And there, beneath a clear, crisp November sky, with
the remnants of autumn's bright leaves rustling in the
trees around them, with the birds and the squirrels and
the rabbits forgetting they were there and scurrying and

scratching through those leaves that had already fallen, Lucy said yes to Walter, yes to everything except the legal bond that would ruin his plans, his future, his life.

They were on their way back to town, hurrying a little to get Lucy home by nine o'clock, when a sheriff's car, lights flashing, drew up alongside them and turned its spotlight on them. Lucy saw Walter glance at the speedometer. He hadn't been hurrying that much, he'd have been crazy to on this road. He frowned, but he pulled onto the shoulder and stopped.

The deputy stepped up to Walter's side of the truck and looked in. "Good," he said. Then, "Briggs." That was meant to be a greeting, Lucy knew, a kind of code between men that said all the things that women had to verbalize. But when he spoke again, she wished he'd had a code so he hadn't said what he did to her.

She'd seen him around, on duty and off, but she didn't know him. Obviously, though, he knew her.

"Lucy, honey," he told her, "you need to get on out to your grandpa's. Your mama needs you out there."

"What's the matter?" Walter asked.

The deputy motioned with his head, jerking it to one side. More code, Lucy recognized, telling Walter to get out of the truck, to step away so she couldn't hear what was said. But she had to hear it. She knew she did. "What's the matter, Deputy?" she asked.

He looked to Walter, but Walter nodded.

"It's your daddy, ma'am. There's been an accident."

Now Walter did step out of the truck. He patted Lucy's hand and walked back by the rear tire, and the deputy followed him.

"What happened?" Walter asked.

The deputy cleared his throat. "That switchback

north of town? His Buick didn't make it. We found him at the bottom."

"How bad?" Walter asked. But Lucy already knew the answer. Aunt Marian had wanted him to take part of the artifacts to the dealer, and Papa had been fool enough, or arrogant enough, or greedy enough to try. She didn't have to listen, but she did.

"I think he might have survived the crash," the deputy said. "He was outside the car. But some animal, bear maybe—something big—found him before a motorist saw the smoke from the burning car. I'm afraid he's dead. Real dead."

17

Annie was in his arms.

David absorbed that fact as he studied his surroundings in the early dawn light filtering through lace curtains on tall, narrow windows. He'd started his night in Annie's bed on top of the covers, telling himself he'd put at least that much distance between himself and temptation. But sometime during the night the room had grown colder and he had grown lonelier, and, less than half awake, he had tunneled under the comforter and electric blanket, wrapped his arms around Anne Locke and dragged her close.

She hadn't awakened—he remembered that much— just given a little sigh as she relaxed against him and slid deeper into sleep.

And she wasn't awake now, just snuggled trustingly against him as though seeking his warmth.

Trustingly.

Well, hell.

He felt his mouth twist in a wry grin. At least something in his life was going well. As an oath, that one had been downright mild. There had been a time in his life, not too long ago, when his thoughts, spoken or not, would have been a lot more colorful.

There had been a time in his life when he wouldn't have had the need to swear, because he wouldn't even have considered what he was now doing: freeing his arms from their protective embrace of the woman they held. Sliding out from under the covers. Feeling the chill of the floor seeping through the braided rug beneath his feet.

Annie moaned softly in her sleep and turned toward him, reaching but finding only empty bed. With another moan, she snuggled into the pillow he had just left.

No. He could not get back in that bed with her. He could not lie there with her as the world came to life, as she awoke. He wanted more from her, much more than she was apparently willing to give. And more than he was able to return. And if he ached, those feelings paled when he considered the ache and emptiness he'd feel if he did something to shatter Annie's trust in him, if he did something that would make her drive him away completely. But he did reach down and brush a wayward, tangled red curl from her cheek. And he could and did lift the comforter to cover her shoulder and the slender arm embracing the pillow he had so recently used.

He helped himself to Annie's shower and to a new toothbrush from the stash she kept on hand. Finding that the razor he had used a week before had not been tossed away, he tested it carefully, then used it again.

He didn't go upstairs.

He stopped with his hand on age-blackened varnish of the newel post and his foot on the bottom step, listening. Had he heard something? God, he hoped not. He had no idea what there was about that room that bothered him so. What there was about that skeleton— even before all the strange happenings began—that . . . haunted him. Yes. Haunted was exactly the word. He'd seen burial exhibits before, numerous times. Even an

Egyptian mummy in its blackened wrappings. But none of those had created more than a vague unease about the just use of a past culture's dead in public exhibits. Homicides, especially those when the body hadn't been discovered until only science could produce identification, were the only things that came close to evoking this reaction in him.

No. He wouldn't go upstairs. Not until he had to. God knew that would be soon enough.

He had the coffee made, the fires turned up, and the chill off the kitchen by the time he heard a pickup climb the driveway and brake to a stop outside.

He met Wayne Samuels at the kitchen door. Margaret waved from the truck but left without coming in.

"Anne's still asleep," he said, warning the other man to silence.

Samuels nodded, shrugged out of his jacket, hung it on a peg, and crossed to the coffeepot. "Rough night?"

Rough night, rough week, David thought. "Yeah. Coffee?"

"Always."

Samuels took his coffee hot and black. He leaned against the cabinet as he sipped it and glanced at the completed ceiling. "Not a bad job for a cop and a lady doctor," he admitted.

David studied Samuels. "Hell, if I'd known you were an expert," he said cordially, "I'd have invited you to help Thursday."

Samuels raised an eyebrow. "And risk having three angry women driving us out of the kitchen for spoiling their meal?"

David shrugged, and Samuels turned serious.

"You want to run out to the Tompkins place and grab some clothes? I can look out after your lady while you're gone."

"I don't think so," David said.

"I didn't either," Samuels admitted. "I know I wouldn't. What is it I'm supposed to be looking for?"

"I told Blake you probably wouldn't find anything this time, either."

"But I'll look anyway. So tell me why he thinks I need to look, and why, after a week you've suddenly decided the doc needs your protection at night."

How much could he tell this man without telling him everything? How much of the truth did he owe Samuels? Enough to keep him from getting killed.

"I don't suppose you and Blake will just go away and let Annie and me work this out by ourselves?"

Samuels gave a short bark of laughter. "Me, Blake, and Maggie," he corrected. "I told you she liked the doc. If it wasn't for Maggie, I never would have come Thursday, and Blake would still be trying to talk me into coming today."

"Right." David motioned toward the table. Samuels shook his head and remained at the counter. With a grimace, David leaned back against the sink. "Friday morning I told Blake what you thought you'd seen up here Wednesday night, and asked him about mountain lions— No, hell no. It goes back farther than that. Probably a lot farther. But for now, let's just go back to Wednesday.

"Anne and I found—a couple of things in the house, things that we now believe her Uncle Ralph brought in when he was dealing in artifacts from the Spiro mounds. Wednesday we sent them out, one to a collector I know in Dallas, another to a pathologist Anne knows in Chicago. Wednesday night you saw the cats. Yesterday, the collector was killed by some sort of wild animal. Also yesterday, a lab tech in Chicago was killed by some sort of wild animal. And last night we heard something, something big, pacing."

"Where?"

That was it? No reaction other than to ask where? As though this were an old story Samuels was hearing repeated?

David glanced at him. No. He saw no mockery, no ridicule, just a patient waiting.

So why not tell him? Why the hell not? "Upstairs."

Samuels scratched at the back of his neck. "And outside?"

"Maybe Wednesday," David admitted. "About the time we found the things."

"Wednesday night?"

"No. Earlier. One, two o'clock in the afternoon."

"You're right. I probably won't find anything. My uncle didn't when Marian Hansom took her dive down the stairs and blamed it on a couple of cats, and he was the best tracker ever born."

"That story again. Anne's mother mentioned it, but she also said Marian is 'crazy as a bessie bug,' whatever the hell one of those is."

"Yeah, she's that all right. Cats and curses. Uncle James said that was all she talked about. He looked for cats, outside, but found no sign of them. And, according to him, the curse sounded like an even bigger figment of her imagination."

"Anne's mother mentioned that, too. She said Marian claimed Ralph had infuriated some ancient god."

David expected Samuels's short bark of laughter. What he got was silence, and a reflective look.

"More than likely he infuriated some supplier or collector," Wayne said finally, "if what I've heard about his business dealings is anywhere near the truth. That would probably explain why his Buick went off the side of the mountain after leaving a quarter of a mile of real erratic skid marks."

"Murder?"

Samuels's mouth twisted in what could have been a smile, could have been a frown. "Maybe."

"Maybe. And nobody checked it out?"

"Hey, I'm telling tales I heard as a kid from someone who wasn't even there years before. But as I recall the story, no one thought old Ralph's death was any big loss to anybody. But it wouldn't explain why— Holy hell!"

"What?" David asked."

Samuels's mouth twisted again, and this time it was obviously into a bitter grin. "Why his body was mauled. Everybody thought it was probably a bear. But nobody checked."

"Your uncle?"

"Was logging at Pine Valley. Didn't come home until a couple of months later."

The two men exchanged troubled, silent questions.

"Look," David said, and knew he was going to have to say more. "I think we're safe. I can't tell you how I know this, but there seems to be a pattern in the attacks, at least the ones yesterday— I won't know about the others until I can talk to someone who remembers, and Annie and I planned to start doing that today. In fact, I had considered asking you to stick around while we're gone, not because of any supernatural threat but because I don't trust Joe not to send someone up to snoop around if he knows we're gone. But for God's sake, be careful."

"And Maggie? She's coming back for me later. Will she be in any danger?"

"No."

Annie's voice sounded from the doorway. Both men swiveled to look at her. She'd dressed warmly for their trip, and had her hair scalped back in that no-nonsense knot she wore it in when working. She looked rested, as though she had gotten a good night's sleep for the first time in a long time. Well, David was glad someone had. But she was pale. Too pale. How much had she heard?

"No," she repeated. "Neither of you will be in danger. Because you won't be here."

"Annie—"

"No, David. I won't put anyone else in jeopardy."

"But we can't leave the house unattended. You know what that could mean. And I won't leave you here alone."

She smiled at him. "If you would leave my friends here, if you're sure they will be safe, why shouldn't I be just as safe, alone, without you?"

"Because you won't stay out of the damned room."

Her smile drained from her. She closed her eyes as a wave of memory moved visibly over her features. "I won't, will I?" she said softly.

"Annie, damn it." In four long strides he was at her side, his arm around her shoulder. Supporting her? Or keeping her from running back to grieve at the feet of a long-dead man? "Here," he said, guiding her to the table. "Sit."

She popped up from the chair like a damned jack-in-the-box, thrusting her chin out. "Don't be silly. I'm all right. And I'm perfectly capable of—"

"Maybe you'd both better sit," Samuels said, stretching up from his slouch at the counter. "I've got work to do outside before the frost melts."

Wayne returned to the house just as David and Anne were leaving.

David didn't have to ask if he'd found anything; Samuels nodded at him as he shrugged out of his jacket.

"What?" David asked.

Wayne crossed the room and waited until David and Anne stepped back into the kitchen before turning and looking at David's boots. "You been out in back lately? Taken anyone with you?"

"I walked around the barn Wednesday, and I took Hank Foresman on a tour of the outbuildings a week ago when he showed up claiming to want work."

Samuels shook his head. "Hank wears Redwing workboots. Whoever was out there hadn't been there when I checked out the place Thursday morning. His tracks cross the ones we left in the soft ground later that day. He was wearing a western boot, riding heel, about a size ten. It could have been Thursday night. It could have been last night. The ground didn't freeze solid till way after midnight this morning."

"It wasn't Thursday night; I checked out the place Friday morning. Hell, I was out there last night, looking for a damned cat. Where?"

"You name it. He scoped out the well house, the barn, most of the windows on the ground floor, came up on that porch outside the room where we watched the game Thursday, maybe tried the doors, maybe just looked."

David felt Anne's fingers clutch his arm. "All the windows?" she asked.

Samuels nodded.

"You'll stay?" David asked. "I'm not sure how long we'll be, I guess that depends on what we find and who we find to talk with, but it's got to take at least a couple of hours just to get up there and back."

"I'll stay. You take as long as you need. Maggie's coming back for me and we don't have anything else planned for the day. But you two be careful."

"Thanks. You, too."

They were on the porch before Samuels spoke again. "What room?"

Annie's hand jerked on his arm. David turned to look at the man.

"I don't intend to prowl your house, Doc. But if I hear something, I need to know which room I shouldn't go in."

Annie looked up at him, her eyes shadowed with the doubts and questions written in them. But damn it, they had to trust someone. And if they trusted Samuels enough to leave him here to guard this mystery, they owed him at least enough knowledge to, maybe, keep himself safe. Annie drew in a deep breath and nodded.

"Marian's sitting room," he said. "The one at the end of the first hall toward the back of the house. The one with the lavatory and parlor stove."

"The one that looks like it doesn't belong in this house?"

"Yeah," David told him. "That one."

They took the Blazer. David drove. Anne stared out into the fog that had descended into the cracks and crevices of the mountains, then down at it when the road climbed to follow the upper ridges. At this altitude, the hardwood trees had shed their leaves, and their bare limbs reached upward toward the pale early-morning winter light. Pleading, or prayer, she wondered as she studied those outstretched branches. Sometimes she wondered if there was a difference. Yes. Yes, there was. At least with prayer you had a hope of being answered.

She glanced at David. He didn't notice. All his attention seemed to be focused on something, probably the twists of the road as it wound along the ridges, dipping into patches of fog, rising out of them into the light.

He'd gone back into her house before they drove away, leaving her in the kitchen while he went into the interior for several minutes. He didn't tell her what he'd done, or what he carried in the small box he placed in the back of the Blazer. She didn't ask. She didn't want to know. Then they'd made a brief stop at his cabin, where he changed clothes and filled a small bag, before they headed north. He was once again crisply starched and pressed, as he had been that first day. And he looked so solemn. So unapproachable. Was this the man who had led her from the upstairs room last night, so fierce and yet so gentle, and who had held her through the night?

What had happened last night? What in God's name had happened?

She never sleepwalked. Not even as a child. But the dream had been so real. So real. And now she couldn't even remember what it had been about. But David had been in it. Oh, yes. David had definitely been in it.

And he had been in the one that followed, the one she remembered too clearly in every intimate detail, after he had returned her to her room. After he had plopped himself down outside the covers and anchored her in place with his arm. After he had burrowed his way under the blanket with her and dragged her against him. He hadn't awakened then, but she had, enough to hear him murmur her name, enough to feel him nuzzle at her throat and moan before dropping deeper into sleep.

The road wound its way down from the ridge into the valley surrounding Fairview just as the fog began to lift. Dim, thin light surrounded them, but it was growing brighter.

"You didn't have any breakfast this morning," David said, breaking the silence. "Do you want to stop? We can have fast food—the real thing."

She heard the teasing in his voice and felt herself relaxing marginally. He hadn't gone completely away from her after all. "Stop if you want. Coffee would be nice, but I'm really not hungry."

"I know what you mean." He stopped at a convenience store on the south edge of town. "Do you want to go in?"

She shook her head.

He came out a few minutes later with two large cups of coffee. He also had a couple of brochures and a bag of fresh doughnuts.

"They had a tourist information rack by the cash register," he told her, handing her the brochures. "These don't look as though they have a whole lot of information, but it's got to be more than we know."

"Spiro Mounds," Anne read aloud from the cover of the first brochure, which bore the picture of some sort of small statue of a kneeling male figure.

She opened the first brochure. "Did you read these?" she asked.

"No." David perched the cups in the slots of the plastic holder some previous owner had rigged on the dash and started the Blazer. "I just grabbed them. Why don't you fill me in as we drive?"

Anne nodded and opened the brochure. A drawing of a man, stretched forward probably in ceremonial dance, dominated the center. "Oh."

"What?" David asked sharply.

She held the brochure so that he could see. The man's legs and feet were bare except for bands of beads, much like bracelets on each ankle and just below his knees. But his upper body and arms were covered in a form-fitting pelt, which flowed into a mask completely covering his head. At least, she thought it was a mask. Four strands of beads circled his neck. Other beads circled his wrists. And his hands— Were they hands? Were those claws part of the costume for the dance? Or were they—

"Jaguar," David said. "Hell. Read."

Anne read. About the twelve mounds the park encompassed. About the civilization that had built them between A.D. 850 and 1450. About the site's importance in the commerce of the day, about its association with other mound sites throughout the southeast. About the ceremonies for the celebration of the seasons and the rituals centered on the death and burial of the elite.

There wasn't much, just enough to whet an appetite for information. But there were pictures. Pictures with no captions showing shells with the designs Anne had been seeing all of her life, pictures of a pleasant, tree-shaded, park-like setting with a series of hillocks.

Anne dropped the brochure to her lap and picked up the next one and turned it over, and then almost dropped it, too.

"Oh. Oh, no. No."

"Annie?"

"It's him," she said, clutching the brochure in both hands. "It's him."

David pulled to the shoulder of the road and set the emergency brake. "Let me see," he said. He reached for the folder. "Annie, let me see."

She gave him the folder, appalled by the protectiveness she felt for no more than a line drawing.

And it was just a line drawing, she realized as David looked at it, as she looked at it again. A face, dark eyes, strong chin, firm lips. The hair, the roach, the back of the head—these were not drawn, merely represented by a series of lines that could indicate shadow. A face. A part of a face. The long forelock drawn through two round beads. The visible earspool carrying the image of—of what?—an elephant? If so, an elephant as she had never seen one. And around the eye, a painted design pointing to the ear.

She traced that design with her fingers.

"It's called forked eye," David told her.

He returned the brochure and sank back against his seat. "It's a drawing. Just a drawing. Probably a composite the artist made up. I'll concede the similarity in the earspool, but there's not an ounce of copper showing. What makes you so sure this is our guy?"

"I don't— Yes. Yes, I do. The medallions. The ones in the cedar box."

"They're symbolic, Annie, and highly stylized. How can you see a resemblance between either of them and this drawing—"

"Because I looked at them, David, really looked, and you didn't. Just as you haven't really looked at this drawing. Why?"

He didn't answer. Instead, he held out his hand. She placed the brochure in it and watched him. He looked, but it was obvious he didn't want to. Why not? What could it cost him to look? But it was costing him something, that much was as evident as his forced examination of the drawing.

"Maybe," he said. He thrust the brochure at her and started the engine. "Maybe."

The state park containing the Spiro Mounds was miles from the little town of Spiro, miles off the state highway, almost on the Arkansas River, and within sight of one of the many lock and dam structures that had made the river once again navigable.

David circled the small, almost empty parking lot and

pulled the Blazer into a slot near the sidewalk leading to the front door.

The building was unobtrusive, built low to the ground and partially earth-bermed, with a concrete and square-post bower guarding the walk, while a concrete table and benches sat beneath a nearby tree. Anne waited quietly while David got out of the Blazer and walked toward the front of the truck. From this angle, she could see a group of low mounds off to the right, against a backdrop of trees as stark and winter-bare as the one that guarded the picnic table. She didn't want to get out. She didn't want to go any closer. But when David started toward her door, she opened it herself and stepped out.

He turned, and she saw that his attention, too, had been trapped by the stepping-stone mounds to the right.

"Those have to be the ones in the brochure," she said.

"Yes." He reached for her hand and clasped it. "Yes."

Why couldn't the place be closed? This was, after all, a holiday weekend. But no, they found the door unlocked, their path unimpeded.

The entryway faced a small counter of what appeared to be gift items and a rack of publications. A guest register lay open on the glass countertop. David picked up the pen but lay it down without signing. She looked at him but recognized the wisdom of remaining at least partially anonymous for the moment. She nodded and turned toward the open area to the right.

Clearly visible through the walls of windows that faced them, the mounds spread out across a well-tended lawn: the stepping-stone ones to the right, a large one almost directly in front of them that beneath its mantle of tan winter grass looked as though someone had taken a backhoe to the very top of it and had left it ravaged, others behind and to the left of that. To the right, below the cluster of mounds, was a primitive thatch-roofed house.

Only then did she notice the display cases of exhibits placed tastefully throughout the room. Only then did she turn and see the mural. She sucked in her breath. There, larger than life, the cat-man of the first brochure crouched in eternal dance among a group of other, symbolic dancers.

She felt David step closer to her and drop his hand on her shoulder. She raised her hand to his and fought the urge to shrink against him. This was a museum, nothing more. Those hills out there had been built hundreds of years before and had been ransacked decades ago. Did anything remain of the people who had built them?

A woman dressed in a pressed khaki uniform stood talking to a family near the doors leading out to the park. Two children, a boy perhaps ten and a girl about eleven, seemed to be the ones questioning the guide. David gave Anne's shoulder a squeeze and guided her into the display area.

Shells. Lots of shells and fragments. A small statue identified as a pipe. Ear spools. Small pieces of what was probably a cedar pole. A tattered remnant of lace. Fragments of a civilization long gone.

Three folio-sized books occupied pedestals placed in front of the waist-high window ledge. Anne walked to them, avoiding the view outside those windows. She scanned the books' captions until she found one containing drawings of the copper artifacts found during the excavations.

Slowly she leafed through the book. Hawks. Dancers. Gorgets. Human heads. Feathers.

She looked up at David in confusion. "There are no cats."

"Sshh." He nodded toward the guide and visitors.

"But where are the bodies?" the boy asked. "Skeletons? Bones? Mummies?"

His parents both gave self-conscious laughs.

"No bodies," the guide said pleasantly.

"Well, what kind of graveyard is this?"

"Daniel! Hush!" The mother took the boy's arm and began leading him toward the front door. "Thank you for your time—"

"Well, where are they?" the boy asked again, with a voice full of unthinking bloodlust.

In my closet, Anne thought. David rubbed his hand up and down her arm as a shudder worked its way through her.

The guide watched quietly until the family left, then shook her head and chuckled. She walked to where Anne stood with David beside the book of drawings.

The badge on the guide's uniform shirt identified her as Frances Collins. The slight, almond slant to her eyes, the café au lait tint to her flawless complexion, and the reddish cast to her straight, dark hair, identified her as a blend—a beautiful blend—of races: Choctaw, black and— What? Irish? Anne felt an instant affinity with her. And why not? If the woman was from this area, they probably had at least one ancestor in common. Wouldn't *that* thrill her mom's cousin Harriet?

"Hello. Can I help you with anything? Answer any questions?"

Lots of questions, Anne thought, if she only had the nerve to ask them.

David stepped forward and extended his hand. "Thank you, Ms. Collins. We're rank amateurs so we'll probably have lots of very basic questions."

"That's my job," she said cheerfully.

"I heard the boy ask about bodies," David said. "These were burial mounds?"

"Some of them." She pointed out the window to the stair-step mounds. "That's Craig Mound, the site of what we call the Great Mortuary, and, to the south, on that smaller mound, the crematory basin." She turned slightly and pointed toward the hillock from which the top had been gouged. "But Brown Mound also contained a significant number of burials."

"Crematory basin?" David asked. "Then the charming little boy who just left would have trouble finding a body, wouldn't he?"

Again the guide chuckled. "Not so much. While most of the burials were secondary burials . . ."

She broke off when she recognized Anne's puzzled glance.

"Secondary, in that the dead were buried once, then later exhumed, the bones cleaned and reinterred."

Anne nodded, an understanding of the term but not of the images it called forth.

"While most of them were secondary burials, a number of the higher ranking burials were primary, or just the one time, litter burials."

"With grave goods?" David asked.

"Yes. That's what makes the Spiro site such an important find." The woman frowned slightly. "And what almost destroyed it."

"Pothunters?" David asked.

"Oh, yes. Full-time, commercial ones."

"Who were they?" Anne asked. "The people who built these mounds?"

Ms. Collins cocked her head slightly, but accepted the change of subject. "They were a Mississippian culture, probably related by trade and religion with other

Mississippian centers, such as that at Cahokia in Illinois and Etowah in Georgia."

"And the Aztec?" David asked. "I see a similarity in some of the designs—the snakes, the speech symbol, the cats."

"You're not such a rank amateur after all, are you?" Ms. Collins said with a grin.

"About Spiro, yes, I really am," David admitted. "But I have done some reading about meso-American pre-history." Anne saw his bad-little-boy smile dart out and waited for whatever outrageous statement he would make to disarm this woman. When it came, it wasn't so outrageous after all. "Searching for my roots."

"Yes, well . . ." But it had disarmed. Frances Collins paused for a moment, smiled her understanding, and continued. "There's been an ongoing controversy about the meso-American connection for the past fifty years. Depending on who you read, and in what decade, either there was no connection whatsoever, or the Spiro people were engaged in trade with the southwest. What has become accepted is that the Spiro site evolved from one of several cultural centers in this area to the major cultural and trade center of the vast interior of this country. We've found evidence of trade with the Great Lakes, or Mexico, once again depending on your source and time frame, in the copper sheets used for engraving, to the Gulf of Mexico, probably the Florida peninsula, for the conch shells that were found in such profusion, and to the Rockies, although that was argued for a while, too, for various Bison products."

"Didn't a number of cultures use the conch shell?" David asked.

"Yes. In small pieces. And even entire, for storage containers, but we've yet to find the intact shells engraved as they have been here."

David walked to another of the large books, which had been left open to a drawing of a small statue that appeared to be a warrior or executioner decapitating the figure over which he crouched. "Young Daniel would have been right at home," he said. "Warlike, weren't they?"

"Maybe. But we found no evidence of any fortification of this site. They did control the river, which was the major trade route. And maybe their spiritual leaders were so strong, they grew out of the need for fortifications."

"What happened to them?" Anne asked.

Ms. Collins shook her head. "No one really knows. The best guess is a prolonged drought and the subsequent reduction in the supply of food to support the population in the villages surrounding Spiro, and perhaps a subsequent reduction in the faith necessary to support the hierarchy of the elite. In any event, by then this location was strictly ceremonial, with only a very few of the highest leaders living on the grounds.

"The villages shrank and finally disappeared as the remaining people became more nomadic, more 'hunter-gatherer' than farmer or craftsman. But we believe descendants of these people were still here at the time of European immigration—still are, as the Caddo or possibly the Wichita peoples."

"They weren't conquered and hauled away as happened in so many other places?" David asked.

"No. This world ended more with a whimper than a bang. However, an early rumor, started, I think, at the time the railroad was built through what was then the Choctaw Nation, held that a huge battle had been fought in the Redland Bottoms just west of here. That rumor persisted for years, still does among some of the locals, even though we've learned that what the railroaders uncovered was probably no more than the cemetery for one or more of the villages surrounding Spiro.

"Then they weren't all buried here?"

"No. At least not in the later days. I don't know what the cut-off rank was, because not all of the burials here were of equal rank, but it was probably pretty high. And there seems to be evidence to support that if one were that rank or above, his body, his grave goods, and maybe even his retainers were brought here for their final rest. Which might account for a number of the secondary burials."

"You're very knowledgeable about these people," Anne said.

Ms. Collins laughed. "I hope so. I grew up three miles away, hearing these stories from before I can remember, and I finished my master's degree in archaeology last spring." She grinned conspiratorially at David. "My own roots, you understand. I start work on my doctorate next fall, but I had to take a year off to be near my grandfather."

"Then you're the archaeologist in charge of this location?"

Ms. Collins' easy smile faded. "No. No way. I'm strictly interim. One year while my grandfather recovers and while the state finds someone qualified to take over here. Why don't we go out into the park? We have an interpretative walk."

Now it was Frances Collins who changed the subject. How interesting, Anne thought, but she followed the guide to the door leading outside, even managed to step one foot through it, when she realized she couldn't go any farther. Not even with David's arm around her shoulder. Not even with him close enough for her to feel his warmth. Not even with the questioning look

Frances Collins shot her as she stopped and refused to move forward.

"Go on," Anne said. "Please. It's— I— I'm sorry. I can't go out there."

Ms. Collins turned abruptly and ushered them back into the building. Taking Anne's arm, she led them through the displays, outside, and to the picnic table. "Sit," she said.

Anne did. Gratefully. While David watched, not puzzled but concerned.

"Annie?"

She felt his hand on the back of her neck. She wanted to speak, to assure him that she was all right, that she was *not* going to faint. What kind of wimp did he think she had become? But she seemed to have lost the strength necessary even to form words.

"It affects some people that way," Ms. Collins said. "Not many, but some. God, I wouldn't have this as a full-time job if my life depended on it."

18

When he was sure Anne wasn't going to keel over in a faint, David went back into the museum, to the vending machine he had seen down the one dark hall to the right, and slugged coins into it. He returned and handed Anne a can of Coke.

"Drink it," he said when she looked up questioningly. "You need the caffeine and the sugar."

"I thought I was the doctor in this road show," she said, but her smile was wan and her voice too weak to reassure him, in spite of her cheeky words, and she clutched the can like a lifeline.

Frances Collins leaned against the end of the table, not quite sitting, not quite hovering. He hadn't forgotten what she'd said, but only when he saw Annie's color returning to something approaching normal did he feel free to turn any attention to the guide.

"You say this happens often?"

"No," she said. "Not to this extent. Never to this extent. Are you all right now?"

Annie reached for his hand and squeezed it. Was she all right? He'd hoped getting her out of that house would get her away from the influence of whatever the hell they'd unlocked in that room. Obviously it hadn't.

"We need some answers," he said.

"Yes. I can see that. Would you like to go into my office?"

Annie glanced at the building. She'd go; he could see that in the determined lift of her shoulders. But she didn't want to.

"No," he said. The fog had lifted entirely. Winter sun warmed the air and the concrete table and benches. "It's pleasant out here, Ms. Collins."

"Frances," she told him, told both of them. "I have a feeling we've just progressed at least to first name status."

Anne managed a smile. "Probably farther than that," she said, extending her hand to the woman. "I'm Anne Locke."

They shook hands, and Frances turned to him.

"David Huerra," he told her, not at all sure they should be divulging any more than absolutely necessary, but recognizing in the sharing of their identities a trade of sorts. Information for information.

"That wasn't so bad, was it?" Frances asked. "Now, what is it you came to learn?"

"Were we that obvious?" Anne asked.

"Other than deliberately not signing the guest book? Other than not seeming surprised by the diversity of the exhibits even though you'd never been in before? Other than seeming to have a purpose in your search of them rather than the usual first-timers' meandering examination? Other than going directly to the book on copper and searching it as though looking for something specific? Well, no."

Frances counted off each point on her fingers and smiled as she said this, and, remarkably, David found himself smiling, too. "You'd make a good cop if you decide against archeology."

"Thanks, but I'm afraid I'm still operating on classroom time. Sorry. So. What do you want to know?"

He glanced at Annie. She nodded. Hell, why not? "Are you familiar enough with Spiro artifacts to be able to identify something for us?"

"Maybe. Most of them are pretty distinctive. There are some designs that overlap with other Mississippian locations, but there are some that are uniquely Spiro."

He'd folded the tracing and stuck it in his windbreaker pocket before they left Anne's house. Now he pulled it out and handed it to Frances Collins.

"Oh."

Her fingers caressed the penciled outlines with a reverence he had seen only a few times before. Jack Townley had almost had it. An ancient man he had met in Mexico City definitely had.

Anne sighed. "I guess that's our answer, isn't it?"

"Yes." David dropped his hand onto her shoulder and left it there, gripping her with a tension he recognized but couldn't seem to subdue. "What would something like that be worth today?"

"Depends." Frances laughed. "Doesn't everything? I heard of a broken one going for twenty-five thousand. But that was probably a rumor. And there are reproductions now being sold as original, points, fragments, things like that." She studied the sketch. "It's original?"

Anne nodded.

"And it wasn't ceremonially killed?"

"No." David answered her this time. None of it had been. Not one item accompanying the warrior had been damaged. Only the slight nick on this piece, and it could have been done before the burial. "Is that significant?"

"Yes. In that it probably denotes a really high-status

burial." She touched the drawing once more before returning it to him. "Conservatively, ten to fifteen thousand without documentation. Fifty to a hundred thousand with documentation."

He felt Anne tense beneath his hand. A fortune. A bleeding fortune. But hadn't they both already known that?

"Where are—" Anne smiled up at him before plunging onward. "You have only a few artifacts here. Where are the rest of them kept?"

"We have *no* originals here."

"What?"

Frances shook her head. "I guess you noticed this is not the most secure location in the world. We simply cannot afford to take the risk of losing another piece, and the insurance on the original of something like, well, like the basalt pipe you saw in the case is unbelievably expensive. The Resting Warrior pipe depicted in so much of the early literature is owned by the University of Arkansas. It's insured for a million and a half."

He felt the breath whoosh out of Annie.

"As for the rest of the artifacts, they're all over the world. During the commercial digging, before Oklahoma's antiquities laws were finally passed and took effect, there were buyers here at the site, literally snatching up everything the diggers brought out. It's been estimated that fully eighty percent of all high-status art in the U.S. was located in the mounds here at Spiro. There were more copper and conch items found here than at all the other North American sites combined. And now it's scattered. France, England, Germany, South America. Even China."

"But surely some of it was—was—"

Again Frances shook her head, but this time she found a smile for Annie. "Sure. Some of it. After the

W.P.A. and the University of Oklahoma took over the excavations. But by that time over four hundred burials, most of them high status, had already been disturbed. The commercial diggers had dug seven tunnels into Craig Mound—they called it the Great Temple Mound—and before they left, they dynamited all but one of their tunnels. Of course, by then, so much damage had already been done, the blasting probably didn't do that much additional damage. When the W.P.A. took over in June of '36 this place looked like a minefield. And much of the record that would have helped us understand a civilization as rich and powerful as the one that flourished here for—what? a thousand years or so, here and in the surrounding area—was gone. Scattered. Irretrievable."

Annie was getting ready to speak. He could sense it in the tension beneath his hand. Getting ready to say something that probably should never be said. "You recognized what was happening to Anne." If he was speaking, she couldn't. Not yet. "And you said you wouldn't have this job full time if your life depended on it."

Frances laughed softly. "I'd hoped you missed that. Now who's acting like a cop?"

David grinned at her, but he didn't relent. "Why, Frances?"

"Fair enough."

She'd said it easily, but now she seemed at a loss for words. With a glance at Anne—for reassurance that she wasn't going to be scoffed at?—she began.

"I told you I'm interim only. I'm not the archaeologist in charge. I refused to be the archaeologist in charge. Winston Harris, my immediate predecessor, youngish—mid-thirties—a classmate of mine in undergrad studies, had a heart attack after only three months on the job. But why should he have been immune?

Everyone in charge of this site has suffered some problem, mental, emotional, physical. Alcoholism, insanity, divorce, a bleeding ulcer—you name it, it's probably happened here.

"One not technically in charge, but closely connected, had his dissertation on Spiro and all his notes go up in a fire in his tent while on another excavation.

"Three members of the W.P.A. crews died in cave-ins on this site.

"And that doesn't even begin to touch the things that happened to some of those involved in the commercial dig; drowning facedown in a dry stream bed; being trapped in a cave-in while everyone else got out; crashing into a tree because the brake line was severed—forged, not cut or worn; painful, disfiguring cancer.

"And then there were those we only suspect were connected to the Spiro site. Collectors who were brutally murdered. One man who locked himself in a bank vault with a basket of Spiro pearls and was found dead the next morning—and the pearls were missing.

"I come out here sometimes at night, not because I want to, but because I can't seem to help myself. There's a heaviness here, after dark, that weighs down on me." She laughed self-consciously. "Even my stomach tingles. And concepts come so vividly—always, here—but more so at night.

"I can almost see . . .

"Some of this comes from growing up here, of hearing the rumors, even of seeing that damned huge feather cloak before the house where it was on display burned. But at night I can almost see that pair of big gold cats the old-timers talked about prowling the mounds.

"And I can almost— I *can* see the aura that seems to hover over the mounds."

She laughed again. "And of course we can't keep one blasted mechanical thing working for any length of time."

Annie had picked up on the word cats; hell, he had too. But not yet. He couldn't let her get into that yet. "Cloak, you said? Feather cloak?"

She nodded. "Six, eight feet long. At least a hundred and twenty pounds. It was supposed to have come out of the central chamber in Craig Mound, the chamber that most experts claim didn't really exist, at least not as more than a collapsed area between litter-borne burials, certainly not as a separate chamber. But Gramps said it did, said that when they broke into it, it whooshed like a sealed vacuum being opened, that big cedar poles making bins lined the walls, that there were boards painted with portraits that looked like Egyptians, and that there were maybe four burials there including the one with the cloak and the copper-covered giant that all the commercial diggers claim to have seen and no one knows what happened to. The experts say it probably didn't exist. My grandfather says it did."

"Who—" Now Annie spoke. "Who would wear a hundred and twenty pound feather cloak?"

"One heck of an important ruler. Maybe *the* priest, or *the* ruler. One thing for sure, he had to have had a fortune in grave goods with him, as well as a lot of faithful retainers and probably wives to follow him into the afterworld."

"Priest," David asked. "Not god?"

"No. Not god." Frances told them. "We think that these people had a naturalist religion that strove to control the forces of the spirits that inhabit animals, maybe even the elements. They probably worshipped to some degree, maybe only symbolically, the sun, moon, maybe the wind, rain, water, soil."

"And the giant?" Anne asked softly, intently. "Do you suppose he was one of the retainers of the priest?"

"No. I don't think so. From the way Gramps described him, he was—had to be—pretty powerful in his own right. He had to have been a high-status warrior who would have earned his own place in the hierarchy and would not accompany the priest in death. Instead he would be accompanied by his own attendants."

"And wives?" Annie asked.

"And wives," Frances said.

But he hadn't been. Or had he? How could they ever know now? How could Annie be so sure he had been alone?

"Can I talk with your grandfather?" Annie asked. "I need to talk with your grandfather."

For a moment Frances looked startled. "I'm sorry," she said finally. "He's had a stroke. That's why I'm home. To help my grandmother. He's recovering. But he still doesn't have his speech back. He may never have."

"No." Annie's voice softened and she reached for Frances's hand. "I'm the one who's sorry."

Frances shrugged off the dark mood that had momentarily claimed her. "You have more reason than just curiosity, don't you?"

Anne nodded. "Yes. You see my great uncle was probably at the digs at the same time your grandfather was. He was a dealer. He— He was responsible for removing a great deal of material from—from here."

Frances cocked her head to one side and stared at the drawing, now anchored to the table by Annie's Coke can. "And that's where that piece came from?"

Annie nodded. "That. And— And others. That I can't understand why he didn't get rid of because I think he died, if not in poverty then at least close to it except for the money his wife's family provided. Your grandfather might know him. And why . . . "

"I can ask. Communication isn't impossible, just horribly difficult. What was his name?"

"Hansom," Annie told her. "Ralph Hansom."

"Oh, shit." Frances had started to rise. Now she sat down abruptly. "The curse. The damned curse. He didn't get rid of it and now you can't."

Anne turned to look up at David. He stepped closer, pulling her back against him. But that wouldn't protect her. Would anything? "You've heard of him, then?"

Frances looked at him, shook her head, and laughed weakly. "Yeah. You might say that. You see, my grandfather wasn't particularly happy with what he had done here. This was during the depression, you remember, and this area had been depressed since before the Choctaw chose the losing side in the Civil War and had to free their slaves, then had to give them citizenship and a piece of the pie when the lands in the nation were allotted to individuals instead of being held in common title by the Choctaw Nation. Anyway, the commercial diggers were offering about the only jobs to be had. I heard Gramps say, more than once, that the items shipped out of the mounds were the major export for the county during that time.

"But, later, after his family was fed and clothed, he worried about his part in the grave-robbing. That's what he called it. The Choctaw had known these mounds were here for over a hundred years and not bothered them. And even though there had been some digging on the sly since—well, since God only knows when, probably since the first farmer managed to clear away the cane that covered most of these river-bottom lands by then and plowed up a conch shell or an ax, there wasn't any serious activity until 1933.

"And he helped. He took money to help desecrate a burial ground. At least that's how he looked at it after the fact. And that's how he told it to me while I was growing up. And when stories about curses and retribution crept in, so did your uncle's name.

"He bought something. Or stole it—Gramps was never very clear on that. And everyone who helped him died a brutal death. And everyone he tried to sell it to died a brutal death. And finally, he died a brutal death.

"Is that about what you'd heard?"

Annie closed her eyes and leaned against David, gathering strength. She reached into her jacket pocket and took out the folded brochure with the warrior's picture on the cover. "This image," she asked. "Where did it come from?"

Frances glanced at the cover; he could tell she didn't have to study it. "From an engraving on a copper plate we found in a burial when we made some trial excavations on the plaza. That's the area between Brown, the mound with the top gouged out of it—the commercial diggers did that, too—and Copple, the mound just barely visible at the back of these grounds. Actually, I'm not sure it was a burial. We trenched through a house mound. There was a great deal of material, so we decided to excavate it completely. We found three bodies, but they didn't fit any of the patterns of burial we know. It was almost as if they had died and the house had been allowed to fall in and cover them. One of them, a woman, was wearing this as a breastplate."

"Can I see it?" Anne asked. "No. I suppose what I mean is, where can I see it?"

"I wish I knew," Frances said. "It— You have to know that Spiro artifacts have a long history of just disappearing. From locked vaults, from archived collections. In recent days, these disappearances haven't been of major items, nothing like the Resting Warrior or Big Boy pipes, but little pieces—a little piece here, a little piece there. This breastplate is one of those pieces. Why?"

Anne reached for his hand. She was going to say it, and nothing he could say or do would stop her. He caught her hand in his and held tightly.

"Because we found the warrior he was modeled after. The one in the central chamber. The copper-clad giant that doesn't exist. And since we found him, two people have died brutal deaths."

They went back inside. Anne knew they would either have to do that, or leave, when a small but steady stream of visitors began arriving at the museum. Parked in Frances's cramped little office, surrounded by magazines, books, and articles about the Spiro people, about the artifacts, about the authorized excavations and the commercial digging, Anne sat with her eyes closed, listening as David paged through book after book. Looking for something. Looking for what? Answers? Did he honestly think he'd find answers to what faced them in those books?

He slammed one shut and scraped his chair as he stood and tried to pace in the crowded room. She opened her eyes and looked up. She'd seen him in many moods this past week, but never agitated like this.

"It's worth a fortune, Annie," he said from a temporary pause in his march at the corner of an overflowing bookcase. "We already suspected that, though, didn't we?"

She didn't answer; he didn't seem to need one.

"But not just in money," he went on. "Do you have any idea how much information can be gained from what your uncle hid in the dark fifty years ago?"

Frances opened the door and stepped into the room as David was speaking. She leaned against the doorjamb, silent, waiting.

"Him," Anne said, tired beyond belief. "He."

David shot her a sharp glance. "Why do I have the feeling I'm not going to like what you say?"

But maybe she wasn't too tired to smile. Just a little. "Probably because you won't. Probably because neither one of you will. He's not an *it*, David, or a *what*. He's a man who was buried with honor and dignity, then ripped from that grave. Aside from the fact that whatever is killing these people won't let us disturb him any more than he's already been disturbed, why on earth should we even want to? Why can't he be left alone? Why should he have to become some sort of encyclopedia? Is desecrating his grave for that purpose really any better than desecrating it for money"

"You don't want the money?"

"Oh, God, no."

He threw his head back and twisted his neck and shoulders, easing tight muscles, before sighing. "Don't you think we have an obligation to science, or history, or even to the people who once lived at this very site, to share what knowledge can be gained from this . . . from *his* burial?"

"I don't know, David. I just don't know."

He walked to where she sat and leaned against the edge of the desk, taking her hand in his. "What do you want, Annie? The decision is up to you. He's yours, you know."

What did she want? What had she wanted last night when she knelt at the warrior's feet, crying. What had she wanted when she held the cedar box and miniatures in her hand and grieved for something and someone she had no way of understanding?

One thing she did understand.

"No, he isn't mine," she said. "If I think that, I'm no different from my uncle. What do I want? I think what I want is for him to be at peace. After all these hundreds of years since he died, is that too much to ask?"

"And if we can do both?" Frances asked softly. "Would you be willing to let me try to find a way to do both?"

Anne turned to face the woman, feeling the strength in David's touch flowing into her as he continued to grasp her hand. "Can you?"

"I don't know. I can only try."

Anne looked up at David, but he offered no opinion, telling her by his silence that this decision was hers alone to make. But was it? Wasn't he as deeply involved in everything that was happening, had happened, as she? But he gave her the decision, and she made it. She nodded. "Yes," she said. "Try. God knows we have to do something."

Anne remained silent during the drive to the highway, There, David hesitated at the stop sign. She'd seemed rested that morning. Had that only been an illusion? Because now she had shrunk back into herself, had shrunk into the corner of the Blazer, shutting him out. Damn it! Why was she shutting him out?

"What is it?" she asked when he remained stopped at the sign long after traffic had cleared.

"You didn't have breakfast," he said. "Frances said Fort Smith is only a few miles to the east. Why don't we find us a really good lunch?"

She dragged her head back and forth against the headrest. "Please. Could we just go home?"

Yeah. They could do that. Hell yes, they could do

that. Why not? Leaving obviously hadn't done her one bit of good. Without speaking, he turned right and headed them toward the road that would eventually take them back to Allegro.

She slept. Not well. With little whimpers and a frown or a grimace of pain on her face. In the mountains just north of the Pitchlyn County line, he debated unsnapping her seat belt and pulling her closer, regardless of the built-in obstacle course of the bucket seats and small console, regardless of the slight risk to her safety. Until he saw emergency lights flashing ahead.

"Damnation." His hand froze on the seat belt release. Slight risk to her safety? In the mountains? On a road with more curves and bumps than a roller coaster?

She awoke as he slowed and eventually stopped in the line of traffic waiting to be directed around the clutter of cars and trucks a hundred yards downhill, but now out of sight behind a slight curve.

"What is it?" she asked.

"A wreck, I think," he told her. "Maybe a pretty bad one if the number of emergency vehicles is any indication."

She blanched. That was the only word to describe what happened. Already pale, already wan, her complexion took on the color of old, grayish parchment. And her eyes filled with a dread as old as the mountains that surrounded them. But when they reached the officer who was directing traffic, she leaned across David, to the window he had opened, and spoke clearly, with no sign of what he would have sworn was panic.

"I'm a doctor," she told the officer. "Can I be of help?"

"Thank God," the young deputy said. "Yes, ma'am, you sure can. Will you park over there, sir?"

David parked on the shoulder of the road, behind a sheriff's cruiser. "Are you up to this?" he asked her.

Anne just looked at him, without answering, but that one look was answer enough. She wasn't up to it. Not in any way, shape, form, or fashion—and *why* wasn't she? the thought nagged at him—but she was going to do it.

She almost spoke, almost reached for his hand, then she drew into herself, even as she seemed to draw on some inner source of strength, and opened the door instead.

"Annie, you don't have to do this."

She turned to look at him for only a second. "Don't I?" she asked. Then she stepped from the Blazer and walked toward the knot of people clustered on the narrow verge beside the pile of cars.

A baby was screaming. A young woman was sobbing and fighting against the restraint of an officer who held her away from the small boy on the shady shoulder of the highway. The boy wasn't crying. His eyes were closed, but his mouth was held in a tight grimace. His pant leg was split from groin to ankle, and a huge open gash exposed muscle on his thigh. A teenage boy knelt beside him, holding a bloody shirt as a makeshift compress against the wound. Once Anne saw the injured boy, she seemed to lose all awareness of anyone else. She shrugged out of her coat and draped it across the child's chest as she dropped to his side. "I'm a doctor," she said again.

"Oh, thank God." The teenager's words echoed the deputy's, and he scurried aside to give her room.

"My bag—" She looked up at David. "Would you—" She took the shirt and pressed it against the wound. "I didn't bring it. What am I going to do? I didn't bring it."

What was happening? This wasn't the Anne Locke he had spent the last week getting to know, the competent woman he had grown to respect. And it had nothing to do with Spiro or her uncle or skeletons in the closet.

"Annie."

His voice stopped her flow of words, thank God. "I have a couple of clean undershirts in my duffel. Will they work for a compress?"

She nodded and turned back to the boy on the ground. While she held pressure on the gaping wound with one hand, she tested the tourniquet on his thigh, sought and found a pulse in his throat, spoke soothingly to him as she lifted his eyelid to check his pupil, and shifted to move closer to him while she crooned words of encouragement and comfort. David watched her for a moment. Yes. This was Anne. Pale. Drawn. But the Anne he knew. And she would be all right.

But the boy wouldn't be, if he didn't hurry.

When he returned with the clean undershirts, Anne looked up at him long enough to smile and check to see how he had folded them before she nodded toward the boy's thigh where the makeshift pad had soaked through.

"Let me," he said. He dropped to his knees beside her and eased the clean pad of his shirt into place and held it there, freeing her to discard the other and hold the boy in both her arms. "Like this?" he asked.

She nodded and moved even closer to the boy, now lying on the rocky ground as she shared her body's warmth and her soft touch. "Yes. Thanks. His name is Wayne. He's ten. I was telling him we have a friend named Wayne who can track wild animals through the woods. Wayne, this is David. He's a police detective in Dallas. I'll bet that if you go to Dallas someday, he'll show you all through the police department and tell you about some of his really big cases. Won't you, David?"

She was crying. Crying like she had last night. Tears streaming unchecked down her cheeks as she held the boy and rocked slightly against him. The people around them were quiet, as though they suspected the doctor and her assistant were merely going though the motions, that the battle had already been lost. Even the baby had stopped screaming and the mother had stopped fighting to get to her son's side.

No, damn it! This boy wouldn't bleed to death while they waited for an ambulance, and he wouldn't surrender to the pain and give up. "I sure will, Wayne," David told him, with not a trace of his frustration evident in his voice. "One of the men I work with played college baseball, almost went pro before he decided he'd rather be a cop. He does a lot of work with the young people in Dallas, and he's been known to get an autographed ball every now and then. You come to see me, and I'll make sure he has one of those balls for you. Who's your favorite player?"

Wayne didn't answer. By then his grimace had faded. David shot a sharp glance at Anne.

"He's passed out," she told him. "But he's still alive."

The scream of the approaching ambulances broke the silence, but even after they screeched to a stop behind the pile-up, it seemed an eternity before one emergency med tech moved in to take David's place with the pressure compress, and another moved to take Anne's place to monitor vital signs.

Only then did David notice another ambulance crew working over another victim. Alive? Or dead? Suddenly he didn't want Annie to know that Wayne hadn't been the only patient. He helped her to her feet, took her ruined coat as their young helper handed it to him, and turned her toward the Blazer, away from the sight of that other crew.

"Where will you take him?" he asked the EMT who had replaced him.

"St. Ed's in Fort Smith," the man told him.

David nodded and hugged Anne to his side. "We'll check later. Let's go now, Anne. Let's let these people do their job."

She didn't resist. Didn't argue. Didn't insist on following the boy to the hospital. And for that he was grateful. Because she looked just about one step from having to be taken there herself.

He loaded her into the passenger seat of the Blazer before he prowled through his duffel and found a teeshirt to sacrifice to the cleanup detail, then used it to wipe the blood from her hands and arms.

"So much blood," she said, not helping him, not fighting him. "So much blood." She looked straight ahead, out the opened door, not at him, not at the wrecked cars, not at the blood on her hands and his. "And I wasn't any more help today than I was then."

19

They stopped at a service station a few miles down the road to wash.

"You folks hurt in that wreck up on Simpson Knob?" the underaged station attendant asked as he followed them to the door of the restroom.

"No." David turned the water on full blast and washed off a grimy bar of soap before he handed it to Annie.

The attendant looked at the evidence of the carnage. "With all the ambulances that went through, it must have been a bad one."

He was a boy, David reminded himself. Just a boy. With no more concept of what carnage and mayhem and death really meant than young Daniel at the museum. Annie didn't answer; he wasn't sure she was able to. He didn't want to.

"Yeah," he said, offering no information, and finally the boy left them to the soap and hot water.

Anne scrubbed for a long time before he took the soap from her and handed her a wad of paper towels. While he scrubbed she dried, then sat on the closed lid of the toilet, her hands clasped between her knees, and stared at something he couldn't see.

He led her back to the Blazer. After a moment's consideration, he left her there and went into the station. There wasn't a big selection, but he bought a half-dozen candy bars, a couple of bags of cashews, and two cans of Coke, and piled it all into a small box he found on the cluttered and grease-stained counter near the cash register. He handed her the box when he returned to the Blazer, but she just held it as he pulled out of the service drive and once again started toward home.

Annie's silence, her near-shock state, was worrying him, a lot.

He saw a sign pointing to a boat landing off somewhere to the right. For a moment he hesitated. Would it be better just to take her on home? No, hell no, it wouldn't. Not in the state she was in. God only knew whatever it was in that house would do to her in this weakened and sensitive condition. He took the turnoff and followed the winding road to a finger of a small Corps of Engineers lake.

The parking area where he braked to a stop led to a boat launch where the water of the lake was beginning to lash angrily at the concrete ramp. The parking area served a picnic site, shaded in summer but now merely surrounded by bare trees. There was no other vehicle, no other person, in sight. One more small favor he'd have to give thanks for.

But the wind had picked up, and the sun had apparently decided to go home for the day. There was no way Anne could be warm enough at one of the picnic tables without her coat, and there was no way he was asking her to put her body in that bloodstained reminder of what she had just had to do. And his windbreaker, stashed now in the back with her coat, was only marginally less stained.

He left the engine running and adjusted the heater.

Then he freed himself from his seat belt, popped the top on a can of Coke, and peeled back the wrapper from a chocolate bar. He propped the Coke in the holder on the dash and rested the candy bar across its top as he turned toward Annie, as he unfastened her seat belt, as he turned her to face him.

He handed her the candy bar and waited, not speaking, until she had taken a bite from it. She chewed and swallowed and looked at him. "I know what you're doing."

He found a smile for her. "I thought you might. Eat. A little sugar rush will be good for you about now. And I have some cashews to force-feed you some protein for when that rush crashes."

She took another bite of the candy. "Damn. I never thought there'd come a time in my life when I'd have to make myself eat chocolate."

Her words were right, but her voice still wasn't. Her color still wasn't. And the time wasn't right, but then the time might never be right for what he was about to ask. And he had to ask. He waited until she finished the candy bar and half the Coke.

"Annie, why did you study medicine?"

She closed her eyes and let her head fall back until it rested against the high back of the seat. "I don't know any more," she said. "Once— Once I thought I might be able to help. Once I thought I had to help, I had to learn to heal."

"Once." The word sounded hollow in the enclosed car. "But not now?"

"You saw how ineffective I was today. You saw how I fell apart."

"I saw how you did your best in adverse circumstances. I saw how you comforted and loved your patient—"

"My best? Yeah. Maybe that was my best. Maybe all I'm capable of doing anymore is holding somebody and crying while he bleeds—while he . . ." Her voice broke, and her face twisted in pain. "While he dies."

And that's when he knew that her reaction had some basis in her concern for the boy they had just left, but even more in the robbery in Chicago that she had barely survived and so many others had not.

"Annie. Oh, God, Annie." He twisted and maneuvered himself across the narrow console into her seat, lifting her onto his lap and wrapping her in an embrace meant to keep her demons at bay.

Maybe it did for a while.

The tension eased from her as finally she took the comfort he offered her and lay against his chest with her face hidden from him against his neck. He couldn't see her tears, but he could feel them. And he could hear the words, as broken as they were, she gasped against his collar.

"I can't do this anymore," she said. To herself? To him? To God? Who knew? "I just can't do it anymore."

And then her sobs came, all the more terrible because at first she tried to hold them back. And couldn't. All the more terrible because he realized they must be the first she had allowed herself since the robbery took place—when?—almost a year ago?

"I begged them," she said, and he knew she was reliving that moment. "One of my patients was thirteen, still just a child. He tried to be a hero and they killed him first. I begged them to let the others go. They thought it was funny. They told me to get down on my knees. I did. I'd do it again. But it didn't matter. They laughed. And then they panicked.

"I can't see a child bleed—I can't see blood—without seeing that room and all the people who had trusted me, who had counted on me, without being back in that room with those half-crazed, half-grown . . . "

"Annie, Annie, you're not there now." He rubbed his hand across her back, trying to soothe her, trying to bring her back from the hell she was trapped in. "I have you. I have you and you're safe. You're not there now. You don't ever have to go back there. You don't have to face it alone. You'll never have to face anything alone again. I'm with you."

She sniffed once and stopped fighting her tears, stopped fighting her sobs. He held her, this strong, confident woman who had been forced to her knees to beg. For others. He hadn't missed that in her tortured stream of words. Not for herself but for others. And he hadn't missed hearing his own words, either, even though he didn't understand where they had come from and why they felt as though they had been too long unsaid. *You'll never have to face anything alone again. I'm with you.*

Anne was still quiet and still emotionally drained when they reached Allegro, but then, so was he. He glanced at her before he turned into the drive leading up to her faded purple house.

"Let me take you someplace else."

She shook her head. "It's okay," she told him. "I'm okay. And going someplace else, for no matter how long, isn't going to make the warrior or the problem of what to do with him go away."

"No, but it might give you time to regain the strength you need to deal with those problems."

She gave a choked, humorless laugh and leaned her head against the back of the seat. "Do you really think anything is going to do that?"

She didn't seem really to want an answer. Maybe there wasn't one. He turned into the drive.

Wayne Samuels's truck was parked near the back porch. And so was the black Jimmy David had seen Blake Foresman driving the night before. Cautiously, he parked between the two vehicles and turned to tell Annie to wait while he checked to make sure they weren't walking in on a problem she didn't need to face. He might as well have saved his energy. She yanked the door open and stepped from the Blazer.

Margaret, Wayne, and Blake sat at the round table in the kitchen. All three looked up when they entered.

Margaret jumped up from the table. "Anne. My God—"

Blake Foresman scooted his chair back and rose to his feet. "Are you all right? Huerra? What happened?"

"A wreck," David said, and then he realized how they must look. "We weren't involved. We stopped to help."

Margaret closed her eyes briefly.

"Where?" Blake asked. "No one contacted me."

"I think the kid at the service station called it Simpson Knob."

Blake nodded. "A dangerous stretch. Thank God it's not in my county. How bad was it?"

"Not now, Blake," Margaret said as she walked to Anne's side. "Be a lawman later. Come on, Doc, you look like you could use a hot shower and a change of clothes."

Anne started to resist. David saw it in her eyes. But after one long, questioning glance at Blake, which he studiously ignored, she smiled at Margaret. "You're right about that."

"I'll come on back with you and tell you about the new paint the town has decided to bestow upon the clinic. It looks like we're going to have to find a gracious way to tell them to stuff their benevolence about ten feet below the town dump."

David waited until the two women had left the room before he leaned back against the cabinet.

"Okay," he said. "Anne didn't ask, but I will. What's going on, Blake? Why are you here?"

"Seems you and the Doc were spotted leaving town this morning," Blake told him. "So you had a visitor. One who didn't know that Wayne was here without a vehicle. One who didn't knock on the door but went to those French doors off the side porch and let himself in."

"I figured I'd call the sheriff while he was letting himself in," Wayne said, taking over the telling. "By the time I did that, he was in, so I moved around behind him and let him know, nice like, that he wasn't alone."

David could just imagine how *nice like* Wayne had been. "I'm glad it wasn't me you surprised. Where?"

Wayne waited a moment before answering. "The landing at the top of the stairs. It looked like he was trying to decide which hall to take."

"Damn! Who?"

"Joe," Blake told him.

"Joe Hansom? Himself? Not just someone he sent?"

Blake nodded.

"Well, hell. I didn't think he was that dumb."

"Or that arrogant?" Blake asked.

David laughed. Nothing about this situation was funny. But, damn, it was either laugh or run his fist through a cabinet door. "So where is he? In custody?"

"No. I told him I ought to run him in. I think I put the fear of God in him, but with Joe you never can tell. I told him to get on home and stay there until I found out for sure if Anne wanted to press charges. Will she?"

"I don't know," David admitted. "I just don't know."

With Wayne and Margaret there for Anne, David

asked Blake to go with him out to the Tompkins place to get the rest of his things and check out of his cabin. Anne might not know it yet, but she had just taken in a boarder. And he figured that if his cabin was no longer available, she might not argue too much about him staying in her house. After all, where else in Allegro could he go on such short notice?

Blake didn't argue. Not about going out to the lake with him. Not about his plans. In fact, he offered his assistance if Anne should argue. Imagine that.

He waited while David showered and changed clothes and packed his few belongings, then flirted unmercifully with Gretta Tompkins when they went to the office for David to check out of the cabin. Blake also told Gretta that Anne had had a burglary, and that he'd asked David to help keep an eye on the place for him. Unofficially, and strictly on the q.t.

"Well, of course," Gretta said with an exaggerated huff of indignation. "If you don't know by now, Blake Foresman, that you can tell me something in confidence, then why on earth have I been feeding you pot roast for the last fifteen years? I did manage to raise a cop, you know."

"I know, darlin'," Blake told her. "But I also know how some of the other ladies—never you—in this town would take an innocent situation and twist it all out of proportion. I was hoping I could count on you to help us keep that from happening?"

Gretta grinned at him. "On the q.t., huh? Maybe connected with some big case he's working on?"

Blake bent and smacked a kiss on her cheek. "You got it, darlin'."

"Pete will have my badge for sure if I drag his mama into this mess," David said on their way back to town.

"You didn't drag her, I did." Blake chuckled. "And you see how hard it was to do. Don't worry. Gretta has helped before. She knows what to do and how to do it."

He negotiated a series of curves before he glanced over at David. "Is there any chance he's going to do that? Take your badge?"

"Maybe," David said. "Oh, hell, no. Probably not. I think he just threatened me with internal affairs so I'd take this damned vacation. But he might. And then again, I might just give it to him."

"You know you've got a place here if you want it."

David twisted his head to the left to look at the man, but Blake was concentrating on the road, not on him.

A place here? Was that an option? He hated small towns. He hated the way they sucked the life out of any-one trapped in them. But Anne didn't see them that way. She looked at Allegro as a haven, a safe place to escape from the danger of big-city crime.

Or maybe as a place to hide?

"Thanks," he said to the sheriff, knowing he had to make some response, and realizing the offer had been made without so much as a question about why his badge might be in danger. "Thanks for the vote of confidence."

"Yeah, you're welcome. I'd appreciate it if you'd return the favor."

"I trust you, Blake. You know that."

Maybe he knew; maybe he didn't. Blake Foresman didn't respond to that statement. "I did some checking on that other matter you asked about," he said instead.

"Other matter?"

"Lucy Hansom."

"Oh. Yeah." So much had happened that Anne's mother's comment about Lucy had completely slipped his mind, and he had no idea how Blake had gone from the subject of trust to an ancient missing person's report. "Did you find anything?"

"Not much. Not nearly enough for the disappearance of a young girl back in those days."

"She did disappear?"

"She and a boy—I guess a young man by then—by the name of Walter Briggs. They'd known each other most of their lives and some said they were planning on getting married. He came home on emergency leave from the army when his mama died just before Thanksgiving of '41, and they vanished. The army carried him as AWOL for years. Maybe still does. And maybe he did go AWOL. Maybe he decided the chances of going to war were looking worse every day so he took Lucy and they lit a shuck for parts unknown."

"And no one looked?"

"No." Blake said. "But that was right at the time Marian took her dive down the stairs and blamed a pair of big yellow cats that no one but her saw, at least no one who was willing to talk. She blamed them for Ralph Hansom's death, too. You did know that he died in a car wreck but his body was mauled? She also said that they'd killed Walter and Lucy, but she wouldn't say where. Or when.

"So we've got a fifty-year-old injury and one death, maybe three, blamed on cats. We've got a brand new death in Dallas and another one in Chicago. We've got you and Wayne Samuels talking about seeing or hearing big cats. We've got you and the doc running all over creation looking for God alone knows what, bringing her back looking like she's barely escaped from a war zone, and you so concerned about her safety you're willing to shred her reputation in this small town. We've got Joe Hansom, who's planning to run for a state senate seat, jeopardizing his chances by breaking and entering. And

all of it seems to be tied to one godawful purple house.
It'd be real nice if someone let me in on what's going on."

"Do you ever call on Anne for emergencies?" David
asked.

Now Blake looked slightly startled at the change of
direction. "Yeah. Some. Not often. If it's in the north
end of the county, it's quicker just to go on into the
Fairview Hospital. Why?"

"You ever notice anything . . . odd about her when
you bring her someone from a wreck or a bar fight?"

"Odd? No. Not what I'd call odd. She does seem a little uptight. Not easygoing like she normally is. I thought
it was— Hell, I don't know what I thought it was.
Why?"

"Because she did escape from a war zone." Blake
Foresman's earlier words were all too descriptive not to
use. "You heard about the clinic robbery in Chicago?"

Blake nodded.

"Well, it seems that our Annie isn't quite over that. It
seems that the sight of blood brings all of those memories back, real up close and personal. Today, she let
down her guard enough to tell me."

"Well, hell." Blake was quiet for a moment. "You
mean she's been carrying all that pain around all this
time and we didn't know it?"

"Yeah. That's what I mean." He didn't have to say
more. He knew from Blake's expression that the man
would cut off his right arm rather than drag Anne back
out for an emergency. Unless there was no other option.

"About the other," David said.

Blake canted his head to one side but kept his eyes on
the road.

"I can't tell you. Not yet anyway. Give us a few more
days. We'll either resolve the problem, or I promise you
I'll fill you in."

"Fair enough. So long as no one else is in danger."

Was anyone else in danger? Was Joe alive only because Wayne had been there to keep him from finding the burial? And what if Frances found a way for them to get rid of the warrior and all his grave goods and the cats wouldn't let him go? Hell, if there were any truth to this curse, why weren't he and Annie dead already?

"*Is* anyone else in danger?" Blake asked.

"I can't be sure," David admitted, hoping he was right. "Probably not, if we're careful. If no one else gets involved."

"That's not good enough, Huerra."

No, it wasn't. Not for Blake. Not even for him. "I know. But it's the best I can do. That, and promise you that if there's any change, I'll fill you in immediately."

They'd reached the outskirts of Allegro. Blake growled out a sound that could have been agreement but probably was disgust.

"Where are we going?" David asked as Blake turned onto Main Street.

"Hardware store. Wayne asked me to pick up a new lock set for the French doors. It seems that Joe was not gentle with the existing one." He braked to a stop in front of the store and turned in his seat. "Tell me, is what you're guarding Anne against outside the house? Or inside?"

"I don't know that either." He looked at the brick facade of the hardware store in front of him, at the slightly shabby but still pleasant-looking downtown business district that stretched only three blocks in any direction. "You didn't ask why Pete was considering yanking my badge, but maybe you ought to know. I'd come dangerously close to being omniscient, at least in my own mind. The last case was just the icing, not the whole cake. I'd see the answer, clear as day, just don't confuse me with conflicting facts. But if the facts do conflict, well, hell, that's no problem. I know who did it; let's just beat those facts to fit and paint them to match."

"You're saying you manufactured evidence?"

"No. Good God no. Not yet anyway. Who knows what I might have done if I hadn't screwed up so bad on this last case."

He might as well spill it out. Blake might never know about Marla Hamilton and her country doctor daddy, but he would understand how unchecked prejudice could subvert an investigation.

"One of the suspects was—hell, he was a surgeon. He had it all, a Mercedes, a condo, a self assurance that came off more often than not as arrogance, and a woman he hadn't had before people around her began getting sliced up. Before long, I was convinced he wasn't just a suspect; he was the only suspect. But before I could prove he was guilty, two more people died, and the real perp almost killed my suspect and his lady.

"And who knows what might have happened if I hadn't realized my unfounded prejudices got so much in the way of being a good cop that I scared myself into knowing I had to change.

"No. What I'm saying is that in the week I've been here, I've gone from being a man who was convinced he knew everything worth knowing, to someone who's been confronted by the fact that he knows almost nothing. And the more I learn, the less I'm sure of anything except that if anything ever again hurts Anne Locke, it'll have to come through me first."

"You know that already. That quick?"

"Yeah," David said. Hell, maybe a small town wouldn't be so bad after all. Maybe this one wouldn't choke the life out of him the way the one where he grew up had. Maybe. Could he risk it? "That quick. And that sure."

Margaret had Anne working with her in the kitchen when they returned to the house, more to keep her busy, David suspected, than because she needed help with the meal preparations.

And they had told her about Joe. That much was evident when she looked at Blake and repeated the words David had used so often that week. "I don't know. I just don't know."

Blake declined her invitation to stay for a late lunch, but before he left he promised to stay in the area that night, when he again took the graveyard shift for an absent deputy.

When just the four of them remained in the kitchen, Wayne reached for the new lock set and turned to David. "Come on, city cop. Let's see if you know as much about locks as you do about ceilings."

Joe had not been gentle with the French doors or the lock. Wayne had already been at work, filling and gluing the damage to the bottom of the doors where the ineffectual stops had been splintered loose by the force of Joe's entry, and removing the old, mangled lock and knobs.

"Sure of himself, wasn't he?" David asked when he realized the amount of noise Joe must have made entering the house.

"Yeah."

"Any chance he wore a size ten western boot with a riding heel?"

"Yeah."

Well, that answered at least one question. "When did you know it was Joe?"

Wayne began pulling supplies from the bag. He examined each of them before placing them with deliberate care on a table he'd brought near to hold his tools. He then rubbed the back of his neck and stared out the doors toward the dining room windows.

David picked up the mangled lock and studied it, waiting for Wayne to work through whatever held him silent. Waiting for him to decide whether or not he'd answer.

"That's a hell of an alarm system the doc's got," Wayne said finally. "I was on my way out, fastest way possible, when I saw Joe coming through the woods toward the house and realized your oversized house kitties were probably just that– an alarm system."

David dropped the lock to the table. "You heard them?"

"Oh, hell, yes. From somewhere upstairs, probably not too far from that room you warned me about."

So, it wasn't his imagination. If he'd ever had the slightest hope that it was, Wayne had just taken that away.

"Did Joe hear them?"

"Now that's the strangest thing. I'd have sworn anybody in a six-county radius could have heard them, but he didn't seem to. Not even after he was in the house, upstairs damn it, with them pacing and grumbling. I'd swear he didn't hear a thing until I stepped up behind him."

"Damn it, Samuels, you took a hell of a chance staying in the house. Why didn't you go ahead and get out when you first heard them?"

Wayne turned to the door and ran skilled fingers over his repair work. "Because after I saw the doc's cousin coming through the woods, and I got over the first panic, I realized something that's about as strange as anything I've ever known. I mean it, Huerra. Whatever they are, and wherever they were, your watch-kitties weren't fussing at me."

It wasn't difficult to talk Annie into moving her bedroom upstairs, at least for a while, especially since she'd learned that someone had been looking in windows the night before. The rooms upstairs had their share of problems too, but eventually they decided on those at the end of the front hall, as far away from Marian's sitting room as it was possible to get. David saw her settled into the room at the end, right over the study.

While the only place David wanted to be was beside her, he knew that the time probably wasn't right for that. She'd rallied some while Wayne and Margaret remained at the house, probably for their benefit, but she had to be feeling battered still from the effects of her little jaunt through memory lane. So he took the room next to hers and settled himself onto the narrow white bed, fully believing he'd spend a sleepless, restless night.

The rooms were stuffy from having been shut up for years, so he'd raised the windows in his and left them opened just enough to let some fresh air in, and he left the door open so that he could hear anything approaching. A slight breeze played through the room, not so cold as to be unbearable, merely touching him lightly before moving into the hall. He tugged the blanket around his shoulders and listened to the sounds of the night, to the whisper of the breeze, to the memory of other nights, other cool breezes, to the memory of laughter, sweet, childish, and loving, but he couldn't remember whose. They beguiled him into the sleep he'd thought would elude him that night.

20

1941

The wind teased Lucy's hair, dragging it across her face as she stood with the small crowd of mourners at the graveside. She held herself very still, ignoring the chill the wind now carried. Her right hand was warm, caught tightly in Walter's, but that was just about all of her that was.

Walter was here. Thank God he'd made it in time for the funeral. There'd been some doubt, even with all the work Reverend Jones had done to get him his emergency leave. As it was, her mama had convinced Reverend Jones to delay the service almost an hour until Walter arrived. She didn't think Walter would ever forgive himself if he'd missed his mother's funeral. She knew he'd have a hard enough time forgiving himself for not knowing Mrs. Briggs was so sick, even though she had made them all promise not to tell him.

He stood straight and tall and proud beside her after the brief graveside service, while friends stopped to shake his hand, to clap a comforting hand on his shoulder, to tell him what a fine woman his mother had been. And he thanked these people, even smiled at some of them, but his eyes had a funny closed-off look, like he wasn't really listening, as if he wasn't really there.

She knew where he was. She'd gone the same place when her papa died, when people who hadn't been his friend in life tried to tell her they had been.

Walter had come there for her and had brought her back. She would do the same for him. But not now. Now was the time for grieving, for saying good-bye. Not for celebration. But it would be soon; so much had to be done in the three days he had been allotted.

But finally all of the mourners were gone. Only Reverend Jones, Lucy and her mama, Walter, and the two men who would close the grave remained. Reverend Jones clasped Walter's hand one more time before leaving, and Mama stepped up.

"Now you come to our house, Walter Briggs. Sara would have wanted that."

"Yes, ma'am," he answered. This time when he smiled, it was real. "I can't thank you for all you did for my mama, Mrs. Hansom."

"Hush, now. There's no talk of thanks between family. And you are family. Have been for a long time." She pressed a key into his hand. "This is to Marian's car. It's parked just outside the gates. Now you hurry on back to your house and change out of that good uniform, gather up your things, and come on home. Lucy? You'll be going with him?"

"Yes, Mama."

"Good. Bring him home now. Real soon."

Walter's house was small and plain and had always been kept scrupulously clean until Sara Briggs took sick a week after he'd left to go to basic training at Fort Sill. The ladies of the church had come in and cleaned it— after it looked like she wasn't going to get any better, and Mama had moved her into their second best upstairs bedroom—but it wasn't clean like Mrs. Briggs had always kept it. And it didn't have the good smells that had always come from her kitchen or the feeling of home that somehow she had always given it.

Walter looked around the empty house and knew. "How long has she been gone from here?"

"A month," Lucy told him. "Mama couldn't convince her to come any sooner."

"And you didn't tell me?"

"I tried, Walter. I begged her to let me. But she was so proud of you. She didn't want to do anything to upset you; she didn't want you trying to get out because of her, and she knew you would if you ever guessed how sick she was."

"Yes. I would have."

Lucy stood just inside the front door studying him. Maybe his mama shouldn't have kept her secret from him; maybe she owed him the right to love her. But he looked so handsome, so right, standing tall and strong in the army olive green. She knew he hadn't had the wool uniform specially tailored, but it looked like he had. Just like the Sam Browne belt, the smart-looking tan leggings and the brown shoes—shiny enough to catch a reflection even after all the miles he'd worn them coming home— looked like they had been made just for him.

Walter belonged in the army. She knew he'd talked about using it as no more than a job. But that had changed. She'd read it—yes *read* it—in his letters, beyond the words he'd written. And he would have left it for his mama. He'd leave it for her if she wasn't careful. But she wasn't in the same situation as Sara Briggs had been. She was healthy and young, and she had her mama and all her mama's family to help her while he was gone.

But if he looked right in his uniform, he didn't look right in this house. Not any more. He'd taken his cap off and folded it, and now he slapped the soft fabric against his thigh as he looked into what had been his mama's bedroom.

She reached behind her and twisted the key in the front door. Yes. It was time to bring him back.

She walked up to him and lifted her hands to his tie. He looked startled for a moment, but she was smiling, and soon he did too. "Careful," he warned her. "That thing has to be ironed."

"You've learned how to do that?" she asked in mock alarm. "My, my, the United States Army must really be something special."

She slid her arms around him. It felt so strange to find wool and leather beneath her touch where always before she had found cotton, or just Walter. But she hugged him, and she held him close, and she knew it the moment he let go of his smile and let go of just a little of the pride that held him aloof and away from his pain.

"Blood brothers, Walter," she reminded him. "We've shared our blood, and we've shared our love, and we can share this. I can help you with this, like you've helped me so many times. Let me. Please."

Then he was holding her, tight. Tighter than he ever had. So tight she could feel the shudders racking through him.

"Lucy. Oh, my God, Lucy. She was so sick, and I didn't even know."

"Sshh," she told him. "She didn't want you to know. She loved you so much, and she knew you loved her. She wanted to give you this, Walter. We had to let her. And you have to accept it the way she meant it, with love. Miss her, yes. I know you will, but she wouldn't want you feeling guilty because you weren't here."

He hugged her again, a quick, fierce hug, and she felt

him pulling his strength back around himself because he couldn't let himself be weak very long. Not even with her. "How did you get to be so wise?" he asked.

"I had help. A skinny little redheaded boy taught me that I wasn't dumb. He taught me that someone besides my mama really can love me. He taught me to love. And Walter, I do love you. So much that sometimes I can't believe it's all coming from just the one person inside me."

She felt tears on her cheeks. She'd already done her crying for Sara Briggs. But Walter hadn't. Maybe he couldn't. But she could do it for him.

He brushed at her tears with incredibly gentle callused fingers. "I love you, Lucy Hansom."

"I know that. I've known that since the day you pulled out that nasty-looking knife and asked me to cut my finger."

"And I want to marry you," he said in a voice thickened by the tears he would not shed. "Today, tomorrow. Before I leave I want you wearing my name. I want everybody knowing you belong to me."

Lucy felt a chuckle building right alongside the sob that forced its way out of her. "I don't think there's going to be any doubt about that. At least not for very long."

He put her away from him slightly, frowning down at her. "What are you talking about?"

"I told your mama. I hope you don't mind that I told her before I told you, but she needed to know. She was happy, Walter, real happy, knowing that you're going to have me to love you all the rest of your life. And that you're going to have our baby to love you, too."

He looked at her for a moment longer, stunned into silence, before his whole face seemed to glow. "You're sure?"

Yes. She'd known he'd be happy. She nodded and touched the wide band of leather that belted his long jacket. "Just as sure as I am that I can't figure out how to get you out of this sophisticated harness."

He whooped and picked her up and spun her around, laughing. "Lucy, honey . . ." He set her on her feet and stroked his hand down over her belly before he knelt and pressed his face against it. "Give me a minute," he said, and she heard his words all choked with the emotion he hadn't let himself show before. "Give me a minute," he repeated, "and I'll give you a lesson in a most improper way to get a soldier out of his uniform."

Marian seldom came to the kitchen for any purpose other than to gather her meal and carry it into the dining room. When Walter and Lucy arrived at the Hansom house, though, hours later, after laughing and loving, and crying some as they stripped the rental house of the last of the personalities of Walter and Sara Briggs, Marian waited for them in the kitchen.

She rose from a chair at the round table and raked her eyes up and down the cotton and denim work clothes Walter had changed into. She held out her hand. "My key," she said.

Lucy had wondered about Marian's generosity; it had seemed completely out of character, and apparently it was. Walter juggled the duffel bag and bag of his clothes he carried into one hand, and held out the key to the woman. She snatched it away.

"I've already told Ellie," she said. "Now I'll tell you so there will be no chance for misunderstanding. That is my car; not hers, certainly not yours. The next time your mother takes it upon herself to lend it to someone, I will see that the person driving it is arrested."

She didn't wait for a response, but she did make a terrific exit, even if that exit had to be through a pantry.

Walter set his duffel and bag on the floor and took the small box containing his mother's treasures from Lucy's hands. "My God, what kind of hold does that woman have on your family? I thought she was bad enough before your father died, worse still when I left two months ago, but this? Lucy, why does your mother put up with her?"

Lucy shook her head. She didn't want to think about Marian now. She didn't know why her mother put up with her. But she did. But for the most part Mama had ignored her after finally telling her that she wasn't her maid, and any cleaning up Marian wanted done, she'd have to do herself.

But she was getting stranger every day. Long before Papa died, Marian had locked the bedroom off her sitting room. She hadn't complained when Mama had asked Walter to close off the windows so no one would accidentally look in and see the man in copper. But lately she had taken to unlocking the door and going in and sitting on the floor by his side. Aunt Marian. On the floor. And—Mama didn't know this—picking up pieces of shell or copper and holding them close while she rocked back and forth.

Marian thought they were hers. Lucy knew that. Her papa had made provisions for Aunt Marian in his will, leaving her some of his business holdings. The only problem was, by the time he died, there were no business holdings.

Only the dead man.

And Mama had been real clear about him. He was in the house, so he was part of the house. *Her* house. Enough people had died already. Mama was not going to let Marian even try to get rid of him again.

And she was not going to run the risk of young Joseph or one of the cousins accidentally wandering into the room where he lay in final rest. She'd changed the lock once already, but Marian had managed to get it open,

and it was downright creepy the way she'd go in there at
all hours of the day and night and *talk* to him. Just like
he could hear her. Just like he'd *want* to hear anything
she had to say to him.

"I don't want to talk about Aunt Marian." Lucy walked
to his side at the table and took the small box from his
hands. She ran her hands over it reverently as she set it
on the table. It contained so little: Sara Briggs's wedding
picture, her silver thimble and hand-carved ivory cro-
chet hook, a few school papers Walter had given her
years before. The few dishes and quilts, which they had
transported in Marian's car and which now sat in a trunk
in the barn. These were all that remained of the things
Sara had considered special—so little compared to the
pile of grave goods that had been buried with the man
upstairs. Yet Sara was at peace. Was he?

Mama made up the big downstairs bedroom for Walter,
the one she hadn't slept in since Papa died. She hugged
him when they told her they were going to be married
before he went back to Fort Sill. Lucy saw a glint of
tears in her eyes, but they were happy tears. Mama
wouldn't let herself cry any other kind.

The church folks had come and gone by the time
Lucy and Walter got back to the house, but they had left
their offerings of food. Mama had them all set out on the
dining room table and sideboard. Now she took a bottle
of her grandma's muscadine wine from the back of the
buffet and three delicate stemmed glasses from the
bow-fronted china cabinet. She poured each of them a
glassful and raised hers. "I've thought of you as family
for years. Now I'm pleased to welcome you as an official
member. May the two of you be as happy together the
rest of your lives as you have been till now."

Walter hugged Lucy, and then he hugged her mama. "Thank you, Mrs. Hansom. I couldn't ask for better family. I just wish—"

Lucy watched Walter change what he'd wish for in mid-sentence.

"I just wish there was some way I could repay you for all the good things you did for my mother."

Mama would say thank you, but payment wasn't necessary. Lucy had heard her say that too many times to think she would ever change. But she did.

"Actually, there is something," she said. "I'd planned to wait a little while before asking you, but it seems we don't have all that much time after all. I have the supplies in the attic; I've had them for months now. Walter, while you're home on leave, I really would appreciate it if you'd build me a wall."

Marian hated the wall. She hated Walter for building it, Lucy for helping, and Mama for asking for it. She screeched out her hatred the next morning until Mama took her arm and shook her and said in a cold, tight voice Lucy had never heard before, "Marian, be quiet, or you and your son are out of my house, forever, and damn the consequences."

Marian got quiet, watching sullenly from her green-striped couch until Joseph wandered into the room. Mama was real quick to close the door then, shutting Lucy and Walter in the room with the skeleton while Walter worked on framing in what would soon look like the back wall of a closet.

Walter rested his hammer on a cross bracing. "She wants to be able to get to him," he whispered. "To sell him?"

Lucy shook her head. "I don't know anymore.

Maybe. Maybe just to be near to him. But with this in place she won't be able to do either. Ever again."

He leaned against one of the many studs already in place. "Lucy, with this wall in place, we won't be able to get to him, either. We won't be able to return him, even if we figure out how, unless—"

"Unless what, Walter?"

"Unless we move him before I finish the wall. Unless we hide him somewhere safe until we can figure out what to do with him. Unless we convince Marian and— damn, I hate this—unless we convince your mama he's still here, behind this wall."

"Mama wouldn't mind us moving him. She thinks he belongs—"

"Where, Lucy? Where does he belong?"

But of course she didn't have the answer for that. "Not here," she said. "Not in a closed-off, dark room behind Aunt Marian's clothes."

"No. And your mama knows that. But she wouldn't want us to move him. Not because we're greedy or malicious or even disrespectful. But because she'd be afraid something would happen to us. And it might."

"Papa moved him before. Nothing happened then. But he came back. He always comes back."

"Maybe because no one's ever moved *all* of him. Not since he was brought here. We could do that."

"Where, Walter?"

"I don't know. But I could find out. Abe McPherson's got a telephone. I could make some calls, ask around, maybe talk to the people from the University of Oklahoma or the Historical Society who've been digging up at Spiro."

Lucy glanced down at the man on the litter. The only light in the room came from a small bulb hanging from a broken fixture. He'd been buried with pride and ceremony. Surely he deserved a better tomb than this. And if anyone could find out, Walter could. They were old enough now, big enough now to do something other than hide and watch. And nothing would happen to them. Nothing could happen to them if all they meant was to bring him peace, could it?

21

She was warm. *Deliciously warm.* Warm and safe. Anne didn't want to wake up, didn't want to open her eyes, didn't want to leave the cocoon of soft mattress and hard muscle. She sighed and turned, snuggling closer to the source of the warmth and felt an arm shift and reshape its hold on her.

An arm? Hard muscle?

Anne blinked open her eyes to dim, early morning light. Good grief. How had she gotten to David's room? To David's bed?

He looked down at her and let his bad-boy grin peek out. "You walked again last night, Annie."

"Oh, boy." She tried to turn her face away, not wanting him to see the embarrassment in hers, not wanting to see ridicule or rejection or even stoic acceptance in his.

"I heard a noise about three o'clock, looked up, and there you were in the doorway."

"Oh, boy," she repeated.

Her gown had ridden up. Her leg brushed against his leg. His bare leg. In turning, she had placed her hand against his chest. His bare chest.

"I thought you might have heard something, but when I spoke to you, you didn't answer. You did look down the hall once, but then you came in here, lifted the covers and crawled in as though you'd been doing it all your life."

"I'm sorry," she muttered, easing her leg away from his and trying to lift her hand.

He caught her hand and held it still above his heart. "I'm not. I knew last night that if you were going to walk in your sleep, I'd rather have you coming to me than going to . . . to him."

She felt his life pulsing beneath her touch. Life. Vibrant, vital life. His pulse grew stronger as she stared up into his eyes, seeing none of those things she'd been afraid of seeing. It was the strangest thing, but she had the feeling his heart beat just for her, that it beat in unison with hers. That it always had. That it always would. And that at this moment, he knew it, too.

"Annie, what's happening to us?"

A glib response wouldn't do here. He knew about physical attraction; so did she. And while, yes, her body was responding to his nearness as his was unmistakably responding to hers, his voice carried too much wonder, too much frustration, and too much confusion to be asking about something so obvious.

He raised his hand to her cheek and trailed his fingers to her throat. There, her pulse leapt beneath *his* touch.

"It took me a while to sort out what I was feeling when I saw you kneeling at his feet Friday night—even longer to admit it to myself. I was jealous. Jealous of a man who's been dead seven hundred years, give or take a century or two. Jealous, when I've no more than kissed you. Jealous, when there's not a hope in hell we can ever mesh our lives and our homes and our careers.

"So when you came to my door last night, when you came to my bed, why did it seem no different than when you went to him?"

There was no answer, glib or otherwise, for that. She could only stare into his eyes, letting him see her own wonder, frustration, and confusion. And need.

"Annie. Oh, God, Annie." He hauled her against him and found her mouth with his. "I don't want this," he muttered when he dragged his mouth from hers. "We don't need this. Not now. There's too much—too much . . . "

"I know," she said. But her hands were as greedy as his; her mouth as needy. Her body as feverish. "I know."

Later, she would wonder how she could have been so rash, how she could have responded to David with no more than a thought that she thrust to the back of her mind about birth control or protection of any kind. But at that moment, all she could do was respond, as though she had been responding to him all her life, as though she had been responding to him the seven hundred years, give or take a century or two, that he had just mentioned, as though his touch and their sharing was as vital to her—to each of them, to *both* of them—as the blood that thundered through his heart and hers.

"Believe me," she murmured against his throat. "I know."

When Anne awoke again, she was alone. The covers were tucked neatly up around her, and her red flannel nightgown lay across the foot of the narrow bed. A slight breeze, more chill than cool, came through the partially opened window. As did light. Enough light to tell her it was past time to get this day started.

Later, dressed and more or less put together for their outing that morning, she went in search of David. She

smelled coffee and bacon before she reached the stairwell. She hesitated a moment with her hand on the
newel post. The warrior lay in the other direction.
Should she check on him first?

*And do what, Annie? Ask him if he wants breakfast,
too?* Her hand clenched on the post as in her mind she
heard David's voice, clearly mocking. Or was it her
own? She shook her head and squared her shoulders
and marched herself down the hall.

Wayne and Margaret had already arrived to keep vigil
for the day. Wayne rose from his chair in a quaint,
faintly courtly gesture when she entered the room.

David turned from his position at the stove and let his
eyes give her a warmer welcome than his almost casual,
"Good morning. Coffee's ready. One egg or two?"

"Good morning." Was she blushing? Good lord, she
didn't blush. She couldn't let herself, because if she did
all her freckles stood up and begged for attention.
Maybe not. Margaret was looking at her, but it was a
speculative look, not a knowing one.

And just how was she supposed to greet David, anyway?

Just like nothing had happened. Just like he greeted
her. That decided, she headed toward the coffeepot.
"Only one egg, please."

He grinned at her. Turned as they were, no one else
could see that grin. And no one else could see the way
he searched her features, as if making sure she was all
right, or the wicked wink he sent her way even though
he didn't seem at all assured that she was. "Coming
right up. I found some juice in your freezer. Hope you
don't mind that I made myself at home."

Wayne and Margaret already had full cups of coffee,
still steaming, so Anne realized they must have arrived
only a few minutes ago, probably while she was in the

shower. She smiled at them and walked to the table. Wayne held a chair for her and only sat down after she did. "I could get used to treatment like this," Anne said.

David turned back to the stove and cracked an egg on the edge of the skillet. "You look like you could use a lot of it, too."

Margaret chuckled. "It does no good to fight it, Anne," she said. "So you might as well enjoy being cosseted. After yesterday, you certainly deserve it."

After yesterday. For a moment the room spun around her. She had forgotten. How had she forgotten? "Did anybody— Is he— How is he?"

Margaret reached over and lay her hand on Anne's, stilling her. "Blake came by our place this morning before he went off duty." she said. "The boy is still in critical condition, but it looks like he's going to make it."

Anne slumped in her chair. "Thank God."

Wayne shook his head. "The way Blake tells it, it's thank God, and you two."

"No. All we did was give rudimentary first aid, the kind anybody can give. The kind those people on the scene were already giving."

Wayne just stared at her. "Rudimentary first aid? Is that what you call taking that boy's fear away? Giving him hope?" He shot a glance at David. "Promising him an autographed baseball?"

"Here. Eat." David put a plate in front of her. The flatware was already on the table, as were butter and blackberry jelly.

He draped a hand on her shoulder for a moment before dragging out his own chair and sinking onto it. He waited only until she had finished her egg and bacon and spread butter and jelly onto a toasted English muffin.

"We don't have to do this today, you know," he said. "We can wait. You can rest."

She carefully set the muffin back on her plate. There was cosseting, and then there was babying. "I'm fine."

"I know you think you are, but you've had a series of— You had a pretty rough day yesterday—"

"Wait until when?" she asked. "It isn't that far, but if we don't go today, it will be Wednesday, or maybe even Saturday before I can take the time to make the trip."

They went. Anne telephoned first, to make sure that Marian Hansom was really a patient in one of the nursing homes in Texarkana. She found her registered in the third one she called.

David drove. "Are you upset with me?" he asked when they were deep in the mountains.

Upset with him? What was he talking about? "No, of course not. Why should I be?"

"Maybe because . . . because I took advantage of you when you were especially vulnerable. Maybe because you regret what happened between us."

She turned her head to look at him. Good lord, he was serious. "You didn't take advantage of me," she told him. "I knew what I was doing, and I wanted to do it. Whatever gave you the idea I regretted anything that we shared?"

He reached across the chasm of the console separating them and lifted her hand in his. "We should have driven your truck. There's a lot to be said for good old-fashioned bench seats."

Anne returned the pressure of his hand, and when he placed hers on his thigh so he could grip the steering wheel, she laughed softly and left her hand where he had placed it.

"That's more like it," he told her. She peered at him and then down at her hand.

"That too," David said with a chuckle, "but what I was talking about was your laugh. I've missed it."

"David, it's only been . . . "

"I've missed it," he repeated.

Anne knew that she had seen Marian Hansom before. Her childhood memories included one of an old, querulous woman in a hospital bed, but where, she couldn't remember. Probably Ellie Hansom's house. Surely her mother had taken her there. She certainly remembered hearing about her. Even if she hadn't heard much, the conversations in the past few days would have filled in any number of gaps.

That had to be why the slender white-haired woman in the wheelchair was such a surprise. Anyone who had acted as ugly as Marian reportedly had, ought to be ugly, not regally beautiful.

The staff at the small, private facility must have told Marian someone had inquired about her, because she was expecting them. She wore a simple silk shirt and skirt. Her hair, thinner now than it would have been in her prime, gleamed like silver in soft finger waves, and her makeup also echoed a restrained version of the style that had been popular in Marian's youth. A delicate lace shawl draped across her shoulders, and a lightweight, woven coverlet lay across the arm of the chair, waiting should she become chilled.

Crazy Aunt Marian looked every bit the regal matri-arch granting an audience. "You wanted to see me?"

David stood a half-step behind Anne and waited for her to speak.

"Yes," Anne said. "I'm Anne Locke. My grandmother was Ellie Hansom's cousin Rebecca."

Marian cocked her head back and studied Anne's

face and hair. "Did the Briggs family manage to insinuate itself into the Hansom family after all? But no, I forgot. You're Katherine's bastard."

Anne felt the blow physically. David gripped her arm, holding her steady.

"Bastard." It was as though Marian tasted the word once again before spitting it out. "That's what they called my Joseph, you know. You're also the one who bought the house. I don't suppose you're here out of family loyalty or love, so perhaps we'd better go somewhere private. You. Yes you, young man. You may push my chair."

David hesitated, but he stepped to the back of Marian's chair. A single glance at her over Marian's head told Anne just where he'd like to push that chair, but he kept his voice calm. "Where?"

Marian directed them to a small, plant-filled room. "No one ever comes in here. There's no television. But shut the door. No one knows my business unless I tell them."

She wheeled herself across the quarry tile floor to a grouping of chairs and waited for them to join her. "You will forgive me if I don't offer refreshments." She nodded toward the rattan chairs. "Well, sit. I don't relish holding this or any other discussion while I have to look up at anyone."

Anne took the chair closest to Marian; David, the other.

"Well, what is it? Why did you drive all the way down here?"

Anne glanced around the room. The plants surrounding the casual, tasteful grouping of furniture were lush and well cared for; the spotless tile floor glowed; the many windows surrounding them gleamed. Anne had visited many nursing homes since starting medical school; this was probably the most luxurious she had ever seen. It was also, undoubtedly, the most expensive.

"This is a lovely facility," she said.

Marian's eyes glittered and she let a small, satisfied smile crease her carefully made-up face. "My grandson takes quite good care of me."

Now that was an understatement. And could Joe really have the kind of money a facility like this charged? "He must love you very much."

Marian's smile faded. "What do you want?"

Anne leaned forward. "I want to know what you know about the man in the hidden room."

Marian sucked in a sharp breath as she drew back. She was quiet for so long Anne began to be alarmed, but just as she reached for the woman's arm, Marian laughed. Harshly. Violently. And Crazy Marian peeked out from behind the regal facade.

"You found him. You found him and you don't know what to do with him. Watch out, Anne Locke. Only I have the key. Only I have the right to him. And look what they did to me."

"Is he why Joe has been trying to buy the house from me? Why he's been sneaking around the outside of the house in the dark? Why yesterday he actually broke into the house?"

"He mustn't. He mustn't."

"Miss Hansom," David said. "It isn't a matter of what Joe must or must not do. He's done it. Did you send him?"

"You didn't tell him? You weren't fool enough to tell anybody?"

Anne sighed. "No. We didn't tell Joe. But why shouldn't we? You obviously have."

Now Marian smiled again. "But not where he is. Don't you see? I promised Joe a fortune, but only I know where he is."

Now Joe's actions toward his grandmother made more sense. Anne hated that she felt easier attributing him with greed rather than familial love, but that hat fit the man she had come to know a lot better.

"Joe mustn't know. The cats won't like that. They're very protective of him, you know. Even with me. Even with me.

"I loved him." Marian tilted her head to one side. In the shade of a leafy palm she looked almost young. "A long time ago, I loved him. And then he took that bitch to mate instead of me. We ruled the heart of this country from the Great Lakes to the Gulf. But we could have ruled the world. Together we would have ruled the world. I got even with him, though, and with her. She thought she was so smart with her herbs and her potions, but my source knew more than simply how to heal. He knew how to take life slowly, steadily. I would have killed her, too, but by then I couldn't get close enough. The cats wouldn't let me. The curse wouldn't let me. But they wouldn't stop me from killing those around her. They couldn't stop me from letting her die.

"And now he's mine. Forever and ever mine.

"All I wanted was the box. I took the things Lucy and that Briggs boy had stolen back to the room, and I picked up the box. I was going to take it with me while I drove to the country. It seemed fitting, you know, that I get rid of her picture, too. The picture should have been mine. And the box should have been mine. It will be mine once he realizes that I only did what I had to do. Once he tells the cats to leave me alone.

"They kill anyone who bothers him. You do know that, don't you?"

Anne nodded. *Crazy as a bessie bug?* Katherine didn't know the half of it.

"Is that what happened to Lucy Hansom and Walter Briggs?" David asked. "You said they had stolen some things from him."

Marian looked up at him. A shadow crossed her face, but she smiled. "You want to know what happened to them?" she asked shrewdly.

"I watched Walter build the wall. Ellie thought she was so smart to close off the room. She thought I wouldn't be able to get to him. I've come across life-times to reach him; why should one wall stop me?

"And it wouldn't have stopped that greedy daughter of hers either. I overheard Lucy and Walter planning to take him away before they closed the wall—take him away and not say anything to Ellie or to me, just let us think he was still back there.

"Didn't they realize I would know? Didn't they real-ize I couldn't let them do that?"

"What happened to them?" David asked.

Marian pulled back in her chair. "Why, the curse got them. I told everyone that. But they wouldn't listen to me."

David leaned forward. "You actually saw the cats kill Walter Briggs and Lucy Hansom? Where? And why didn't you go for help at that time?"

Marian dragged her head from side to side, slowly, deliberately. "Oh, no you don't. I know what you're try-ing to do, but I won't let you.

"I was in the hospital for weeks, you know. And Ellie went with me. She didn't want to, but her pride wouldn't let her go off and leave me alone, even if it meant missing the wedding. And she stayed with me. Weeks and weeks and weeks. When we came back to her house, there was no sign of them. She knew they were dead. She just didn't want to believe it. But she got even with me. She sent my Joseph away. She said she couldn't take care of him and me, too. And she made me watch as she finished the wall and locked the closet and left me so close to him and unable even to see him.

"Oh, yes. She got even."

She heard David's sigh. Somewhere in Marian's story ran a thread of truth, but where?

"Got even for what?" David asked. "Why did she keep you in her house when obviously there was no love between the two of you, Miss Hansom?"

"It's Mrs. Hansom," Marian said coldly. "And she kept me because she couldn't bear the thought of the scandal or the shame it would bring to Lucy and to her if anyone knew that I'd married Ralph before he ever met her, that he only married her because of her family's money, and that he promised me he'd leave as soon as he had acquired enough of the mineral interests, enough of the land, and later, enough of the artifacts that so enchanted him. But he didn't. No. The curse got him too. But if he'd listened to me . . ."

Anne sat bolt upright in her chair. All sorts of rumors had been whispered in the family, but never this. "You're saying that Ralph and Ellie weren't legally married?"

Marian smiled. "Is bigamy legal?"

"And this is what you held over her to stay in her house, with the man everyone thought was her husband?"

"No, no, dear. Blackmail is only good if it's used properly. It's what I held over Ralph. Ellie didn't know. Then."

David dropped his hand on Anne's shoulder, calming her, as he took over the questions. "But she obviously found out. How?"

"How? While building that damned wall she searched the room. My room. And she found my marriage license. She was stunned, but not surprised. She burned it. In my large crystal ashtray that had been empty for months because she refused to buy me cigarettes. She burned it and then she bought paint for the house. Purple. 'A fitting color for a brothel,' she said. 'Isn't that what they call a place where whores live?'

"I almost died when she got sick. Joseph was dead. My sweet Joseph that she turned against me died working on the dam for that lake. It wouldn't have happened if Ellie had let him stay. I would have seen that he got to college, that he didn't have to work like a slave for wages. But he was dead. And no one came to see me but his son, Joe. I'd talk to him; I always knew how much I could tell him and how much I couldn't. He's more like me than his father ever was, but that's all right. I understand that. I know how to use that."

Anne swallowed her distaste. "So he keeps you here in exchange for the promise of a fortune later."

Marian nodded, and her eyes glittered.

"After you die?"

Again, Marian nodded.

"Tell me," Anne asked. "If everyone who tries to claim this treasure dies, just how is Joe going to collect?"

"Now dear, why on earth will I ever have to worry about that?"

Anne stood. She'd been in this woman's presence too long. David reached for her hand but Anne stepped away from him. She glanced at him and knew he had more questions to ask, but she didn't care how much more Marian could or might tell them; she'd heard more than she wanted to hear. She had to leave. She didn't want him staying with this vicious old woman either, but he would. She knew he would. Just as she knew she wouldn't argue with him in front of Marian Hansom. She gave him a brief, tight smile and walked from the room, but in her heart she was running as fast as she could, as far away from Marian Hansom as possible.

David joined Anne a few minutes later at the Blazer. Without speaking, he took her in his arms and just held her.

"I'm going to paint the house," she said against his jacket.

He rubbed his hand over her back but remained silent.

"The first few days that are warm enough and clear enough, I'm going to have a crew up there. I thought she was just eccentric. I could live with that. But my God, what she must have gone through. Poor Aunt Ellie."

"You have to know that woman is capable of making up any story she wants to serve any purpose she might have."

"You think she was lying about being married to Ralph?"

"Annie, all she had to do to prove it was to write for a duplicate marriage license. And if she couldn't do it, she could have told Joe where to write and had him do it."

"Do you think she did? Tell Joe?

"I don't know. Would it be better for him politically to have an unmarried ancestor, or a bigamous one?"

"Poor Joe," she said, "what a quandary."

"That's better." David said, easing his hand to the nape of her neck and massaging the tension knotted there.

She sighed and relaxed into his touch before she opened her eyes to find him looking down at her with a gentleness she had felt so often coming from him. Felt, but not recognized. Needed, but not returned. "You're so good for me," she whispered.

"I try to be, Annie. I try."

"What are we going to do?"

And he knew without asking what she meant. Out of all of the problems facing them, he zeroed in on the one that should have been the easiest to solve. But wasn't. *What are we going to do about us?* What were they going to do about the attraction between them when his vacation was over, when he had to leave, and she couldn't. "I don't know, Annie."

"Kiss me?" She couldn't believe she'd said it. Kiss me. Here. In the parking lot in front of anyone who happened to look. But she had. And meant it. And wanted it regardless of who might be watching.

"And take away the taste of our visit with Marian?"

Was that why? As she looked into his eyes she knew that was a part of it. But only a part. "Yes," she said, knowing she had to be honest with him. She felt his arms tense around her, saw his eyes begin to take on a hardness alien to the David he had shown her, and knew she couldn't leave him with less than the complete answer. "Yes," she repeated. "That, too."

There was no question that night where either of them would sleep. While Anne readied for bed, David made one last sweep of the yard and the locks on the windows and doors. Then they went up the stairs together, to the room at the end of the front hall where she had begun the night before. It was cold, and Anne shivered in her long robe and flannel nightgown. David opened one window just a crack; Anne switched on the electric blanket she had brought upstairs, shed her robe, and crawled between frigid sheets.

David gave her one of his lethal grins as he scooted in beside her. "You don't really think you're going to need that blanket, do you?"

Anne swallowed once and looked at him. No. He

didn't really feel any humor; he was only trying to distract her from the path her thoughts had taken. And why? Unless his thoughts had gone there, too.

And why now had her thoughts chosen that path? She'd known from the beginning his time here was limited. Why, tonight, had that taken on such sinister overtones? But it had. When he moved closer to her, she raised her hands to his face. "You're going to leave me, aren't you? As soon as your time is finished here, you'll go back to Dallas, back to your life."

He pulled her close and bent his head to rub his cheek against her hair. "I don't know what I'm going to do, Annie, and that's the God's truth." His arms tightened fractionally. "Blake offered me a job."

Was that the answer? The answer to *what*? What was wrong with her tonight that made her see everything so fatalistically?

"Could you be happy as a county cop? Could you really live in a small town with all of its limitations and none of the city's advantages and not go stark raving crazy?"

"I don't know. What do you want me to say, Annie? That I love you? I don't know that, either. I only know that I've never felt this way about another woman. If I hadn't met you I wouldn't even have considered Blake's offer. If I hadn't met you I probably would already be back in Dallas, cursing my leave, prowling through all the alleys of my life trying to find out what I was going to do with the rest of it."

"Sshh," she whispered, stopping his flow of words with gentle fingers across his lips. Did she want him to say he loved her? Or would that cause more problems? "I only wanted you to know I understand. I— I wanted you to know that I . . . I don't expect more. I wanted you to know that I can't leave."

There. She'd said it. She'd warned him not to care too much. So why did it feel as though that wasn't what needed to be said? Why did she feel as though what she wanted was to beg him never to leave her again?

"I know, Annie," he said. "If I ever had any doubts about that, I lost the last one yesterday."

Well, damn it, she was crying, and her tears felt like ice on her cheeks. Why was she crying? She'd had to reassure him that she wasn't asking for forever, hadn't she? Because forever wasn't for them. Their meeting was a fluke, an accident, something that never should have happened, wasn't it?

Now he lifted his fingers to her face and traced her tears.

"Ah, damn it, Annie. We'll get through this. We'll find a home for your skeleton and scrape that damned purple paint off your house. You'll be happy here because this is where you need to be. And if you don't want to practice medicine, if you want to make jewelry, that's okay too. You're strong, sweetheart, strong enough to know yourself. Strong enough to do what's right for you."

She sniffed once and felt a sob bubble out. He was so good for her. So good to her.

"And if I want to be with you?"

With gentle pressure beneath her chin, he lifted her face toward his. "I'm here, Annie. With you. *Is* that what you want?"

She felt the soft brush of his breath against her forehead. Carefully, cautiously, she lifted her hand to his chest and felt his heart beating beneath her palm. For her. With her.

"Yes," she whispered. "That is exactly what I want."

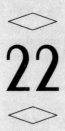

22

Monday morning came all too soon. Anne rode to the clinic with Margaret, and they left David and Wayne discussing painters and the problems of stripping the purple paint from the house and replacing it in the erratic November weather, and probably Joe Hansom, although both men were careful not to mention his name as Anne was gathering up keys and bag and coat.

Any Monday at the clinic, but especially one after a four-and-a-half-day holiday, ought to have been hectic. It was hectic, for about an hour and a half, but primarily because a half-dozen patients without appointments were waiting for the doors to open, and Nellie didn't show up. Working together, Anne and Margaret pulled files and shuffled patients from the reception area to examination rooms, filled out billing slips, and grabbed the phone. Eventually, though, the small crowd thinned, the phone quieted, and Margaret signaled she would make coffee as Anne saw the final waiting patient.

Bobby Preston sat on the examination table, bouncing his dangling feet back and forth as he drummed out a vaguely military rhythm on the metal base of the table with his heels. His mother stood against the back wall, holding his jacket and looking harried.

Anne leaned against the closed door and manufactured a stern frown for this tiny terror. "Well, tiger, what have you done this time?"

He held out his arm and the towel wrapped around it. "Darned old stitches just came out."

Anne glanced at his mother and lifted her hand to her mouth to try to hold back a chuckle. It wouldn't do to let Bobby think she was laughing at him; at eight, he had an abundance of male pride. Toni Preston understood that all too well. She had clasped her own hand across her mouth, and her eyes wore an expression of equal parts chagrin, frustration, and love for this male creature who seemed bent on driving her crazy. Anne exchanged a brief, surreptitious smile with her before she advanced on the boy.

"I guess I'd better see what damage those stitches did. Just came out, you say? All by themselves?"

"Well . . . almost."

Anne lifted the towel and studied her once neat row of sutures. "And the bandage? Did it come off by itself, too?"

Bobby gave another bang to the table with his heel and looked away from her, staring steadily at the bright red thumbtack she had stuck into the wall for her younger patients to focus on while she looked into their eyes. "I kind of . . ." His words got lost in a maze of mumble. Anne waited. When she remained silent, he grimaced at her. "I kind of sold it."

Anne choked. Toni Preston was having a similar reaction. "You . . . You *kind of* sold it? A bloody bandage?"

"Yeah." His face split in a gap-toothed grin. "I cut it up in a bunch of pieces. I got more for it than for just a look at my stitches."

Anne couldn't help it. She reached out and ruffled his hair. "Oh, Bobby. Bobby, Bobby, Bobby, what am I going to do with you?"

"Sew me back up?"

She nodded. "You've got that right. I hope you got enough out of your venture into capitalism to make this worthwhile, because it's going to hurt."

He nodded too, solemnly. "That's what Mom said. She promised me ice cream if I don't say any bad words." He stuck out his jaw. "So go ahead, Doc. I can take it."

Margaret slipped into the room as Anne finished replacing Bobby's bandage and pulled his sleeve into place over it. "Don't sell this one, Bobby," she warned. "And don't let these stitches escape. There's a limit to how many times I can stick a needle through your hide and still have enough skin to hold the thread."

He giggled at that, and Toni stepped forward to drape his jacket over his shoulder. "Don't worry, Dr. Locke. His father has already explained just what will happen if he sells anything else without getting permission first."

Anne chuckled again, and bent to give Bobby a quick hug. "See you in a week, tiger. And not a day before. Got that?"

He shrugged out of her hug but grinned at her. "Got it."

Anne started to follow the Prestons to the front desk to take care of the checkout procedure, but Margaret stopped her. "Exam room two," she said softly. "I'll take care of Toni."

Another patient? Anne hadn't heard anyone else come in. But then, she hadn't been paying a whole lot of attention to anything except an eight-year-old heart stealer.

No chart waited in the slot outside the closed door of

exam room two. Anne frowned. This wasn't like Margaret. Still frowning, she opened the door.

Nellie sat on the chair at the small built-in desk. Huddled there. With her face turned toward the wall, and her shoulders hunched.

"Nellie?"

The young woman turned slowly. When Anne saw her face, she crossed the few steps and knelt in front of her. "Oh, God, Nellie. What happened to you?"

"I'm sorry. I shouldn't have come here. I didn't know where else to go."

"Oh, honey." Carefully, not knowing the extent of Nellie's injuries, Anne took the young woman in her arms.

Nellie held herself erect within Anne's loose embrace. "I thought I was free of him," she said in the emotionless voice of one who had endured too many violent emotions. "I thought at last I could make a life for myself and for Lilly."

"A man did this to you?" Anne asked in shock. But she wasn't really surprised, was she? David's words of Thanksgiving day played through her mind. "Someone you know did this?"

Nellie's only answer was a stifled sob.

"Is Lilly all right? Where is she?"

"I couldn't risk taking her to her regular sitter. I called Gretta Tompkins and asked if she could keep her today. I didn't tell her why. I didn't get out of the car when I took her out there. I told her—I told Lilly not to say anything. I can't put my baby through this. What am I going to do?"

Anne drew back and brushed Nellie's hair away from her battered face. "First, I'm going to examine you and treat what needs to be treated, and then we're going to call Blake and have him put that bastard where he belongs. Behind bars."

"No!"

The sheer panic in Nellie's voice rocked Anne back on her heels. "No?" she asked softly. She heard the exam-room door open and looked up to see Margaret slip inside and lean against the closed door. "Nellie, you can't let him get away with this."

"No." Nellie grabbed her arm. "You don't understand. He'll take Lilly away from me. He promised me that."

Anne glanced up at Margaret. "He can't do that, honey."

"Yes. Yes, he can. He got me evicted. I don't have a home. I can't work—"

"Sshh." Anne rose to her feet and held out her hand for Nellie. "It will be all right," she promised. "Somehow we'll make it all right. Now let's get you put back together."

Anne's tiny office contained a couch, which had as its only redeeming factor a sublime comfort. After assuring herself that Nellie's injuries were painful but not threatening, Anne gave the young woman acetaminophen and a mild muscle relaxant and insisted she lie down. Now Nellie slept a tortured sleep, covered by a light afghan that one of the grandmothers Anne treated had given her as a welcoming gift.

Margaret had finally found the time to make coffee. Anne joined her near the coffeepot in the supply room at the back of the building and held her mug in both hands, aware of the chill in the unfinished room. Aware of the chill in her.

"I want to hurt someone," she said. "I never thought I'd say that, but I think I would take great pleasure in hurting whoever it was who did this to Nellie."

"Yes." Margaret didn't say more. She didn't have to.

"She says she's been evicted. She needs a place to go. I have the room . . . "

"That's not a good idea, Anne."

"I know. I can't jeopardize her or Lilly by bringing them into that house until we—" She broke off abruptly. Margaret didn't know; no matter how much it seemed as though she was as deeply involved with the man in the closet as Anne, she wasn't.

"Yes," Margaret said again.

"Do you know who it is?" she asked, suspicious of Margaret's easy acquiescence. And then another doubt struck her. "We can keep her safe, can't we? We can protect her?"

Margaret stared up at the ceiling. "We have room for them; we can see that no one harms them."

"But Wayne— Excuse me, Margaret, but I got a clear impression that Wayne is extremely careful about who he allows near him. How will he feel about you inviting two almost strangers into your house?"

Margaret gave her a twisted smile. "Wayne knows suffering, and he knows refuge. He's really much better than when he first came home. Besides, he's a real sucker for a little kid, and Lilly's already captured a piece of his heart. It will be all right. It will be more than all right. It just might be what he needs to finish bringing him back into the world."

The town fathers' generosity hadn't extended so far as to provide carpet for the unseen portions of the clinic, so the sound of a man's booted footsteps echoed through the hallway. Anne glanced in alarm at Margaret, forgetting immediately that she hadn't completely answered her questions. Margaret calmly reached across the counter and picked up a new, unopened bottle of ketchup by its neck and held it up loosely, warily, more or less like a baseball bat.

"Anne? Annie? Are you back here?"

Both women relaxed when they recognized David's voice. Margaret smiled sheepishly and looked at the bottle in her hand.

"Yes. Back here," Anne called out before cocking an eyebrow at Margaret. Stately looking Margaret. "Neat trick," she said. "I'll have to remember that."

Margaret shrugged. "A long-necked beer bottle makes a fine weapon. At least it did back in the days of my misspent youth. There is a resemblance."

Anne had both hands over her mouth to stifle her laughter, and Margaret was still looking with dazed confusion at the ketchup bottle she gripped by the neck when David rounded the corner.

He glanced first at Anne and then at Margaret. Anne saw the moment he considered the bottle as a weapon and then dismissed that idea. Margaret. No way. Or was there? "Is everything all right back here?"

And suddenly it wasn't funny anymore. Anne shook her head. "Someone beat up Nellie."

"Son of a bitch! How is she? Is Lilly okay? What did Blake say? Has he caught the bastard?"

Margaret quite carefully replaced the bottle on the counter. "Lilly is fine, or at least safe with Gretta Tompkins. Nellie won't let us call in the police."

"Why the hell—"

"Sshh," Anne whispered. "Nellie's asleep in my office."

"Was it the same guy?"

Margaret cocked her head at David in a silent question.

"David told me Thanksgiving day he thought Nellie had been abused," Anne told her before answering David. "I don't know. Probably. She said she thought she was free of him."

"Damn!"

Which echoed Anne's sentiments exactly. "What brought you down here? Something wonderful, I hope, like telling me to pick out paint colors."

"Oh. Oh, hell."

No. Not wonderful. She braced herself.

"Frances called. She's set up a meeting."

Anne slumped against the cabinet. "Oh, hell." That, too, echoed her sentiments. "When?"

"Today. This afternoon."

"This afternoon? I can't take the time right now—"

Margaret looked from David to Anne. "Does this have something to do with that room upstairs and the reason why Wayne has been patrolling your house but barely tolerates my being there?"

"Yes." Anne's voice was almost gone. "Yes."

"Then you can take the time. You only have two firm appointments this afternoon. Neither one of them is critical. I'll call and reschedule."

"Why today, David?" Anne asked. "Why not tonight? Or Wednesday afternoon?"

"She said this was the only time the museum rep could make it."

"And you believe her?"

"Yes. It's the rep I'm not too sure about."

"So what do we have to do?"

"Excuse me," Margaret said. "Do you really want me hearing this?"

At their stunned silence, she grimaced. "Thought so. Go. Talk about it in private. But do one thing first. I'll keep Nellie with me, but I took a look out the back door a while ago. Her car is there, and unless I miss my guess, she managed to get back in her house long enough to grab what's really important to her. The car doesn't need to stay in sight, here, or anyplace else, until we're sure she's safe. Take it back to your place and stash it. Okay? Then go do what you have to do, and if it's half as dangerous as Wayne's actions make me believe, then for God's sake, be careful."

Anne drove Nellie's Escort to her house. David followed closely. When she reached the top of her driveway, she glanced around. Even behind the house, the car could be spotted if someone were really looking for it. She hesitated only a moment before she drove to the old barn at the back of the drive and stopped in front of its doors.

David walked to the side of the car, and she cranked the window open. "Inside?" he asked.

She wondered at the reluctance she heard in his voice. "Isn't the building sound enough?" she asked.

"Yeah," he said. "Yeah. I guess it is that."

He unbarred the doors and opened them, and Anne drove through them into the shadowed interior. She'd forgotten how grim it was inside, had almost forgotten the hole in the roof. She stepped out of Nellie's car and locked it before giving in to a curiosity that approached reluctant fascination to look around.

Fallen leaves. Pieces of discarded furniture. An open, abandoned trunk. An ancient, dead car.

Almost without realizing what she was doing, she circled Nellie's Ford and headed to the other Ford that sat neglected and lonely, lord, so lonely, beneath the overhanging loft.

"Annie?"

David had waited at the doors. Now he entered the barn and put his arm over her shoulder, stopping her forward progress.

"That car?" Anne asked. "I wonder how long it's been here."

"It hasn't been tagged since 1941."

"'41? When Marian fell? Do you suppose it was hers?"

"Maybe. That might explain it. It was a pretty spiffy model when it came out back in '35. Would it have been in Ellie to let it sit here and rot, maybe remind Marian every once in a while that it was out here?"

"Or like Mom said, for Marian to refuse to allow her to sell it?"

She felt a shudder work through him. He was wearing a windbreaker, but in here, out of the weak sun, the air seemed colder than outside. Much colder. "Let's go in the house," she said on a shudder of her own. "I want to hear what Frances said."

"Yeah. Good idea. Go on in and I'll get these doors closed."

Anne hesitated on the back porch and looked back at David as he worked at putting the bar back across the now closed doors. Firmly putting it back. But when he joined her on the porch and they went into the warmth of the kitchen he said nothing about his puzzling actions.

Wayne nodded at her and left them alone in the kitchen.

David put his hands on her shoulders. "The rep wants to see a picture of the burial, and a few of the actual pieces."

It took a moment for his words to register. "A few of the pieces? The whole idea was to find someplace where it wouldn't have to be separated, ever, and their representative wants to see *a few* of the pieces?"

"Yes. That's what he wants. Actually, he was more specific than that. He wants samples of shell, pottery, copper, and the skeleton itself."

She couldn't do it. She couldn't go in that room and tear loose a bone for someone to poke and pry at. But somehow, worry for her safety and David's seemed a more valid argument than her reluctance to play ghoul. "And just how are we supposed to get them there without getting ourselves killed?"

"We don't have to go, Annie. We can bring him here. For that matter, you can call Joe, tell him where his grandmother's treasure is and let him have it and the responsibility for it today. Right now. But I thought you wanted to find a way, a safe and reasonable way for him to be at peace and yet of value to the scientific community. And it seems to me that Frances's call might be that way. Or it might not. The only way we're going to find out is to meet with this man. Away from here, in case he's not able to meet your requirements. And the only way he's going to be sure of what we have is if we take him samples."

"And how do we do that? How in God's name do we do that?"

"I think I know."

She stepped back, just looking at him. He dropped his hands from her shoulders and let her go.

"Why didn't something happen to us when we brought the pieces downstairs, or to you or Margaret when you took them to be mailed, or for that matter to an unsuspecting mail carrier?"

"All right," she said slowly. "Why?"

"I think it must have something to do with the dirt that's so prevalent up there. I'm not sure what, but something. We didn't clean the pieces. But when they came back, they had been cleaned. Maybe the dirt— I know it's crazy, but what the hell about this whole thing isn't? Maybe the dirt acts as some sort of connective tissue. As long as it's there, with the piece, some . . . supernatural force tells the cats it's okay. Or maybe just doesn't tell them it isn't."

"So as long as we leave an amount of dirt on each piece, we should be safe?"

"Yeah."

"And if you're wrong?"

"I'll go alone. But I'm not wrong."

He'd go alone? Did he really think she'd let him do that? Take the risk of being trapped in a closed car on a mountain road with—with . . . Oh, no. If nothing else, she'd go just so she could throw everything out the window if they were threatened. But she'd argue that later. "How can you be so sure you're not wrong?"

He looked at her in stark despair. "Because I'm a stupid, arrogant, ignorant son of a bitch, Anne. Because in spite of what had already happened, I didn't realize the danger I was putting you in. I've already proved this theory."

"What?"

"Yeah. Saturday. I took a gorget with us when we went to Spiro."

23

Anne sat stiffly erect in the split and sprung passenger seat of the Blazer. In her lap she held a sturdy, square box with its flaps securely closed. Inside, in a nest of crumpled paper for protection of the items, and a generous layer of dirt for protection of a different kind, they had placed an engraved, intact conch shell, a delicate pottery cup no taller than three inches, a small rock crystal pipe bowl in the shape of a jaguar, an engraved copper plate from the warrior's right shoulder, and one of his earspools showing the image of what she could only describe as an abstract elephant.

The museum representative had requested a bone, but Anne had flatly refused to separate any of the skeleton. Instead, she had moved the copper covering the right femur and knelt by that bone with a yardstick as David took a picture with the Polaroid camera he had picked up at the drugstore in town before he came to the clinic for her. That photograph and three others, each taken carefully to show the burial in its best light but mask its surroundings, were now tucked securely into the pocket of her jacket.

She slipped her hand into her pocket and touched them.

Were they doing the right thing?

David glanced at her as she shifted in her seat. Without speaking, he reached across the narrow console and took her hand. He clasped it tightly and pressed it against his thigh. Beneath the starched crisp denim, he was warm, so warm, living flesh and muscle, with life's blood pulsing through him. When he died, as he must, as they all must . . .

Her fingers dug into his thigh as that thought lodged in her heart. Of course he would die. Of course she would. That was a given, a part of the journey.

"What is it?" he asked.

"I was—" She turned slightly in the seat to look at him. The box grew heavy against her thighs. The pictures in her pocket burned her fingers. He would leave her. She'd known that since the first day. They'd talked about it last night. She just hadn't thought of that leaving in terms of death. She shivered, and he gripped her hand, lending her warmth.

"I was just wondering if, oh, say a thousand or so years in the future, someone will be digging up our bones and analyzing the innerspring mattresses and custom coffins we'll probably be buried in to try to determine what we ate and worshiped, how we lived, how we died."

"And if they do?"

"I guess it will mean that the civilization we know now didn't survive."

"Yeah. Probably. But it won't matter to us, Annie. Not by then. Just as it can't matter to your warrior. We'll be dead. Just like he's dead. And the spirit that animates us will be long gone from the empty shell that housed it. Just like it is from his."

His voice took on a new intensity. Who was he trying to convince? Her? Or himself?

"He's bones, Annie. Just bones. And because his burial survived, the memory of a way that is as dead as he is has a chance for survival. I don't know what this is that's protecting the shell that remains, but that's all it is. A shell. The life, the essence that was him, is gone. The civilization that honored him in burial is gone. All that remains is a small collection of *things*. Things that if shared can give the memory of that civilization a semblance of life. But not your warrior, Annie. Not as he truly was. He will never live again."

No. He wouldn't. She turned her hand in David's and interlaced their fingers. It was foolish, probably even dangerous; he couldn't drive that way for long. But right now, she needed the connection.

The museum and park were closed on Monday and Tuesday. Frances had explained that to them. She had also suggested that the closed museum would give them the privacy and the anonymity they insisted upon for their meeting.

Two cars waited in the parking lot. One, an elderly pickup of indeterminate years, probably belonged to Frances or to her grandparents. The other, a big Mercedes sedan with Oklahoma tags but a prefix Anne didn't recognize, had to belong to the museum rep. David parked in a slot well away from both vehicles and sat frowning at the Mercedes for several seconds after he had turned off the key to the Blazer.

"Is there a problem?" Anne asked at his continued silence.

He shook himself and turned to her. He lifted his hand and brushed a stray curl back from her cheek. "Probably not," he said. "Are you ready?"

Was she? Somehow, Anne didn't think so. But she

had to be. She gave David a quick nod and an equally quick smile.

His fingers lingered on her cheek. "It will be okay," he promised. "Somehow. Some way." And she wanted to believe him. Oh, how she wanted that.

Frances opened the outer door only moments after David's knock. She glanced at the box Anne carried but didn't reach to take it. "I've set up a table in the room where we normally project the slide show. He's waiting." She closed and locked the door behind them. "I— He just got here a few minutes ago. He's . . . He's . . . Dr. Tilman apparently was not able to come. This man is not who I expected."

"Do his credentials check out?" David asked.

"Yes. Oh, yes. There's no doubt he's who he says he is. I've seen him at a distance a number of times. But I took the liberty of telling him that I had to wait for you to contact me because I didn't know how to contact you."

"You don't trust him?"

"I don't know. Dr. Tilman, yes. I'd trust him with my life and everything I own. But there's something—" She grinned ruefully. "I get paranoid periodically, and downright offensive when people look right at me and don't see me. I could be wrong. I have been before."

David nodded and draped his arm around Anne, and they walked into the exhibit hall. In front of the windows, Anne paused for a moment, looking out at the mounds. Timeless. Quiet. But somehow, underlying the sense of peace the park tried to portray, she sensed something ominous waiting. Just waiting.

"Annie?"

She glanced up at David. He too was looking out over the park, toward Craig Mound and its stair-step companions. She straightened within the loose embrace of his arm. "I'm ready."

The man seated at a table in the adjacent room looked as though he would be at home in the car in the parking lot. He rose gracefully when they entered the room and closed the folio of pottery artifacts that had been placed on the table. Although Anne hadn't had much money of her own, she had been exposed to it, lots of it, during her years in Chicago. Anthony had come from a monied background and during their courtship, brief though it had been, had insisted on dragging her to charity fund-raisers and intimate gatherings, either truly small ones or those with only a few hundred or so of the host's closest friends.

She took quick inventory of the man who had insisted on seeing them so quickly. Thousand-dollar suit, five-thousand-dollar watch, hand-tailored silk shirt, custom-designed tie, special-order-only Italian shoes, two-hundred-dollar haircut, subtle more-precious-than-gold aftershave or cologne.

And he took a quick and equally thorough inventory of them. Anne had wanted to change into what in Chicago she had laughingly called her going-to-the-bank clothes, the kind that told the man whom you were begging for money, for yourself or your clinic or your favorite charity, that you really didn't need it. She'd thought that perhaps that would give them better footing in their negotiations.

"Why do we need a better footing?" David had asked. "Annie, you have what he wants. That's all the bargaining power you can possibly need. Besides, you might not see the real him if you go dressed for success."

So they had worn jeans, casual sweaters, and casual shoes. David, of course, was as starched and pressed as he always was except when dressed for physical labor. And she—well, the jeans were only six months old, and they were clean, and still, mostly, blue. But everything she and David wore could have been purchased in any small town in the state for a lot less money than the museum rep's shoes. And he knew it.

She watched the appraisal and the faint, barely perceptible dismissal that flicked through his eyes when he finished. The faint, but more perceptible distaste he revealed when he let his eyes be drawn back to the healing bruise on David's slightly Hispanic features. And she knew what Frances had meant. This man had looked right at them, but he didn't see them, only stereotypes. Stereotypes beneath him, way beneath him.

She set the box on a cleared space on the table between them and rested her right hand on it as she reached up to cover David's hand on her shoulder with her left.

Frances stepped into the room with them and closed the door. She glanced at Anne's defensive posture but nodded toward the rep. "This is Stephen Carlton," she said. "He represents the Carlton Foundation, which has endowed an Oklahoma prehistory room at the Winchester Museum in Tulsa."

Carlton stepped forward, hand extended. "And you are?"

David returned a smile as false as the one the man offered them. "Anonymous."

The man dropped his hand but held on to his smile. "Yes, well, I think we've gone beyond that now that we've met. I understand you have Spiro artifacts for which you wish to find a home."

"The right home," Anne corrected gently. "An appropriate home. One that can give us certain guarantees."

"I think you'll find the Winchester more than adequate. We're a small facility, but well endowed and well staffed. Your artifacts will have a more than appropriate display area, and more than adequate climate-controlled storage for those items which, for some reason or other, are not included in the public viewing."

Point one. Anne felt David's fingers flex beneath hers. "No," she said, just as gently as she had spoken before.

Carlton glanced at her. "No? No to what?"

She rubbed her hand over David's, drawing strength from him. "I'm not at all sure I want the artifacts on public display. The only reason I'm even considering placing them anywhere is because of their value in leading us to understanding the culture that once thrived here. But whether or not they are ever placed on public display isn't really the issue. Whatever we decide about that, I must have your assurance—written, legal, binding—that the artifacts will never be separated."

"Separated from what?"

"From each other. The collection must be kept intact."

"I can assure you that we would never sell or donate any part of the collection without your permission."

"No. Please listen to me, Mr. Carlton. The collection must be stored in the same location, in the same room, together, touching, at all times."

He glanced at her and then at the box. "With demands like that I certainly hope you have more than the contents of that box."

Almost feeling as though she were abandoning it, Anne slid her hand from the top of the box and into her jacket pocket. She retrieved one of the Polaroid snapshots and handed it to Stephen Carlton.

He glanced down at it, and his brows drew together. "This is a hoax, right? Ms. Collins, if I can prove you're party to this, I'll have your job."

Anne took the other snapshots from her pocket and handed them to Frances. The woman looked at them, visibly stunned. "Oh, my sweet lord," she whispered. Her hands trembled when David took the photographs from her and placed them on the table. He shared a long questioning glance with Anne. Did she want to go on with this? No. Would she go on with it?

Now her fingers trembled as she worked them under the flaps of the box and opened it. "Frances?" she asked. "Will you help me?"

Frances walked to her side and looked down into the box as Anne lifted the large conch shell from its nest. She turned to hand it to Frances, but while the woman touched it with loving, wondering hands, she refused to take it. "Oh, no. No, I don't think so. Not in this lifetime."

Carlton had no such compunctions. He reached across the table for the box. "I wouldn't do that if I were you," David warned softly. "The lady will take them out of the box and put them on the table."

And Anne did. The conch shell, the copper plate, the delicate cup, the rock crystal jaguar, the earspool.

Unable to restrain himself any longer, Carlton snatched up the earspool. "A long-nosed god?"

Beside Anne, Frances nodded confirmation.

Carlton pulled a spotless linen handkerchief from his pocket and began to rub the earspool. "There aren't— what? more than two of these known to have survived from this site?"

With an alarmed glance at David, Anne reached out her hand. "Don't!"

He glared up at her, annoyed, angered, or maybe just so surprised that she had dared to order him that he failed to hide his condescension. "I certainly know how to clean an artifact without injuring it."

"That isn't the issue," David said coldly. "She said don't, and unless you reach an agreement with her, she has every right to direct the care and handling of her property."

Anne noticed that he had said unless, not until, and she was very much afraid that until was getting farther and farther away.

She chuffed out a sigh and began lifting items back into their nested box. Carlton took the conch as she reached for it and turned it to look inside the bowl of the shell. They had filled it with grave dirt. Now he upended it. "Is it stained from the black drink?" he asked as he began shaking the soil onto the tabletop.

The growl started low and grew until it swirled through the room. Frances stiffened beside her, her hand stilled in its gentle tracing of the crystal jaguar Anne had already returned to the box.

"Put it down!" David ordered.

Carlton frowned at him and continued dumping soil and rubbing at the bowl with his fingers as the growl surrounded them, growing in intensity. Unbelievably, the man seemed totally unaware of it.

David reached across the table and yanked the shell from Carlton's hands.

"My God, why did you do that? You could have broken it, jerking it away like that."

But the growling faded to a low grumble.

Anne took the man's linen handkerchief from the table where he had dropped it and began sweeping the spilled soil across the table to her waiting hand. And when David placed the conch shell in the box, she scattered the soil over and into it and over the other items.

"I believe we have our answer," she said as she closed the box.

"Yes." David picked up the photos.

"I'll need those for our Board of Trustees," Carlton said, reaching as though to take them.

"No." Calmly, competently, David stacked the four photos together and then, with no apparent effort, ripped the pile in half, and in half again. He tucked the pieces in his windbreaker pocket and picked up the box. "Thank you, Frances. We appreciate your efforts."

She shook her head, let out a closely held breath, and placed her hand over her heart. "I can't say it's been a pleasure, but it's certainly been an experience. I'm sorry it didn't work out."

"Something will," Anne told her. "Something will have to."

"What the hell are you people talking about? Is everybody in this godforsaken corner of the world crazy?"

"He hasn't a clue, has he?" Frances asked.

Anne shook her head. She didn't understand; she might never understand. "I don't think so."

David took Frances's hand and held it in a moment of silent thanks. "Can you give us five minutes, maybe ten? It will be safer if he can't follow or trace us."

"The key's in the lock. If you'll leave it outside, I'll call someone to come and let us out."

Anne gave the woman a quick hug, which Frances returned. "Go," she said. "I'll be fine."

They went, hurrying out of the small room. As the door closed behind them, she heard Carlton's voice raised in protest, and Frances's voice, slurred now in the soft dialect of the area, the dialect she knew Carlton had expected simply because she looked the way she did.

"No, you wait just a minute," Frances said. Her words sounded clearly through the closed door as Anne followed David toward the locked front door, and while her accent was soft, her words were anything but. "You came down here under false pretenses. You have single-handedly destroyed any chance of the Winchester or probably any other museum gaining an invaluable collection. You have insulted possible donors. You have insulted me, and you have threatened my job . . ."

David thrust the box into Anne's hands as they reached the front door. He twisted the key from the lock, pulled the door closed behind them, and quickly locked it. Together, without speaking, they sprinted for the Blazer, but at the Mercedes, David stopped. The car wasn't locked. He opened the driver's door and tugged on a lever just inside, then opened the hood and fumbled in there. He grinned at her as he eased the hood closed. "That'll stop him."

"What?"

"Just a couple of loose wires. Want to bet our buddy has absolutely no knowledge of how this baby works?"

Anne felt a laugh building. God. Was it just a laugh? Or was it hysteria threatening to break free?

"Want to bet no one closer than Fort Smith knows how to work on a Mercedes?" she asked.

"No way," he told her as he took her elbow and hurried her to the Blazer. "I'm relatively sure that Frances will help you win that bet, hands down."

They met few cars on the road to the highway, and although Anne kept her eyes focused on the side mirror and the road they had traveled, she saw no big Mercedes roaring up behind them.

"He didn't hear them," she said. "My God, they were all around us, and he didn't hear them."

"Wayne said Joe didn't hear them either."

Anne twisted in the seat. "Wayne heard them? In the house?"

"Yes. The day Joe broke in. He said the cats warned him."

"Oh, lord." Anne hugged the box to her. "What are we going to do, David? What on earth are we going to do?"

"Something," he promised. "Something."

At the highway, he turned left.

"Where are we going?"

"Into Fort Smith. If somebody is following, if somebody was posted along the road, we'll lose them in city traffic."

Her pulse rate had returned to almost normal. The traffic along the state highway grew heavier, but no one appeared to be paying any attention to the battered Blazer. Eventually the two-lane highway became a divided interstate. A sign directed them to an off-ramp, and they took it and the well-traveled road toward town.

"You can let go of your death grip on that box now," he told her.

She glanced down. Her knuckles were white where they clutched the edges of the box. Her fingers didn't want to straighten. She laughed self-consciously and laced them together, stretching them, coaxing circulation back into them.

"Why don't you stick that behind the seat? I think we've been assured we're safe."

"I guess we have at that." She twisted within the confines of the seatbelt and tucked the box behind David's seat, and then, because the day had taken one of the November weather's quirky turns into a late, late Indian summer and the sunlight streaming into the Blazer had become uncomfortably warm, she shrugged out of her jacket and dropped it on top of the box.

"Better?" he asked.

She stretched and eased tight muscles and reached to touch his shoulder. "Yes."

They reached the downtown area, a blocks-long stretch of red brick buildings, some of them appearing a hundred years old or more, many of them charming, a few in sad need of repair. They drove the length of it, from the huge, closed hotel and a vibrant, old church at one end, to the high, arching bridge that spanned the width of the Arkansas River at the other.

David turned off the main street and drove past the courthouse and federal buildings, eventually winding past the entrance to the military cemetery and the restored buildings that remained from the fort that had given the city its name.

But this was not a sightseeing trip. Anne sensed that in David's constant vigilance of oncoming traffic as well as of the vehicles behind them. She looked out at the stately white-trimmed red brick building across the wide lawn and wondered if one day they might return as tourists. It didn't seem likely.

David returned to the main street, traveled a few blocks, and pulled into an angled parking space at the curb.

"What?" she asked.

"I think we made our getaway without being followed." He nodded toward the building in front of them. "And I know I'm hungry."

And so was she. But there was the box on the floor behind his seat.

"Leave it," he said. "It's covered by your jacket, and I'll lock the Blazer. We're on a busy street, parked at a busy sidewalk."

She nodded and got out of the car and waited for him at the parking meter. He stuffed a quarter in the slot and grinned at her. "Your hair's all falling down," he said.

She swiped an anxious hand to her hair.

"It looks great," he said, giving her one of his killer smiles. "Leave it?"

She chuckled. "I think I'll have to. I only brought identification and a little mad money with me."

"Good."

"Good? You're on the streets with someone who has to look like a mad woman and you say good?"

He took her arm and pulled her close into a loose hug. "Yeah."

What they found in the storefront restaurant wasn't the fast food she suspected David was addicted to, but it was the best burger Anne had ever eaten. Thick, juicy, on a homemade roll, served with huge wedges of roasted potato, and coffee to die for.

They were seated at a dark pine booth against bare brick walls and gleaming hardwood floors. At the front of the room, against the storefront glass, a profusion of plants grew, but none were allowed to encroach past a certain point. And near the antique cash register stood what looked to be an authentic gravity-flow, glass-bulbed gas pump, with the top cleaned and fitted as an aquarium.

Anne loved it.

She loved the stream of nonsense conversation David kept flowing.

She loved him.

Damn.

Well, she'd gotten through worse; she'd get through this.

And she'd enjoy the time she had with him.

She would.

Anne was sated with good food and their conversation when they left the restaurant, almost content but with her senses humming with awareness of him. He'd taken her arm, and they were chuckling softly over some bit of nonsense when they reached the Blazer.

David tensed. "Damn it all to hell!"

Anne had idly glanced toward a mother and three small children making an awkward, ambling journey down the sidewalk. At David's fierce oath, she turned toward the Blazer. The driver's side window had a gaping hole in it, surrounded by spidery veins in the shattered but still connected safety glass.

David reached for the door handle but jerked his hand back. Instead, he stepped to the door and looked into the Blazer, stepped back and glanced into the back.

"It's gone, isn't it?"

"Yes, and so is your jacket."

"Well, great. Just great. What do we do now?"

"Oh, Annie." He shook his head. "I don't want to do this. If this were my car, I'd be tempted to just get the hell out of Dodge. But it isn't. I've got to report it."

"And what do we tell the police officer?"

"As much of the truth as we can."

"A lady's jacket and an empty box." The officer repeated David's words and shook his head. "Damn, Huerra. Welcome to Arkansas."

"Actually, it's a gentler welcome that the one he got to Oklahoma," Anne said. "There, one of our natives knocked his car into the rear end of a log truck. With him in it."

"This is a heck of a way to spend a vacation. Are you sure you wouldn't rather be back on duty? No offense, Dr. Locke."

Anne laughed softly. Officer Stanton had been a pleasant surprise. Well into middle age and comfortable with who he was and the work he did, he'd gone about taking their report with a minimum of discomfort. And she didn't feel too badly about lying to him. If the box were found, it would be empty. "None taken."

"Okay," he said, closing his pad holder on the brief report. "Tell the dealership in Fairview this will be ready for their insurance company tomorrow, day after at the latest. I'm really sorry—"

A harsh scream ripped through whatever Stanton would have said, and repeated, echoing its cry of terror and pain. The three of them turned. It had come from a nearby alley, probably magnified and tunneled toward the street by high brick walls.

"What the—" But Stanton was already turning, tossing his pad holder down, reaching for his service revolver, running.

David put his hand on Anne's arm. "Stay here. I'll go."

Stay. Oh, yes. Definitely. There was no way she wanted to know what caused that cry, no way she wanted to see the result of that pain. There was no way she could help, she knew that already. She could only follow David as he ran toward danger and death.

"The hell I will . . ."

And they were all running, fighting to get through the small crowd of people that had already clogged the opening to the alley.

"Let me through," Stanton ordered. "Come on, move it, folks, let us through."

And remarkably, they did.

The screams had stopped. The snarling had stopped. The growls had stopped.

The body lay in an alcove off the alley. Stanton approached it cautiously. David grabbed Anne's arm and hauled her to a stop. "Let me go," she told him.

"You don't want that."

No, she didn't, but that didn't, couldn't, make any difference. Maybe she wasn't too late. Maybe she could . . . something. "I have to help if I can," she said as she jerked her arm from his grasp.

"Annie! Wait!"

But she didn't. She couldn't. She reached the alcove just as Officer Stanton turned from the crumpled mass in the doorway and staggered toward her. He caught her in his arms but not before she saw what was left of—of a man?

She gagged and whirled away from the body. David grabbed her and held her face against his chest.

"Get her out of here," Stanton ordered. "There isn't anything she can do. See if you can keep the lookers back, and call for help. Homicide, Animal Control, God, I don't know. I'll stay here and . . ." He looked around the alley. It was empty. Anne could have told him that. As empty as the cardboard box at the entrance to the alcove. But Stanton wouldn't believe her. He stood there, an incredibly brave man protecting a dead man and a crime scene from something so far beyond his experience he could only imagine the danger, while he urged David to get her to safety.

David did. She stopped at the end of the alley. "Go for help. I'll keep them from going back there."

"And just how do you plan to do that, Annie. You don't know what ghouls some people can be."

"Simple." She reached out and touched the sleeve of a man who crowded against them. "I don't think you want to go back there, sir. There's a real serious gas leak. I think it's going to blow at any minute."

David grabbed her to him and just held her as the shudders racked him. "Don't go back there. Don't put yourself in danger. Promise me."

She nodded abruptly. She'd used her supply of words and her bravado. Only then did she remember what Karen had said about the killing in her lab.

David used the radio in Stanton's police cruiser. His first words were guaranteed to get the maximum help in the minimum time and cut through the bullshit of bureaucracy demanding to know who he was and why he was on a restricted radio. "Officer needs assistance."

For a small department, an amazing number of official vehicles swarmed the scene. David had his shield in his hand and his hands in plain sight when the first car arrived. "Block the alley," he said. "Keep those civilians out. Stanton's in there guarding the crime scene."

He hadn't a hope in hell that would work, at least not without a lot of explanation on his part. But it did. The officer ran his car up on the sidewalk and closed off the alley entrance. But he yelled down the alley. "Stanton? You okay back there?"

A siren coming up the alley from the other end cut off Stanton's reply, but not until at least one reinforcement had heard his voice.

Annie. Where was Annie? A man in a suit forced his way through the throng to David's side and shoved a badge in his face. "What's happened here?"

There she was. Pale. God, she looked like she might pass out at any moment. But she was coming to him. If she could reach him through the press of officers surrounding him.

He took a step toward her, only to be stopped by a hand on his arm. He glared at the hand; he glared at the man who put it there. "Let her through."

The man nodded and the crowd surrounding him parted. Annie stumbled and he caught her. She sobbed once and leaned into his strength. He looked over Annie's head at the man obviously in command.

"Officer Stanton was taking a burglary report from us," he said. "He has our names and addresses. He had finished the report and was leaving when we heard a scream from the alley. I'm a police officer from Dallas. Anne is a doctor. We accompanied him into the alley approximately fifty yards to an alcove and a doorway where we found a body. We saw no one. He asked for our assistance while he guarded the scene. Anne blocked the alley and I used his radio."

"Is that how you remember it, ma'am?" the man asked Anne.

She nodded.

"And you didn't stay to see if you could give medical aid?"

Anne raised her head and looked at her interrogator, and David thought he would never forget the sick revulsion in her eyes. "Go look at him," she said. "Go look at him and then come back and ask me that question."

24

No one reported hearing growls or snarls, not Stanton, not any of those who had been drawn to the alley by the screams. Certainly not David or Annie. The Fort Smith police let them go. There was, after all, nothing more to be said or done by them, and that department had all it could handle.

The Blazer's heater had all it could handle, too, fighting the increasingly cooler outside air of late afternoon as it whistled and roared through the shattered window.

David had taken off his windbreaker and draped it around Anne's shoulders, but it wasn't enough.

He stopped in Fairview. The Chevy dealer was remarkably unconcerned about the damage to the loaner, maybe because David's car still sat, untouched, in the back lot. "You're hell on cars, Huerra," was all he'd said, and cheerfully at that, before he'd lent him still another vehicle, a modified Suburban.

Blake had not been available when he called the sheriff's office, but the dispatcher promised to find him and relay the message that David needed to talk to him. It was time to live up to his promise to the sheriff, and he wasn't looking forward to it.

And he wasn't looking forward to taking Annie back to that house. But he had to.

He'd seen her look like this once before. Damn it. Only two days before. At the fork in the highway just outside Allegro, he pulled to a widened place on the side of the road and stopped.

This truck had bench seats.

He unsnapped his seat belt and hers and dragged her to his side.

She was cold. Still cold. Little shivers shook her. And she wasn't with him. Where was she? In Chicago pleading futilely for the lives of those who had trusted her? At the top of Simpson Knob, physically holding life and blood in a small boy? Or in an alley in Fort Smith witnessing a sight that rivaled any nightmare he had seen in fifteen years as a cop?

He rubbed his hands up and down her arms, across her back, and finally just wrapped her as close to him as he could and held her. "It will be all right, Annie girl. We'll make it all right. We can do it. Somehow."

He felt her drag in a tortured breath and rock against him. "It isn't supposed to happen here. I came here because this kind of thing isn't supposed to happen here. No violence. No blood. No crime. Harriet Nelson or June Cleaver in every kitchen. Who was he, David? Someone sent by that awful man from the museum? Someone sent by Joe? Or just a thief who picked the wrong car? And what difference does it make who he was? This place is supposed to be safe. Damn it! Bad things don't happen in little towns like this. That's why I'm here; that's why I have to stay. It's the big cities where greed and death rule not—"

"Annie, Annie, it can happen anywhere. Some places are safer than others, but no place is completely safe."

"No, you don't understand. I won't let it happen

here; I can't let it happen here. I need someplace in the world, someplace in this whole big world where I won't be afraid."

He felt his throat tighten, felt the pressure of not being able to promise her that he would always keep her safe. Because he couldn't promise her that.

"You're safe here, Annie," he said around the constriction in his throat. "And now. Right here and right now you don't have to be afraid. Start with that, darlin'. Build on that. You can do it."

"And when you leave? What do I do then?"

She was sure, so sure he would leave her. Was she right? Could he survive in this corner of the world where she had chosen to hide? Could she?

Anne seldom saw a sunset. The hill behind her house cut off any view of one from her home. Her home. Only a week before those words had brought her great pride. Now— Now she suppressed a shudder as David turned the Suburban into her driveway and downshifted for the climb. Twilight already hid the yard and lower windows, and from the kitchen a light gleamed.

Margaret's truck sat parked in the turnaround. Of course. The clinic would be closed by now, and she and Wayne wouldn't leave the house unguarded.

God. Did any human have to guard the house?

David parked and took the key from the ignition. He, too, looked up at the house, at the back wall bare of windows, at the overgrown hillside behind them, at the closed and barred doors of the sagging barn.

"I should have run with you that first day," he said softly. "I should have said, 'I'm not going in that house, and there's no way in hell I'm letting you go back in without me.' I should have stuffed you back in that brown truck of yours and hauled us both out of this county."

She fumbled for his hand and held on.

"We're not in any danger from what's in there," he said. "I'm pretty sure of that. But I'm not so sure we're safe from anyone who decides to come looking. I'm sorry, Annie."

"Why are you sorry? If it weren't for my crazy, greedy family, there'd be no problem."

"Now that I'm not so sure of."

A shadow separated from the side of the house and moved forward, just before the bright beam of a flashlight trapped them in its glare. Anne could have sworn her heart stopped, then started again at double speed.

"Damn. It's okay, Annie. It's okay." David opened the truck door, and when the interior light came on, the flashlight went off. "Sorry, Wayne. I should have realized you wouldn't recognize the truck."

Anne watched as Wayne stopped and examined both of them in the dim light. "You two okay?"

"Yes." David slid from the seat, still holding Anne's hand. He bent toward her, looking at her face, her eyes, focusing for a moment on her lips. His own quirked ruefully, and he gave her another of his wicked grins. "We'll neck later," he whispered. "This will be a great truck for it. Much better than the Blazer."

With a sob or a chuckle, she wasn't sure which, Anne slid from the truck. With a little effort, she convinced her knees to support her, and she convinced her legs to work as she walked with David up onto the porch and into the warmth of her kitchen.

Wayne came in with them. Margaret entered the room from the hallway, and the two of them shared a silent communication before Wayne shrugged out of his coat and hung it on a peg. "Don't suppose you'd want to tell us what happened to the Blazer, or to Anne, or just in general what in the hell is going on, would you?"

"Wayne." Margaret's soft voice both chastised and invited his silence.

"No, hell, no, Maggie. If it were just me, I would keep my mouth shut. But you're here, and that poor, hurt little girl and her baby, and this is the second trip out of three in as many days that he's brought Anne back looking like death warmed over. It's time to ask questions."

David looked down at Anne. He was going to tell— she knew that—with or without her permission. And he was right to do so. Slowly she nodded.

"And it's time for answers." Still looking at her, David spoke to Wayne and Margaret. "Just as soon as Blake gets here."

David met Blake on the back porch when he arrived.

"Tell me that homicide in Fort Smith doesn't have anything to do with the problems coming from this house," the sheriff said without preamble.

"I can't do that, Blake."

Blake slumped slightly. He scrubbed at the back of his neck. "Well, hell."

David opened the screen and stepped back. "Come inside."

Nellie had joined them in the kitchen for a few minutes. She'd even been persuaded to drink a cup of soup. But the two men and undercurrents she had no way of understanding obviously made her uneasy, even though she tried to hide it. Margaret fixed her a cup of hot tea, gave her more analgesics, and convinced her to rest in the downstairs bedroom.

Gretta Tompkins, perhaps understanding the need

for an early bedtime, had kept Lilly up and active all afternoon. So after a quick supper for her, even though it was not late, it wasn't difficult for them persuade the little girl to take a nap with her mama.

That left Wayne and Margaret, David and Anne, and Blake, seated at the round table in the kitchen.

Still pale, still wearing his windbreaker, Anne had her hands stuffed in its pockets. An unpleasant, expectant hush had settled over the room. She looked up at David. "Where do I start?"

"I'll do it." Somehow it seemed the least he could do for her. "If you'll let me."

"Oh, please."

Now, all he had to do was figure out how to explain the unexplainable. But maybe that wouldn't be completely impossible. Wayne met his glance from across the table and gave him an almost imperceptible but nonetheless encouraging nod.

He supposed he'd have to start at the beginning. And where else would that be but with the man upstairs? His gesture at the museum, tearing up the photographs, had been more for security than for dramatic emphasis; in the wrong hands those pictures could be dangerous. He'd meant to shred them further and dispose of the pieces, but he hadn't yet.

"Annie," he said softly. "Give me the pictures. In the jacket pocket," he added when she just looked at him, confused.

She remembered. Nodding, she withdrew her hand from the pocket and handed him the pieces of photographic paper.

The puzzle wasn't difficult; he'd only torn them twice—four parts to each of four distinctive portraits. With only a moment's study he pieced them together and lay them in the center of the table, clearly visible by the three people—friends, good friends, trustworthy friends—across from them.

Wayne gave a low whistle and looked up, understanding. "Ralph Hansom's treasure."

"Yes."

"Is that what got him killed?"

"Probably."

Blake looked up from the photo he had been tracing the perimeter of in fascinated disbelief. "You're saying he was murdered?"

"No." David hurried to stop that misconception. "I believe his car went off the mountain with him in it, and that no other person was involved."

"Then what—" Wayne stopped, finding the answer to his own question. "The cats? Inside with him?"

David nodded. "I think so."

"Cats," Blake said. "Like these cats you've been hearing, seeing, tracking?"

"Not like them, Blake," David told him. "The same ones."

"Wait a minute. That was almost fifty years ago. Are you telling me that you've been tracking geriatric mountain lions?" He gave a short laugh. "Or maybe their ghosts?"

Wayne leaned back in his chair and reached for Maggie's hand. "Maybe," he said. "That would explain why Uncle James didn't see them."

"Wait a minute," Blake said, looking from Wayne to David. "Hold on. Stop."

Wayne stopped.

David stopped. He recognized the need Blake felt to deny the unbelievable. He'd done it himself. He recognized Blake's need to orient himself with something familiar and real. He'd done that, too. But Blake had now had his moment to do that; it was time to move on.

"In the last three days, we've spoken to Frances Collins, the interim director at the Spiro Mounds Park, and to Marian Hansom, Joe's grandmother, as well as to you, Blake, looking for answers to questions we didn't even know how to ask. Each answer we got led us deeper into confusion, but there were some things that kept recurring. Cats. And curses. And death."

Blake shifted in his chair, but he gave David his full attention.

"In 1935, Ralph Hansom apparently either stole this burial," David told them, indicating the photographs, "or hired someone to steal it. Everyone who helped him, everyone he tried to sell it to, died a brutal death.

"Frances's grandfather was a digger at the site. She heard this from him. She says the old-timers talk about big golden cats prowling the mounds. She didn't tie the deaths she told us about to the cats. She did tie them to the curse.

"Marian Hansom blames everything on the curse: Ralph's death, her poverty, her injury." He glanced pointedly at Blake. "The deaths of Lucy Hansom and Walter Briggs. She also admitted that the reason Joe is supporting her is because she has told him about the fortune this represents, but not where it is."

Wayne and Blake knew the next part of the story; he doubted that Margaret did. "We found the burial on Wednesday. That was the first time we heard what could have been a large cat. We sent a shell to a collector in Dallas. He was murdered. We sent a femur to a friend of Anne's in Chicago. It was stolen from her. The thief was murdered. Both by large animals."

Margaret gasped and clutched Wayne's hand. "These are the cats he's heard?"

"Yes, Margaret, I believe they are."

He turned to Blake. "The day Joe broke in, the cats

warned Wayne. He heard them, before and after the break-in. Joe didn't.

"We asked Frances to help us find a way to let archaeologists and historians benefit from the knowledge this burial can reveal and yet protect anyone who might come in contact with it in the future.

"We met today with a representative from a private museum in Tulsa. We took him these four pictures and five items from the grave goods. All Anne asked in exchange for turning this collection over to him was a legally binding promise that it would be kept secure and together. He gave lip service, but it was apparent he didn't intend to do that. It was also apparent that the cats didn't like his treatment of the artifacts."

"You heard them?" Blake asked.

David nodded. "I heard them. Anne heard them. And Frances Collins heard them. God, Wayne, I know now what you mean about the volume. We were in a windowless room, maybe fifteen by thirty. They were all around us. And Stephen Carlton didn't hear a thing."

"So I was right." Wayne grimaced. "They weren't fussing at me, were they?"

"Oh, they were fussing, all right. They only stopped when we forcibly took the last artifact from him and packed it away with the others. I don't know what would have happened to us if we hadn't done that."

"And Fort Smith?" Blake asked. "How did they get from the Mounds park to Fort Smith?"

"We went into the city to make sure no one from the museum followed us home," David said. "I would have sworn I wasn't followed. We stopped to eat. While we were in the restaurant someone broke into the car and stole the box of artifacts."

"The man who was killed in the alley?"

"Yes, Blake. I saw the empty box just outside the doorway where he had been trapped."

Anne laid her hand on his, seeking his attention. "We have to call Frances," she said. "We left her locked in the museum with that awful man. We have to make sure she's all right."

"Huerra, damn it!" Blake rose with a roar. "What the hell kind of path are you cutting through this part of the country?"

"With her permission, Blake." Annie said quickly. "She told us to. She kept him locked in with her so that we could leave. Please. Please . . ."

David turned his hand and laced his fingers with hers.

She returned the pressure. Whatever she had been about to beg for, she didn't. "Would you please see if you can get in touch with her? She lives with her grandparents, but I don't know their names."

Blake dragged his chair around, scooted it back up to the table, and rested his hands on the back of it. "Sorry, Doc. Sure. Sure. I'll have my dispatcher call the sheriff's office up there. They'll know. But first—" Now he was the one giving a pointed look—at David. "You said the box was empty. Any idea what happened to the items that were in it?"

He felt Annie's fingers jerk within his. He drew her hand up and clasped it in both of his, rubbing it. Warming it. "They ought to be back by now, don't you think?"

"Yes."

Oh, hell. If the first part of this story had been hard for Blake to believe, how much more difficult would be the rest of it?

"Have I been upstairs since we came in this afternoon, Wayne?"

"No."

"Has Annie?" he asked, knowing that not even his Annie would be safe from suspicion.

"Thanks," David said when Wayne dragged his head to one side in a negative gesture. "Remember that, please. Make the call, Blake," he suggested. "Then we do have to go upstairs. All of us."

Blake called his office and requested the information, then hauled the telephone back over to the table and set it in front of his chair. It rang in only minutes—minutes that had dragged because of the silence around the table. Blake noted a number, said a few terse words to the caller, then scooted telephone and the scrap of paper with the number on it across the table.

David considered giving the telephone to Annie to make the call. Considered it for about the space of two heartbeats. She had rallied, but not that much, and not that well. He dialed the number.

Frances answered on the second ring.

"Are you all right?" he asked. "Annie wanted to be sure you survived confinement with Carlton."

"Yes," Frances said over the mumble of a television in the background. "But I'm not sure he did. He was looking awfully ragged by the time Gramma got there to unlock the door."

He patted Annie's hand and mouthed the words, "She's all right."

"I'm sorry we had to do that," he told the woman on the phone.

"Those are the magic words, aren't they, David? Had to. I'm sorry I got you nice folks involved with him."

"Will there be any repercussions for you?"

"No, I . . . " Her voice faded as the sounds from the television grew louder. "Wait a minute. What? What Gramps? Oh, my lord."

"What is it, Frances?" he asked sharply.

"What it is, is the Fort Smith news," she said eventually, and he knew what story she must be seeing, but not how much was being told. Their names shouldn't be mentioned. There wasn't any reason for them to be dragged into the news story. But the mangled body was news. Big news.

"Yeah," he said without her having to ask. "Someone broke into the car and stole the box of artifacts."

"Oh, shit."

He listened to the faint hiss of the line and the rumble of the television newscaster.

"How is Anne?"

How was Anne? He glanced at her. About at the end of her endurance? Holding on by a thread and sheer determination? "Better," he told her, praying it was true.

"I'm coming down there," Frances said abruptly. "Something's got to be done. Carlton's going to try to find you. God only knows what he'd do if he got his hands on the burial. Do you suppose he was responsible— Never mind. We can talk about that when I get there. Maybe— Maybe together we can come up with something."

"Can you—" Hell, why not? "Can you make sure you're not followed?"

For reply, she only gave a wicked laugh. "Give me finding directions for where you are."

Maybe his paranoia was working overtime. Maybe it was time for his paranoia to start doing just that. If Blake had found her telephone number so easily, who else might have? "No," he said. "Call when you get to town. Then we'll either give you directions or come and lead you here."

Anne looked in on her other guests before they went upstairs. Lilly lay curled against her mother with her thumb securely in her mouth. Nellie slept heavily, her battered face cushioned against a down pillow, unaware that Anne watched. Unaware of anything, not even dreams at this level of sleep. Good. That was what she needed. Sleep to let her body heal. Sleep to give her a chance to recapture her strength.

Was that what she herself was doing, Anne wondered as she pulled the door shut against any noise they might make going upstairs. Retreating from the shock and the pain to recover? Or had she finally reached the limit of what she could endure? She wasn't sure.

Neither was David. He thought she didn't know; he was careful not to be too obvious as he hovered over her. She knew. What she didn't know was how to bring herself out of this cushioned fog that had enveloped her.

"How is she?" David asked at her side.

"Asleep."

"Good."

The two of them led the way upstairs. Anne might have resisted the way David held her arm if she hadn't glanced back and seen that Wayne had taken the same protective posture with Margaret.

The door was closed, as they had left it. David pushed it open and flipped the switch for the overhead light. They'd left the small stove lighted, burning low.

Marian had lived in this room for how long? Years and years and years as a bitter, vindictive, and greedy woman. The hate that fueled her, the madness that governed her, ought to have permeated even the boards beneath their feet.

But it hadn't. The room was warm. Warm and as inviting as its shabby sophistication would allow.

Margaret looked with interest at the art deco sofa and parlor stove. Wayne glanced at the off-center light fixture and then at the closet wall.

"That's what raised Anne's suspicions," David told him.

"A false wall?" Wayne asked.

"Yes, but not where we thought."

David opened the closet and then discovered he either had to let go of her arm or drag her into the closet with him. He patted her arm—he'd done a lot of that since they left the museum—but he let go of it and walked into the closet. She heard the sounds of him wrestling the panel away and stepped back, indicating that Blake should follow him into the closet.

He did. Wayne followed him. Margaret remained by her side. "Should we go back downstairs?" she asked.

Only that morning, Anne had thought that it seemed as though Margaret had been involved forever. Now that feeling doubled. How strange. "No," she said.

The three men stood at the foot of the skeleton. Anne and Margaret stepped to one side, standing together. And he was a skeleton, Anne told herself. No longer a warrior. No longer a man. Bones. Just bones, as David had said, with the spirit that animated him long gone.

But why did the loss seem so recent? Why did the separation seem so new? She felt Margaret's arm come around her waist in silent support and looked up to see moisture glistening in her friend's eyes.

And why did it seem as though she had stood just here, before, with this woman, sharing her support as she grieved for this man?

Blake broke the spell. "Wait a minute. You said you sent the femur, the *right* femur, to Chicago."

Anne slipped from Margaret's side and went to kneel beside the litter. "Yes," she said. She shifted the copper slightly. "This one." She didn't look at Blake's face; she knew she'd see blatant skepticism there. "And this gorget is the one we sent to Dallas." All of the other items except the crystal jaguar had already settled into place. It still rested on the edge of the litter. One by one she touched them. "And these were in the box that was stolen from the car in Fort Smith." Now she turned to look at Blake. "We told the police officer the box was empty, because we knew it would be when they found it."

Blake was dragging his head from side to side. "I trust your word, Anne Locke, but I'm having a whole lot of trouble with this."

"Frances is coming," David told him. "She can identify the pieces that we showed Carlton."

"There's another way," Anne said. "Pick out a piece, Blake. One that you can easily recognize."

"Annie—"

"It's all right, David. We've done it. And maybe this is the only way Blake will truly understand."

Blake approached the foot of the litter warily and went down on one knee. Just as warily he reached toward the heaped up treasures. When she saw that he picked up the cedar box containing the miniatures, Anne wanted to call back her words, wanted at least to cry out, *Not that one. Anything else, but not that.*

She didn't have to. A low rumbling came from her left, not really threatening—not yet—just making its presence known. Blake tossed down the box and backed carefully away from the litter.

"That's it?" he asked softly. "That's the sound you heard?"

"Not quite," David stepped between Blake and the warrior. "I don't think it was really pissed off at you, just moderately upset. You read it that way, Wayne?"

Wayne had already thrust himself between Margaret and the sound. "Yeah. That about describes it. Why don't we take the women downstairs."

The crystal jaguar had not moved. Anne scooped a

little loose dirt from the floor of the litter and sprinkled it on and in the pipe bowl. "How about this piece, Blake? Would you be able to recognize it?"

"Anything. Anything, Anne. Don't you think you should move away from there?"

Should she? Anne looked at the litter, at all that remained of the man who had amassed such wealth and power. Someone who for some reason unknown by them, and in spite of what was now believed about the religion of his time, had gone to his grave and his after-life alone. And he was still alone. Anne knew that as certainly as she knew he had been torn from his grave.

"Annie."

David had moved to stand beside her. Now he held his hand for her to help her to her feet. He was right. She knew he was right. Only bones and a lingering memory. And he was worried about her. Concern tightened his features and darkened his eyes. And maybe he was right about that, too, because no matter how much David meant to her, a part of her wanted to stay right where she was. With a man who had been dead for seven hundred years.

But of course she wouldn't do that.

She shifted the crystal jaguar into her left hand and took David's hand with her right as she rose to her feet. Such a fierce frown he had. Such a possessive grip. Did he realize that? She gave him a smile to ease his frown. He closed his eyes briefly, and when he opened them both his frown and his grip eased.

They left the light on in the room. David and Blake settled the panel into place and closed the closet door. They waited in the hall while David closed the door to the room behind them. "We can't lock it," he said. "We haven't found a key or changed the lock. But I think we can find a way to convince you."

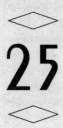

25

Anne watched how each person dealt with the story David had told.

Maybe she hadn't wimped out, after all. Maybe her way was just as valid as any other for dealing with an unbearable situation.

Blake had wanted to leave the rock crystal jaguar in plain sight so that he could watch it constantly. Because neither she nor David knew exactly how the transfer worked, they'd argued against that as potentially dangerous. Instead, Blake had pulled his car in front of the porch steps, in full view of the window in the kitchen door. After David lightly dusted the ancient pipe, Blake had locked it in the glove compartment and then had locked all of the car's doors. He'd also gone with Wayne and David to check the locks on all the doors and windows on the ground floor of the house.

Now he paced, and all too often he walked to the back door and looked out as though he half expected to find the door ripped from his Jimmy.

Although he tried not to be too obvious, David watched Anne.

Margaret faced the time by digging into Anne's pantry and freezer and putting together a meal.

Anne spent the time knitting herself back together. Thread by thread, by thread.

The only one who seemed unbothered by the wait was Wayne, and Anne suspected he had learned places inside himself where he could go and no one would ever know.

When Frances telephoned, everyone in the room seemed to breathe a sigh of relief. They'd been on hold, waiting for something. Now they knew what.

Blake wouldn't leave. Wayne drove into town to lead her back to the house. And Margaret began setting the meal on the table.

They heard the cars climbing the drive, and each moved in an action determined by God alone knew who. It reminded Anne of a funeral gathering, each person going through the motions of a normal life when everything normal had been shattered by death.

Wayne opened the door and ushered Frances in. She stopped just inside the door and looked around the kitchen as she shed her coat. "Wow," she said. "This is going to be great. Is it as huge as it looks in the dark?" But when Wayne took her coat from her, she turned and noticed Blake and her smile faded. "Sheriff? Is there a problem?"

"No." Anne handed her a cup of coffee. "Blake's here because we asked him, and I hope as a friend."

"We're all friends," Margaret said from her place at the stove.

And they were. More than that. Anne's eyes sought out David. Some much more than that. He held the chair for Frances, a courtly gesture he seemed to have picked up from Wayne, or maybe not. Maybe it had already been ingrained in him. How truly strange,

Anne thought. A week before she had known only two of these people, and those two in a professional capacity.

Now they would forever be a part of her life.

Even when they left her.

Damn! She had to get out of this morbid mood. Not everybody was destined to leave her. Why did she keep coming back to that thought? No. No, no, no. Before it had been David, only David, she'd known would go. Now it was *all* of them. Ridiculous. In all the emotional knitting she'd been doing, she must have dropped a stitch.

"Did you have any problems getting here?" David asked.

"No more than any other person who's been spoiled by flatland river bottoms," she said.

Blake still prowled. Now he glanced at Frances. "Ms. Collins?"

She turned questioningly toward him.

"Could you recognize the artifacts that David and Anne brought to the park today?"

"Well, yes. Of course. They were unique in design. Have they been recovered?"

Margaret closed the oven door with a determined thump. "Oh, go on and check, Blake Foresman. No one's going to want dinner until this is resolved anyway."

Blake turned toward Anne. "Do you suppose . . ."

"I don't know," she told him.

David went with him. Frances looked puzzled but resisted asking any questions. At least for the moment. Anne was sure the woman would have plenty of them later.

When the men returned Anne knew from Blake's ashen face that the jaguar had disappeared from his truck.

David moved to her side. Blake stopped inside the door and just stood there. Anne remembered all too well those first moments when she and David knew that the warrior's grave goods returned to him. She remembered the suspicion that David, and even she, had felt before believing the unbelievable.

"Go," she told David. "Take him upstairs and get it over with."

Now more than ever the gathering took on a funereal air. She hadn't been able to go to Anthony's funeral; she'd still been in the hospital. But she remembered her grandmother's, with all the family coming home. Singly or in groups, all of them had gone to the funeral home to view the body—the shell—that had been her grandmother. Anne had slipped away by herself to say good-bye to her grandmother. She hadn't wanted to share what little time she had to say good-bye to her with others. As strange as it seemed, she felt the same way now.

Did the others?

"Will you come with us?" David asked her.

"No." She glanced at the woman sitting quietly, if not completely patiently, at the table. "Frances, would you like to see the burial?"

Frances clutched her hands together in front of her on the table. "I don't know. I find I'm having a surprising amount of trouble with this." She laughed shakily. "It's a hell of a note for a woman who has worked most of her life trying to get an advanced degree in archaeology, but since you showed me those photos earlier, he's become a person to me, not just a study, and I'm having a real hard time with the fact that someone, thief or scientist, it doesn't really matter to me right now, ripped him out of his grave."

"I know," Anne told her. "But maybe that's a good reason for you to see him."

"Besides," Blake said, still a little subdued, "I'd like you to confirm something for me."

Frances went upstairs with the men.

"Are you all right?" Margaret asked when the two of them were alone in the kitchen.

"I'm getting there," Anne told her. And she truly believed she was.

The others were all quiet when they returned to the kitchen. Frances smiled uncertainly at Anne. "I'm still not comfortable with the questions I've had to ask myself today, Anne Locke, but I will forever thank you for sharing that treasure with me."

Blake lapsed into silence, only occasionally rousing himself to mutter the three syllable *hell* that was the one sure sign he was disturbed.

Wayne walked over to Margaret and without warning hugged her tight to his chest. "I love you, woman. I don't think I've told you that in a long time. Too long."

Margaret's eyes filled. No tears fell, but her voice quivered slightly. "I know that, Wayne Samuels. I've always known that."

And David—David who, more than she, had been able to come and go from the room without seeming to be affected by the man who lay there—David seemed strangely subdued.

Of course Frances identified the items that she had seen at the park. Of course the crystal jaguar had returned from Blake's locked truck.

And of course, with the close of the meal they ate simply because they had to, and because Margaret put it on the table in front of them, the questions began. Tentatively. Touching first on what was real, normal, and known, before moving into speculation. Crazy Marian. Joe and his greed. Ralph and his greed. Frances's grandfather's part in the commercial digs.

The deaths of diggers and dealers. The disappearance of Lucy and Walter. The three brutal deaths that had taken place in the last four days.

Anne listened, not sharing, allowing David to speak for them. Thinking about the man upstairs. Thinking about the world he must have known. Thinking about the world that had dragged him back.

Thinking about David, as he glanced up sharply at something that was said. As he frowned later at something else. As he reached for her hand and held it against his thigh, massaging her fingers almost unconsciously as one portion of his fertile mind worked on some problem while another engaged in the conversation now flowing around the table.

Did he know he touched her as though she had been a part of his life forever?

During the meal and discussion, Blake had regained his voice and his vocabulary. "So what we're saying is, if we don't protect that not-so-small fortune Anne found, the cats are going to do it for us?"

Anne shuddered at his choice of words.

"That about sums it up, Blake," David told him.

"Well, hell." The sheriff in Blake took over. "Let's see who knows about this. Marian Hansom. Now she's a wild card in any deck. Who knows what she's liable to say or to whom? Joe Hansom, who apparently wants it bad enough to spend a fortune on care for a grandmother he must know is using him, bad enough to risk his political campaign and future as a free man to break into this house at least once already. Stephen Carlton, who might not know who you two are now but probably has the resources to find out." He did a quick head count. "The six of us. Anybody else? Nellie? The little girl?"

David shook his head. "No. I don't think so. Wayne?"

"Not from us. She came in with Maggie after the clinic closed and except for the little bit of time she was in the kitchen earlier, she's shut herself up in that front bedroom, sleeping."

"That's another thing," Blake said. "Somebody want to tell me what happened to her?"

"Not now, Blake," Margaret said. "I think she should, and Anne thinks she should, but Nellie is scared to death to get you involved—"

"Well, hell, that's reason enough—"

"And as soon as I can convince her of that, I will call you," Margaret promised.

"The problem is, what to do with a monetary and scientific fortune," Wayne said. "A deadly fortune."

"Yep. That about says it," David admitted. He turned to Frances. "Tell me, now that you've seen it, now that you've heard what can happen, do you think there's a snowball's chance that *any* museum would honor a requirement not to separate the burial?"

"I want to say yes," Frances said slowly. "But there's been so much competition over the years, so much rivalry, and so many items that have simply disappeared, that I'm afraid I can't."

"Marian doesn't want Joe to get his hands on it before she dies," Blake offered. "There's always a possibility she'd keep her mouth shut about its location. Could we maybe build a vault around it and just leave it here? At least until you folks found someone you could trust to turn it over to?"

"I'll go along with whatever Anne decides," Wayne said, "but Blake, do you really think that would be a wise course of action?"

"Hell, no, I don't think it's wise. I want it out of my county. I just don't know how to get it gone without risking more lives."

"Annie." David lifted her hand from his thigh. She missed the warmth and nearness until he clasped it in both of his. "Even though I agree with Blake on this, I'll go along with whatever you want done. But we have to hear from you. What do *you* want to do?"

She looked around the table at the small coterie of caring people gathered there. What did she want? She wanted the impossible. She wanted him at peace. "I just want to put him back."

She saw sympathy in their eyes. And compassion. And regret for what couldn't be.

Frances propped her elbows on the table and clasped her hands under her chin. And looked at Anne. Really looked at her. And opened her mouth on a silent word. And lifted her head. "Well, why not?"

"What?" That was the last thing Anne had expected anyone to say.

Apparently it was the last thing any of them expected anyone to say. Her question was only one of five.

Frances held up her hands, asking for silence. "Wait a minute. Let me think. Oh, God, let me think." She caught her hands to her mouth and rocked back and forth in silence for what seemed like forever as Anne waited, scarcely daring to breathe. *Could they do this? Could they restore him to the grave that had been stolen from him?*

"Okay." Frances pulled her hands from her mouth and stopped her rocking. "Craig Mound is sterile soil. What that means is that it was dug out and dynamited by the pothunters, and sliced away in thin vertical layers by the W.P.A. and the university, until there was nothing left on the original location. Nothing. Down to a depth low enough that the excavators were sure was below the level of any possible archaeological find. Then the dirt was sifted and sieved until the tiniest fragments were found and removed and catalogued. And then the soil was replaced and shaped to the measurements and specifications and photographs that were available at the time.

"There's no reason for anyone ever to dig in that mound again. Except . . . "

Anne realized she had been holding her breath. She released it, but she didn't release her grip on David's hand. "Except for what, Frances?"

"Except for a rumor that crops up every few years about constructing a viewing chamber in Craig. But you know how state government works. And since the oil bust, finances are really tight. We can't even get authorization for more excavation—Brown hasn't been completed, Copple barely started, the Plaza only sampled—so the chances of something like a viewing chamber are almost nonexistent. Almost, I have to say. But if we're careful, we can put him away from where any possible chamber should be located."

Now they all looked at Anne. *Whatever she wanted to do.* The decision was hers. David endured the pressure of her fingers on his, even gave hers a slight squeeze in encouragement.

Yes. This seemed right. She leaned against David's shoulder and let the rightness wash over her. "Yes," she said. "Yes. Let's do it."

"When?" David asked.

"The park's closed tomorrow," Frances said.

"The sooner the better," Blake added.

Margaret glanced at Anne. "Then the clinic is closed tomorrow, too. I'll need a few minutes in the morning to reschedule the appointments."

As quickly as that, it was decided.

Wayne and Margaret opted to stay there the rest of the night rather than wake up Nellie and Lilly and move them for what could be no more than a few hours.

Anne invited Frances to stay, but she insisted she had

to get back to her grandparents, and that she needed time in the morning at the park before they arrived. Agreeing on when and telling them where they should meet the following day, she said good night. "Just hope the blasted tractor won't decide that tomorrow is a good day for it to go on strike," she said on her way out the door, and Anne knew she was only half joking. "It does that with disgusting regularity."

Blake left with Frances, promising to escort her safely at least as far as the county line.

Anne showed Margaret and Wayne to an upstairs room and found linens for them, but when she offered to help make the bed, Margaret shooed her away. "Go on," she said. "You have to be dead on your feet."

And she was. Almost. Until she was ready for bed. Until David and Wayne were making one last check around the outside of the house. Until she accepted that there was something she had to do.

Removing the panel had become almost easy over the last few days. Now Anne slipped it aside and entered the room. She considered not even turning on the light, but she wanted to see him one last time. She pulled the cord, flooding the room with light from the bare bulb, and looked around the shabby chamber where a once powerful ruler had lain hidden for half a century. As tombs went, it wasn't much.

She knelt at his feet and lifted the small cedar box containing the miniatures. Nothing growled at her when she picked it up. Why? Because she realized how special it must have been to him and to the woman pictured? She didn't open it. She didn't need to; the images were engraved on her memory. Instead, she touched it reverently and placed it where she had first seen it, where it had returned after Blake had tossed it down. Near that fragile, vulnerable left foot.

She felt tears on her cheeks and let them fall freely.

"Are we doing the right thing?" she asked.

But of course he didn't answer. He would never again answer anyone.

"Annie. Oh, Annie." She heard a wealth of anguish in David's voice as he dropped his hands to her shoulders and pulled her back against his thighs.

"I'm just saying good-bye," she told him. "I need to do that."

He didn't argue with her. Perhaps he had his own need to say good-bye, perhaps he only felt he had to guard her. He kept his hands on her shoulders, standing over her, until something within her told her it was time to let go. She looked up at him, and he helped her to her feet. Only then did he touch her in any other way. He lifted his hands to her face and traced the path of her tears. "He's dead, Annie. He's been dead for a long, long time."

"Yes," she said. "I know." And she knew something else. The reason for the anguish in David's voice and in his eyes as he looked down at her. This man loved her. Whether he admitted it or not.

"I learned something today," she told him.

She knew why he touched her face, because she felt the same need to touch him, to affirm that he was real, that he was here, with her. She lifted her hands and traced his cheekbones, the fading bruise, the fine line of his nose, his cleanly sculpted lips. She saw the pulse beating in his temple and touched her fingers to it, feeling its echoing beat in her own heart.

"You may not want to hear this," she warned, "but I don't think I can fail to tell you."

He tensed beneath her touch, but she wouldn't let him pull away from her. Sighing, she leaned forward, feeling the beat of his heart beneath her cheek, feeling the strength of muscle beneath her arms as she held him to her.

"I learned I love you, David Huerra. Whether you stay in Allegro or return to Dallas, whether you want me for a lifetime or only for a month, I love you."

She heard what sounded suspiciously like a groan before he tightened his arms around her, pulling her impossibly close. "Oh, God, Annie, I was going out of my mind thinking about you in here grieving for your warrior—"

"I was, David," she told him. "I believe there's a part of me that always will, and *please* don't ask me to explain that because I don't think I can. But there's another part of me, the part that lives and feels and wants and dreams, that is so glad you came into my life."

"Annie—" His breath whispered on her cheek before he turned with her, reaching one-handed for the light cord. "Let's get out of here."

Loving was a celebration, Anne realized when they returned to their room and David took her in his arms. A celebration of living, of the spirits of each of the lovers. Or was there no separation of spirit? Because David's touch, his caress, his need, blended so completely with her touch, her caress, her need, that she was no longer sure where Anne stopped and David began. *If* Annie stopped and David began.

Morning dawned gray and cold, probably little, if any, above freezing. David eased into the morning warily, watching his breath condense in the frigid, unheated room.

Annie had burrowed under the covers and lay as close to him as she could get without crawling inside of him. He could just see the top of her head beneath the edge of the blankets, but he could feel her warmth along the length of him, the soft cushion of her breast against his side, her leg wrapped over his, her foot seeking his calf for warmth. He could feel the beat of the pulse in her arm where it rested across his ribs and feel the puff of her slow, steady breath against his throat.

Annie loved him. Anne Locke loved him, David Huerra, beat-up, washed-up cop.

What the hell was he supposed to do about that?

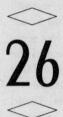

26

A few harsh, dry snowflakes dusted the tops of the vehicles in the driveway when Anne made her way to the kitchen to begin preparations for breakfast, but by the time Blake arrived and Wayne and Margaret returned, they had melted, though the day still promised to remain a grim and chilly gray.

Lilly bounced into the kitchen as the conspirators ate a hasty meal, followed by Nellie, whose bruises were even more prominent, and who walked as though each step had to be taken with painful deliberation.

Nellie. Oh, lord, Nellie. How could she have forgotten about her? Anne rose to go to the young woman, but Nellie spotted Blake at the table and stopped with a sharp gasp. "Sheriff?"

Blake rose. Anne saw the moment he realized the extent of the beating Nellie had taken, but to his credit, he hid that response from Nellie. "Morning, Nellie. You're just in time for breakfast. Come on over and have some orange juice, honey."

Nellie cast a wounded, betrayed glance at Anne, but with Lilly bubbling through her good morning greetings to Wayne and David, she had little choice but to continue into the room.

David stood and held a chair for her, and by the time Nellie reached it, she was too weak to do more than collapse gratefully onto it.

David's eyes met hers over Nellie's head. Anne recognized his silent message. Nellie needed more medical help than a few aspirin and bed rest. She needed someone to take the responsibility of caring for her child while she healed; she needed someone to tend to her meals and her medication, and to see that her physical needs were met. She needed warmth and caring and loving.

And soon, very soon, all of those who could have given her that care and love would be leaving this house for several hours.

Nellie was also a wild card in their hasty and secret plans.

Could they trust her? Should they trust her? Or would confiding in her only give her a burden she wasn't equipped to carry?

Having completed her flirting, Lilly climbed into Margaret's lap and demanded juice. Wayne laughed. "Well, I guess that tells us who she thinks is really important."

"Not so." Margaret glanced up at her husband with a smile so full of love it hurt Anne to watch. "We saw who she went to first."

Already standing, David brought glasses, plates, and flatware from the cabinet to the table.

Nellie cringed from him. Without seeming to notice, David poured juice in her glass, passed her the toast, and spooned scrambled eggs onto her plate. Only then did he return to his chair by Anne's side.

Nellie looked at the food on her plate, at her

daughter happily seated on Margaret's lap, and the people around the table who welcomed her into their midst and asked no questions. Her eyes filled. With a moan she stumbled to her feet. "I— I'm— Excuse me."

Anne watched as Nellie made her way from the room. No, damn it! The girl didn't need to be alone. And she was just a girl, even if she did have a four-year-old daughter. A girl who had to be in as much emotional pain as she was in physical pain. And if Anne understood anything, it was emotional pain. She tossed her napkin to the table as she stood. "Excuse me," she said. But without waiting for response she followed Nellie.

Nellie sat on the edge of the bed. Her tears streamed unchecked; her fragile shoulders shook. "You think I should talk to Blake, don't you?"

Anne sat beside her and carefully pulled Nellie against her, cradling her, for the moment, against the pain of the world. "Yes, I do. But that isn't why he's here."

"It isn't?"

"No."

"I'm such a coward. My daddy always told me that. I thought— I thought when I saw all of you there that you were going to make me tell."

"But you came on into the room. And you sat there, even though you were obviously terrified. That doesn't sound very cowardly to me."

"But I—"

Anne held her shoulders and she leaned away and looked at Nellie's ravaged face. "Blake is here, and Margaret and Wayne, too, because something pretty serious happened yesterday. To . . . To David and to me. Something we need their help to deal with."

"Do you want me to leave?"

This child thought she was a coward? Good lord, did

she know how much strength it would have taken for
Anne to have asked that question?

"No. But we're going to leave you. I don't think you
should be alone. What I think we should do is take you
to Gretta for the day."

"And let her see . . ."

"And let her take care of you and Lilly. The other
option is to leave you here alone. Lilly is wonderful, but
she's an active four year old, and while I think you'll be
safe here, I don't think you're strong enough to care for
her right now. Not by yourself."

"Can I think about it a little while? Is there time for
me to do that?"

"Yes. Yes, of course there's time. Why don't you lie
back down. We'll send Lilly to you after breakfast, and
you can give me your answer then."

The five of them crowded into the hidden room. David
knew they had to begin. Frances would already have
begun excavation. The longer they postponed this, the
harder it would be.

Wayne had suggested one solution to the transport.
To the burial. Tarps and sleeping bags. Anne had suggested another. Her vacuum cleaner looked incongru-
ous beside a prehistoric relic.

She had gathered a great deal of soil with her hands
and sprinkled it on the one opened sleeping bag they
had spread to the immediate right of the warrior. Now
the men exchanged troubled glances. It would either
work, or it wouldn't.

Some sort of canvas lay across the ribbing of cedar
poles. Would it hold?

David stepped to the head of the burial, Blake to the
right, Wayne to the left. With quiet, drill-like precision

each bent and grasped the visible tarp. Anne watched quietly from the foot until they started to rise. Then she stepped closer and grasped the tarp. And Margaret moved to stand beside Wayne, also sharing the responsibility for disturbing the grave.

The contents shifted and slid as they lifted, and the ancient tarp ripped in places, threatening to tear completely, and sending dirt slithering down to the old wooden floor, but it held while they moved the few feet necessary and lowered it to the waiting bag.

The cats remained quiet.

Or maybe this was one of those times when they wouldn't hear them.

"Whatcha doin'?"

David jerked to his feet. Anne whirled around. The others seemed frozen in place.

Lilly. Four-year-old Lilly, who was supposed to be safely downstairs in her mother's care, stood at the opening from the closet.

All innocence, the girl came into the room and walked to Wayne's side. "Will you play hide and seek with me?" Trusting, totally ignorant of the danger she was in, she lifted her arms to Wayne to be picked up, and when he did she plopped her thumb in her mouth and looked down at the copper-covered skeleton.

"Did he get dead?"

Anne's eyes met David's, begging for guidance. Hell! How was he supposed to know what to do?

"Yes," he said. "But it was a long, long time ago."

"And it's a secret, Lilly. A big secret."

Lilly studied Anne's words. "Like the man who hurt my mama?"

"Yes, darling," Anne told her, finding words David couldn't. "But it's a secret even your mama doesn't know. A secret that she must not know. No one else must know."

"What you don't know can't hurt you?"

"What?"

Lilly slid her little arm around Wayne's neck. "My grandma told me. I'd ask her, and she'd say that. But it did. My mama kept saying she didn't know, but he didn't believe her. That kind of secret?"

Annie's smile almost faltered, but she managed to hold onto it. "Yes, darling. That kind of secret."

"Okay," she said, squirming. Wayne shrugged, but he let her down. What else could he do?

Lilly bent to the jumbled pile of grave goods. The crystal jaguar had shifted to the top of the pile. She picked it up. David sucked in a breath, but nothing growled or menaced, and after a moment, she put it down and looked at the copper mask covering the skull. "Will you put him someplace where nobody can hurt him again?"

He saw Anne's eyes close. In prayer? Maybe.

"Yes, darlin'," he promised her. "That's what we're doing now."

"Okay." She flashed him a brilliant grin. "I've got to go back to my mama now."

The five of them watched in stunned silence as she skipped from the room.

Blake broke the silence. "What will we do?"

"Nothing," Wayne said. "There's nothing we can do."

"Yes, there is." Annie picked up her vacuum cleaner hose and switched the machine on, sucking the spilled dirt into the clean bag.

Yes. There was. David recognized the wisdom of her actions. He reached for the second sleeping bag and shook it open over the burial, then knelt to connect the zippers.

It wasn't a perfect solution. The grave goods jostled together inside the combined sleeping bags, and Annie hadn't been able to get all of the soil. The floorboards had dried out over the years of darkness, had shrunk and separated, and now a generous portion of the grave dirt lay between them and the subflooring or the ceiling of the room below. But it was a solution.

The rear seats of the Suburban had already been removed by a previous owner in an attempt to convert a nine-passenger truck to a hunting camper. It all would fit. They'd make sure of that. Anne and David had decided they couldn't risk separating any part of it at this point, not even with the dirt. And they couldn't risk the lives of any of their friends by asking someone else to transport any of it. The three men maneuvered the sleeping bags into the back of the truck. The poles were the problem. But they, too, fit. Barely, by extending them over the back of the front seat and bracing them between the windshield and the rear cargo door.

David slammed the cargo door and turned to Anne. "We need to go."

"Yes."

But first there was something else that must be done. He went with Anne back into the house. The bedroom door was open. Lilly played quietly on the floor beside the bed where Nellie slept. Anne sat on the side of the bed.

"Nellie."

The young woman moaned and turned her head on the pillow.

"Nellie. Wake up. We need to take you to Gretta's now."

"Oh."

Nellie eased up against the headboard, grimacing and holding herself against her pain. "Now?" she asked.

"Now." Anne told her.

"Let me— I—" Nellie shook her head and then sucked in a sharp breath. "I was going to say, let me wake up, but I think that just did it." She fell quiet, breathing with deliberate care. "I don't think I can. Not just yet. In a little while, maybe. Probably."

"We have to leave now, Nellie."

Nellie bit at her lip. "I can call Gretta in a few minutes. I can ask her to come for me. I will. I promise I will."

Anne didn't look convinced, but she knew they had to go. She gave Nellie a gentle hug and Lilly a fiercer one. "Take care of your mama, cupcake. Do you know how to dial zero for help?"

"Of course."

Anne brushed her lips across Lilly's hair. "Of course. How silly of me."

"We had to leave her, Annie," David told her later, on their way to the mounds.

"I know."

"She'll be all right."

Anne looked at him over the barrier of the cedar poles separating them. "I know that, too."

Frances had told them where to park. A road ran along the east side of the park, back out of sight to a parking area where the archaeology students had camped the summer they helped excavate the Plaza. From there, half hidden now by briars, a stile crossed the fence and led to the north side of Craig Mound.

Blake led the way in his Jimmy, insisting they might need his police radio to summon help.

David and Anne followed in the Suburban.

Wayne and Margaret guarded the rear and brought the tarps and shovels they might need.

Frances met them at the stile. "We have freezing rain, maybe snow in the forecast for this morning."

Damn! Nothing about this was going to be easy.

But maybe it was. The tractor had started. And Frances had been busy. Very busy. She had already stripped sod from the back of the mound and stacked it neatly to one side and had opened a pit low in the back side of the mound. It was much lower than the relatively late burial of this man would have put him. But it was wide enough to accommodate the width of the poles and the litter burial, and it was long enough to accommodate his height.

They hurried. Even Anne, who'd visibly had to force herself to climb the stile and help carry the warrior into the park. The chances of being seen from the distant road were slim, and Frances argued that because she occasionally gave private tours she could explain their presence, if necessary.

They lay the poles in place over an all-weather tarp, lay the sleeping-bag-encased warrior on top of the poles, as he had been placed centuries before, straightening the bag even while knowing the goods would probably resettle themselves the way they had over the last fifty years, and finally they covered the entire burial with another all-weather tarp.

The six of them stood silently. David felt he ought to say something. His Catholic God was used to words at a time like this. He saw Anne's lips moving in familiar ritual and pulled her close with an arm over her shoulder. Each of them was having a similar problem.

Each of them was forgetting something very important. He looked around at the cluster of friends, so like mourners, who shared this moment. Six of them. Burying a fortune without one complaint about the loss of that fortune. Burying a man that none of them had known but who would forever be a part of their lives. "The words he would want to hear have already been said."

Anne smiled up at him through misty eyes. "Yes." She too looked around at the conspirators. "Thank you. All of you."

"One last thing." Frances pulled a plastic bag from her pocket and knelt beside the grave where she tagged the bag to a zipper pull.

"What?" Anne asked.

"Just a warning," Frances told her. "In case he's ever found, those who find him have to be warned to keep this burial together."

It was done.

All that remained was to close the grave.

Wayne commandeered the tractor, freeing Frances from this last, heavy work, and when the bulk of the soil had been replaced, they all took shovels and rakes and tamped and packed and filled, and eventually covered the raw wound on the mound with the waiting sod.

The snow started as they were gathering tools, preparing to leave. Frances looked up as the wet, fluffy flakes began drifting to the ground in rapid succession. "Thank you," she whispered.

She straightened and handed the shovel and hoe she had picked up to David. "Go now," she said. "These roads can get treacherous."

They went. At Fairview they all pulled into the parking lot at the sheriff's office. They looked at each other, but there didn't seem to be anything further to say. At least not now. Without speaking, Blake left his Jimmy and walked toward the courthouse, Wayne and Margaret turned toward an alternate route that would lead to their isolated mountain, and David and Anne headed for a purple house now emptied of its curse.

But maybe not quite.

◇ ◇ ◇

David had expected the eerie sensation that first warned him of something ominous in the house to be gone when they returned.

It wasn't.

Or maybe it was his own depression he felt settling over him as they reached the top of the driveway and he parked the Suburban. Depression caused by the knowledge that he still had nothing to offer Anne Locke.

He turned off the key and sat in the truck and looked at that damned blank wall that he had first seen—what?—ten days ago? Only ten days? Eleven now. It seemed as though this house and this woman had been a part of his life for years. If they had been, would David now be considering telling Annie they had no future?

He felt her hand on his cheek, turning him to face her. "Don't say it," she told him. "Don't even think it. Not yet. We have the rest of your month. Besides," she said with a tremulous smile, "we haven't necked in this wonderful truck yet."

He pulled her against him and buried his face in her glorious hair. *Annie, my Annie,* he cried silently. *I don't want to leave you. I never wanted to leave you.*

But he would.

It was inevitable.

Why?

The snow had followed them south and intensified in the higher elevations of the mountains surrounding Allegro. In the minutes since they had stopped it had gathered in the corners of the windshield and built up against the wiper blades, although it still melted when it touched the hood. He glanced around. The outbuildings were already dusted white.

"We'd better go in," he told her and watched his breath condense in the rapidly chilling air.

She rubbed her cheek against his chest and rested it a moment over his heart, but eventually she lifted her head and pulled away from him. A seductive smile softened her eyes and parted her lips. "Yes," she said. "I think we'd better."

They made it into the kitchen before she turned to him again. The door had been unlocked. He frowned at it, trying to remember if they had left it that way. Surely not, not with Nellie in the house. But Annie shrugged out of her jacket and dropped it to the floor, and she lifted her hands to peel him out of his.

Annie, an intentionally seductive Annie, was almost more temptation than he could resist. He caught her hands with his, stilling her. "Do you know what you're doing?"

She grinned at him. "I hope so. But if I don't, can you teach me?"

"It's called an affirmation of life, Annie."

She looked at him, all seriousness now. "I certainly hope so. But it's also called love, David. Something we're going to have to talk about. But not yet. Not just yet."

No. Please, God. Not yet. He wasn't ready to leave her yet. "Right. So what do you say to closing up the house, taking the phone off the hook, and locking ourselves in an upstairs bedroom for the next three weeks or so?"

She lifted her hands to his neck and stretched against him. "Sounds good to me."

"I'm afraid that will have to wait a while."

Anne's hands clenched on his neck. David jerked his head up to confront the menace in the words that had just echoed across the kitchen. She tried to turn, but he pressed her face against his chest and held her still.

Joe Hansom stood in the door to the butler's pantry. He looked as immaculate as the last time—the only time—David had seen him. From his black, western-cut leather coat, black denim jeans, black triple-stitched custom boots, to the .38 Colt revolver held in his black-leather gloved hand.

"This is not a good idea," David said, moving to place Anne behind him. He'd hidden his pistol inside a tin on the top shelf of a cabinet near the sink when he'd realized Lilly would be in the house. Fifteen endless feet away.

"Don't move."

Maybe not as immaculate. And definitely not as contained. There was a wildness about Joe, in his eyes and in the jerky motions of his head, that David had not seen at the café. And he was, after all, Crazy Marian's grandson.

"Is whatever you want worth this, Hansom?"

"I said don't move."

David opened his hands behind Annie's back, but he refused to release her. If necessary, he could spin with her held this way, turning to put himself between her and Joe.

"Step away from her. My argument's not with you."

"Oh, I think you just invited me into it."

"Hush, David," Annie murmured against his chest. "Don't antagonize him."

Tiny tremors worked their way through her in wave after wave. Oh, hell. It was Chicago all over again. She had to be thinking that. There was no way he was letting her go. "It's all right, Annie," he said softly. "It's all right.

"What is it, Hansom? What do you want?"

"I want to know if she's going to file charges. I want to know why you've been spending all this time with Blake Foresman. I want to know where that secret room is. And you're going to help me find it.

"It's all connected. I know that. I just had no idea it

was here, in the house. If she'd told me that in time, I could have bought it. I would have bought it. And then the two of you wouldn't have been snooping where you have no right to snoop.

"So move away from her and come on, slowly, carefully. It's upstairs. I know that much. I've been talking to that crazy old woman for years, and she finally gave me enough of the pieces to figure that much out.

"*Move!*"

"Annie," David said, feeling the shudder that wracked her at Joe's sharp command. "You can do this, darlin'." She nodded her head against his chest once, quickly, and raised her head. Maybe she could do it. And maybe this was the final straw that would send Anne Locke so far inside herself she'd never find her way out. "We can do it," he promised her, "together."

She took one step back from him, under her own power, and stood waiting. "Together," he said again.

"Upstairs," Hansom said. "Come on. Let's go."

David didn't know how Annie made it up the stairs unless it was by raw nerve. Each time David reached to help her, Hansom poked the gun in her back, far enough away that David had no chance of disarming him.

At the top of the stairs Hansom stopped them. "Now," he said, "where do you think my crazy grandmother would hide a secret room?"

Annie raised her head and looked at Joe with eyes that had already seen too much death to doubt what would follow. "Where do you think, Joe? Someplace where she could have easy access."

She was going to tell him. And why not. A protracted search might have given David more opportunities for a chance at overpowering Joe, but perhaps the shock of discovering he was only hours too late might do the same.

"You know!"

Anne drew herself tall. "Of course I know. But it will do you no good."

Joe gestured with the gun.

Damn it, Annie, David thought. Take your own advice. Don't antagonize him. Not now. Not until I can take advantage of it.

She led Joe directly to Marian's old room. Directly to the closet. Directly to the panel. Opened it for him. And stepped out of sight into the hidden room.

"Damn it!" Joe yelled. "Come out of there!"

"Don't you want to come in, Joe? Don't you want to see what your grandmother has kept hidden for fifty years?"

David's mind raced through a quick mental inventory of what was left in the room. A couple of barrels. A broken and discarded bed frame. A chest of drawers against the windowless wall. Anne's vacuum cleaner with its metal wand. Maybe. Maybe, if he could just get to it. If he could just make a moment for surprise. Don't do anything rash, Annie. He sent the thought silently. Please don't do anything rash.

She turned on the light.

Joe waved him forward and through the opening, but he followed too quickly for David to do more than reach Anne's side.

Inside the room the man stopped and stared at the siding visible through the windows, at the tattered floral wallpaper, at the dismal furniture and bare-bulbed light. He shook his head and turned in a wide circle, searching the room but never completely taking his attention from David or Anne.

"Where are they!?"

His cry rang through the room, shocking even him. He rocked back on his heels and took a deep breath. "Where are they?"

Yes, where were they? David wondered, but about something that had to be completely different. A pair of golden attack cats would come in handy right about now.

But they were gone.

Protecting the dead.

"This is all there is," David said. "This is what you have been paying for, for how many years, Joe?"

"No. You've found them. You've done something with them. But you haven't told Foresman. Not yet. I'd have known if you had. So there's hope. There's hope."

Was there?

"Found what, Joe?"

"Oh, no. No you don't."

And when Joe Hansom looked at them with Marian's eyes, David knew that there would be no escape. Not for both of them. But if he was careful, if he played the man just right, maybe Annie would live. Please, he prayed, to his God, to the god of the man they had just reburied, to any god who would listen. Please let Annie live.

David took a half-step forward. "Found what, Joe? Or who?"

Beside him, Anne sucked in a sharp breath and tensed. But she wasn't staring at Joe; she was staring past him.

Oh, God. He almost moaned. Lilly stood in the opening. There was no way he could tell her to run or hide without calling Joe's attention to her, and she did that herself, darting past him to run to Anne.

"What the—" Joe spun around and fired a shot that went wide. Wildly wide.

Now or never, David thought. I love you Annie. He sent that thought to her. Be safe. Please, God, be safe.

He felt the blow. It knocked him to his knees before he reached Joe. Too soon. Too soon.

And finally he heard the sound. Annie's body jerked as though she had been shot, too.

Beg, darlin', he tried to say. Do what you have to, but live. God, yes. Please live.

But Annie didn't beg. With a screech, she thrust Lilly behind her and ran at Joe. "You will not kill him," she screamed. *"You will not kill him!"*

He couldn't move. His legs wouldn't work. His knees wouldn't straighten. Not even his hand would raise. He could only watch as Annie, brave, foolish Annie, tackled a man with a loaded revolver and as Joe—two Joes now in his rapidly blurring vision—caught her and twisted her around, holding the gun at her throat, as a shadow—someone—edged from the opening into the room, swinging something . . . swinging something high and hard and connecting with the back of Joe Hansom's head as the noise echoed through David's and finally his knees gave out and he fell the rest of the way to the floor.

"Damned hard head."

"Hush, Blake."

David swam back to consciousness and a ringing in his head that resembled Big Ben at noon inside a closed car.

Consciousness.

He didn't die.

Annie leaned over him with a cloth in her hand. A bloody cloth. God. A head wound? How bad?

He could think. He could see. And even with that infernal clanging in his head, he could hear.

He could feel. Hands. Feet. Arms. Legs.

Annie's expression as she looked down at him was grave. But her eyes were clear. She had cried. He could see the evidence of that on her cheeks. But she wasn't crying now. And she was here, fully here, with him. Not locked inside herself.

"I don't believe it, Huerra," Blake said. "Yeah, I do. Pete said you were stubborn. Just thank your lucky stars that your skull's so thick and Joe was such a bad shot."

"Hush, Blake," Annie said again.

He'd been moved, stretched out on that hideous sofa in Marian's sitting room.

That was a good sign, wasn't it? He tested moving his tongue and his lips. "Lilly?" he croaked.

Anne's hand stilled on his head. Her eyes closed and her head bent forward. Almost touching his. Almost.

"She's fine," Anne said. "She came to tell us that she had dialed zero and told the operator that the bad man who hurt her mama was here, that Doc Anne needed Sheriff Blake right now, and that she'd found the key and let her mama out of the closet where Joe had locked her."

Joe. Damn! He was the one who had terrified Nellie. "Who— Who took him out?"

"Nellie." Anne's eyes filled with more tears and her voice caught. "She swears she's never going to cower from anyone or anything again as long as she lives."

"Is she—"

"She'll be all right." Annie answered before he had to force out all the words. "Margaret and Wayne are here. Margaret's with her."

"You?"

She touched her palm to his cheek. "I think I know how Nellie feels."

It was good—it was more than good—having her hovering over him, touching him with such tender care, if the damned bells would quit long enough for him to remember what had seemed so clear just before Lilly burst into the hidden room.

He shifted on the sofa and dragged himself up.

"Be still," Anne ordered.

"I'm fine."

She choked on a laugh. Or was it a sob? "You're not fine. You've very probably got a concussion."

"And a dashing bullet wound?" he asked. He had a feeling she would be leading him a merry chase for the rest of their lives. Hell, might as well play this damned headache for a little sympathy. It would probably be the last he got from her.

She shook her head. "Close, but no cigar."

He turned his head—bad mistake—to look at the bloody cloth she had stashed in the basin beside him and the suture tray beside it.

Once again she lay her hand against his cheek. Tears and laughter mingled in her eyes, but it was Foresman who spoke. "Hell, Huerra. The really spectacular wound came from hitting your head on Annie's vacuum cleaner when you passed out."

"No hospital."

He remembered saying those words, and apparently someone had listened, because when he awoke again, he was in bed. His and Annie's bed. He was alone, covered against the cold with the electric blanket turned on, staring at a buildup of fat, wet snow in the window ledges.

And the ringing—the *gong*ing—had stopped.

Damn! A head hard enough to deflect a bullet. And taken out by a vacuum cleaner. If Pete found out, he was never going to live this down.

But he was going to live. For a while there he'd been too damned sure he wouldn't. And Annie was going to live. With him.

He made a few tentative stretches with his legs. They

worked. They worked just fine. He eased himself to the side of the bed and sat up.

And he was still dressed, except for his boots and shirt. That simplified matters. He looked around the room and found his duffel bag. Carefully he knelt and rummaged through it until he came up with a pair of loafers. Better than boots anyway, right now. No tugging. No jarring. He slipped his feet into them and stuffed his arms in a soft, worn flannel shirt. Then he turned and came face to face with his bandaged, battered reflection in the dressing table mirror.

Matched bruises.

Damn.

If Joe had to shoot him in the head, why hadn't he had the decency to keep the bruise on the side that was already discolored? Now he really would look like an outlaw.

Joe. Joe. *Where are they?* Found what, Joe? Or who? *Where are they?*

And then he remembered what he had seen so clearly just before Lilly ran into the room.

"Oh, hell."

The cops were gone. Nellie and Lilly were gone. Everyone was gone except Wayne and Margaret, Blake, and Anne. David found them in the kitchen, still the only warm room in the house, all looking frazzled and about as bad as he felt.

"Caffeine," he said from the door to the hallway, remembering a morning only a few days before when he had teased and bullied Annie into feeding him and giving him coffee and letting him out of a trip to the hospital.

Anne jumped up from her chair and started toward him. Halfway across the room she stopped and frowned at him. "You belong in bed."

He grinned at her. "Go with me?"

Blake choked back a laugh.

David looked at the three still seated at the table. Now was as good a time as any, better than most. "I'm going to marry Anne Locke. The sooner the better. You're all invited."

Wayne smiled at Margaret and lifted his hand in salute. "Don't you think you ought to ask her?"

"Good idea. Annie, can I please, please have a cup of coffee?"

Anne closed her eyes, shook her head, and sighed. "Sit down," she insisted. "At least do that."

Gladly. Maybe he wasn't up to all that still had to be done. Nonsense. It *had* to be done. He pulled out a chair and eased himself onto it.

"Do me a favor, Huerra," Blake said. "Next time you decide you need a little peace and quiet, may I suggest Alaska for your vacation? Antarctica? Anywhere but my county? I'll be doing paperwork and fighting reporters over this day's work, and that's just the part we'll tell them about, clear up until time for reelection. What in the hell got into Joe? What *they* was he screaming about? He didn't see the cats, did he?"

Annie leaned against him, her arm over his shoulder. David drank in the warmth of her closeness. "Is it time for some more of those nice horse aspirin yet, Doc?"

Anne shook her head. "Don't press your luck. Blake can have an ambulance here in a heartbeat."

"Yeah." And the time for teasing had passed. "How about the county coroner?"

"What?"

David slipped his arm around Annie's waist and returned her hug. "Joe may have meant the burial and the artifacts, but I think the *they* he was talking about was much more current than the cats. I think he was talking about Walter and Lucy.

"I think Marian was holding him to her with more than the promise of a fortune, even a sizable one. That she was probably up to her old tricks of blackmail and coercion.

"With Joe's political aspirations and their family history, that wouldn't have been too difficult. And if bigamy or adultery or incest, take your pick depending on Marian's mood, wasn't enough of a scandal to keep him in line or was too far removed, why not throw in a couple of murders?"

"Marian killed them? Not the cats?"

"She never really said the cats killed them. Not to us. She quite pointedly didn't answer when I questioned her on that. What she said was the curse killed them. What she said was that they were trying to move the burial, maybe like we did, to keep it safe, but we'll never know for sure. That she returned the items that they had taken and picked up the cedar box to take it to the country with her and get rid of the woman's miniature, *too*. Remember, Anne?"

"Yes." She pulled a chair close and sank onto it. "But where are they? And why didn't anyone find them?"

"I think because no one was looking in the right place. She was in the hospital for weeks, Marian said, weeks and weeks and weeks. Ellie went with her. While they were gone, no one would have come up here, at least not after the original search, because of the story of Ralph and the curse, because of Marian's insistence on supernatural, killer cats. And when Ellie and Marian finally returned, no one could find Walter and Lucy.

"The car in the barn, Anne. The one your mother said Marian wouldn't let anyone drive. The car that sat through World War II with all its tires intact and the key in the ignition?

"I don't think Walter and Lucy went anywhere, because I believe Marian took her dive down the stairs before she had a chance to get rid of their bodies."

Blake and Wayne lifted the bar and opened the doors to the barn, but when they found the trunk lid on the old Ford coupe stuck, Wayne brought a pry bar from his truck and handed it to David.

The miasma of despair surrounding the car hadn't weakened. Beside him, Anne shuddered. Did she feel it, too? Or was he the only one?

He swallowed once—did he really want to do this?— and jammed the pry bar under the trunk lid, beneath the lock. It didn't budge; he simply didn't have the strength. Annie stepped aside as Wayne moved forward. He put his hands on the pry bar beside David's. "Let me help."

David searched Wayne's eyes and saw an acceptance of what was and what must be that was older than time. Yes. It was right for him to help. Together they bent over the bar, joining their efforts, until the old lock snapped and the lid popped loose.

"Blake?" David stepped back in acknowledgment of Blake's jurisdiction.

Blake fitted a towel under the edge of the trunk and lifted.

"Hell."

One syllable. Not three. But containing a wealth of emotion.

Annie clutched his arm. David dropped the pry bar and clutched her.

Was this the way she had felt when she grieved for the warrior? It felt as though it must be.

The two skeletons lay in the bottom of the trunk. Walter, for that was who it had to be, the larger of the two, lay on the bottom. The side of his skull that was visible clearly showed the fracture that had killed him. Lucy, smaller, almost tiny, lay draped over him, her arms and legs positioned awkwardly behind her as though she had been bound, but looking as though even in death she comforted him.

Annie burrowed her face against David's chest and moaned. Too much. This time it was too much for him. He turned, holding her tight and walked from the barn into the bright, harsh light reflected off the snow covering the yard, leaving the others there to deal with the reports and the realities.

He'd never be able to prove how Lucy Hansom died, but he knew. She'd died in the trunk of that car huddled over the body of the man she loved, hearing the cars and ambulance arrive for Marian and then the silence as she waited and no one came for her.

He stopped and grabbed Annie to him. "Whatever you want to do, Anne Locke, and wherever you want to live, I'm going to be there with you. City. Small town. Mountaintop. Deserted island. Somewhere. Anywhere. It doesn't matter anymore. Just as long as we're together."

Had he known all this on some level when he made his declaration in the kitchen? Somehow he thought he must have, that he must have known since the day he woke up on the side of a road and found her ordering him around and working her way into his heart. *Back* into his heart?

"And don't think you're getting out of this deal in thirty days," he warned. "This is forever, lady. Forever."

She turned her face up to his. Her eyes were washed with tears, but he saw enough love in them to last more than a couple of lifetimes. "Yes," she said. Just, "Yes."

It was more than enough.

Epilogue

1990

Katherine Maria Huerra, named for her two grandmothers, decided to be born the night before Thanksgiving, two weeks early, in Dallas, Texas, at the hospital where her mother, who had at long last found her career home in pediatrics, practiced medicine.

Anne had been busy at her workbench when she admitted to herself that Katie was determined to make an appearance. She'd had time to put the finishing touches on the latest of the engraved copper plates that once again fascinated her, and to stack it with the others she had been almost driven to complete during her pregnancy. And then she reached for the telephone to call David.

David had returned to the Dallas P.D. Pete Tompkins hadn't taken his badge. Instead, when Pete retired he'd recommended David for promotion, citing intuition, integrity, and common sense among his numerous qualifications for the job. Now he found himself more often corralling reports and officers than criminals. But that was okay. That job was a necessary part of police work, too. And if it bought him more time with Anne, it was better than okay.

David let himself into the house through the garage door before Anne finished dialing. He grabbed the bag they had already packed, bundled her into the car, and hurried her to the hospital. He didn't tell her that the reason he had come home early was that for the first time in five years, he had heard the cats. Grumbling, fussing, but not angry. Not this time.

He might never tell her that.

He thought more often than he wanted to admit about Walter and Lucy, and about the warrior they had reburied. All of those involved did. That was obvious from their silence about it when they got together at the Hansom house in Allegro for their annual Thanksgiving dinner.

Only Blake would be sharing the meal with them tomorrow. Because of Anne's advanced pregnancy, their regular dinner had been held a month early this year. At that time Frances had quietly given him a copy of the legislation that had been introduced the year before giving federal protection to Native American funerary and sacred objects. It was too early to tell just how this legislation would develop and how it would work in actuality, but maybe, just maybe if the warrior were ever found there would be protection in place for him and because of that, for those who found him.

Frances Collins, on leave from the University of Oklahoma where she taught anthropology, heard the wind rising and looked out the window of her grand-mother's house, toward the line of trees that marked the curve of the river, then farther, to the lights of the lock and dam, and then to the west, toward the park where the warrior lay buried. Her stomach tingled. Something was happening. Something completely unrelated to her grandfather's funeral, which she had attended that morning. She felt it. And then she saw the glow. Golden. Hanging low over the mounds. Circling them.

Wayne Samuels looked up from his woodcarver's bench as wind rattled the windows in the glass-walled room adjoining the kitchen in the house he and Margaret had bought from Anne. He didn't like living in town, even one as small as Allegro. He might never like it. But here at least he could walk in the woods when people crowded him too much. And Margaret needed to be here. She still worked at the clinic, keeping it open for the doctor who came three half-days a week. There was talk—just talk so far—of the possibility of a nurse practitioner license for registered nurses in rural areas of the state. Maggie would like that. And because she would, he would.

The house was big, too big for just the two of them. So, surprising himself, he had suggested they invite Nellie and Lilly to share it with them while Nellie finished high school and then began work on a degree at the community college in Fairview. And Nellie, surprising herself, he suspected, had agreed.

But right now, the house wasn't big enough. Wayne put down his carving and walked to the back door. Something was happening. Something he had to investigate.

In Dallas, caught in the grip of a powerful contraction, Anne clutched her husband's hand. He was there for her. Always. As he had promised.

Near Spiro, Frances climbed over the stile into the park and walked toward Craig Mound. Yes. The cats were there. Visible. Pacing, but not anxious.

The wind whistled down from the river, lifting the edge of her coat, then hesitated and with a sigh, stilled. And the cats were gone.

In Allegro, Wayne followed the wind to the restored

barn on the rear of the lot. Lilly had discovered it and used it as a playhouse, coming and going through a loose board beneath the rear window. She thought no one else knew about it. He thought that maybe she was what he heard in the barn tonight.

But that couldn't be. Lilly had gone into Fairview with her mother and the young man Nellie was dating.

So what . . .

Wayne opened one of the doors to the barn and stepped inside. The wind followed him, grabbing the door and banging it back, then hesitated, and with a sound as gentle as a sigh, left the barn in silence.

In Dallas, at 11:59, Katherine Maria gave her first triumphant cry. The lights in the hospital flickered once, probably because of the wind that had whipped itself into an almost unheard of frenzy for Dallas in November, but then steadied. David took his daughter from the doctor and held her in trembling arms. Little Katie was as beautiful as her mother, and Anne was so beautiful he sometimes wondered how he could have been so blessed. Not trusting himself not to drop her, he lay her on her mother's breast. Anne lifted one hand to Katie's back and the other to David, asking for his touch. She smiled at her daughter and then at him through a shimmer of tears.

She heard them, too. He knew she did when her hand tightened on his and her eyes widened, but not in fear. Not this time. Maybe never again. Against the backdrop of the hospital noises, the conversation between doctor and staff in the room with them, the bleeps and gurgles and thunks of machinery, and their awareness of the tiny miracle of Katie, the two of them heard the unmistakable sound of the cats. Not angry. Far from it. Not even fussing. The sound they heard could almost be described, if ever they dared describe it, as a contented purr.

Let HarperMonogram Sweep You Away

❦

BURNING LOVE by Nan Ryan
Winner of the *Romantic Times* Lifetime Achievement Award
While traveling across the Arabian desert, American socialite
Temple Longworth is captured by a handsome sheik.
Imprisoned in *El Süf*'s lush oasis, Temple struggles not to lose
her heart to a man whose touch promises ecstasy.

A LITTLE PEACE AND QUIET by Modean Moon
Bestselling Author
A handsome stranger is drawn to a Victorian house—and the
attractive woman who is restoring it. When an evil presence is
unleashed, David and Anne risk falling under its spell unless
they can join together to create a powerful love.

ALMOST A LADY by Barbara Ankrum
Lawman Luke Turner is caught in the middle of a Colorado
snowstorm, handcuffed to beautiful pickpocket Maddy
Barnes. While stranded in a hostile town, the unlikely couple
discovers more trouble than they ever bargained for—and
heavenly pleasures neither can deny.

DANCING MOON by Barbara Samuel
Fleeing from her cruel husband, Tess Fallon finds herself on the
Santa Fe trail and at the mercy of Joaquin Morales. He brands
her with his kiss, but they must conquer the threats of the past
before embracing the paradise found in each other's arms.

And in case you missed last month's selections...

MIRANDA by Susan Wiggs
Over One Million Copies of Her Books in Print
In Regency London, Miranda Stonecypher is stricken with
amnesia and doesn't believe that handsome Ian MacVane is her
betrothed—especially after another suitor appears. Miranda's
search for the truth leads to passion beyond her wildest dreams.

WISH LIST by Jeane Renick
RITA Award–Winning Author

Only $5.99

While on assignment in Nepal, writer Charlayne
Pearce meets elusive and irresistibly sensual Jordan Kosterin.
Jordan's bold gaze is an invitation to pleasure, but memories
of his dead wife threaten their newfound love.

SILVER SPRINGS by Carolyn Lampman

Only $5.99

Independent Angel Brady feels she is capable of
anything—even passing as her soon-to-be-married twin
sister so that Alexis can run off with her lover. Unfortunately,
the fiancé turns out to be the one man in the Wyoming
Territory who can send Angel's pulse racing.

CALLIE'S HONOR by Kathleen Webb

Only $3.99

Callie Lambert is unprepared for the handsome
stranger who shows up at her Oregon ranch determined
to upset her well-ordered life. But her wariness is no match
for Rafe Millar's determination to discover her secrets, and
win her heart.

*Harper
Monogram*